BETTY NEELS

Her Special Charm

MILLS & BOON

HER SPECIAL CHARM © 2023 by Harlequin Books S.A.

ROMANTIC ENCOUNTER
© 1992 by Betty Neels
Australian Copyright 1992
New Zealand Copyright 1992

First Published 1992
First Australian Paperback Edition 2023
ISBN 978 1 867 27210 6

NEVER SAY GOODBYE
© 1983 by Betty Neels
Australian Copyright 1983
New Zealand Copyright 1983

First Published 1983
First Australian Paperback Edition 2023
ISBN 978 1 867 27210 6

THE CHAIN OF DESTINY
© 1989 by Betty Neels
Australian Copyright 1989
New Zealand Copyright 1989

First Published 1989
First Australian Paperback Edition 2023
ISBN 978 1 867 27210 6

FSC
www.fsc.org
MIX
Paper | Supporting responsible forestry
FSC® C001695

Published by
Mills & Boon
An imprint of Harlequin Enterprises (Australia) Pty Limited (ABN 47 001 180 918), a subsidiary of HarperCollins Publishers Australia Pty Limited (ABN 36 009 913 517)
Level 13, 201 Elizabeth Street
SYDNEY NSW 2000
AUSTRALIA

Printed and bound in Australia by McPherson's Printing Group

CONTENTS

Romance readers around the world were sad to note the passing of **Betty Neels** in June 2001. Her career spanned thirty years, and she continued to write into her ninetieth year. To her millions of fans, Betty epitomized the romance writer, and yet she began writing almost by accident. She had retired from nursing, but her inquiring mind still sought stimulation. Her new career was born when she heard a lady in her local library bemoaning the lack of good romance novels. Betty's first book, *Sister Peters in Amsterdam,* was published in 1969, and she eventually completed 134 books. Her novels offer a reassuring warmth that was very much a part of her own personality, and her spirit and genuine talent live on in all her stories.

Romantic Encounter

CHAPTER ONE

FLORENCE, CLEANING THE upstairs windows of the vicarage, heard the car coming up the lane and, when it slowed, poked her head over the top sash to see whom it might be. The elegant dark grey Rolls-Royce, sliding to a halt before her father's front door, was unexpected enough to cause her to lean her splendid person even further out of the window so that she might see who was in it. The passenger got out and she recognised him at once. Mr Wilkins, the consultant surgeon she had worked for before she had left the hospital in order to look after her mother and run the house until she was well again—a lengthy business of almost a year. Perhaps he had come to see if she was ready to return to her ward; unlikely, though, for it had been made clear to her that her post would be filled and she would have to take her chance at getting whatever was offered if she wanted to go to work at Colbert's again; besides, a senior consultant wouldn't come traipsing after a ward sister…

The driver of the car was getting out, a very tall, large man with pepper and salt hair. He stood for a moment, looking around him, waiting for Mr Wilkins to join him, and then looked up at her. His air of amused surprise sent her back inside again, banging her head as she went, but she was forced to lean out again when Mr Wilkins caught sight of her and called up to her to come down and let them in.

There was no time to do more than wrench the clean duster off her fiery hair. She went down to the hall and opened the door.

Mr Wilkins greeted her jovially. 'How are you after all these months?' he enquired; he eyed the apron bunched over an elderly skirt and jumper. 'I do hope we haven't called at an inconvenient time?'

Florence's smile was frosty. 'Not at all, sir, we are spring-cleaning.'

Mr Wilkins, who lived in a house with so many gadgets that it never needed spring-cleaning, looked interested. 'Are you really? But you'll spare us a moment to talk, I hope? May I introduce Mr Fitzgibbon?' He turned to his companion. 'This is Florence Napier.'

She offered a rather soapy hand and had it engulfed in his large one. His, 'How do you do?' was spoken gravely, but she felt that he was amused again, and no wonder—she must look a fright.

Which, of course, she did, but a beautiful fright; nothing could dim the glory of her copper hair, tied back carelessly with a boot-lace, and nothing could detract from her lovely face and big blue eyes with their golden lashes. She gave him a cool look and saw that his eyes were grey and intent, so she looked away quickly and addressed herself to Mr Wilkins.

'Do come into the drawing-room. Mother's in the garden with the boys, and Father's writing his sermon. Would you like to have some coffee?'

She ushered them into the big, rather shabby room, its windows open on to the mild April morning. 'Do sit down,' she begged them. 'I'll let Mother know that you're here and fetch in the coffee.'

'It is you we have come to see, Florence,' said Mr Wilkins.

'Me? Oh, well—all the same, I'm sure Mother will want to meet you.'

She opened the old-fashioned window wide and jumped neatly over the sill with the unselfconsciousness of a child, and Mr Fitzgibbon's firm mouth twitched at the corners. 'She's very professional on the ward,' observed Mr Wilkins, 'and very neat. Of course, if she's cleaning the house I suppose she gets a little untidy.'

Mr Fitzgibbon agreed blandly and then stood up as Florence returned, this time with her mother and using the door. Mrs Napier was small and slim and pretty, and still a little frail after her long illness. Florence made the introductions, settled her mother in a chair and went away to make the coffee.

'Oo's that, then?' asked Mrs Buckett, who came up twice a week from the village to do the rough, and after years of faithful service considered herself one of the family.

'The surgeon I worked for at Colbert's—and he's brought a friend with him.'

'What for?'

'I've no idea. Be a dear and put the kettle on while I lay a tray. I'll let you know as soon as I can find out.'

While the kettle boiled she took off her apron, tugged the jumper into shape and poked at her hair. 'Not that it matters,' she told Mrs Buckett. 'I looked an absolute frump when they arrived.'

'Go on with yer, love—you couldn't look a frump if you tried. Only yer could wash yer 'ands.'

Florence had almost decided that she didn't like Mr Fitzgibbon, but she had to admit that his manners were nice. He got up and took the tray from her and didn't sit down again until she was sitting herself. His bedside manner would be impeccable…

They drank their coffee and made small talk, but not for long.

Her mother put her cup down and got to her feet. 'Mr Wilkins tells me that he wants to talk to you, Florence, and I would like to go back to the garden and see what the boys are doing with the cold frame.'

She shook hands and went out of the room, and they all sat down again.

'Your mother is well enough for you to return to work, Florence?'

'Yes. Dr Collins saw her a few days ago. I must find someone to come in for an hour or two each day, but I must find a job first.' She saw that Mr Wilkins couldn't see the sense of that, but Mr Fitzgibbon had understood at once, although he didn't speak.

'Yes, yes, of course,' said Mr Wilkins briskly. 'Well, I've nothing for you, I'm afraid, but Mr Fitzgibbon has.'

'I shall need a nurse at my consulting-rooms in two weeks' time. I mentioned it to Mr Wilkins, and he remembered you and assures me that you would suit me very well.'

What about you suiting me? reflected Florence, and went a little pink because he was staring at her in that amused fashion again, reading her thoughts. 'I don't know anything about that sort of nursing,' she said, 'I've always worked in hospital; I'm not sure—'

'Do not imagine that the job is a sinecure. I have a large practice and I operate in a number of hospitals, specialising in chest surgery. My present nurse accompanies me and scrubs for the cases, but perhaps you don't feel up to that?'

'I've done a good deal of Theatre work, Mr Fitzgibbon,' said Florence, nettled.

'In that case, I think that you might find the job interesting. You would be free at the weekends, although I should warn you that I am occasionally called away at such times and you would need to hold yourself in readiness to accompany me. My rooms are in Wimpole Street, and Sister Brice has lodgings close by. I suppose you might take them over if they suited you. As to salary…'

He mentioned a sum which caused her pretty mouth to drop open.

'That's a great deal more—'

'Of course it is; you would be doing a great deal more work and your hours will have to fit in with mine.'

'This nurse who is leaving,' began Florence.

'To get married.' His voice was silky. 'She has been with me for five years.' He gave her a considered look. 'Think it over and let me know. I'll give you a ring tomorrow—shall we say around three o'clock?'

She had the strong feeling that if she demurred at that he would still telephone then, and expect her to answer, too. 'Very well, Mr Fitzgibbon,' she said in a non-committal voice, at the same time doing rapid and rather inaccurate sums in her head; the money would be a godsend—there would be enough to pay for extra help at the vicarage, they needed a new set of saucepans, and the washing-machine had broken down again…

She bade the two gentlemen goodbye, smiling nicely at Mr Wilkins, whom she liked, and giving Mr Fitzgibbon a candid look as she shook hands. He was very good-looking, with a high-bridged nose and a determined chin and an air of self-possession. He didn't smile as he said goodbye.

Not an easy man to get to know, she decided, watching the Rolls sweep through the vicarage gate.

When she went back indoors her mother had come in from the garden.

'He looked rather nice,' she observed, obviously following a train of thought. 'Why did he come, Florence?'

'He wants a nurse for his practice—a private one, I gather. Mr Wilkins recommended me.'

'How kind, darling. Just at the right moment, too. It will save you hunting around the hospitals and places…'

'I haven't said I'd take it, Mother.'

'Why not, love? I'm very well able to take over the household again—is the pay very bad?'

'It's very generous. I'd have to live in London, but I'd be free every weekend unless I was wanted—Mr Fitzgibbon seems to get around everywhere rather a lot; he specialises in chest surgery.'

'Did Mr Wilkins offer you your old job back, darling?'

'No. There's nothing for me at Colbert's...'

'Then, Florence, you must take this job. It will make a nice change and you'll probably meet nice people.' It was one of Mrs Napier's small worries that her beautiful daughter seldom met men—young men, looking for a wife—after all, she was five and twenty and, although the housemen at the hospital took her out, none of them, as far as she could make out, was of the marrying kind—too young and no money. Now, a nice older man, well established and able to give Florence all the things she had had to do without... Mrs Napier enjoyed a brief daydream.

'Is he married?' she asked.

'I have no idea, Mother. I should think he might be—I mean, he's not a young man, is he?' Florence, collecting coffee-cups, wasn't very interested. 'I'll talk to Father. It might be a good idea if I took the job for a time until there's a vacancy at Colbert's or one of the top teaching hospitals. I don't want to get out of date.'

'Go and talk to your father now, dear.' Mrs Napier glanced at the clock. 'Either by now he's finished his sermon, or he's got stuck. He'll be glad of the interruption.'

Mr Napier, when appealed to, giving the matter grave thought, decided that Florence would be wise to take the job. 'I do not know this Mr Fitzgibbon,' he observed, 'but if he is known to Mr Wilkins he must be a dependable sort of chap! The salary is a generous one too...not that you should take that into consideration, Florence, if you dislike the idea.'

She didn't point out that the salary was indeed a consideration. With the boys at school and then university, the vicar's modest stipend had been whittled down to its minimum so that there would be money enough for their future. The vicar, a kind, good man, ready to give the coat off his back to anyone in need, was nevertheless blind to broken-down washing-machines, worn-out sauce-pans and the fact that his wife hadn't had a new hat for more than a year.

'I like the idea, Father,' said Florence robustly, 'and I can come home at the weekend too. I'll go and see Miss Payne in the village and arrange for her to come in for an hour or so each day to give Mother a hand. Mrs Buckett can't do everything. I'll pay—it is really a very generous salary.'

'Will you be able to keep yourself in comfort, Florence?'

She assured him that she could perfectly well do that. 'And the lodgings his present nurse has will be vacant if I'd like to take them.'

'It sounds most suitable,' said her father, 'but you must, of course, do what you wish, my dear.'

She wasn't at all sure what she did wish but she had plenty of common sense; she needed to get a job and start earning money again, and she had, by some lucky chance, been offered one without any effort on her part.

When Mr Fitzgibbon telephoned the following day, precisely at three o'clock, and asked her in his cool voice if she had considered his offer, she accepted in a voice as cool as his own.

He didn't say that he was pleased. 'Then perhaps you will come up to town very shortly and talk to Sister Brice. Would next Monday be convenient—in the early afternoon?'

'There is a train from Sherborne just after ten o'clock—I could be at your rooms about one o'clock.'

'That will suit Sister Brice very well. You have the address and the telephone number.'

'Yes, thanks.'

His, 'Very well, goodbye, Miss Napier,' was abrupt, even if uttered politely.

* * *

The Reverend Napier, his sermon written and nothing but choir practice to occupy him, drove Florence into Sherborne to catch the morning train. Gussage Tollard was a mere four miles to that town as the crow flew, but, taking into account the elderly Austin and the winding lanes, turning and twisting every hundred yards or so, the distance by car was considerably more.

'Be sure and have a good lunch,' advised her father. 'One can always get a good meal at Lyons.'

Florence said that she would; her father went to London so rarely that he lived comfortably in the past as regarded cafés, bus queues and the like, and she had no intention of disillusioning him.

She bade him goodbye at the station, assured him that she would be on the afternoon train from Waterloo, and was borne away to London.

She had a cup of coffee and a sandwich at Waterloo Station and queued for a bus, got off at Oxford Circus, and, since she had a little time to spare, looked at a few shops along Oxford Street before turning off towards Wimpole Street. The houses were dignified Regency, gleaming with pristine paintwork and shining brass plates. Number eighty-seven would be halfway down, she decided, and wondered where the lodgings were that she might take over. It was comparatively quiet here and the sun was shining; after the bustle and the noise of Oxford Street it was peaceful—as peaceful as one could be in London, she amended, thinking of Gussage Tollard, which hadn't caught up with the modern world yet, and a good thing too.

Mr Fitzgibbon, standing at the window of his consulting-room, his hands in his pockets, watched her coming along the pavement below. With a view to the sobriety of the occasion, she had shrouded a good deal of her brilliant hair under a velvet cap which matched the subdued tones of her French navy jacket and skirt. She was wearing her good shoes too; they pinched a little, but that was in a good cause…

She glanced up as she reached the address she had been given, to see Mr Fitzgibbon staring down at her, unsmiling. He looked out of temper, and she stared back before mounting the few steps to the front door and ringing the bell. The salary he had offered was good, she reflected, but she had a nasty feeling that he would be a hard master.

The door was opened by an elderly porter, who told her civilly that Mr Fitzgibbon's consulting-rooms were on the first floor and would she go up? Once on the landing above there was another door with its highly polished bell, this time opened by a cosily plump middle-aged lady who said in a friendly voice, 'Ah, here you are. I'm Mr Fitzgibbon's receptionist—Mrs Keane. You're to go straight in…'

'I was to see Sister Brice,' began Florence.

'Yes, dear, and so you shall. But Mr Fitzgibbon wants to see you now.' She added in an almost reverent voice, 'He should be going to his lunch, but he decided to see you first.'

Florence thought of several answers to this but uttered none of them; she needed the job too badly.

Mr Fitzgibbon had left the window and was sitting behind his desk. He got up as Mrs Keane showed her in and wished her a cool, 'Good afternoon, Miss Napier,' and begged her to take a seat. Once she was sitting he was in no haste to speak.

Finally he said, 'Sister Brice is at lunch; she will show you exactly what your duties will be. I suggest that you come on a month's trial, and after that period I would ask you to give three months' notice should you wish to leave. I dislike changing my staff.'

'You may not wish me to stay after a month,' Florence pointed out in a matter-of-fact voice.

'There is that possibility. That can be discussed at the end of the month. You are agreeable to your working conditions? I must warn you that this is not a nine-to-five job; your personal life is of no interest to me, but on no account must it infringe upon your work here. I depend upon the loyalty of my staff.'

She was tempted to observe that at the salary she was being offered she was unlikely to be disloyal. She said forthrightly, 'I'm free to do what I like and work where I wish; I like to go to my home whenever I can, but otherwise I have no other interests.'

'No prospects of marriage?'

She opened her beautiful eyes wide. 'Since you ask, no.'

'I'm surprised. I should like you to start—let me see; Sister Brice leaves at the end of next week, a Saturday. Perhaps you will get settled in on the Sunday and start work here on the Monday morning.'

'That will suit me very well.' She did hide a smile at his surprised look; he was probably used to having things his own way. 'Will it be possible for me to see the rooms I am to have?'

He said impatiently, 'Yes, yes, why not? Sister Brice can take you there. Are you spending the night in town?'

'No, I intend to go back on the five o'clock train from Waterloo.'

There was a knock on the door and he called 'come in', and Sister Brice put her head round the door and said cheerfully, 'Shall I take over, sir?' She came into the room and shook Florence's hand.

The phone rang and Mr Fitzgibbon lifted the receiver. 'Yes, please. There's no one until three o'clock, is there? I shall want you here then.'

He glanced at Florence. 'Goodbye, Miss Napier; I expect to see you a week on Monday morning.'

Sister Brice closed the door gently behind them. 'He's marvellous to work for; you mustn't take any notice of his abruptness.'

'I shan't,' said Florence. 'Where do we start?'

The consulting-rooms took up the whole of the first floor. Besides Mr Fitzgibbon's room and the waiting-room, there was a very small, well-equipped dressing-room, an examination-room leading from the consulting-room, a cloakroom and a tiny kitchen. 'He likes his coffee around ten o'clock, but if he has a lot of patients he'll not stop. We get ours when we can. I get here about eight o'clock—the first patient doesn't get here before half-past nine, but everything has to be quite ready. Mr Fitzgibbon quite often goes to the hospital first and takes a look at new patients there; he goes back there around noon or one o'clock and we have our lunch and tidy up and so on, he comes back here about four o'clock unless he's operating, and he sees patients until half-past five. You do Theatre, don't you? He always has the same theatre sister at Colbert's, but if he's operating at another hospital, doesn't matter where, he'll take you with him to scrub.'

'Another hospital in London?'

'Could be; more often than not it's Birmingham or Edinburgh or Bristol—I've been to Brussels several times, the Middle East, and a couple of times to Berlin.'

'I can't speak German…'

Sister Brice laughed. 'You don't need to—he does all the talking; you just carry on as though you were at Colbert's. He did mention that occasionally you have to miss a weekend? It's made up to you, though.' She opened a cupboard with a key from her pocket. 'I've been very happy here and I shall miss the work, but it's a full-time job and there's not much time over from it, certainly not if one is married.' She was pulling out drawers. 'There's everything he needs for operating—he likes his own instruments and it's your job to see that they're all there and ready. They get put in this bag.'

She glanced at her watch. 'There's time to go over to my room; you can meet Mrs Twist and see if it'll suit you. She gets your breakfast and cooks high tea about half-past six. There's a washing-machine and a telephone you may use. She doesn't encourage what she calls gentlemen friends…'

'I haven't got any…'

'You're pretty enough to have half a dozen, if you don't mind my saying so.'

'Thank you. I think I must be hard to please.'

Mrs Twist lived in one of the narrow streets behind Wimpole Street, not five minutes' walk away. The house was small, one of a row, but it was very clean and neat, rather like Mrs Twist—small, too, and bony with pepper and salt hair and a printed cotton pinny. She eyed Florence shrewdly with small blue eyes and led her upstairs to a room overlooking the street, nicely furnished. 'Miss Brice 'as her breakfast downstairs, quarter to eight sharp,' she observed, 'the bathroom's across the landing, there's a machine for yer smalls and yer can 'ang them out in the back garden. I'll cook a meal at half-past six of an evening, something 'ot; if I'm out it'll be in the oven. Me and Miss Brice 'as never 'ad a cross word and I 'opes we'll get on as nicely.'

'Well, I hope so too, Mrs Twist. This is a very nice room and I'm sure I shall appreciate a meal each evening. You must let me know if there's anything—'

'Be sure I will, Miss Napier; I'm one for speaking out, but Mr Fitzgibbon told me you was a sensible, quiet-spoken young lady, and what 'e says I'll believe.'

Sister Brice was waiting downstairs in the prim front room. 'There's time to go back for half an hour,' she pointed out. 'I'm ready for the first patient; Mr Fitzgibbon won't be back until just before three o'clock, and Mrs Keane will already have got the notes out.'

They bade Mrs Twist goodbye and walked back to Wimpole Street, where Mrs Keane was putting on the kettle. Over cups of tea she and Sister Brice covered the bare bones of Mr Fitzgibbon's information with a wealth of their own, so that by the time Florence left she had a sound idea of what she might expect. Nothing like having a ward in the hospital, she reflected on her way to the station. She would have to make her own routine and keep to it as much as possible, allowing for Mr Fitzgibbon's demands upon her time. All the same, she thought that she would like it; she was answerable to no one but herself and him, of course—her bedsitter was a good deal better than she had expected it to be, and there was the added bonus of going home each weekend. She spent the return journey doing sums on the back of an envelope, and alighted at Sherborne knowing that the saucepans and washing-machine need no longer be pipe-dreams. At the end of the month they would be installed in the vicarage kitchen. What was more, she would be able to refurbish her spring wardrobe.

'Mr Fitzgibbon seems to be an employer of the highest order,' observed her father when she recounted the day's doings to him.

She agreed, but what sort of a man was he? she wondered; she still wasn't sure if she liked him or not.

She spent the next two weeks in a burst of activity; the spring-cleaning had to be finished, a lengthy job in the rambling vicarage, and someone had to be found who would come each day for an hour or so. Mrs Buckett was a splendid worker but, although Mrs Napier was very nearly herself once more, there were tiresome tasks—the ironing, the shopping and the cooking—to be dealt with. Miss Payne, in the village, who had recently lost her very old mother, was only too glad to fill the post for a modest sum.

Florence packed the clothes she decided she would need, added one or two of her more precious books and a batch of family photos to grace the little mantelpiece in her bedsitter, and, after a good deal of thought, a long skirt and top suitable for an evening out. It was unlikely that she would need them, but one never knew. When she had been at the hospital she had never lacked invitations from various members of the medical staff—usually a cinema and coffee and sandwiches on the way home, occasionally a dinner in some popular restaurant—but she had been at home now for nearly a year and she had lost touch. She hadn't minded; she was country born and bred and she hadn't lost her heart to anyone. Occasionally she remembered that she was twenty-five and there was no sign of the man Mrs Buckett coyly described as Mr Right. Florence had the strong suspicion that Mrs Buckett's Mr Right and her own idea of him were two quite different people.

She left home on the Sunday evening and, when it came to the actual moment of departure, with reluctance. The boys had gone back to school and she wouldn't see them again until half-term, but there was the Sunday school class she had always taken for her father, choir practice, the various small duties her mother had had to give up while she had been ill, and there was Charlie Brown, the family cat, and Higgins, the elderly Labrador dog; she had become fond of them during her stay at home.

'I'll be home next weekend,' she told her mother bracingly, 'and I'll phone you this evening.' All the same, the sight of her father's elderly greying figure waving from the platform as the train left made her feel childishly forlorn.

Mrs Twist's home dispelled some of her feelings of strangeness. There was a tray of tea waiting for her in her room and the offer of help if she should need it. 'And there is a bite of supper at eight o'clock, it being Sunday,' said Mrs Twist, 'and just this once you can use the phone downstairs. There's a phone box just across the road that Miss Brice used.'

Florence unpacked, arranged the photos and her bits and pieces, phoned her mother to assure her in a cheerful voice that she had settled in nicely and everything was fine, and then went down to her supper.

'Miss Brice was away for most weekends,' said the landlady, 'but sometimes she 'ad ter work, so we had a bite together.'

So Florence ate her supper in the kitchen with Mrs Twist and listened to that lady's comments upon her neighbours, the cost of everything and her bad back. 'Miss Brice told Mr Fitzgibbon about it,' she confided, 'and he was ever so kind—sent me to the 'ospital with a special note to a friend of 'is. 'E's ever so nice; you'll like working for him.'

'Oh, I'm sure I will,' said Florence, secretly not at all sure about it.

She arrived at the consulting-rooms well before time in the

morning. A taciturn elderly man opened the door to her, nodded when she told him who she was, and went to unlock Mr Fitzgibbon's own door. The place had been hoovered and dusted and there were fresh flowers in the vase on the coffee-table. Presumably Mr Fitzgibbon had a fairy godmother who waved her wand and summoned cleaning ladies at unearthly hours. She went through to the cloakroom and found her white uniform laid out for her; there was a frilled muslin cap too. He didn't agree with the modern version of a nurse's uniform, and she registered approval as she changed. She clasped her navy belt with its silver buckle round her neat waist and began a cautious survey of the premises, peering in cupboards and drawers, making sure where everything was; Mr Fitzgibbon wasn't a man to suffer fools gladly, she was sure, and she had no intention of being caught out.

Mrs Keane arrived next, begged Florence to put on the kettle and sorted out the notes of the patients who were expected. 'Time for a cup of tea,' she explained. 'We'll be lucky if we get time for coffee this morning—there's old Lady Trump coming, and even if we allow her twice as long as anyone else she always holds everything up. There's the phone, dear; answer it, will you?'

Mr Fitzgibbon's voice, unflurried, sounded in her ear. 'I shall be about fifteen minutes late. Is Sister Napier there yet?'

'Yes,' said Florence, slightly tartly, 'she is; she came at eight o'clock sharp.'

'The time we agreed upon?' he asked silkily. 'I should warn you that I frown upon unpunctuality.'

'In that case, Mr Fitzgibbon,' said Florence sweetly, 'why don't you have one of those clocking-in machines installed?'

'I frown on impertinence too,' said Mr Fitzgibbon, and hung up.

Mrs Keane had been listening; she didn't say anything but went and made the tea and sat down opposite Florence in the tiny kitchen. 'I'll tell you about the patients coming this morning. One new case—a Mr Willoughby. He's a CA, left lobe, sent to us by his doctor. Lives somewhere in the Midlands—retired. The other three are back for check-ups—Lady Trump first; allow half an hour for her, and she needs a lot of help getting undressed and dressed and so on. Then there is little Miss Powell, who had a lobectomy two months ago, and the last one is a child, Susie Castle—seven years old—a fibrocystic. It's not for me to say, but I think it's a losing battle. Such a dear child, too.'

She glanced at the clock. 'He'll be here in about two minutes...'

She was right; Mr Fitzgibbon came in quietly, wished them good morning and went to his consulting-room.

'Take Mr Willoughby in,' hissed Mrs Keane, 'and stand on the right side of the door. Mr Fitzgibbon will nod when he wants you to show the patient into the examination-room. If it's a man you go back into the consulting-room unless he asks you to stay.'

Florence adjusted her cap just so and took herself off to the waiting-room in time to receive Mr Willoughby, a small, meek man, who gave the impression that he had resigned himself to his fate. An opinion not shared by Mr Fitzgibbon, however. Florence, watching from her corner, had to allow that his quiet assured air convinced his patient that it was by no means hopeless.

'This is a fairly common operation,' he said soothingly, 'and there is no reason why you shouldn't live a normal life for some years to come. Now, Sister will show you the examination-room, and I'll take a look. Your own doctor seems to agree with me, and I think that you should give yourself a chance.'

So Florence led away a more hopeful Mr Willoughby, informed Mr Fitzgibbon that his patient was ready for him, and retired discreetly to the consulting-room.

Upon their return Mr Fitzgibbon said, 'Ah, Sister, will you hand Mr Willoughby over to Mrs Keane, please?' He shook hands with his patient and Florence led him away, a much happier man than when he had come in.

Lady Trump was quite a different matter. A lady in her eighties, who, at Mr Fitzgibbon's behest, had undergone successful surgery and had taken on a new lease of life; moreover, she was proud of the fact and took a good deal of pleasure in boring her family and friends with all the details of her recovery…

'You're new,' she observed, eyeing Florence through old-fashioned gold-rimmed pince-nez.

'Sister Brice is getting married.'

'Hmm—I'm surprised you aren't married yourself.'

Ushered into the consulting-room, where she shook hands with Mr Fitzgibbon, she informed him, 'Well, you won't keep this gel long, she's far too pretty.'

His cold eyes gave Florence's person a cursory glance. His, 'Indeed,' was uttered with complete uninterest. 'Well, Lady Trump, how have you been since I saw you last?'

Mrs Keane had been right: the old lady took twice as long as anyone else. Besides, she had got on all the wrong clothes; she must have known that she would be examined, yet she was wearing a dress with elaborate fastenings, tiny buttons running from her neck to her waist, and under that a series of petticoats and camisoles, all of which had to be removed to an accompaniment of warnings as to how it should be done. When at last Florence ushered her back to Mrs Keane's soothing care, she breathed a sigh of relief.

'Would you like your coffee, sir?' she asked, hoping that he would say yes so that she might swallow a mug herself. 'Miss Powell hasn't arrived yet.'

'Yes,' said Mr Fitzgibbon without lifting his handsome head from his notes, 'and have one yourself.'

Miss Powell was small and thin and mouse-like, and he treated her with a gentle kindness Florence was surprised to see. The little lady went away presently, reassured as to her future, and Florence, at Mr Fitzgibbon's brisk bidding, ushered in little Susie Castle and her mother.

Susie was small for her age and wore a look of elderly resignation, which Florence found heart-rending, but even if she looked resigned she was full of life just as any healthy child, and it was obvious that she and Mr Fitzgibbon were on the best of terms. He teased her gently and made no effort to stop her when she picked up his pen and began to draw on the big notepad on his desk.

'How about a few days in hospital, Susie?' he wanted to know. 'Then I'll have time to come and see you every day; we might even find time for a game of draughts or dominoes.'

'Why?'

'Well, it's so much easier for me to look after you there. We'll go to X-ray...'

'You'll be there with me? It's always a bit dark.'

'I'll be there. Shall we have a date?'

Susie giggled. 'All right.' She put out a small hand, and Florence, who was nearest, took it in hers. The child studied her face for a moment.

'You're very pretty. Haven't you met Prince Charming yet?'

'Not yet, but I expect I shall one day soon.' Florence squeezed the small hand. 'Will you be my bridesmaid?'

'Yes, of course; who do you want to marry? Mr Fitzgibbon?'

Her mother made a small sound—an apology—but Florence laughed. 'My goodness, no... Now, supposing we get you dressed again so that you can go home.'

It was later that day, after the afternoon patients had gone and she was clearing up the examination-room and putting everything ready for the next day, that Mr Fitzgibbon, on his way home, paused beside her.

'You are happy with your work, Miss Napier?'

'Yes, thank you, sir. I like meeting people...'

'Let us hope that you meet your Prince Charming soon,' he observed blandly, and shut the door quietly behind him.

Leaving her wondering if he was already looking forward to the day when she would want to leave.

CHAPTER TWO

THE DAYS PASSED QUICKLY; Mr Fitzgibbon allowed few idle moments in his day, and Florence quickly discovered that he didn't expect her to have any either. By the end of the week she had fallen into a routine of sorts, but a very flexible one, for on two evenings she had returned to the consulting-rooms to attend those patients who were unable or who didn't wish to come during the day, and on one afternoon she had been whisked at a moment's notice to a large nursing home to scrub for the biopsy he wished to perform on one of his patients there. The theatre there had been adequate, but only just, and she had acquitted herself well enough. On the way back to his rooms she had asked if he performed major surgery there.

'Good lord, no; biopsies, anything minor, but otherwise they come into Colbert's or one of the big private hospitals.'

They had already established a satisfactory working relationship by the end of the week, but she was no nearer to knowing anything about him than on the first occasion of their meeting. He came and went, leaving telephone numbers for her in case he should be needed, but never mentioning where he was going. His home, for all she knew, might be the moon. As for him, he made no attempt to get to know her either. He had enquired if she was comfortable at Mrs Twist's house, and if she found the work within her scope—a question which ruffled her calm considerably—and told her at the end of the week that she was free to go home for the weekend if she wished. But not, she discovered, on the Friday evening. The last patient didn't leave until six o'clock; she had missed her train and the next one too, and the one after that would get her to Sherborne too late, and she had no intention of keeping her father out of his bed in order to meet the train.

She bade Mr Fitzgibbon goodnight, and when he asked, 'You're going home, Miss Napier?' she answered rather tartly that yes, but in the morning by an early train. To which he answered nothing, only gave her a thoughtful look. She had reached the door when he said, 'You will be back on Sunday evening all right? We shall need to be ready on Monday morning soon after nine o'clock.' With which she had to be content.

It was lovely to be home again. In the kitchen, drinking coffee while her mother sat at the kitchen table, scraping carrots, and Mrs Buckett hovered, anxious not to miss a word, Florence gave a faithful account of her week.

'Do you like working for Mr Fitzgibbon?' asked her mother.

'Oh, yes, he has a very large practice and beds at Colbert's, and he seems to be much in demand for consultations…'

'Is he married?' asked Mrs Napier artlessly.

'I haven't the slightest idea, Mother; in fact, I don't know a thing about him, and he's not the kind of person you would ask.'

'Of course, darling—I just wondered if his receptionist or someone who works for him had mentioned something…'

'The people who work for him never mention him unless it's something to do with work. Probably they're not told or are sworn to secrecy…'

'How very interesting,' observed her mother.

The weekend went too swiftly; Florence dug the garden, walked Higgins and sang in the choir on Sunday, made a batch of cakes for the Mothers' Union tea party to be held during the following week, and visited as many of her friends as she had time for. Sunday evening came much too soon, and she got into the train with reluctance. Once she was back in Mrs Twist's house, eating the supper that good lady had ready for her, she found herself looking forward to the week ahead. Her work was by no means dull, and she enjoyed the challenge of not knowing what each day might offer.

Monday offered nothing special. She was disconcerted to find Mr Fitzgibbon at his desk when she arrived in the morning. He wished her good morning civilly enough and picked up his pen again with a dismissive nod.

'You've been up half the night,' said Florence matter-of-factly, taking in his tired unshaven face, elderly trousers and high-necked sweater. 'I'll make you some coffee.'

She swept out of the room, closing the door gently as she went, put on the kettle and ladled instant coffee into a mug, milked and sugared it lavishly and, with a tin of Rich Tea biscuits, which she and Mrs Keane kept for their elevenses, bore the tray back to the consulting-room.

'There,' she said hearteningly, 'drink that up. The first patient isn't due until half-past nine; you go home and get tidied up. It's a check-up, isn't it? I dare say she'll be late—a name like Witherington-Pugh...'

Mr Fitzgibbon gave a crack of laughter. 'I don't quite see the connection, but yes, she is always unpunctual.'

'There you are, then,' said Florence comfortably. 'Now drink up and go home. You might even have time for a quick nap.'

Mr Fitzgibbon drank his coffee meekly, trying to remember when last anyone had ordered him to drink his coffee and get off home. His childhood probably, he thought sleepily with suddenly vivid memories of Nanny standing over him while he swallowed hot milk.

Rather to his own surprise, he did as he was told, and when Florence went back to the consulting-room with the first batch of notes he had gone. He was back at half-past nine, elegant in a dark grey suit and richly sombre tie, betraying no hint of an almost sleepless night. Indeed, he looked ten years younger, and Florence, eyeing him covertly, wondered how old he was.

Mrs Witherington-Pugh, who had had open chest surgery for an irretractable hernia some years previously, had come for her annual check-up and was as tiresome as Florence had felt in her bones she would be. She was slender to the point of scragginess and swathed in vague, floating garments that took a long time to remove and even longer to put back on. She kept up what Florence privately thought of as a 'poor little me' conversation, and fluttered her artificial eyelashes at Mr Fitzgibbon, who remained unmoved. He pronounced her well, advised her to take more exercise, eat plenty and take up some interest.

'But I dare not eat more than a few mouthfuls,' declared the lady. 'I'm not one of your strapping young women who needs three meals a day.' Her eyes strayed to Florence's Junoesque person. 'If one is well built, of course...'

Florence composed her beautiful features into a calm she didn't feel and avoided Mr Fitzgibbon's eye. 'None the less,' he observed blandly, 'you should eat sensibly; the slenderness of youth gives way to the thinness of middle age, you know.'

Mrs Witherington-Pugh simpered. 'Well, I don't need to worry too much about that for some years yet,' she told him.

Mr Fitzgibbon merely smiled pleasantly and shook her hand.

Florence tidied up and he sat and watched her. 'Bring in Sir Percival Watts,' he said finally. He glanced at his watch. 'We're running late. I shan't need you for ten minutes—go and have your coffee. I'll have mine before the next patient—' he glanced at the pile of notes before him '—Mr Simpson. His tests are back; he'll need surgery.' He didn't look up as she went out of the room.

Sir Percival was on the point of going when she returned, and she ushered in Mr Simpson; at a nod from Mr Fitzgibbon she busied herself in the examination-room while he talked to his patient. She could hear the murmur of their voices and then silence, and she turned to find Mr Fitzgibbon leaning against the door-frame, watching her.

'I'll be at Colbert's if I'm wanted; I'll be back here about two o'clock. You should be able to leave on time this evening. I expect you go out in the evenings when you're free?'

'Me? No, I've nowhere to go—not on my own, that is. Most of my friends at Colbert's have left or got married; besides, by the time I've had supper there's not much of the evening left.'

'I told you the hours were erratic. Take the afternoon off tomorrow, will you? I shall be operating at Colbert's, and Sister will scrub for me. I shall want you here at six o'clock in the evening—there's a new patient coming to see me.'

He wandered away, and Florence muttered, 'And not one single "please"...'

Save for necessary talk concerning patients that afternoon, he had nothing to say to her, and his goodnight was curt. He must be tired, Florence reflected, watching from the window as he crossed the pavement to his car. She hoped that his wife would be waiting for him with a well-cooked dinner. She glanced at her watch: it was early for dinner, so perhaps he would have high tea; he was such a very large man that he would need plenty of good, nourishing food. She began to arrange a menu in her mind—soup, a roast with plenty of baked potatoes and fresh vegetables, and a fruit pie for afters. Rhubarb, she mused; they had had rhubarb pie at home at the weekend with plenty of cream. Probably his wife didn't do the cooking—he must have a sizeable income from his practice as well as the work he did at the hospital, so there would be a cook and someone to do the housework. Her nimble fingers arranged everything ready for the morning while she added an au pair or a nanny for his children. Two boys and a girl... Mrs Keane's voice aroused her from her musings.

'Are you ready to leave, Florence? It's been a nice easy day, hasn't it? There's someone booked for tomorrow evening...'

Florence went to change out of her uniform. 'Yes, Mr Fitzgibbon's given me the afternoon off, but I have to come back at six o'clock.'

'Ah, yes—did he tell you who it was? No? Forgot, I expect. A very well-known person in the theatre world. Using her married name, of course.' Mrs Keane was going around, checking shut windows and doors. 'Very highly strung,' she commented, for still, despite her years of working for Mr Fitzgibbon, she adhered to the picturesque and sometimes inaccurate medical terms of her youth.

Florence, racing out of her uniform and into a skirt and sweater, envisaged a beautiful not-so-young actress who smoked too much and had developed a nasty cough…

The next day brought its quota of patients in the morning and, since the last of them went around noon, she cleared up and then was free to go. 'Mind you're here at six o'clock,' were Mr Fitzgibbon's parting words.

She agreed to that happily; she was free for almost six hours and she knew exactly what she was going to go and do. She couldn't expect lunch at Mrs Twist's; she would go and change and have lunch out, take a look at the shops along the Brompton Road and peek into Harrods, take a brisk walk in the park, have tea and get back in good time.

All of which she did, and, much refreshed, presented herself at the consulting-rooms with ten minutes to spare. All the same, he was there before her.

He bade her good evening with his usual cool courtesy and added, 'You will remain with the patient at all times, Miss Napier,' before returning to his writing.

Mrs Keane wasn't there; Florence waited in the reception-room until the bell rang, and opened the door. She wasn't a theatre-goer herself and she had little time for TV; all the same, she recognised the woman who came in. No longer young, but still striking-looking and expertly made-up, exquisitely dressed, delicately perfumed. She pushed past Florence with a nod.

'I hope I'm not to be kept waiting,' she said sharply. 'You'd better let Mr Fitzgibbon know that I'm here.'

Florence looked down her delicate nose. 'I believe that Mr Fitzgibbon is ready for you. If you will sit down for a moment I will let him know that you're here.'

She tapped on the consulting-room door and went in, closing it behind her. 'Your patient is here, sir.'

'Good, bring her in and stay.'

The next half-hour was a difficult one. No one liked to be told that they probably had cancer of a lung, but, with few exceptions, they accepted the news with at least a show of courage. Mr Fitzgibbon, after a lengthy examination, offered his news in the kindest possible way and was answered by a storm of abuse, floods of tears and melodramatic threats of suicide.

Florence kept busy with cups of tea, tissues and soothing words, and cringed at the whining voice going on and on about the patient's public, her ruined health and career, her spoilt looks.

When she at length paused for breath Mr Fitzgibbon said suavely, 'My dear lady, your public need know nothing unless you choose to tell them, and I imagine that you are sufficiently well known for a couple of months away from the stage to do no harm. There is no need to tamper with your looks; your continuing—er—appearance is entirely up to you. Fretting and worrying will do more harm than a dozen operations.'

He waited while Florence soothed a fresh outburst of tears and near-hysterics. 'I suggest that you choose which hospital you prefer as soon as possible and I will operate—within the next three weeks. No later than that.'

'You're sure you can cure me?'

'If it is within my powers to do so, yes.'

'I won't be maimed?'

He looked coldly astonished. 'I do not maim my patients; this is an operation which is undertaken very frequently and gives excellent results.'

'I shall need the greatest care and nursing—I am a very sensitive person…'

'Any of the private hospitals in London will guarantee that. Please let me know when you have made your decision and I will make the necessary arrangements.'

Mr Fitzgibbon got to his feet and bade his patient a polite goodbye, and Florence showed her out.

When she got back he was still sitting at his desk. He took a look at her face and observed, 'I did tell you that it was hard work. At Colbert's I see as many as a dozen a week with the same condition and not one of them utters so much as a whimper.'

'Well,' said Florence, trying to be fair, 'she is famous…'

'Mothers of families are famous too in their own homes, and they face a hazardous future, and what about the middle-aged ladies supporting aged parents, or the women bringing up children on their own?'

Florence so far forgot herself as to sit down on the other side of his desk. 'Well, I didn't know that you were like that…'

'Like what?'

'Minding about people. Oh, doctors and surgeons must mind, I know that, but you…' She paused, at a loss for getting the right words, getting slowly red in the face at the amused mockery on his.

'How fortunate it is, Miss Napier,' he observed gently, 'that my life's happiness does not depend on your good opinion of me.'

She got off the chair. 'I'm sorry, I don't know why I had to say that.' She added ingenuously, 'I often say things without thinking first—Father is always telling me…'

He said carelessly, 'Oh, I shouldn't let it worry you, I don't suppose you ever say anything profound enough to shatter your hearer's finer feelings.'

Florence opened her mouth to answer that back, thought better of it at the last minute, and asked in a wooden voice, 'Do you expect any more patients, sir, or may I tidy up?'

She might not have spoken. 'Do you intend to leave at the end of the month?' he asked idly.

'Leave? Here? No...' She took a sharp breath. 'Do you want me to? I dare say I annoy you. Not everyone can get on with everyone else,' she explained in a reasonable voice, 'you know, a kind of mutual antipathy...'

He remained grave, but his eyes gleamed with amusement. 'I have no wish for you to leave, Miss Napier; you suit me very well: you are quick and sensible and the patients appear to like you, and any grumbling you may do about awkward hours you keep to yourself. We must contrive to rub along together, must we not?' He stood up. 'Now do whatever it is you have to do and we will go somewhere and have a meal.'

Florence eyed him in astonishment. 'You and I? But Mrs Twist will have something keeping warm in the oven for me...'

He reached for the telephone. 'In that case I will ask her to take it out before it becomes inedible.' He waved a large hand at her. 'Fifteen minutes—I've some notes to write up. Come back here when you're ready.'

There seemed no point in arguing with him; Florence sped away to the examination-room and began to put it to rights. Fifteen minutes wasn't long enough, of course; she would have to see to most of the instruments he had used in the morning—she could come early and do that. She worked fast and efficiently so that under her capable hands the room was pristine once more. The waiting-room needed little done in it; true, on her way out the patient had given vent to her feelings by tossing a few cushions around, but Florence shook them up smartly and repaired to the cloakroom, where she did her face and hair with the speed of light, got out of the uniform and into the jersey dress and matching jacket, thrust her feet into low-heeled pumps, caught up her handbag and went back to the consulting-room.

Mr Fitzgibbon was standing at the window, looking out into

the street below, his hands in his pockets. He looked over his shoulder as she went in. 'Do you like living in London?' he wanted to know.

'Well, I don't really live here, do I? I work here, but when I'm free I go home, so I don't really know what living here is like. At Colbert's I went out a good deal when I was off duty, but I never felt as though I belonged.'

'You prefer the country?'

'Oh, yes. Although I should think that if I lived here in surroundings such as these—' she waved an arm towards the street outside '—London might be quite pleasant.'

He opened the door for her and locked it behind him. 'Do you live in London?' she asked.

'Er—for a good deal of the time, yes.' There was a frosty edge to his voice which warned her not to ask questions. She followed him out to the car and was ushered in in silence.

She hadn't travelled in a Rolls-Royce before and she was impressed by its size; it and Mr Fitzgibbon, she reflected, shared the same vast, dignified appearance. She uttered the thought out loud. 'Of course, this is exactly the right car for you, isn't it?'

He was driving smoothly through quiet streets. 'Why?'

'Well, for one thing the size is right, isn't it?' She paused to think. 'And, of course, it has great dignity.'

Mr Fitzgibbon smiled very slightly. 'I am reassured to think that your opinion of me is improving.'

She couldn't think of the right answer to that; instead she asked, 'Where are we going?'

'Wooburn Common, about half an hour from here. You know the Chequers Inn? I've booked a table.'

'Oh—it's in the country?'

'Yes. I felt that it was the least I could do in the face of your preference for rural parts.'

'Well, that's awfully kind of you to take so much trouble. I mean, there are dozens of little cafés around Wimpole Street—well, not actually very near, but down some of the side-streets.'

'I must bear that in mind. Which reminds me, Mrs Twist asks that you should make sure that the cat doesn't get out as you go in.'

'Oh, Buster. She's devoted to him—he's a splendid tabby; not as fine as our Charlie Brown, though. Do you like cats?'

'Yes, we have one; she keeps my own dog company.'

'We have a Labrador—Higgins. He's elderly.' She fell silent, mulling over the way he had said 'we have one', and Mr Fitzgibbon waited patiently for the next question, knowing what it was going to be.

'Are you married?' asked Florence.

'No—why do you ask?'

'Well, if you were I don't think we should be going out like this without your wife… I expect you think I'm silly.'

'No, but do I strike you as the kind of man who would take a girl out while his wife actually sat at home waiting for him?'

Florence looked sideways at his calm profile. 'No.'

'That, from someone who is still not sure if she likes me or not, is praise indeed.'

They drove on in silence for a few minutes until she said in a small resolute voice, 'I'm sorry if I annoyed you, Mr Fitzgibbon.'

'Contrary to your rather severe opinion of me, I don't annoy easily. Ah—here we are. I hope you're hungry?'

The Chequers Inn was charming. Florence, ushered from the car and gently propelled towards it, stopped a minute to take a deep breath of rural air. It wasn't as good as Dorset, but it compared very favourably with Wimpole Street. The restaurant was just as charming, with a table in a window and a friendly waiter who addressed Mr Fitzgibbon by name and suggested in a quiet voice that the duck, served with a port wine and pink peppercorn sauce, was excellent and might please him and the young lady.

Florence, when consulted, agreed that it sounded delicious,

and agreed again when Mr Fitzgibbon suggested that a lobster mousse with cucumber might be pleasant to start their meal.

She knew very little about wine, so she took his word for it that the one poured for her was a pleasant drink, as indeed it was, compared with the occasional bottle of table wine which graced the vicarage table. She remarked upon this in the unselfconscious manner that Mr Fitzgibbon was beginning to enjoy, adding, 'But I dare say there are a great many wines—if one had the interest in them—to choose from.'

He agreed gravely, merely remarking that the vintage wine he offered her was thought to be very agreeable.

The mousse and duck having been eaten with relish, Florence settled upon glazed fruit tart and cream, and presently poured coffee for them both, making conversation with the well-tried experience of a vicar's daughter, and Mr Fitzgibbon, unexpectedly enjoying himself hugely, encouraged her. It was Florence, glancing at the clock, who exclaimed, 'My goodness, look at the time!' She added guiltily, 'I hope you didn't have any plans for your evening—it's almost ten o'clock.' She went on apologetically, 'It was nice to have someone to talk to.'

'One should, whenever possible, relax after a day's work,' observed Mr Fitzgibbon smoothly.

The nearby church clocks were striking eleven o'clock when he stopped before Mrs Twist's little house. Florence, unfastening her seatbelt, began her thank-you speech, which he ignored while he helped her out, took the key from her, unlocked the door and then stood looming over her.

'I find it quite unnecessary to address you as Miss Napier,' he remarked in the mildest of voices. 'I should like to call you Florence.'

'Well, of course you can.' She smiled widely at him, so carried away by his friendly voice that she was about to ask him what his name was. She caught his steely eye just in time, coughed instead, thanked him once again and took back her key.

He opened the door for her. 'Mind Buster,' he reminded her,

and shut the door smartly behind her. She stood leaning against it, listening to the silky purr of the car as he drove away. Buster, thwarted in his attempt to spend the night out, waited until she had started up the narrow stairs and then sidled up behind her, to curl up presently on her bed. Strictly forbidden, but Florence never gave him away.

If she had expected a change in Mr Fitzgibbon's remote manner towards her, Florence was to be disappointed. Despite the fact that he addressed her as Florence, it might just as well have been Miss Napier. She wasn't sure what she had expected, but she felt a vague disappointment, which she dismissed as nonsense in her normal matter-of-fact manner, and made a point of addressing him as 'sir' at every opportunity. Something which Mr Fitzgibbon noted with hidden amusement.

It was very nearly the weekend again, and there were no unexpected hold-ups to prevent her catching the evening train. It was almost the middle of May, and the vicarage, as her father brought the car to a halt before its half-open door, looked welcoming in the twilight. Florence nipped inside and down the wide hall to the kitchen, where her mother was taking something from the Aga.

'Macaroni cheese,' cried Florence happily, twitching her beautiful nose. 'Hello, Mother.' She embraced her parent and then stood her back to look at her. 'You're not doing too much? Is Miss Payne being a help?'

'Yes, dear, she's splendid, and I've never felt better. But how are you?'

'Nicely settled in—the work's quite interesting too, and Mrs Twist is very kind.'

'And Mr Fitzgibbon?'

'Oh, he's a very busy man, Mother. He has a large practice besides the various hospitals he goes to…'

'Do you like him, dear?' Mrs Napier sounded offhand.

'He's a very considerate employer,' said Florence airily. 'Shall I fetch Father? He went round to the garage.'

'Please, love.' Mrs Napier watched Florence as she went, wondering why she hadn't answered her question.

Sunday evening came round again far too soon, but as Florence got into the train at Sherborne she found, rather to her surprise, that she was quite looking forward to the week ahead. Hanging out of the window, saying a last goodbye to her father, she told him this, adding, 'It's so interesting, Father—I see so many people.'

A remark which in due course he relayed to his wife.

'Now, isn't that nice?' observed Mrs Napier. Perhaps by next weekend Florence might have more to say about Mr Fitzgibbon. Her motherly nose had smelt a rat concerning that gentleman, and Florence had barely mentioned him…

Florence, rather unwillingly, had found herself thinking about him. Probably because she still wasn't sure if she liked him, even though he had given her a splendid dinner. She walked round to the consulting-rooms in the sunshine of a glorious May morning, and even London—that part of London, at least—looked delightful. Mrs Keane hadn't arrived yet; Florence got the examination-room ready, opened the windows, put everything out for coffee, filled the kettle for the cup of tea she and Mrs Keane had when there was time, and went to look at the appointment book.

The first patient was to come at nine o'clock—a new patient, she noted, so the appointment would be a long one. The two following were short: old patients for check-ups; she could read up their notes presently. She frowned over the next entry, written in Mrs Keane's hand, for it was merely an address—that of a famous stately home open to the public—and when that lady arrived she asked about it.

Mrs Keane came to peer over her shoulder. 'Oh, yes, dear. A patient Mr Fitzgibbon visits—not able to come here. He'll go straight to Colbert's from there. Let's see, he'll be there all the afternoon, I should think—often goes back there in the evening on a Monday, to check on the operation cases, you know.

So there's only Lady Hempdon in the afternoon, and she's not until half-past four.' She hung up her jacket and smoothed her neat old-fashioned hairstyle. 'We've time for tea.'

The first patient arrived punctually, which was unfortunate because there was no sign of Mr Fitzgibbon. Mrs Keane was exchanging good-mornings and remarks about the weather, when the phone rang. Florence went into the consulting-room to answer it.

'Mrs Peake there?' It was to be one of those days; no time lost on small courtesies.

'Yes, just arrived, sir.'

'I shall be ten minutes. Do the usual, will you? And take your time.' Mr Fitzgibbon hung up while she was uttering the 'Yes, sir'.

Mrs Peake was thin and flustered and, under her nice manner, scared. Florence led her to the examination-room, explaining that before Mr Fitzgibbon saw new patients he liked them to be weighed, have their blood-pressure taken and so on. She went on talking in her pleasant voice, pausing to make remarks about this and that as she noted down particulars. More than ten minutes had gone by by the time she had finished, and she was relieved to see the small red light over the door leading to the consulting-room flicker. 'If you will come this way, Mrs Peake—I think I have all the details Mr Fitzgibbon needs from me.'

Mr Fitzgibbon rose from his chair as they went in, giving a distinct impression that he had been sitting there for half an hour or more. His, 'Good morning, Mrs Peake,' was uttered in just the right kind of voice—cheerfully confident—and he received Florence's notes with a courteous, 'Thank you, Sister; be good enough to wait.'

As Florence led Mrs Peake away later she had to admit that Mr Fitzgibbon had a number of sides to him which she had been absolutely unaware of; he had treated his patient with the same cheerfulness, nicely tempered by sympathetic patience, while he wormed, word by word, her symptoms from her. Finally when he had finished he told her very simply what was to be done.

'It's quite simple,' he had reassured her. 'I have studied the X-rays which your doctor sent to me; I can remove a small piece of your lung and you will be quite yourself in a very short time—indeed, you will feel a new woman.' He had gone on to talk about hospitals and convenient dates and escorted her to the door, smiling very kindly at her as he had shaken hands.

Mrs Peake had left, actually smiling. At the door she had pressed Florence's hand. 'What a dear man, my dear, and I trust him utterly.'

There was time to take in his coffee before the next patient arrived. Florence, feeling very well disposed towards him, saw at once that it would be a waste of time. He didn't look up. 'Thank you. Show Mr Cranwell in when he comes; I shan't need you, Sister.'

She wasn't needed for the third patient either, and since after a cautious peep she found the examination-room empty, she set it silently to rights. If Mr Fitzgibbon was in one of his lofty moods then it was a good thing he was leaving after his patient had gone.

She ushered the elderly man out and skipped back smartly to the consulting-room in answer to Mr Fitzgibbon's raised voice.

'I shall want you with me. Five minutes to tidy yourself. I'll be outside in the car.'

She flew to the cloakroom, wondering what she had done, and, while she did her face, set her cap at a more becoming angle and made sure her uniform was spotless, she worried. Had she annoyed a patient or forgotten something? Perhaps he had been crossed in love, unable to take his girlfriend out that evening. They might have quarrelled… She would have added to these speculations, only Mrs Keane poked her head round the door.

'He's in the car…'

Mr Fitzgibbon leaned across and opened the door as she

reached the car, and she got in without speaking, settled herself without looking at him and stared ahead as he drove away.

He negotiated a tangle of traffic in an unflurried manner before he spoke. 'I can hear your thoughts, Florence.'

So she was Florence now, was she? 'In that case,' she said crisply, 'there is no need for me to ask where we are going, sir.'

Mr Fitzgibbon allowed his lip to twitch very slightly. 'No—of course, you will have read about it for yourself. You know the place?'

'I've been there with my brothers.'

'The curator has apartments there; his wife is a patient of mine, recently out of hospital. She is a lady of seventy-two and was unfortunate enough to swallow a sliver of glass during a meal, which perforated her oesophagus. I found it necessary to perform a thoracotomy, from which she is recovering. This should be my final visit, although she will come to the consulting-room later on for regular check-ups.'

'Thank you,' said Florence in a businesslike manner. 'Is there anything else that I need to know?'

'No, other than that she is a nervous little lady, which is why I have to take you with me.'

Florence bit back a remark that she had hardly supposed that it was for the pleasure of her company, and neither of them spoke again until they reached their destination.

This, thought Florence, following Mr Fitzgibbon through a relatively small side-door and up an elegant staircase to the private apartments, was something to tell the boys when she wrote to them. The elderly stooping man who had admitted them stood aside for them to go in, and she stopped looking around her and concentrated on the patient.

A dear little lady, sitting in a chair with her husband beside her. Florence led her to a small bedroom presently, and Mr Fitzgibbon examined her without haste before pronouncing her fit and well, and when Florence led her patient back to the sitting-room he was standing at one of the big windows with the curator, discussing the view.

'You will take some refreshment?' suggested the curator, and Florence hoped that Mr Fitzgibbon would say yes; the curator looked a nice, dignified old man who would tell her more about the house…

Mr Fitzgibbon declined with grave courtesy. 'I must get back to Colbert's,' he explained, 'and Sister must return to the consulting-rooms as soon as possible.'

They made their farewells and went back to the car, and as Mr Fitzgibbon opened the door for her he said, 'I'm already late. I'll take you straight back and drop you off at the door. Lady Hempdon has an appointment for half-past four, has she not?'

She got in, and he got in beside her and drove off. 'Perhaps you would like to drop me off so that I can catch a bus?' asked Florence sweetly.

'How thoughtful of you, Florence, but I think not. We should be back without any delay!'

Mr Fitzgibbon, so often right, was for once wrong.

CHAPTER THREE

MR FITZGIBBON IGNORED the main road back to the heart of the city. Florence, who wasn't familiar with that part of the metropolis, became quite bewildered by the narrow streets lined with warehouses, most of them derelict, shabby, small brick houses and shops, and here and there newly built blocks of high-rise flats. There was, however, little traffic, and his short cuts would bring him very close to Tower Bridge where, presumably, he intended to cross the river.

She stared out at the derelict wharfs and warehouses they were passing with windows boarded up and walls held upright by wooden props; they looked unsafe and it was a good thing that the terrace of houses on the other side of the street was in a like state. There was nothing on the street save a heavily laden truck ahead of them, loaded with what appeared to be scrap iron. Mr Fitzgibbon had slowed, since it wasn't possible to pass, so that he was able to stop instantly when the truck suddenly veered across the street and hit the wall of a half-ruined warehouse, bringing it down in a shower of bricks.

Mr Fitzgibbon reached behind for his bag and opened the door. 'Phone the police—this is Rosemary Lane—lock the car, and join me.' He had gone striding up the road towards the still tumbling bricks and metal. There was no sign of the truck.

Florence dialled 999, gave a succinct description of the accident and its whereabouts, and added that at the moment the only people there were herself and a doctor and would they please hurry since whoever had been in the truck was buried under the debris. It took no time at all to take the keys, lock the car and run up the street to where she could see Mr Fitzgibbon, his jacket hanging on a convenient iron railing, clearing away bricks and sheets of metal, iron pipes and the like.

'They're coming,' said Florence, not wasting words.

Mr Fitzgibbon grunted. 'Stand there—I'll pass back to you and you toss it behind you, never mind where. The cabin will be just about here—if I could just get a sight of it…'

He shifted an iron sheet very gently and sent a shower of bricks sliding away so that he was able to pull out a miscellany of bricks and rubble. He passed these back piece by piece to Florence, stopping every now and then to listen.

There was a great deal of dust and they were soon covered in it. A sudden thought made Florence say urgently, 'Oh, do be careful of your hands…' She wished she hadn't said it the moment she had spoken—it had been a silly thing to say. What were cuts and bruises when a man's life was possibly at stake? Only the hands belonged to a skilled surgeon…

Seconds later Mr Fitzgibbon stopped suddenly, and Florence, clasping a nasty piece of concrete with wires sticking out of it, stood, hardly breathing, her ears stretched. Somewhere inside the heap of debris a voice was calling feebly. 'Oi,' it said.

Mr Fitzgibbon passed a couple of bricks to Florence. 'Hello, there!' He sounded cheerful. 'Hang on, we're almost there.'

It took several more minutes before he pulled another lump of concrete clear, exposing part of a man's face, coated with dust, just as an ambulance came to a halt beside them, and hard on its heels a police car and a fire engine.

Mr Fitzgibbon withdrew his head cautiously. 'There's a sheet of metal holding most of the stuff—we need the bricks and rubble out of the way so that we can get at him.'

The newcomers were experts; they widened the gap, shored up the metal above the man's head and brought up their equipment for Mr Fitzgibbon's use. He was head and shoulders inside now; Florence could hear him talking to the man, but he emerged very shortly. 'I need access to his legs. Can you clear the rubble from that end? As far as I can see, he's lying in a tunnel. It seems safe enough above his head, but I need to look at his legs. I believe he's pinned down.' He looked over his shoulder. 'Florence, my bag—I want a syringe and a morphia ampoule.'

He checked the drug and told her to draw it up, and slid into the gap again. The men were already busy, carefully shifting rubble from one end over the man's foot, and presently a boot came into view, and then the other foot, and Mr Fitzgibbon went to have a look.

'I'll have my bag,' he said to Florence. 'Tell the medics I want the amputation kit, then cram yourself through the gap and be ready to do what I tell you.' He spoke to the two men who had come to help him, and she slid carefully towards the man, already drowsy from the morphia.

'Cor, lumme,' he whispered, 'getting the VIP treatment, ain't I? And what's a pretty girl like you doin' 'ere?'

The space was small around the man, and Florence found Mr Fitzgibbon's face within inches of her own. He was applying a tourniquet above the man's knee. He said easily, 'Oh, Florence is my right hand. Pretty as a picture, isn't she? You ought to see her when her face is clean. Now, old chap, I'm afraid I shall have to take off part of your leg; you won't know anything about it, and I'll promise you'll be as good as new by the time I've finished with you in hospital. Just below the knee, Florence; let go when I say, and keep an eye open for everything else.'

He stretched behind him. 'I'll have that drip—hang on to your end, will you, while I get the needle in?'

He was busy for a few moments, talking quietly to the man as he worked, and when Florence moved a little and something tore he said, 'I hope that's nothing vital, Florence,' and the man chuckled sleepily.

''Old me 'and,' he told Florence, 'and keep an eye on old sawbones…'

Florence gave the grimy fist a squeeze. 'That's a promise.'

Mr Fitzgibbon shifted his bulk very slightly, and another face appeared. A young cheerful face, which winked at Florence. 'Going to put you off to sleep, old chap.'

He had the portable anaesthetic with him, and she said in a comfortable voice, 'And while he's doing it you can tell me about yourself. Are you married? Yes? And children, I expect… Three? I always think that three is a nice number…' She rambled on for a few more moments until the man was unconscious, then she took her hand from his and leaned forward as far as she could, ready to do whatever Mr Fitzgibbon wanted done.

He was working very fast, his gloved hands, despite their size, performing their task with gentleness, cutting and tying and snipping until he said, 'Let go slowly, Florence.'

She loosened the tourniquet very slightly, and then gradually slackened it. Everything held. Mr Fitzgibbon put his hand behind him for the dressings, and his helper had them ready. 'How's his pulse?'

'Strong, fast, regular. You'll take him out from your end?'

'Yes, support his head as far as you can reach.'

He disappeared from her view, but presently he and one of the medics crawled in again and began to shift the man while the third steadied the leg. It took some time; to Florence, her shoulders and arms aching from keeping the man's head and shoulders steady, it seemed like hours. At last he was free, loaded on to a stretcher and taken to the ambulance. She began to wriggle out backwards, and halfway there was caught round the waist and swung on to her feet by Mr Fitzgibbon.

'Stay there,' he told her and went back to talk to the ambulancemen, and she stayed, having no wish to move another step. She ached all over, she was filthy dirty, her mouth was full of dust and she wanted a cup of tea and a hot bath at that very minute; she also wanted to have a good cry, just by way of relieving her feelings.

Her wishes, however, were not to be granted, at least for the moment. Mr Fitzgibbon came back, took her by the arm and walked her to his car. 'In you get; I want to get to Colbert's at the same time as that ambulance.'

He waved to the police car and the fire engine as he came abreast of them, and the police car went ahead, its lights flashing and its siren wailing, and the fire engine brought up the rear.

They went very fast and the traffic parted for them rather like the waters of the Red Sea; at any other time Florence would have enjoyed it immensely.

'Has he got a chance?' she asked.

'Yes. I don't think there's much else damaged, but we can't be sure until he's X-rayed. I want to get at that leg, though—I'll need Fortesque! Ring Colbert's, will you, and see if you can get him?'

Mr Fortesque, the orthopaedic consultant, was found, and yes, he would make himself available, and yes, he'd get Theatre Sister on to it right away. Florence relayed the information as Mr Fitzgibbon drove, and was about to hang up when he said, 'Tell them I want a taxi at the hospital to take you home to Mrs Twist. You're not hurt or cut?'

'No, I don't think so.'

'Make sure of that. Go to Casualty if you have any doubts.' He gave her a brief grin. 'Good, we're here. I'll see you later.' He got out and opened her door. 'Get hold of Mrs Keane. I'll phone later.'

He had gone, but not before giving her an urgent shove towards the taxi waiting for her.

The driver got out and helped her into the cab. 'Been in an accident, love?' he wanted to know. 'Not hurt, are you?'

'No, I'm fine, just very dirty. We stopped to help a man trapped in his truck.' She gave him a shaky smile. 'If you'd take me to my rooms, then I can go back on duty...'

'Right away, love...where to?'

He got out and helped her from the cab, and she said, 'Can you wait a minute? I've not got any money with me but I can get some from my room...'

'All taken care of, love. Head porter at Colbert's told me to call back for it. Just you go in and have a nice cuppa and a lay down.'

He went to the door with her and thumped the knocker and, when Mrs Twist came, handed her over in a fatherly manner. ''Ad an accident,' he told her erroneously. 'I'll leave 'er to your loving 'ands.'

Florence thanked him. 'I'm sure Mrs Twist will give you a cup of tea.'

'Ta, love, but I'd best get back. Take care.'

Mrs Twist shut the door. 'Whatever's happened?' she wanted to know. 'Are you hurt? You're covered in dirt...'

Florence said, 'Not an accident. If you would let me have an old sheet or something I could take these things off here; otherwise the house will get dirty.'

'That's a bit of sense.' Mrs Twist bustled away, arranged an old tablecloth on the spotless lino in the hall, and begged Florence to stand on it. She peeled off everything, with Mrs Twist helping. 'And this dress is ruined,' declared that lady. 'There's a great piece torn out of the back; lucky there wasn't anyone to see your knickers.'

Mr Fitzgibbon must have had a splendid view when he had lifted her out of the truck. 'If I could have a bath and wash my hair, Mrs Twist?'

'That you may, love, and a nice hot cup of tea first. And how about a nice nap in bed?'

'I haven't the time. Mr Fitzgibbon has a patient at half-past four; I must get back to get ready for her.'

'You've not had your dinner?'

'No.'

'I'll have a sandwich or two for you when you've had your bath. Now off you go.'

Later, her head swathed in a towel, comfortable in a dressing-gown and slippers, Florence sat in Mrs Twist's kitchen, gobbling sandwiches and drinking endless cups of tea while she told her landlady all about it. Halfway through she remembered that she had to phone Mrs Keane and, since it was an emergency and Mrs Twist found the whole thing exciting, she was allowed to use the phone. Mrs Keane reacted with calm. 'You come over when you're ready,' she told Florence. 'We'll have a cup of tea, and by then I could ring Colbert's and see if Mr Fitzgibbon has any instructions for us. You're sure you're all right?'

'I'm fine.' Florence put down the phone and, urged by Mrs Twist, went on with her account of the morning's events.

There was more tea waiting for her when she got to the consulting-rooms, and Mrs Keane, despite her discreet manner, was avid to hear the details.

'What I don't understand,' said Florence, 'is why Mr Fitzgibbon was going to operate on the patient—he's a chest man…'

'Yes, dear; he specialises in chest surgery, but he can turn his hand to anything, and this Mr Fortesque is an old friend and colleague. Mr Fitzgibbon is a man who, once having started something, likes to see it through to the end.' She passed the biscuit tin. 'And you, dear, were you hurt at all?'

'No, but my uniform is ruined and I caught the back of the skirt on a nail or something and tore a great rent in it. Mrs Twist said she could see my knickers, which means everyone else saw them too.'

'Knickers?' asked Mrs Keane. 'I didn't think girls wore them any more—only those brief things with lace.'

'Well, yes, but I didn't tell Mrs Twist that—she was horrified enough.'

'Probably no one noticed.'

'Mr Fitzgibbon lifted me down from the truck; I was coming out backwards.'

'Mr Fitzgibbon is a gentleman,' declared her companion. 'Have another cup of tea! We have twenty minutes or so still.'

Florence was arranging the surgical impedimenta Mr Fitzgibbon might need when he came into the consulting-room and thrust wide the half-open door connecting the examination-room. If Florence had hoped for a slightly warmer relationship after their morning's experience she saw at once that she was going to be disappointed. He looked exactly as he always did, immaculate, his linen spotless, not a hair out of place, his manner coolly impersonal.

'Ah, Sister, none the worse for your experience, I hope? You feel able to finish the day's work?'

'Yes. What about that poor man? Did he have any other injuries?'

'Fractured ribs, a perforated lung and a fractured humerus. We've patched him up and he should do. He had plenty of pluck.'

'His wife...?'

'She's with him. She'll stay in the hospital for tonight at least.'

'The children?' Florence went on doggedly.

'With Granny.'

'Oh, good. Someone must have organised everything splendidly.'

'Indeed, yes,' agreed Mr Fitzgibbon, who had done the organising, getting this and that done, throwing his weight around rather, and no one daring to gainsay him. Not that he had been other than his usual cool, courteous self.

'Be good enough to give Mrs Keane details of your ruined uniform so that you can be reimbursed, and—er—for any other garment which may have suffered.'

Florence blushed.

No further reference was made to the morning's happenings, and she went off to her room feeling slightly ill done by. Mr

Fitzgibbon could have thanked her, or at least expressed concern as to her feelings—did he consider her to be made of stone? Florence, very much a warm-hearted girl, reflected that there must be something wrong with his life, something which made him uncaring of those people around him. But that wasn't true, she had to remind herself; he had been marvellous with the man in the truck—indeed, he had sounded quite different talking to him. Getting ready for bed, she decided that she was sorry for him; he needed someone or something to shake his unshakeable calm. Underneath that he was probably quite nice to know. Her eyes closed on the praiseworthy resolve to treat him with understanding, not to answer back and to show sympathy if he ever showed signs of needing it.

Full of good resolutions, she went to work the next morning, but there was little opportunity of carrying any of them out. Mr Fitzgibbon was decidedly abrupt in his manner towards her, and in the face of that it was hard to remain meek and sympathetic. Nevertheless, she fetched his coffee and bade him drink it in a motherly fashion, pointed out that it was a lovely morning and suggested that a weekend in the country would do him a world of good, adding that he probably didn't take enough exercise.

He raked her with cold eyes. 'Your solicitude for my health flatters me, Florence, but pray confine your concern to the patients.'

So much for her good intentions.

It was towards the end of the week as she was tidying up after a patient that Mrs Keane came in. 'There's Miss Paton here, Mr Fitzgibbon, wants to see you.' She hesitated. 'I did say that you were about to leave for the hospital.'

He looked up from his desk. 'Ask her to come in, will you, Mrs Keane?' He looked across to the half-open door of the examination-room, where Florence was putting away instruments. 'I shan't need you, Florence; if you haven't finished there perhaps you will come back presently?'

He spoke pleasantly but without warmth. She closed the door

and crossed the consulting-room, and reached the door just as it was opened from the other side. Out of the corner of her eye she saw Mr Fitzgibbon get to his feet as a girl came in. Not a girl, she corrected herself, taking in the details with a swift feminine eye, but a woman of thirty, good-looking, delicately made-up, dressed with expensive simplicity. She went past Florence with barely a glance.

'Darling, I simply have to see you. Naughty me, coming to your rooms, but you weren't at the party and I have so much…'

Florence reluctantly closed the door on the rather high-pitched voice, but not before she had heard Mr Fitzgibbon's, 'My dear Eleanor, this is delightful…'

'Who's she?' asked Florence, and Mrs Keane for once looked put out.

'Well, I can't say for certain, dear. She seems to be very friendly with Mr Fitzgibbon—she's always phoning him, you know, and sometimes he rings her. She's a widow; married an old man. He died a year or so ago. Very smart, she is—goes everywhere.'

'And does she…does he…? Are they going to get married?'

'If she gets her way they will, but you can't tell with him, dear. Never shows his feelings. Very popular he is, lots of friends, could go anywhere he chooses, but you never know what he's thinking, if you know what I mean.'

Florence thought she knew. 'But she's all wrong for him,' she said urgently.

Mrs Keane nodded, 'Yes, dear, he needs someone who doesn't butter him up—someone like you.'

'Me?' Florence said and laughed. 'Are you going home? I'll have to stay and finish the examination-room. I hope they won't be too long. I said I'd be at Colbert's at seven o'clock.'

'Of course, you've got friends there, I expect. I'll be off. The first patient is at nine o'clock tomorrow—a new one, too.'

After Mrs Keane had gone Florence went and sat in the kitchen, and it was another ten minutes before Mr Fitzgibbon and his visitor came out. She came out to meet him and asked if she should lock up, and then bade them goodnight. 'Who's that girl?' she heard Eleanor ask as they left the waiting-room. She wondered what he had replied, then shrugged her shoulders, finished her work and went home in her turn.

She had her supper on a tray in her room, changed quickly and went to catch a bus to Colbert's. The man who had been in the truck was out of Intensive Care and, since she had been on the hospital staff, she had no difficulty in obtaining permission to visit him.

She found him propped up in bed, looking very much the worse for wear but cheerfully determined to get better. His wife was with him; a small, thin woman whose nondescript appearance Florence guessed held as determined a nature as his. She didn't stay long; she arranged the flowers she had brought with her in a vase, expressed her delight at seeing him already on the road to recovery, and prepared to leave.

'Owes 'is life to you and that nice doctor,' said his wife as Florence prepared to say goodbye. 'Bless yer both for saving 'im. And that doctor. 'E's a gent if ever there was one. 'Aving me fetched like 'e did, and all fixed up to stay as long as I want, and the kids seen to. Not to mention the money. A loan, of course; as soon as we can we'll pay 'im back, but there's no denying the cash'll come in handy.'

Going back to her bedsit, Florence reflected that Mr Fitzgibbon was a closed book as far as she was concerned. And likely to remain so.

The next day was Friday and she would be going home in the evening. The day was much as any other; Mr Fitzgibbon never lacked for patients—his appointments book was filled weeks ahead and a good deal of each day was spent at the hospital. Florence cleared up after the last patient that afternoon, glad to be going home. Mr Fitzgibbon had been his usual terse self, and she felt the strong need for the carefree atmosphere of the vicarage.

She tidied away the last dressing towels, wiped the glass top of the small table to a brilliant shine and opened the door into the waiting-room. Mr Fitzgibbon was sitting on the corner of Mrs Keane's desk, talking to her, but he turned to look at Florence and got to his feet.

'I have just agreed to see a patient this evening, Florence. He is unable to come at any other time so we must alter our plans. You were going home this evening?'

She wouldn't have minded so much if she had thought he had sounded even slightly sympathetic. 'Yes, but there are plenty of morning trains—I can go tomorrow. At what time this evening do you want me here, sir?'

'Half-past six. Telephone your home now, if you wish.'

He nodded and smiled at Mrs Keane, and then went away.

'Hard luck, dear,' said Mrs Keane. 'Is there a later train you could catch?'

'It takes two hours to get to Sherborne and it would be too late for anyone to fetch me. No, it's all right, I'll go on the early train in the morning.'

'Is Mrs Twist home? What about your supper?'

'She's going out, but that's all right, I can open a tin of beans or something. I told her I'd be going home, you see.'

'It's spoilt Mr Fitzgibbon's evening too—he was to have taken someone out to dinner. I dare say it's that woman who came here—that Eleanor…'

'Well, it's nice to know that his evening is spoilt too,' said Florence waspishly. She smiled suddenly. 'And hers.'

Mrs Keane laughed. 'I'll be off; you're coming?'

They went out together, and Mrs Keane said cheerfully, 'See you Monday. He's operating at eight o'clock, so we'll have the morning to ourselves.'

Mrs Twist was put out. 'If I'd known I'd have got you a bit of ham for your supper…'

Florence hastened to placate her. 'If I may open a tin of beans? I'll do some toast. I've no idea how long it's going to take; Mr Fitzgibbon didn't say. I'll catch the early train tomorrow morning...'

'Well, if that's all right with you,' said Mrs Twist reluctantly. 'Just this once. Seeing it's for Mr Fitzgibbon.'

Florence let that pass. She doubted if he would need to open a tin of beans for his supper. She had her tea, tidied her already tidy person, took a quick look at Mrs Twist's *Daily Mirror* and went back to the consulting-room.

Mr Fitzgibbon was already there, brooding over some X-rays. 'Ah, there you are,' he observed, for all the world as though she were late instead of being five minutes early. He went back to his contemplation of the films and she took herself off to the waiting-room, ready to admit the patient.

He arrived fifteen minutes late, and Florence opened the door to him, recognising the famous features so often pictured on the front pages of the daily Press and the evening news on TV. She hoped that her face betrayed no surprise as she wished him good evening and begged him to take a seat. 'Mr Fitzgibbon is here,' she said, 'if you'll wait a moment.'

It struck her much later that one didn't ask men like that to wait a moment, but Mr Fitzgibbon had at that moment thrust open his door and come to shake hands with his patient. He nodded to Florence and she followed them into the consulting-room to hear him assure the man that she was utterly reliable and discreet. 'Sister will prepare the examination-room while I check the details your doctor has given me,' suggested Mr Fitzgibbon smoothly, and Florence, taking the hint, slid away and closed the door.

It seemed a long time before the two men came to the examination-room, and an even lengthier time before Mr Fitzgibbon was finished with his examination. The pair of them went back into the consulting-room, leaving Florence to clear up. Mr Fitzgibbon appeared to have used almost everything usable there—an hour's work at least, she thought, and it was already almost eight o'clock.

She was half finished when he came in. His patient had gone and there was only the reading-lamp on his desk to light the consulting-room.

He said pleasantly, 'I'm sorry that your evening has been spoilt.' He picked up a hand towel from the pile she had just arranged. 'Mrs Twist has supper waiting for you?'

'Oh, yes,' said Florence airily, 'something special.' She said, 'She's a good cook, and I expect we shall have it together...'

Mr Fitzgibbon replaced the towel carefully. 'In that case, there's no point in suggesting that we might have had a meal somewhere together.'

'Was your evening spoilt too?' asked Florence, aware that it had been, but hoping for a few details.

'Spoilt? Hardly. Shall I say that it necessitated a change of plans?'

'Me too,' agreed Florence with a cheerful lack of grammar. 'Never mind, you have the whole weekend.'

'Indeed I have. Be outside Mrs Twist's at half-past eight tomorrow morning, Florence: I will drive you home.'

She arranged everything just so, put the hand towels out of his reach and finally said, 'That is most kind of you, sir, but there is a train I can catch... It only takes two hours; I can be home well before lunchtime.'

'Two hours? I can do it in an hour and a half in the car. I need a breath of country air too.'

'Won't it spoil your day?' asked Florence feebly.

'My dear Florence, if it were going to spoil my day I should not have suggested it in the first place.'

She looked extremely pretty standing there, the last of the sun turning her hair to burnished copper, her face a little tired, for it had been a long day. She gave him a clear look, making sure that he had meant what he had said. 'Then I'd like that very much,' she told him quietly.

'Go home now, Florence. I have some writing to do, so I'll lock up.' He turned back to his desk. 'Goodnight.'

She wished him a good night and made her way to Mrs Twist's, where she kicked off her shoes, opened a tin of baked beans, took the pins out of her hair and sat on the kitchen table, eating her supper. Of course, supper with Mr Fitzgibbon would have been quite a different matter—a well-chosen meal at the end of the day would have been very acceptable, but not acting as a substitute for the glamorous Eleanor.

She fed Buster, had a bath and presently went to bed.

It was a glorious morning; it was almost June and a lovely time of the year. She swapped the dress she had been going to wear for a much prettier one, telling herself it was because it was more suited to the bright sunshine outside, and she skipped downstairs to make a cup of tea. Mrs Twist took things easy on Saturdays and there would be no breakfast, although Florence knew she was free to help herself. The note she had left on the kitchen table for her landlady had gone, and in its place Mrs Twist had left one of her own. 'Don't let Buster out. Have a nice trip, you lucky girl.'

Florence drank her tea, gave Buster his breakfast, picked up her weekend bag and let herself out of the house. She was closing the door gently behind her when the Rolls came to quite a quiet halt and Mr Fitzgibbon got out to open her door.

She wished him good morning and thought how nice he looked in casual clothes; he looked younger too, and his 'good morning' was uttered in a friendly voice. Emboldened, she remarked upon the beauty of the morning, but beyond a brief reply he had nothing to say and she supposed that he wasn't in the mood for conversation. She let out a small surprised yelp when a warm tongue gently licked the back of her neck. She turned her head and found herself looking into a pair of gentle brown eyes in a whiskered face, heavily shrouded in eyebrows and a great deal of light brown hair.

'Ah, I should have mentioned,' said Mr Fitzgibbon casually, 'Monty likes the country too. You don't mind?'

'Mind? No, of course not. She has a beautiful face. What is she?'

'We have often wondered… We settled for a mixed parentage.'

'Did you get her from a breeder or a pet shop?'

'Neither—from a doorway in a street full of boarded-up houses. It took some time for her to achieve the physical perfection she now enjoys, but, even now, it is difficult to decide what her parents might be.'

Florence exchanged another look with the brown eyes behind her. 'She's awfully sweet. Higgins will love her. I'm not sure about Charlie Brown, though—he's our cat.'

'Monty likes cats. Our cat had kittens a couple of weeks ago and she broods over the whole basketful whenever Melisande goes walking.'

'Melisande—the cat?'

'Yes. Does your mother know that we're coming?'

'Yes. My brothers are home again for half-term.'

They lapsed into silence again, broken only by Monty's gentle sighs and mutterings. They were on the A303 by now and the road was fairly clear, for it was still early. Florence, sitting back in the comfortable seat with the dog's warm breath on her neck, felt happy and, since there seemed to be no need to talk, she took time to wonder why. Of course, being driven in a Rolls-Royce was enough to make anyone happy, but it was more than that: she was enjoying Mr Fitzgibbon's company, even though he was doing nothing at all to entertain her. She felt quite at ease with him, and the thought surprised her, for until that moment she had got used to the idea that she didn't much like him, only, she had to admit, sometimes.

Presently she ventured to remark that he could turn off at Sparkford, and then added, 'Oh, sorry, you came with Mr Wilkins.' Then, because he didn't answer, 'Do you like this part of England?'

'Very much; an easy drive from town and, once one is away

from the main road, charmingly rural.' He turned off the A303 and took a minor road towards Sherborne, and presently left it for a narrow country road, its hedges burgeoning with the foliage of oncoming summer.

Gussage Tollard lay in a hollow; they could see the housetops as they went down the hill, and Florence gave a contented sigh. 'Oh, it is nice to be home,' she said.

'You regret taking the job?' Mr Fitzgibbon wanted to know sharply. 'You do not like working for me?'

'Of course I like working for you, it's a super job. Only I wish I knew you better…' She stopped, very red in the face. 'I'm sorry, I don't know what made me say that.'

'Well, if you ever find out, let me know.' He didn't look at her, for which she was thankful. 'The vicarage is past the church and along the lane, isn't it?' He sounded so casual that she hoped he might not have heard what she had said, but he must have done because he had told her to tell him… It had been a silly remark and easily forgotten.

She said cheerfully, 'Here we are.' She glanced at her watch. 'It took an hour and twenty-five minutes. You were right.'

'Of course I was.' He spoke without conceit as he got out, opened her door and then let Monty out, giving her the chance to run into the house first.

CHAPTER FOUR

FLORENCE HADN'T REACHED the door before her mother came to meet her, and hard on her heels were her two brothers, with Higgins shoving his way past them to jump up at her, barking his pleasure.

Florence said breathlessly, 'Hello, Mother—boys…here's Mr Fitzgibbon.'

He had followed more slowly, and stood quietly with Monty beside him as they all surged towards him.

'You've met each other,' said Florence to her mother, and added, 'these are my brothers—Tom and Nicky. Oh, and this is Higgins…'

Higgins had sat down deliberately in front of Monty, and presently bent his elderly head to breathe gently over the little dog.

'Oh, good, they're going to be friends,' said Mrs Napier. 'Come in—the coffee is ready. Did you have a decent drive from London?'

She led the way indoors, and Mr Fitzgibbon, at his most urbane, gave all the right answers and, when asked, declared that there was nothing he enjoyed more than coffee in the kitchen.

'You see, I'm getting lunch and we can all talk there while

I'm cooking.' Mrs Napier gave him a sweet smile. 'Sit here,' she told him, offering a Windsor chair by the big scrubbed table. 'I'm afraid we use the kitchen a great deal, especially in the winter. This is a nice old house but it is all open fireplaces—there's no heating otherwise, and we spend hours lugging in coals just to keep the sitting-room fire glowing. Thank heaven for an Aga.' She beamed at him. 'Have you one in your home?'

Mr Fitzgibbon hesitated for a moment. 'Er—yes, I believe we have.'

'Well, I'm sure you must need it, leading the kind of life you do...at everybody's beck and call, I dare say.'

She was pouring coffee as she spoke, and Florence picked up a jug of hot milk. 'Black or white?' she asked him. She had been listening to her mother rambling on in her gentle way and not minding in the least; if he didn't like it it was just too bad.

Apparently he didn't mind; he accepted milk and sugar and a large slice of the cake on the table, and entered into a spirited conversation with her brothers concerning cars, although he interlarded this with small talk with her mother, and presently, when she remarked that the vicar had gone to Whitehorse Farm a mile the other side of the village, he suggested he might take the car and give him a lift back. An idea which appealed to the boys and which Mrs Napier instantly accepted. 'Do leave your little dog here if you like; she seems happy enough with Higgins...'

They all went out to the car again, and when Mr Fitzgibbon opened the car doors both dogs got in as well. Florence stood with her mother, watching the car turn smoothly out of the gate, and her mother said, 'I do hope he doesn't mind taking the boys and Higgins; he seems such a nice man—charming manners too. Very considerate to work for, I've no doubt, love.'

'I suppose so, Mother. Nothing is allowed to stand in the way of his work, though, and he's very reserved. He doesn't talk much, only to tell me what he wants done...'

'But, darling, you're not working all the time; you had a two hours' drive from London—you must have talked…?'

Florence cast thoughts back to the morning's journey. 'Well, no, only this and that, you know.'

'I'm surprised that he isn't married,' observed Mrs Napier chattily.

They were in the kitchen, clearing up the coffee-cups. 'I honestly don't think he's had the time to fall in love, although he must know any number of suitable women…'

'Suitable?'

'Well, you know what I mean, Mother. His kind of female, beautifully dressed and made-up and entertaining and witty and not needing to work…'

Mrs Napier gave a mug an extra polish. 'What makes you think that is his kind of female?'

'A girl—no, a woman came to the consulting-rooms, Eleanor something or other, and he seemed awfully pleased to see her. She had one of those voices you actually hear from yards away even though they're not speaking loudly—you know what I mean?'

'I don't know Mr Fitzgibbon well, but he strikes me as a man who is unlikely to succumb to such a woman. Do you suppose he might stay for lunch?'

'I doubt it,' said Florence. 'Here they are now.'

Her father was the only one to come into the kitchen; the others were outside, and Florence could see two youthful heads on either side of a grizzled one, peering into the Rolls's engine.

Her father kissed her and patted her on the shoulder in a paternal fashion.

'My dear, what a very pleasant man your doctor is…'

'He's a surgeon, Father, and he's not mine…'

'No, no, my dear, I speak lightly. So kind of him to drive over to fetch me, and he's so patient with the boys.' He looked at his wife. 'Might he not be invited to lunch?'

'Of course, it's Saturday—he must be free. I'll ask him.'

Presently, back in the kitchen, he refused. 'There is nothing I would have enjoyed more,' he assured Mrs Napier, 'but I have a date this afternoon, added to which I must get back to town.'

'Well, of course you must,' declared Mrs Napier comfortably. 'I don't suppose you have much time in which to enjoy yourself. It was very kind of you to drive Florence here. It's not like her to miss the train.'

'Ah, but that's why I brought her—she didn't miss the train, she had to stay on Friday evening to attend a patient; I sometimes have consultations at awkward hours.'

Mrs Napier, who had been nurturing the beginnings of a possible romance between this nice man and her daughter, was disappointed.

They went to the door to see him off, and Mrs Napier said wistfully, 'A pity you couldn't stay; I would so enjoy hearing about your work—I really am quite vague as to what exactly Florence does…'

He was getting into the car. 'Works very hard, Mrs Napier; she is also clear-headed and brave, and doesn't make a fuss when her clothes get torn and she gets covered in dust.' He turned to grin at Florence's annoyed face. 'Do ask her about it.'

He waved a hand, and drove away with the minimum of fuss.

'What exactly did he mean?' asked Mrs Napier. 'Come indoors, love, and tell us about it. Have you been in an accident?'

'No,' said Florence crossly, 'and I wasn't going to say anything about it. How tiresome he is.'

'Yes, dear. Now sit down and tell us what happened.'

There was nothing for it but to do as her mother asked. 'Really, I didn't do anything; I mean, only what anyone else would have done. It was Mr Fitzgibbon who rescued the man and amputated his leg. He did it on his hands and knees and it must have been very uncomfortable for him as he's so very large. He went straight to Colbert's and there was further surgery to do. He sent me back to my bedsit in a taxi.'

'How very kind.'

'Yes? He expected me to be on duty at the consulting-rooms later that afternoon.' Florence gave an indignant snort. 'He doesn't spare himself, and he doesn't spare anyone else either.'

'He did bring you home in that Rolls,' Tom pointed out. 'I think he's absolutely super...'

'So do I,' said Nicky. 'He knows a lot about cars too.'

'Pooh,' said Florence, 'who wants to know about cars anyway?' And she flounced out of the room and up to her bedroom, where she hung out of the window and brooded, although she wasn't sure what she was brooding about.

It was impossible to brood for long. The garden below her window was bursting with a mixture of early-summer flowers: roses, entangled with soldiers and sailors, wallflowers, forget-me-nots, pansies, lilies of the valley and buttercups rioted all over the rather neglected flowerbeds of the vicarage garden. Florence took herself off downstairs, firmly resolved to bring a little order to the colourful chaos.

The weekend was over far too quickly; she left the half-weeded garden with reluctance, aware that the hard work she had put into it had done much to assuage the feeling of restlessness. Sitting in the train on the way back to London, she reflected that a week's hard work would get her back to her normal acceptance of life once more.

Her room looked cramped and dreary after the comfortable shabbiness of the vicarage; she arranged the flowers she had brought back with her, unpacked her overnight bag and took a bunch of roses down to the kitchen for Mrs Twist, who was so delighted with them that she opened a tin of soup to add to their supper of corned beef, lettuce and tomatoes.

She walked to work the next morning, the early sunshine already warm. It was going to be a lovely day, and her thoughts turned longingly to the garden at home and all those roses needing her attention. Once at the consulting-rooms and in Mrs Keane's company, she became her usual self. With Mr Fitzgibbon at the hospital, there was the opportunity to give the examination-room a good clean, check the instruments, see that the cupboards and the drawers were stocked, and have a leisurely cup of coffee with Mrs Keane.

'You got home, then?' asked that lady as they drank it.

'Mr Fitzgibbon gave me a lift on Saturday morning.'

'Well, I never did—how very kind of him. Was he spending the weekend in your part of the world, I wonder?'

'Oh, no. He only stayed for a cup of coffee; he said he had a date...'

'That Eleanor woman, I have no doubt. There were two calls from her on the answering machine. Well, he's not likely to take her out this evening—he won't get away from Colbert's much before one o'clock, and there are five appointments starting at two o'clock.'

Mrs Keane took another biscuit. 'He'll be a bit terse, I dare say. Monday morning and all that.' She asked abruptly, 'Are you going to stay? I do hope so.'

'Heavens, the month is almost up, isn't it? Yes, I hope he'll decide to keep me on. The work's interesting, isn't it? And it's nice being able to go home each weekend. And the money, of course...'

'Well, I don't expect you'll get home every weekend. There's an appointment for Wednesday—a query. In the Midlands. You'll probably have to go with him, perhaps stay overnight; it could easily have been the weekend, even though it isn't this time.'

'Well, that's all right.'

'Good. Do you mind if I go out for half an hour? I must get something for supper tonight and we'll probably be too late for the shops this afternoon.'

Left to herself, Florence did some more turning out of cupboards and drawers, and she answered the phone several times and then turned on the answering machine and listened to Eleanor's voice. She sounded snappy; Mr Fitzgibbon hadn't turned up to take her to the theatre, nor had he bothered to let her know why. The second message was even snappier. Florence, while conceding that Mr Fitzgibbon wasn't a man who needed sympathy, being well able to look after himself, felt quite sorry for him.

Mrs Keane was back, and they had eaten their lunch when he came in. His 'good afternoon' was austere, and he looked tired, which wasn't surprising, since he had been operating since eight o'clock, but as Florence ushered in the first of the patients she saw that he had somehow shed his weariness, presenting to his patients a sympathetic calm and a complete concentration.

The last one went just before five o'clock, and she took in a cup of tea Mrs Keane had ready for him.

He glanced up as she went in. 'I'm going back to Colbert's,' he told her. 'My first appointment is for nine o'clock tomorrow morning, isn't it? If I'm late say all the usual, will you? I'll hope to get here, but I can't be certain.'

She murmured and went to the door, to be halted by his, 'By the way, I have to go to Lichfield on Wednesday—a little girl with cystic fibrosis. She's been a patient of mine for some time, but her parents insisted on taking her home… She's a difficult child and I shall want you with me. It is possible that we shall have to spend the night, so bring a bag with you. We shall leave around midday after the morning appointments. I've engaged to meet her local doctor at half-past two.'

'Uniform, sir?'

'Oh, decidedly, and your starchiest manner. The poor child is spoilt by her parents and an old nanny, but she responds quite well to calm authority.'

Florence said, 'Yes, sir,' and took herself out of the room. A couple of days away from the consulting-rooms would be a nice change, but it sounded as though she was going to have her work cut out. She found Mrs Keane in the kitchen, drinking tea, and she poured herself a cup.

'I'm to go to Lichfield,' she explained, 'and probably stay the night there, as you thought.'

'Oh, Phoebe Villiers—Sister Brice dreaded that visit; the

child's very difficult and the parents absolutely refuse to let her have further treatment in hospital. They had a house somewhere in Hampstead, and that's how Mr Fitzgibbon took her on as a patient; got her into Colbert's and there really was an improvement, but the parents moved to their other house at Lichfield and discharged her. He could have refused to go on treating her as a patient, but he would never do that, not while there was a chance of keeping the child as fit as possible.'

'So he goes all the way up there to see her?'

'Yes, every three months—she's a private patient, of course, but even if she weren't I believe that he would still go. He doesn't give up easily.'

The next day went smoothly enough; it was just as Mr Fitzgibbon was leaving in the evening after a long afternoon that Florence asked, 'Do I have time to go back to Mrs Twist's tomorrow and fetch my overnight bag?'

'I think not. I want to get away in good time. We shall have to stop for a meal of sorts on the way; you can do whatever you do to your face and hair then.'

Florence muttered a reply. The man needed a wife so that he might have some insight into female ways. She wondered if he treated Eleanor in such an arbitrary fashion, and how she responded if he did. Of course, the occasion would never arise; Eleanor had all the time in the world to make herself ready for any social outing, and this, Florence reminded herself briskly, was by no means to be a social visit—not one of them was likely to notice if her hair was all anyhow and her nose shining.

All the same, she washed her hair that evening, attended to her nicely kept hands and packed an extra uniform. She had dealt with difficult children in hospital and knew how prone they were to throw things…

It wanted ten minutes to noon as Mr Fitzgibbon eased the Rolls away from the kerb. Florence, sitting silently beside him, thought of the small tasks she hadn't had time to do, made a mental inventory of the contents of her overnight bag, and tried not to think about lunch. Her breakfast had been a sketchy one that morning and there had been no time for coffee. She hoped her insides wouldn't rumble. Anyone else, she reflected, and she wouldn't have hesitated to say that she was hungry, but a quick peep at her companion's severe profile made it obvious that he wasn't concerned about food. Getting out of London was uppermost in his mind.

Not knowing that part of the city well, she became quite bewildered with the short cuts and the ins and outs of nondescript streets, and once or twice she wondered if he had got lost, but suddenly they were on the M1, going north, and his well-shod foot went down on the accelerator.

'You're a girl after my own heart,' he said, 'you know when to hold your tongue.' After which astonishing remark he lapsed into silence once more, leaving her to wonder whether he had meant that as a compliment or merely an expression of relief; either way it seemed a good idea to stay silent.

The miles flew by, and they had passed the outskirts of Luton when he slowed the car and turned into Toddington Service Station.

'Twenty minutes and not a minute more. Out you get.'

She got out and followed him into the vast and busy cafeteria. 'Coffee and sandwiches?' he asked as he sat her down at a table. 'Any preference?'

'Cheese, and tea, not coffee.' She added after his retreating back, 'Please.'

The place wasn't too full; he was back quickly with his tray: sandwiches for both of them, coffee for him and a little pot of tea for her—she liked him for that.

They didn't waste time talking, but she liked him even better when he said, 'This is hardly the kind of place to which I would take you, Florence, but we are rather pressed for time. You must allow me to give you dinner one evening as recompense.'

She paused before taking another bite. 'That's all right, sir. These sandwiches are very good, and the tea is heavenly.'

She swallowed a second cup and stood up when he asked her if she was ready.

'I'll meet you at the car—I'll be very quick.' She had whisked herself away, not seeing his quick smile at the unselfconscious remark. The image of Eleanor crossed his mind; in like circumstances she would have talked prettily about powdering her nose and kept him waiting for ten minutes. Of course, she would never allow herself to be in surroundings such as these in the first place.

He was back in the car by now and watched Florence emerge from the Ladies' and make a swift beeline towards him.

He opened the door, shut her in once more and got in beside her. The motorway wasn't busy, since it was the lunch-hour, and the Rolls, kept at a steady pace of seventy miles an hour, made light of the distance. Florence, busy with pleasant plans as to the laying out of her first pay cheque, due the next day, was surprised to see the sign to Lichfield ahead of them. Mr Fitzgibbon turned off the motorway. 'Around twelve miles,' he remarked. He glanced at his watch. 'You will probably have five minutes or so before you meet Phoebe.' He glanced at her. 'You look remarkably neat and tidy.'

'I should hope so,' said Florence tartly. 'You wouldn't employ me for long if I weren't.'

'True. Which reminds me—you intend to stay on?'

'Well, yes, if you're quite satisfied with me, sir.'

'Given time, I see no reason why we shouldn't deal excellently with each other.'

The kind of quelling remark which was enough to tempt a girl to give in her notice then and there.

The Villiers lived a few miles from the town, and Florence glanced around as they drove through the double gates and along a driveway as smooth as silk, running through gardens so well laid out that it might have been painted instead of planted.

A far cry from the vicarage garden, always in need of a good weed and the pruning shears, and twice as beautiful. The house matched the garden: with its pristine white walls, sparkling windows and glossy paint, it seemed rather like a stage setting. Mr Fitzgibbon, apparently oblivious to his surroundings, got out, opened her door and walked with her to the wide porch.

Florence, still feeling as though she were on a film set, was ushered into the hall by a maid, very correctly dressed, even to a cap on her head, and stood quietly waiting for whatever would happen next.

'Mr Fitzgibbon and Sister Napier—we are expected,' said Mr Fitzgibbon, and she walked beside him as they were shown into a large room with a lofty ceiling and french windows opening on to the garden, and furnished with modern chairs, deep couches and glass-topped tables. Florence, brought up among well-polished oak and mahogany pieces, winced.

The man and woman who came to meet them matched the room. Well-dressed, the woman beautifully made-up and coiffeured, they were as modern as their surroundings.

Mrs Villiers spoke first. 'Mr Fitzgibbon—so good of you to come. Dr Gibbs will be joining us shortly.' Her eyes swept over Florence. 'A new nurse? What happened to the other one?'

'Sister Brice left me to get married—may I introduce Sister Napier, Mrs Villiers?'

Mrs Villiers nodded in Florence's direction without looking at her. 'Well, do sit down and have a drink… Nurse can go to her room for a moment or two.'

'I should prefer her to meet Phoebe before we examine her.' Mr Fitzgibbon's courteous manner was very cool.

'Oh, if she must. The child's with Nanny. I'll get someone to take her up.'

'I think it might be better if I go too. Perhaps I might be told when Dr Gibbs arrives?'

Mrs Villiers laughed and shrugged her shoulders. 'You must

do what you think best, I suppose.' She glanced at her silent husband. 'Archie, ring the bell, will you?'

They were led upstairs by the maid, and then through a closed door and down a passage, which led to the nursery, a room that overlooked the grounds at the back of the house, comfortably furnished with rather a shabby lot of furniture, and much too warm. No wonder, thought Florence; there were no windows open, and there was a quite unnecessary fire in the old-fashioned grate too.

Phoebe was sitting at the table, a painting book and a paint-box before her, and opposite her was an elderly woman with a round, pasty face and beady eyes. She got up as they went in, wished Mr Fitzgibbon a good afternoon and stared at Florence.

He brought his considerable charm to bear upon her, so after a moment she relaxed, nodded a greeting to Florence and told Phoebe to say 'how do you do?' like a little lady.

'Hello,' said Phoebe, and went back to her painting. She would have been a pretty child but her illness had given her the look of an under-nourished waif, with eyes too big for her face and no colour in her cheeks.

Mr Fitzgibbon wasted no time. 'And how is the tipping and tapping going?'

'Well, sir, we don't bother with it—Phoebe doesn't like it, poor little lamb; she's happy to stay in this nice warm room with her old nanny, aren't you, love?'

Phoebe didn't answer her, but after a moment looked sideways at Florence. 'Who's she?'

'I've come to look at you and Sister Napier is here to help me. Dr Gibbs will be here directly.'

'I shan't,' said Phoebe.

Florence pulled out an armchair and sat down beside her. 'Why not?' she asked cheerfully. 'Do tell.'

'Just because...'

'We've come a long way,' said Florence, 'and Mr Fitzgibbon is a very busy man. Still, if you won't there's nothing for us to do but get into the car and drive all the way back to London.' She had picked up a paintbrush and was colouring an elephant bright red.

'Elephants aren't red!' said the child scornfully.

'No. But it's nice to do things wrong sometimes, isn't it? Roses are red…do you go into the garden each day and smell them?'

'I'm too ill.'

'That's why Mr Fitzgibbon has come to see you; he'll examine you, and perhaps he'll tell you that you're not so ill any more, and then you can go into the garden.'

Florence finished the elephant and started to paint a zebra with purple stripes.

'I'm very highly strung,' said Phoebe, 'did you know?'

'I've often wondered what that meant—do you suppose you swing from the ceiling?'

Phoebe chuckled. 'I like you. I didn't like the other nurse—I bit her.'

'Ah, but you won't need to bite anyone today because you're getting better.'

Mr Fitzgibbon had been talking to Nanny, but he turned to look at Florence now. He asked, 'Aren't you afraid to get bitten, Florence?'

'Me, sir? Not in the least; in any case, I always bite back.'

He laughed, but Nanny frowned, and it was just as well that the door opened then and Dr Gibbs came in. He was elderly with a nice kind face, and he greeted Mr Fitzgibbon warmly.

'This is Sister Napier, who has replaced Sister Brice, and, since we're all here, shall we have an examination and then discuss the situation later? We are to spend the night. Sister Napier will carry out the tipping and tapping in the morning and let me know what progress has been made. I understand that it has been discontinued.'

'Yes, well, I'll tell you about that.' Dr Gibbs shook Florence's hand. 'If Nanny will allow us we can go into Phoebe's room…'

Phoebe was by no means an easy little patient; the examination took twice as long as it needed to, while Florence used all her patience and ingenuity to keep the child reasonably calm and still. The two men went away presently, leaving her to pacify Phoebe as she dressed her again and then handed her back to a suspicious Nanny.

Florence explained that she would have to rouse Phoebe in the morning and bore meekly the other woman's resentment. 'I'm sorry,' said Florence, 'but Mr Fitzgibbon has told me to do this, and he is in charge of the child. I'm sure you want the best possible treatment for her.'

She bade the still complaining child goodbye for the moment and found her way downstairs. Poor little Phoebe was an ill child and she need not have been—given a longer period in hospital and the proper treatment, she would have had a chance to live longer. Florence thought that once they had gone again Nanny would do exactly what she wanted, and any treatment Mr Fitzgibbon had ordered would be ignored.

She wasn't sure where she should go or what she should do—there was no sign of anyone. The two men would be discussing their findings or having tea with the Villierses, which reminded her that a cup of tea would be welcome. As there was no one in sight, she walked through the hall and out of the front door, and strolled along the carefully tended paths; they looked as though no one ever walked along them…

Mr Fitzgibbon, standing at the drawing-room window, listening to Mrs Villiers's peevish voice assuring him that she was far too sensitive to see that the treatment he had ordered was properly carried out and adding a list of her own ailments, allowed his eyes to stray to Florence, strolling along in the afternoon sunshine. Her copper hair glowed under the neat cap, and he thought that even in her severe uniform she looked exactly right in a rose garden.

He heard Mrs Villiers say fretfully, 'Well, I suppose we had better have a cup of tea. Do sit down, Mr Fitzgibbon, and you, Dr Gibbs. I suppose your nurse will want tea?'

'I am sure that Sister Napier would like that. I see that she is walking in the garden.'

'Archie, go and fetch her, will you?'

Conversation over tea was constrained, and Phoebe wasn't mentioned, but when the teacups had been carried away Mr Fitzgibbon observed, at his most bland, 'If I may I shall take Sister Napier into the garden and brief her as to tomorrow morning, and then perhaps we may have a talk about Phoebe.'

They were well away from the house when he asked, 'Well?'

'Well what, sir? If we're talking about Phoebe I think it's a crying shame that her treatment has been so neglected. If it had been carried out properly and she could have gone back into hospital… Can't you make them?' she asked fiercely.

'My dear girl, short of living here and sharing Phoebe's nursery, I see no way of altering things. I have suggested that they employ a nurse to care for the child. Mrs Villiers tells me, however, that Nanny wouldn't agree to that and she categorically refuses to discuss it. Dr Gibbs does what he can but, as you know, one cannot insist on treatment against the patient's wishes or, in the case of Phoebe, her parents'.'

'Nanny is angry that I must disturb Phoebe tomorrow morning.'

'I thought she might be. Would you like me to come along too?'

'At six o'clock in the morning?' She turned to look up at him. 'That wouldn't do at all.'

'I want to be away by nine o'clock. Dr Gibbs will be here at half-past eight—you will be ready?'

'Yes, sir.'

'Do you suppose,' asked Mr Fitzgibbon smoothly, 'that when there is no one around you might stop calling me sir with every other breath?'

Florence considered this. 'No, it wouldn't do at all.'

'It makes me feel elderly.'

'Nonsense, you're not in the least elderly. Do you suppose I'm to dine with you this evening, or have something on a tray?'

He stopped to look down at her with an air of cold surprise which quite shook her. 'Do you imagine that I would allow that? I am surprised at you even suggesting such an idea.'

'Well, I dare say you are, but Mrs Villiers wouldn't be…'

'Let us not waste time talking about her.' They turned to walk back towards the house. 'I'm operating tomorrow afternoon at two o'clock. Theatre Sister is on holiday, so I shall want you to scrub.'

'You tell me now!' exclaimed Florence. 'Really, you are—'

'Yes?' asked Mr Fitzgibbon softly.

'Never mind, sir. What are you going to do?'

'A lobectomy—you can manage that?'

'I shall do my best, sir.' She spoke sweetly, but her blue eyes flashed and the colour came into her cheeks.

'You are quite startlingly beautiful when you're cross,' said Mr Fitzgibbon, and opened the doors into the drawing-room so that she might go ahead of him.

She had been given a room near the nursery. It was pleasant enough, given that it was furnished with the impersonal style of a hotel bedroom. There was a bathroom next door, and she whiled away the hour before dinner lying in a very hot bath, thinking about Mr Fitzgibbon. The thoughts were wispy—odds and ends of conversations, the manner in which he could change from a pleasant companion to a reserved consultant, the expert way in which he handled his car, the way he had tackled what had appeared to be the hopeless task of freeing the man in the truck. 'I shall end up liking him if I go on like this,' said Florence, peering at her lobster-red person in the bathroom mirror.

Later, in bed and half asleep, she went over the evening. Dinner had been very formal, and the sight of Mrs Villiers in black chiffon and sequins had made her very aware of her uniform, even though it was the pristine one she had packed. The conversation had been stilted, with Mrs Villiers talking about her delicate constitution, her husband making very little effort to take part in the conversation, and Mr Fitzgibbon, with his beautiful manners, saying the right things at the right time. As for herself, she had answered when spoken to, listened to Mrs Villiers's grumbles with what she privately called her listening face, and allowed her thoughts to wander. They wandered all over the place and ended up at Mr Fitzgibbon as she fell asleep.

They left at nine o'clock the next morning, and Florence heaved a sigh of relief as Mr Fitzgibbon turned the car on to the road. The morning so far had been horrendous. Phoebe had been a handful, and Nanny had made her worse. Florence had longed to tell her that her cosseting of the child was doing more harm than good, but she guessed that Mr Fitzgibbon had already made that plain. She had eaten a solitary breakfast while he and Dr Gibbs had talked to the Villierses. She stole a look at his stern profile, and decided not to speak until spoken to.

They were more than halfway to the motorway before he said anything.

'We could have done a great deal for that child. Dr Gibbs will continue to urge them to let her go into hospital, but I'm afraid that by the time he does it may be too late to be of much help.'

Florence, despite her kicked shins, agreed with him. 'Poor scrap,' she said.

'You did very well, Florence, and I'm sorry that you weren't treated with better manners.'

'That didn't matter.'

He gave her a quick glance. 'You're a kind girl and you haven't uttered a single grumble. We'll stop at Milton Keynes and have a pot of coffee.'

They joined the M1 presently, travelling for the most part in silence. Florence was quite glad of that: it gave her a chance to check up on her theatre technique.

They stopped at the Post House in Milton Keynes and had their coffee and a plate of buns, not hurrying, and talking in a desultory fashion, and, although they didn't say much for the rest of the journey, Florence found the silence comfortable. Perhaps their relationship was getting on to a more friendly footing. She was surprised to realise that she very much hoped so.

CHAPTER FIVE

MR FITZGIBBON LEFT his consulting-rooms within minutes of arriving, staying only long enough to check Mrs Keane's carefully written messages and go through his post, leaving Florence with the advice that she should be at Colbert's not later than a quarter-past one. 'I have my own instruments there,' he went on, 'but it would be as well for you to check everything before we start.'

Well, of course it would, she agreed silently, and what about her lunch? He had gone without another word.

She said rather worriedly to Mrs Keane, 'Do you suppose I dare pop over to Mrs Twist's and ask her for a sandwich? She doesn't like me going there during the day...'

'I thought of that, dear.' Mrs Keane's cosy voice sounded pleased with itself. 'I bought some sausage rolls for you as I came in this morning. I remembered how poor Sister Brice would come back from somewhere or other, quite famished. I've got the kettle on; we'll have a cup of tea, and I'll eat my sandwiches at the same time and you can tell me all about it.'

Before she went to catch the bus to Colbert's Florence took a look at the appointments book. There were two patients for later that afternoon. She reckoned that Mr Fitzgibbon would have finished before four o'clock, but there were still his instruments to check before they went down to be sterilised and repacked. The first patient was booked for five o'clock; with luck she would be back at the consulting-rooms by then. She joined the queue for the bus and wondered just how quickly she would be able to change back into uniform.

Although she had worked as Staff Nurse in Theatre for some months, she felt uncertain about her reception, but she need not have worried. The staff nurse on duty was newly qualified and nervous.

'I'm glad it's you,' she confided as Florence got into her theatre kit, 'he scares me stiff, and he looks at you…'

'Well, yes,' agreed Florence, and thought that his eyes were rather nice; they could, of course, look like grey steel, but on the other hand they could look warm and amused. 'Now I'd better lay up my trolley.'

The anaesthetist remembered her as she walked in with the trolley, and he nodded to her in a friendly fashion. 'Hello, Florence, how nice to see you back. No chance of you staying with us?'

He checked his patient and settled down on his stool, and when she shook her head observed, 'Working for Fitzgibbon, aren't you? He's a lucky chap!'

Florence's lovely eyes crinkled in a smile behind her mask; a pity Mr Fitzgibbon wasn't there to hear that. He came a moment later, towering over everyone in his green gown. He wished everyone an affable good afternoon, and got down to work. He had his registrar with him and a houseman, rather timidly assisting, very much in awe of his chief. He had no need to be; Mr Fitzgibbon shed the light of his good humour over everyone there, so that the houseman became quite efficient and the little staff nurse, who was good at her job, forgot to be nervous of him. He worked unhurriedly and with the ease of long practice, and Florence, all the well-remembered routine taking over, handed instruments seconds before he held out a hand for them. All the while he carried on a casual conversation with the other men, so that the atmosphere, which had been rather fraught when he had first come in, became decidedly relaxed. In all, reflected Florence, getting out of the gown, a pleasant afternoon. She was carefully checking his instruments, which one of the nurses was washing before sending them to be sterilised, and she was still in her green theatre smock, when he came back into Theatre.

'How long will you be?' he asked.

'Me? Oh, fifteen minutes, sir. I'll be back in time for the first patient.'

'Make sure it is fifteen minutes—I'll be outside in the forecourt.'

'There's no...' She caught his eye, grey steel. 'Very well, sir,' she said, outwardly meek.

'He's never going to take you back with him?' said the little staff nurse.

'Well, I have to be at his consulting-rooms for the first patient, and I might get held up catching a bus,' said Florence practically.

She finished what she was doing calmly, got back into her dress and went down to the forecourt.

He was there, leaning on the car's bonnet, reading the first edition of the evening paper. He folded it away tidily and opened her door. Sitting beside her before starting the engine, he observed, 'You did very well, Florence.'

Her, 'Thank you, sir,' was uttered with just the right amount of meekness.

There was still a little time before the patient would arrive; she was pleased to see that Mrs Keane had the tea-tray ready and surprised when that lady said blithely, 'Tea is made, Mr Fitzgibbon, and I popped out for some of those biscuits you like. How handy the telephone is, to be sure, otherwise I wouldn't have known when you were coming back. I'll bring you a cup...'

'Thank you, Mrs Keane. The second patient has an appointment for half-past five, hasn't he? When you've shown him in, go home. Florence can do whatever else is necessary.'

'Well, if she doesn't mind...'

'Of course I don't mind; there'll be little enough to do anyway.' She eyed the biscuits hungrily. 'I'll get changed before I have my tea...'

Mr Fitzgibbon paused at the door. 'Did you have lunch?' he wanted to know.

'Mrs Keane was kind enough to get some sausage rolls for me this morning.'

'Sausage rolls?' He eyed her shapely person thoughtfully. 'An insufficient diet for one of your build, Florence.'

If he heard her indignant gasp as he turned away he gave no sign.

She had time for three cups of tea and almost all of the biscuits before the patient arrived, a youngish woman with her husband. She was a little frightened, and it was fearfully difficult to get clear answers to Mr Fitzgibbon's gently put questions. Florence, in attendance, reflected that he must be a kind man under his reserved manner. She mulled over the surprising information Mrs Keane had given her over their tea; he didn't only have a large out-patients clinic at Colbert's and operate there twice a week, but he also had another clinic in Bethnal Green, which dealt with the sad regiments of the homeless, sent to him from various charities. So many of them refused to go to a hospital, but the clinic was a different matter. He had willing helpers too—retired nurses, local doctors, social workers. 'Don't you ever mention it,' warned Mrs Keane. 'He never talks about it to anyone. He has to tell me, of course, because I keep his notes and do the bills and the rent and so forth for him. He's helped a good many there, I can tell you; gives them money, finds them jobs, and sometimes helps get them somewhere to live. I don't know how he finds the time, and him with a busy social life too.'

Florence showed the patient and her husband out, saw Mrs Keane on her way and, observant of Mr Fitzgibbon's bell, showed in the last patient.

An elderly, rather shabby man, but very neat; his manners were nice too. He wished her a polite good afternoon, volunteered his name—Mr Clarke—and sat down with the air of one expecting to wait.

'There's Mr Clarke, sir,' said Florence, sliding into the consulting-room.

'Ah, yes. Show him in, Florence, will you? I shan't be needing you for the moment. You could start tidying up.'

She gave him a cross look. Tidying up was none of his business—she was well aware of what had to be done and when. He was writing something, and without looking up he murmured, 'You wished to say something?'

'Yes, but I won't,' said Florence, and swept back into the waiting-room to usher Mr Clarke in.

As she closed the door she heard Mr Fitzgibbon's voice, friendly and calm. 'Mr Clarke, I'm so glad that you could come...'

She went and looked out of the window for a few moments, and then began her clearing up. There wasn't much to do. She put things ready for the morning and went to look at the appointments book. There was a slip of paper tucked into it and she looked at it idly. It was a note in Mr Fitzgibbon's scrawling handwriting, addressed to Mrs Keane, telling her to make an appointment for Mr Clarke, who should by rights have attended his out-patients clinic at Colbert's, but, owing to family circumstances, was unable to do so. 'No fees,' it ended.

Florence put it back where she had found it. It was getting very hard to dislike Mr Fitzgibbon.

She was roused from her thoughts by his voice on Mrs Keane's intercom, bidding her return. Mr Clarke had to be weighed, his blood-pressure taken, his pulse recorded and his respirations noted, and while she did these things she could see that the nice little man was upset and quite determined not to show it. Her small chores done, she went away again and presently showed him out before going into the examination-room to replace towels and the couch cover, clean up generally and stow everything that had been used in the laundry bag. She didn't hurry over this; the evening stretched before her and, although it was a lovely summer one, she was tired, mentally as well as physically. She would eat whatever supper Mrs Twist put before her and go to bed with a book. The appointment book was crammed for the next day and she felt reasonably sure that she wouldn't be able to get the evening train home. That couldn't be helped; she would go on Saturday morning, and in the afternoon she would take her mother into Sherborne and they would buy the washing-machine. Florence fingered the pay envelope in the pocket of her uniform and decided that, uncertain hours or not, it was worth it.

There was no sign of Mr Fitzgibbon and, since she was quite finished, she tapped on his door and went in. 'Is there anything more you would like done, sir?' she asked.

He closed the folder in which he had been writing. 'Nothing—I think we've crammed as much into today as we can, don't you? We've earned ourselves a meal. I've some work to finish here and I must go home. I'll call for you at Mrs Twist's house in an hour's time.'

'Are you inviting me out to dinner, Mr Fitzgibbon?' Her voice was tart.

He looked up briefly. 'Well, of course I am; had I not made myself plain?'

She hesitated: the invitation had sounded more like an order; on the other hand, the dinner he was offering would surely be more appetising than Mrs Twist's reliable but uninspired cooking. 'Thank you, sir, I should like to come.'

'Good, and for God's sake stop calling me sir.'

'Very well, Mr Fitzgibbon,' and then a little shyly, 'Do I need to dress up?'

His fine mouth twitched. 'No, no, there's a nice little place just off Wigmore Street, five minutes' walk from here.' He looked up and smiled at her, a slow, comforting smile. 'You must be tired.'

'I'll be ready in an hour, Mr Fitzgibbon.' She whisked away, very quickly got out of uniform and sped back to Mrs Twist, ready with apologies for not eating the supper which that good lady would have prepared for her, but she had no need of them: Mr Fitzgibbon had telephoned, and her landlady met her with a simpering smile and the opinion that Mr Fitzgibbon was a gentleman right enough, and was Florence likely to be late back?

'Most unlikely,' said Florence in a matter-of-fact manner. 'We're both tired and tomorrow is booked solid. I may have to stay Friday night and catch an early train home on Saturday morning.'

'Perhaps he'll drive you home again?' suggested Mrs Twist, a woman with a romantic turn of mind.

'Most unlikely, Mrs Twist. Would you mind if I had my bath now instead of this evening?'

'You go ahead, and make the best of yourself,' advised Mrs Twist.

Advice which Florence intended to take. Nicely refreshed from her bath, she examined her wardrobe, searching for something suitable to wear to a nice little place within five minutes' walk. It was a pity, she reflected, that she had no idea what a nice little place consisted of in Mr Fitzgibbon's mind. She decided on a leaf-green crêpe dress with a square neckline and a little matching jacket, piled her copper hair into a chignon, thrust her feet into white sandals, found the little white handbag and put all that she might need into it, and took a last look at herself in the old-fashioned wardrobe mirror. Not being a conceited girl, she decided that she looked all right, thanking heaven that it was a fine evening and that she wouldn't need to take a coat. She hadn't got a suitable one anyway. She would get one on Saturday, she promised herself, and went downstairs, a few minutes early.

Mr Fitzgibbon was in Mrs Twist's front parlour, making himself agreeable to that lady. He had changed into a lighter suit and his tie was slightly less sombre than usual, and gold cuff-links gleamed discreetly from snow-white cuffs. He looked, thought Florence, extremely handsome; no wonder that Eleanor woman was after him. He stood up as she went in.

'Ah, Florence, punctual as always.' He studied her person without appearing to do so, bade Mrs Twist farewell and ushered her outside. 'You don't mind a very short walk? The car is outside the consulting-rooms if you would prefer to drive?'

'I'd like a walk. We don't have much time to take walks, do we?'

'Very little. Do you walk a lot at home?'

'Oh, yes. Miles—I sometimes cycle, though. Father has two villages in the parish as well as Gussage Tollard; when I'm at home I often have to help out with the Mothers' Union and choir practice, and then the bike comes in handy.'

'Do you like country life?'

'I was born and brought up in the vicarage—I went away to boarding-school, but only to Sherborne. I hated London when I came to Colbert's to train.'

'It is hardly a good part in which to live.'

They were walking through the quiet, dignified streets, and she looked round her. 'Well, no, but this is quite different; one could live in any of these streets and be quite content. Though I'd miss the country…'

'A weekend cottage in the country would settle that question, wouldn't it?'

Florence laughed. 'Very nicely. I must look round for a wealthy man with a house round about here and another one in some pretty village.'

He said dreamily, 'There are plenty of wealthy men living in and around this area…'

'I'm sure that there are, only I don't have the chance to meet any of them.'

She looked up at him and laughed. 'Isn't it nice to talk nonsense sometimes?' They were in a narrow side-street, and a moment later he ushered her down some steps into a quite small restaurant, its tables covered in snowy linen and set with gleaming cutlery and lighted by candles. It was fairly full, and Florence was relieved to see that her dress would pass muster. She sat down and glanced around her unselfconsciously with frank pleasure. It was an attractive place with white walls, upon which hung some rather nice flower paintings, and the seats were comfortable, the tables not too close together and the waiter, when he came, most attentive.

The menu was impressive and there were no prices upon it, a fact which left her in some doubt as to what to order. Small it might be, but she had a suspicion that it was expensive.

Mr Fitzgibbon, watching her from under drooping lids, smiled to himself.

'I don't know about you,' he observed, 'but I'm hungry. How about crab mousse to start with, noisettes of lamb—they do a splendid sauce with them—and we can choose a sweet later?'

Much relieved, she agreed at once, and agreed again when he suggested a dry sherry while they waited. 'This is a delightful place—why, you wouldn't even know it was here, would you?'

He understood her. 'Nicely hidden away and quiet.'

For something to say she asked, 'I expect you've been here before?'

'Several times.' He smiled at her across the table; she really looked charming sitting there opposite him, the candlelight turning her hair to burnished gold. The dress, he decided, was by no means new or in the forefront of fashion, and she had no jewellery, only a plain gold chain and her watch. He found himself comparing her with Eleanor, who had phoned that evening and demanded that he should take her to some party or other. He had drifted into a casual friendship with her over the years, and although he wasn't in love with her he had found himself wondering if he might marry her. He wanted a wife, a home life and children, but not with Eleanor; the certainty of that had been in his mind for several weeks, although he had ignored it. Now, watching Florence, he acknowledged it.

He began a trivial conversation, touching on a variety of subjects. Over the lamb he asked casually, 'You like reading?'

She popped some delicious garden peas into her mouth. 'Oh, yes. Anything I can lay hands on…'

'Poetry?'

'Well, yes, I like John Donne and the Brownings—oh, and Herrick; I'd rather read a book, though.'

'*Jane Eyre*?' he asked with a twinkle. '*Pride and Prejudice*, *Wuthering Heights*, anything by—what is her name?—M M Kaye?'

Florence speared a baby carrot. 'However did you know? Yes, I read all those. I like gentle books, if you see what I mean.'

'Yes, I see. You're a gentle girl, Florence. Because you're a parson's daughter?'

She took the remark seriously. 'Yes, probably, but I do have a very nasty temper.'

'So do I, Florence, although I flatter myself that I can control it unless I'm severely provoked.'

'Well, I don't suppose that happens very often,' said Florence comfortably. 'People always seem to do what you want straight away, but, of course, you're important, aren't you?'

She looked up, smiling, and met a steely grey stare. 'Are you buttering me up, Florence?'

She refused to be intimidated. 'Good heavens, no. Why should I do that? Anyway, it's true, and I'm sorry if you're mad at me. Father is always telling me to think before I speak.'

'It is I who should apologise, Florence. Feel free to say what you want without thinking first.'

'Excepting when I'm at work, of course.'

'Having settled the matter, let us turn our attention to a sweet. Biscuit glacé, perhaps, with strawberries? Or a crème brûlée?'

'I'd like the biscuit glacé, please; I can make a crème brûlée at home…'

He ordered, and asked for the cheese board for himself. 'You can cook?'

'Well, of course I can, and I had plenty of opportunity to try out recipes while I was looking after Mother. I suppose all women can cook; it comes naturally, like making beds and ironing shirts.' She was matter-of-fact.

He reflected that he had never had the opportunity of knowing if Eleanor could do any of those things, but it seemed unlikely. He must remember to ask her next time they met. The thought that he was enjoying himself engendered a wish to repeat the occasion.

They had their coffee and walked back presently, and at Mrs Twist's door he took the key from her. 'Do we have to look out for Buster?'

'No, he'll be with Mrs Twist upstairs.' She took back the key. 'Thank you for my dinner, Mr Fitzgibbon; it was a lovely evening.'

'It was a pleasure, Florence.'

He opened the door and she went inside. 'Goodnight, and thank you again.'

His 'Goodnight, Florence,' was quietly said as she closed the door.

She wasn't quite sure what she expected when she got to work the next morning, but it certainly wasn't Mr Fitzgibbon's cold stare and equally cold 'Good morning.' He was seated at his desk, looking so unlike the pleasant companion of the previous evening that the smile faded from her pretty face, and at the first opportunity she sought out Mrs Keane to ask her if she had done or not done something.

'Don't worry, dear,' soothed Mrs Keane, 'I know he's very

pleased with your work. Something's on his mind—or someone; that Eleanor, I suppose...'

'Are they engaged or—or anything?'

'No, nor likely to be: he's no more in love with her than I am. He's thirty-six now, and if you ask me he's never been in love—not enough to want to marry. For one thing he's too busy, and for another she'd have to be a girl who could get past that austere manner.'

'He's not always austere,' said Florence, remembering the previous evening.

Mrs Keane gave her a quick look. 'No, dear, but only a few people know that.' She put on the kettle. 'There's time for a cup of tea now if we're quick, before the first patient comes; we can have coffee later. I'll see to the percolator and have the coffee ready, and you can take him a cup then.'

The first patient arrived and Florence turned into an impersonal automaton, doing what was required of her and then melting into the background until she was needed again, carefully not looking higher than Mr Fitzgibbon's firm chin, and when the patient had gone she fetched his coffee and set the cup and saucer down on his desk gently, suppressing a sudden and surprising wish to throw the lot at him. She wasn't at all sure why, but it might have relieved her feelings.

The last patient for the morning had gone when he was called away to the hospital, and half an hour later he rang to say that the afternoon patients would have to be notified that he would be delayed. 'Postpone the first appointment for half an hour,' he told Mrs Keane, 'and the rest for the same time.'

'There goes my chance to get the evening train,' said Florence crossly. 'That's two weekends running. Do you mind if I use the phone to let Mother know?'

'Perhaps that nice Mr Fitzgibbon will drive you down again, love,' said her mother in a pleased voice.

Florence snorted. 'It's the last thing he'll do,' she said snappily, 'and he's not all that nice.'

She was instantly sorry. 'I didn't mean that, Mother. I'm to stay, and I've got my pay packet—we'll go into Sherborne tomorrow afternoon and buy a washing-machine.'

'Oh, darling, how lovely, but I think you should spend your money on some new clothes.'

'Next month, Mother. I must go—see you tomorrow. Let Father know, won't you?'

There were four appointments in the afternoon, and Mr Fitzgibbon took his time over each one of them. Since one patient telephoned to say that she would be unable to come until later in the afternoon, there was a half-hour's wait. Mrs Keane made tea and Florence got as far as she could with the clearing up, but since there were still two patients to come it seemed a waste of time. She took him a cup of tea, outwardly serene and inwardly seething with impatience.

'You will be unable to go home this evening,' remarked Mr Fitzgibbon. 'A pity, but it cannot be helped. Our friend from the truck had a secondary haemorrhage, and it was necessary to take him back to Theatre.'

'Oh, how awful. Will he be all right? Was it his stump?'

'No, the chest wound. I've had another look and found the trouble. He should do now.' He bent his head over the papers on his desk and she went away, feeling that she would have liked to tell him how mean she felt, moaning because she had had to miss her train while all the while he had been dealing with an emergency. She told Mrs Keane while they drank their tea and was comforted by her sensible observation that, since she hadn't known about it, she had no need to feel guilty.

The delayed patient had come for a check-up and took up a mere twenty minutes of Mr Fitzgibbon's time, but the last patient, a middle-aged and timid lady, accompanied by her husband, took up twice that time, partly because before any examination could be done she needed to be soothed and encouraged. Afterwards, when Florence was helping her to dress again, she felt faint, which delayed her departure for even longer. Florence tucked her up on the examination couch and put a comforting arm around her shoulders while she had a little weep. 'Why does it have to be me?' she demanded tearfully. 'I don't even smoke cigarettes. Do you suppose that Mr Fitzgibbon can really cure me?'

'Certainly he can if he said so,' said Florence stoutly, 'and you don't have to worry about the operation; you really won't know anything about it, and you'll be well again within weeks—you heard him say so. Now I'm going to tell him that you're ready, and you'll go back into the consulting-room and he'll explain everything to you. You can ask him any questions that you want to; he's a kind man and very clever.'

'You are a dear, sweet girl, putting up with an old woman's nonsense.' She patted Florence's arm. 'Shall I see you again?'

'Oh, yes, in a few weeks' time when you come for a check-up after surgery. I shall look forward to seeing you then.'

There was quite a lot to do once the elderly pair had left. Florence took herself off to the examination-room and began to set it to rights, and then put her head round the door to ask if Mr Fitzgibbon would like a cup of coffee.

He refused, still working at his desk, and as she withdrew her head the phone rang. 'Answer that, will you,' he asked her, 'and see who it is?'

Eleanor, thought Florence, and she was right. The piercing voice sounded petulant and demanding, and asked to speak to Mr Fitzgibbon.

'Miss Paton wishes to speak to you, sir.'

He growled something softly and took the phone from her. As Florence went out of the room, closing the door very, very slowly, she heard him say, 'Eleanor, I am extremely busy…' She held the door-handle so that there was still a crack before she closed it, and nodded her head with satisfaction at his, 'No, quite impossible, I shall be working…!'

Mr Fitzgibbon, watching the door-handle soundlessly turning, smiled, paying not the slightest attention to Eleanor's petulant voice.

When Florence went back presently to say that everything was attended to and did he wish her to remain any longer? he lifted his head from his writing to tell her baldly that he needed nothing more and she had no need to stay. He wished her a good night in a voice which suggested that he had no wish to enter into conversation of any kind, and picked up his pen again.

Florence's 'Goodnight,' was crisp. He might at least have expressed regret at her having to miss her evening train. I hope she pesters him to take her out and makes him spend a lot of money at some glitzy restaurant, thought Florence, going back to one of Mrs Twist's wholesome suppers.

Mr Fitzgibbon went home to the charming little Georgian house not ten minutes' drive from his rooms, changed into elderly, beautifully tailored tweeds, told Crib, the elderly man who ran his home with the help of his wife, that he would be back on Sunday night, whistled to Monty, that dog of no known breed, and got back into his car.

Once out of London, he took the A30 and just over two hours later slowed the car as he reached the first grey stone thatched cottages of Mells. It was a small village with a lovely church, a manor-house and a cluster of these same cottages in a charming group dominated by the church and the village inn. Mr Fitzgibbon drove through the centre of the village, and half a mile along a narrow lane turned the car through an open gate and stopped before a low, rambling house built of the same grey and yellow stone as the cottages, but with a red-tiled roof. The front door stood open and he was met on the doorstep by a short, stout woman with a round rosy face and grey hair screwed up into a fierce bun.

'There you are, Mr Alexander, right on time, too. Good thing you phoned when you did—I had time to get Mr Letts to come up with the nicest piece of steak for your supper.' She paused and he bent to hug her.

'Just what I need, Nanny, and how nice to see you.' He let Monty out of the car and they all went indoors, through the stone-flagged hall to a low-ceilinged room with a great inglenook and lattice windows. Doors opened on to the garden behind the house, a lovely place, a riot of roses and summer flowers, with a wide lawn leading down to a narrow stream.

'You're on your own?' asked Nanny unnecessarily.

'Yes, Nanny...'

'Doesn't like the country, does she, that Miss Paton?'

He said evenly, 'No, I'm afraid it isn't quite the life for her.' He had sat down in a great chair and Monty had flopped at his feet. Presently he went on, 'You were quite right, Nanny...'

'Of course I was, Mr Alexander. You just wait until the right girl comes along.'

'She has, but she doesn't know it yet.'

Nanny sat down on a small chair opposite him. She didn't say a word, only waited.

'She's a parson's daughter, a nurse, and she works for me.'

'She likes you?'

'I think so, but not at first, and even now I catch her looking at me as though she wasn't sure of that. On the other hand...'

'Give her time, Mr Alexander.' Nanny got up. 'I'll get your supper; you must be famished, and that nice dog of yours.'

He was up early the next morning and, with Monty beside him, inspected the garden before breakfast. The thought that he was barely an hour's drive away from Florence's home was persistent in his mind but he refused to listen to it. After breakfast he went into the village, where he met the rector and returned with him to have coffee at the rectory. The rector was a keen gardener and the hours passed pleasantly. After lunch he stretched out on the lawn and slept until Nanny called him in to tea. Then he and Monty took themselves off for a long walk before spending a convivial hour in the Talbot Arms. In the evening, after the splendid dinner Nanny put before him, he sat in the lovely drawing-room, thinking about Florence. At length he got up to go to bed, saw Monty into his basket in the kitchen, locked up and turned off the lights before going up the oak staircase to his room. The night was clear and there was a waning moon. He stood by the open window, wondering if Florence was looking at the same moon, and then laughed wryly. 'I'm behaving like a lovesick boy,' he muttered, 'and more than likely she doesn't give a second thought to me…'

Florence wasn't looking at the moon, she was in bed and asleep, but she had from time to time during the day thought about him. She had taken herself to task over this. 'We haven't anything in common except our work,' she told Charlie Brown, snoozing on her bed. 'He lives in London, though I don't know where—in some hideously expensive modern flat, I suppose—and he likes expensive restaurants and big cars, and he hardly ever laughs. And he never looks at me…'

She was wrong, of course, about that.

It was at Sunday lunch that her mother asked, 'I suppose that nice Mr Fitzgibbon has to work at the weekend?'

'I've no idea,' said Florence, 'but I shouldn't think so—he must have a private life.'

'A great many firm friends if he's not married, I expect,' suggested Mrs Napier. 'Handsome single men are always in great demand.'

Florence was filled with a sudden fierce dislike of that. She said, 'I dare say; I really don't know anything about him, Mother.' As she spoke she wished that she did. Where did he go when he left the consulting-rooms, for instance? Did he have parents and live with them, or brothers and sisters? And his friends—surely there must be others than the horrid Eleanor? She could think of no way of finding out, and suddenly she wanted to know quite badly. She reminded herself once again that she was getting too interested in him, and spent the rest of the day gardening with unnecessary energy, and, although she hated leaving home that evening, there was a spark of excitement deep down inside her at the idea of seeing him again.

She went to work a little earlier than usual, a habit she had formed on a Monday morning, to make sure that everything was just so. She was rearranging flowers in a bowl kept filled throughout the year in the waiting-room when Mr Fitzgibbon came in.

A small wave of pleasure at the sight of him left her feeling surprised; there was no particular reason why she should be glad to see him—he hadn't been over-friendly on Friday evening. She bade him good morning and was relieved when he answered her with brisk cheerfulness and a quick smile. He didn't stop to talk; he went straight to his consulting-room and began on his post, so that when Mrs Keane arrived he called her in at once to take his letters. He saw two patients and then took himself off to Colbert's, leaving Florence and Mrs Keane to get ready for the busy afternoon ahead of them.

Mrs Keane, her hands poised over her typewriter, waited until his footsteps had ceased in the house before observing, 'I wonder what is making him so thoughtful? And absent-minded—he usually rattles off his letters, but this morning he kept going off into a world of his own. There's something on his mind…'

'That Eleanor—she phoned on Friday evening,' said Florence, tucking a clean sheet on the couch and raising her voice through the open door. 'But he said he couldn't take her out. Do you suppose he's met someone he likes better?'

Mrs Keane bent over her notebook. 'I've no doubt of it,' she said with quiet satisfaction.

CHAPTER SIX

THE DAY'S WORK went smoothly; Mr Fitzgibbon returned directly after lunch and the whole afternoon was taken up with his patients. Usually Mrs Keane booked appointments so that there was a brief lull halfway through the afternoon, enabling them to have a cup of tea, but today there was no let-up, and by five o'clock Florence was tired and a little cross beneath her seemingly composed appearance, and the prospect of the evening spent alone in her room was uninviting. Mrs Twist would be out, spending the evening with friends, and there would only be Buster for company. Showing the last patient out with smiling friendliness, she decided to go out for the evening herself. She had money—not a great deal, but quite enough to take her to some quiet little restaurant where she could get a modest meal. She would have to get a bus to Oxford Street, where there was bound to be somewhere to suit her taste. She bustled around, drank her tea thankfully, took a cup to an unsmiling Mr Fitzgibbon, and, everything being in apple-pie order, asked if there was anything else he wished her to do.

He looked up briefly. 'No, thank you, Florence; enjoy your evening. Are you going out?'

She beamed at him. 'Yes—for a meal. Goodnight, sir.'

He bade her goodnight in a cool voice and sat looking at the closed door after she had gone. It was, he argued to himself, most irritating that the girl treated him in such a manner; he had no idea what she really thought of him. At times he thought that she liked him, and then she withdrew, becoming a cross between tolerant youth making allowances for middle age and a waspish young woman ready to answer back. He sighed, admitting at last to himself that he wanted Florence for his wife but that persuading her to be of like mind would probably be a delicate undertaking. Mr Fitzgibbon sat back and considered how best to set about the matter, unaware that kindly providence was about to lend him a hand.

Florence let herself into Mrs Twist's house, fed Buster, inspected the corned-beef salad in the fridge for her supper, put it back and went to her room to change. It was well past six o'clock but she took the opportunity to have a bath, since Mrs Twist was prone to remind her that hot water cost money so that she felt compelled to have a shower when that lady was home. Now she luxuriated at some length in an extravagant amount of hot water, dressed unhurriedly, coiled her hair in a smooth chignon, made sure that she had her key and enough money, and left the house. Outside on the pavement, she remembered that Mr Fitzgibbon had still been in his rooms when she had left and, for all she knew, he might still be there. She had no wish to encounter him and, remembering Mrs Twist telling her that there was a short cut which would bring her out almost by Cavendish Square, well past the consulting-rooms, she decided to take it.

It was a narrow street with small, neat houses on either side; there were cars parked on one side of it, but otherwise it was empty. It was later than she had intended, for she had dawdled over her dressing and spent ten minutes sitting on the stairs with Buster, who had been feeling lonely, but the June evening was still light and would be for some time to come. She walked on, hardly noticing that the houses were becoming shabby, for she was allowing her imagination full rein; Mr Fitzgibbon would be spending his evening with Eleanor, no doubt; she didn't think that he was very in love with her, though, but Florence guessed that she was too clever to give him a chance to know that. Men, she thought, might be very clever and all that, but they could be singularly blind at times. She looked around her then and saw how the street had changed from neatness to a neglected, rubbish-strewn thoroughfare with paint peeling off the front doors and grubby curtains at the windows. She must have mistaken Mrs Twist's directions, and she was relieved to see a main street ahead of her, busy with cars. She stepped out more briskly and at the same time became aware that she was being followed.

She didn't turn round, nor did she increase her pace, although it was the one thing she would have liked to do. Common sense told her that she was near enough to the end of the street to scream for help if she needed to, and to show unease might spur on whoever it was behind her… Getting closer, too…

She hadn't realised how close: a large, heavy hand caught her by the shoulder and forced her to stop.

Mr Fitzgibbon, on the way home and the last in the queue at the traffic-lights, looked round him idly, marvelling for the hundredth time how it was possible for such neglected, down-at-heel streets to be cheek by jowl with the elegance around them. It was then that providence, metaphorically speaking, tapped him on one massive shoulder so that his glance strayed into the street alongside the car. He saw that copper head of hair immediately; he also saw that its owner was in difficulties. He was out of the car and into the street, oblivious of anything other than the need to get to Florence as fast as possible. For a man of his size, he was a quick mover. He was very nearly there when he saw her kick hard backwards with sufficiently good result to make the man yelp. He was on him then, removing him with a great arm, shaking him like a terrier shook a rat.

'I advise you not to do that again, my man,' said Mr Fitzgibbon without heat, 'or it will be the worse for you.' He let him go and watched him run back down the street before he turned to Florence.

'And what the hell were you doing, strolling down this back street, asking for trouble—a great girl like you…?'

Florence gulped. Being called a great girl in that coldly furious voice was upsetting; worse, it sparked off the temper her parents had been at pains to teach her to control from an early age. She was a bit shaken and a trifle pale, and her voice wobbled just a little, but more with temper than fright. She said with great dignity, 'I am not a great girl…'

'We'll argue about that in the car—I'll be had up for obstruction…'

He took her by the arm and marched her along willy-nilly. 'I don't wish—' she began, but he stowed her into the car without a word, got in himself and drove on.

'A miracle that there is no traffic or police around,' he observed grimly. It wasn't a miracle but providence, of course.

He took the car round Cavendish Square and into Regent Street, turning off into side-streets before he reached Piccadilly and coming out at the lower end of Park Lane and so into Knightsbridge.

Florence, who had sat silently fuming, said, 'This is Knightsbridge; why are you bringing me here?'

He didn't answer but turned into a quiet side-street lined with rather grand houses, and presently turned again under an archway into a narrow tree-lined street. The houses were smaller here but very elegant, painted white, their front doors gleaming with black paint. He stopped before the end house, got out, opened her door and invited her to get out.

'No,' said Florence, and then, catching the look in his eye, she got out, but once on the pavement she didn't budge. 'Why have you brought me here? And where is it anyway? I'm obliged to you for your—your help just now, but…' she paused, pink in the face, her blue eyes flashing '…a great girl like me can look after herself.' She frowned because she suspected that she had got the grammar wrong somewhere.

Mr Fitzgibbon smiled, not very nicely, took her by the arm in a gentle but firm grasp, and marched her to his front door. Crib opened it, and if he was surprised he showed no sign of it, but bade his master a good evening and added a respectful good evening to Florence.

'Ah, Crib, this is Miss Napier, my practice nurse; she has had an unfortunate encounter in the street. Will you ask Mrs Crib to show her where she can tidy herself?' And, when Crib bustled off down the narrow hall and through a baize door at its end, Mr Fitzgibbon observed in an aloof way, 'You will be better when you have had a drink and a meal.'

'I feel perfectly all right,' snapped Florence, but she couldn't go on because a tall thin woman in a severe grey dress had come through the door and was advancing towards them.

'Good evening, sir,' she smiled at Florence, 'and good evening to you too, miss. If you will come with me?'

She led Florence, speechless and cross, up the graceful little staircase to one side of the hall. 'I hear you've had some kind of accident, miss,' she remarked as they reached the landing. 'There is a cloakroom in the hall, but I dare say you might like a few minutes' peace and quiet if you have been upset.'

She opened a door and ushered Florence into a charming bedroom; its windows overlooked the back of the house and gave a view of a small pretty garden. It was furnished in maplewood, carpeted in white and curtained in apricot silk. The bedspread on the small bed was of the same material and so were the lampshades, and the walls were a pale tint of the same colour. 'Oh, what a darling room,' said Florence, quite forgetting that she was annoyed.

'One of the guest rooms, miss. The bathroom is through the

door there, and if you fancy a nice lie down the *chaise-longue* is very comfortable.'

The housekeeper gave her a kindly smile and went away, and, left to herself, Florence inspected her surroundings more thoroughly. The room was indeed delightful and so was the bathroom, stocked with towels, soap and everything a guest could wish for. Perhaps it had been left ready for a visitor; it seemed a shame to use the soap and one of the fluffy towels so enticingly laid out on one of the glass shelves. However, she had to wash; the man's hand had been dirty, and she could still feel its grimy, sweaty fingers as she had instinctively tried to drag it from her shoulder. She took a look at herself in the wide mirror. There was a dirty mark on her dress and her hair was a mess…!

She went downstairs again some ten minutes later, once more nicely made-up, her fiery head of hair brushed smooth. Her dress had been creased but she couldn't do anything about that, although she had got rid of most of the dirty mark.

There was no one in the hall and she stood, irresolute, at the bottom of the staircase, but only for a moment. Mr Fitzgibbon flung open a door opposite her. 'Come in, come in.' He sounded impatient. 'That's a comfortable chair by the window. What would you like to drink?'

She stood by the door. 'Nothing, thank you, sir. You've been very kind, but I won't trespass upon your time any more.' When he didn't speak she added, 'I'm most grateful…'

He crossed the room, took her by the arm and sat her down in the chair he had indicated. 'A glass of sherry,' he observed, and handed it to her. 'There's nothing like it for restoring ill-humour.'

'I am not ill-humoured,' began Florence, determined to make it clear, which, seeing that she was boiling with rage, hardly made sense.

'You are as cross as two sticks,' said Mr Fitzgibbon genially. 'You are also foolish and most regrettably untruthful.'

Florence had taken a sip of sherry and choked on it, but before she could summon breath to utter he had sat down opposite her, a glass in his hand, the picture of good-natured ease. 'When you have your breath back,' he suggested, 'I should like to know why you were in that disreputable street and why, having told me that you were going out for a meal, you had done no such thing. Did he stand you up?'

'Stand me up? Who?'

'You were intending to dine out alone?'

'Well, what's so funny about that? And I wasn't going to dine. How can you be so silly? On my salary? I was going to Oxford Street to McDonald's or somewhere like that.' She added to make things clearer, 'Mrs Twist's out this evening and it was corned beef and tomatoes.'

Mr Fitzgibbon hid a smile. 'Did you need to fib about it? I am afraid I can't quite see…' He watched the lovely pink creep into her face and saw. 'You were afraid that I might think you were fishing for another meal…'

'What a simply horrid thing to say,' she burst out.

'It's the truth,' he pointed out blandly.

'Well, even if it is, you don't have to say it—I mean, you can think it if you want to but you don't have to put it into words.'

She tossed off the sherry in a defiant way, and he got up and refilled her glass. 'Now I want to know why you were wandering around, asking to be mugged. If you intend to go to Oxford Street you could have kept to Wimpole Street until you came to the bus-stop.'

She managed not to blush this time, but she looked so guilty that Mr Fitzgibbon, watching her from beneath his lids, knew that she was about to tell him some more fibs.

'Well,' began Florence, 'Mrs Twist told me about this short-cut, and it was such a nice evening and the street really looked quite respectable when I started. I thought it would make a nice change.'

It sounded a bit thin, and she could see that Mr Fitzgibbon thought it was too, for his rather stern mouth was turned down at the corners. All the same, what he said was, 'Oh, indeed?' and then, 'I do hope you will give me the pleasure of your company at dinner. I'll drive you back presently.' When she hesitated he added, 'Oxford Street will be packed out with people wanting a meal after the cinema.'

A statement made at random but which reassured her. 'Oh, will it? I hadn't thought of that. We used to go to the local cinema when I was at Colbert's. Are you sure that Mrs Crib won't mind? I mean, will she have cooked enough for two?'

He assured her gravely that Mrs Crib always allowed for the unexpected guest, and began to talk gently about nothing much, putting her at her ease, and when Monty came prancing in from the garden and offered her head for a scratch, looking up at her with melting eyes, she felt all at once quite at home.

'This is a beautiful room,' she told her host. 'You must enjoy coming home to it each evening.'

It was a lovely room, comfortably large, and furnished with a nice mixture of Regency pieces and large chairs and sofas, the kind of sofas where one might put one's feet up or curl into a corner. The curtains at the windows were brocade in what she imagined one would call mulberry-red, and the thin silk carpets scattered on the polished wood floor held the same colour mixed with dull blues and greens. The walls were panelled and for the most part covered by paintings, and there was a bow-fronted cabinet along one wall, filled with fine china and silver. The fireplace was at one end of the room—Adam, she guessed—and in the winter it would hold an open fire. She gave a small sigh, not of envy but of contentment, just because she was enjoying all these things, even if only for an hour or so.

Crib came in to tell them that dinner was served, and they crossed the hall to a smaller room with crimson wallpaper and a rectangular mahogany dining-room table, large enough to seat eight people and set with lace table-mats, sparkling glass and silver. There was a bowl of roses on the table, and Florence asked, 'Are they from your garden?' and, when he nodded, 'The yellow one—isn't that Summer Sunshine? Father plans to get one for next year. I don't suppose you have much time for gardening?'

Crib put a plate of soup before her, and her lovely nose twitched at its delicious aroma. Mr Fitzgibbon studied the nose at some length without appearing to do so. 'No, I should like more time for it. I do potter at intervals, though.'

Florence addressed herself to the soup. Lettuce and cucumber, and not out of a tin either. She had quite forgotten how annoyed she had been at Mr Fitzgibbon's high-handed treatment; indeed, she hadn't felt so happy for a long time, although she didn't trouble to wonder why. The soup plates were removed, and cold chicken, salad and a snowy mound of creamed potatoes were offered. Mr Fitzgibbon poured white wine, passed the pepper and salt and made conversation in an easy manner while he watched Florence enjoying the meal with unselfconscious pleasure, comparing her in his mind with other dinner companions who had shuddered at the idea of a second helping and shunned the potatoes. He frowned a little; he was allowing himself to get too interested in the girl…wanting her for his wife had been a flight of fancy.

Florence saw the frown and some of her happiness ebbed away. After their rather unfortunate encounter that evening—well, fortunate for her, she conceded—even though they hadn't seen eye to eye to begin with, the last half-hour had been delightful, but now he looked forbidding and any moment she would find herself addressing him as 'sir'. She declined more potatoes politely and refused more wine. As soon as she decently could she would think of some excuse to get her out of the house, and the sooner the better.

First there was apple pie and cream to be eaten and polite small talk to be maintained. The small talk became so stilted that he looked at her in surprise. Now what was the matter with the tiresome girl? Still polite and beautifully mannered, but stiff as a poker. She responded willingly to his remarks, but the pleasant feeling that they were old friends, even though they knew very little about each other, had vanished.

They went back to the drawing-room for their coffee, and after half an hour of what Florence privately called polite conversation she said that she should be getting back. 'Mrs Twist might be worried…' she suggested, to which Mr Fitzgibbon made no reply, merely lifted the receiver and phoned that lady, who, it seemed, wasn't in the least worried.

'But, of course,' he said smoothly, 'you would like a good night's sleep—we have a busy day ahead of us tomorrow.'

A gentle reminder that she worked for him and it behoved her to be on duty at the right time. Or so it seemed to her.

She thanked him once again on Mrs Twist's doorstep, and later, getting ready for bed, reflected on her evening. There had been no need for Mr Fitzgibbon to take her to his home and ask her to dinner, so why had he done it? And why had he become remote, evincing no wish to hinder her from going back to her room at Mrs Twist's? She had thought once or twice just lately that they were on the verge of a cautious friendship. There was no understanding the man, she thought, punching her rather hard pillows into a semblance of softness.

In the morning everything was as usual; he arrived punctually, reminded her that his first patient was deaf, commented upon the delightful morning and made no mention of the previous evening. There was, of course, no reason why he should—all the same, she was unreasonably put out.

The deaf patient took up a good deal of time and made everyone else late, but Mr Fitzgibbon went placidly on as though the morning had ten hours to it instead of five, so that their usual lunch-break was cut short about ten minutes. She and Mrs Keane ate their sandwiches and drank a pot of tea between them, thankful that Mr Fitzgibbon had taken himself off, leaving them free to get the place straight for the afternoon patients.

'Quite a busy day,' said Mrs Keane placidly, arranging the patients' notes in a neat pile on his desk while Florence restored the examination-room to a pristine state. He returned five minutes before his first appointment and spent them on the phone to Colbert's, and after that there was no let-up until after five o'clock. Mr Fitzgibbon was at his desk, writing and being interrupted by the telephone, Mrs Keane had just made a pot of tea, and Florence was carrying a cup to him, when the waiting-room door was thrust open and Eleanor Paton came in on a wave of exquisite scent and looking ravishing in a wild-silk outfit which Florence, in a few seconds' glance, instantly coveted.

Eleanor went past her without speaking, taking the cup and saucer from her as she went, opening the consulting-room door without knocking and going inside.

'Who was that?' asked Mrs Keane, poking her nose round the kitchen door.

'Miss Paton,' said Florence quietly while she damped down rage. 'She just walked in, took his tea and went inside...'

'I'd like to be a fly on the wall,' said Mrs Keane. 'Come and have your tea, dear. Do you suppose we should take in another cup for her?'

'I don't think she would like tea-bags.'

They drank their tea and Florence, who had excellent hearing, listened to Eleanor's high-pitched voice and the occasional rumble of Mr Fitzgibbon's. There was no laughter—it sounded more like an argument, as Eleanor's tones became shrill and his became briefer.

Presently they heard the door open, and the pair of them crossed the waiting-room and out of the door, the signal for Florence to nip to the window. Mr Fitzgibbon's car was outside but he wasn't getting into it, and in a moment she saw Eleanor walking away down the street. And she didn't look round.

Florence withdrew her head cautiously and stepped back; she didn't want Mr Fitzgibbon to see her peering from his window. Her fears were ungrounded, however; he hadn't got into his car—indeed, he was standing so close to her that she felt his waistcoat sticking into the small of her back.

'Snooping?' he asked gently.

She didn't turn round but edged away from him. 'Certainly not,' she said with dignity, fingers crossed because she was telling a fib. 'I thought that you might have gone and forgotten to let us know…'

Being a parson's daughter was a terrible drawback sometimes. She turned to face him. 'No, that was a silly excuse. I looked out of the window to watch you drive Miss Paton away.'

'However, I didn't, and does that please you?'

She met his cold grey eyes steadily. 'It's none of my business, sir. I'm sorry I was—was nosy.'

'You are a very unsettling girl, Florence.' He went into his consulting-room and closed the door quietly, leaving her prey to the thought of getting a month's notice; it seemed like a strong hint that he had changed his mind about taking her on permanently. Perhaps Eleanor had persuaded him that she had been unsuitable, and she had played right into the girl's hands, hadn't she?

She went back into the examination-room, made sure that it was quite ready for the next day and then washed the cups and saucers and tidied everything away while Mrs Keane did the last of her filing. Ten minutes later Mr Fitzgibbon reappeared, bade them both a civil good evening, and went away, so that they were free to leave.

After she had eaten her supper Florence sat in Mrs Twist's small back garden; she had no heart for a walk and, since her landlady was going to spend her evening with a neighbour and had no objection to Florence sitting there if she wished, it offered a few hours of fresh air while she got on with a sweater she was knitting for her father's birthday. Not that the air was all that fresh; Mrs Twist had a neat garden, the tiny grass patch in its centre clipped to within an inch of its life, the flowers planted in rows against the low fence which separated it from the neighbours. Florence, used to a rather untidy garden with not a neighbour in sight, found the next-door children, who hung on the fence on one side, and the garrulous old man on the other side a bit distracting. However, she answered the children's questions readily enough, and when they were sent to bed entered into conversation with the old man, leaning on the top of the fence, smoking a pipe. She wondered what tobacco he used; it smelled like dried tea-leaves and charred paper and caused him to cough alarmingly. However, he was a nice person, prepared to reminisce by the hour about his youth. She gave him her full attention until he went indoors for his supper.

Daylight was fading and she let her knitting fall into her lap, finally allowing her thoughts to turn to what was uppermost in her head: the likelihood of being sacked at the end of the month. It seemed to her that it was what she could expect; looking back over the last few weeks, she reflected that she and Mr Fitzgibbon had an uneasy relationship. It had been her fault; she should never have had dinner with him in the first place—it had allowed her to glimpse him in quite a different light from the impersonal courtesy and rather austere manner he habitually wore. She went to her room and got ready for bed, and then sat up against the pillows with a pen and paper, reckoning what she should do with her salary. Even if he asked her to leave, she would have to wait until he had a replacement and they had agreed on a month's notice on either side, so she could count on six weeks' pay. Thank heaven she had got the washing-machine…

She went to work the next morning resigned to her future. It surprised her a little that she should feel so very sad, and she came to the conclusion that it was because she would be unable to buy all the things she had planned to get. Since she had felt secure in her job, the list was a long one, and now she would only be able to get a very few of the things.

The porter admitted her, wished her a good morning and volunteered the information that Mrs Keane had not yet arrived. Florence let herself into the waiting-room, changed into her uniform, adjusted her cap just so on her bright head, and went to put on the kettle. The first patient wouldn't arrive for another hour, and everything was as ready as it could be. She was in the tiny kitchen when she heard the door open. 'The kettle is on,' she called. 'Were you held up by the buses?'

She turned to see Mr Fitzgibbon, in a thin sweater and flannels, leaning against the door. 'Good morning, Florence; I've been held back by a stove-in chest.' He looked very tired and he needed a shave, and Florence, looking at him, knew why she was feeling sad: it was because if she left she would never see him again, and her heart would break because of that. Why she should have fallen in love with him she had no idea; he had given her no encouragement to do so, and why should he when he had the lovely Eleanor waiting to drop into his arms?

She asked gently, 'If you will go and sit down, will I bring you a cup of tea, sir? I'm sorry you've had a busy night.' He went away and she busied herself with a tray, thinking that she had done this once before, only then she hadn't felt as she did now. She muttered to herself, 'Now, Florence, no nonsense,' and bore the tea and biscuits into the consulting-room and found him writing.

'Must you do that?' she cried. 'Can't it wait until you've had a short sleep and a good hot breakfast?'

He put down his pen. 'You sound like a wife. Unfortunately this can't wait, but when it's done I'll go home and have breakfast and change. Does that satisfy you?'

'Oh, that isn't what I meant, sir. I didn't mean to be bossy, only you do look so tired.' She poured a cup of tea and put it beside him. 'There's Mrs Keane.'

She left him sitting there, staring at the notes he had been writing. She had made him feel every year of his age. He drank his tea, reflecting that she had never looked so young and beautiful. He had no doubt that there were other men who thought the same.

An hour later he was back at his desk, having every appearance of a man who had had a good night's sleep, ample time in which to eat a good breakfast and nothing on his brilliant mind other than his patients. Florence, ushering in the first patient, had time to take a good look at him, back at his desk, immaculately dressed as usual, getting up to shake hands with his patient, a loud-voiced young woman with an aggressive manner which, she suspected, hid nervousness. Mr Fitzgibbon ignored the aggression, examined her with impersonal kindness and finally broke the news to her that she would need to have a bronchoscopy, adding, in his most soothing manner, that if, as he suspected, she might need surgery, he would be prepared to do it. He then waited with patience while Florence dealt with his patient, who had burst into tears, followed by some wild talking. A cup of tea, a handful of tissues and gentle murmurs from Florence worked wonders, so that presently she was able to listen to Mr Fitzgibbon's plans. Showing her out into Mrs Keane's hands, Florence reflected that underneath her aggression she was really quite a nice person.

The next patient was a different kettle of fish: a thin, scholarly man of middle age, who listened quietly to what Mr Fitzgibbon had to tell him, made arrangements to go into hospital without demur and shook hands as he left, expressing his thanks for what could only be described as bad news.

The last two appointments were with children, both with bronchiolitis. Mr Fitzgibbon dealt with them very gently, making them laugh, allowing them to try out his stethoscope, making jokes. Like a nice uncle, thought Florence, stealing a loving glance at his bowed pepper and salt head bending over one small boy.

He had a teaching round that afternoon and there were no patients until four o'clock. She and Mrs Keane ate their lunch together, and then went about their various chores until Mr Fitzgibbon returned just before four o'clock.

'Tea?' he enquired as he went into his room, but before closing the door he turned to say, 'This first appointment—the patient is a frail lady, Florence; be ready with tea and sympathy—they help a lot when it's unpleasant news.'

The little old lady who came ten minutes later looked as though a puff of wind might blow her away, but she had bright blue wide-open eyes and a serene face. Florence settled her in a chair on the other side of the desk and melted into a corner of the room until she would be needed, realising that the two already knew each other, and after a few minutes' chatting Mr Fitzgibbon said, 'Florence, Miss MacFinn was Theatre Sister at Colbert's when I was a very junior houseman—I was terrified of her!'

'Now I should be terrified of you—or at least of what you're going to tell me.' She looked across at Florence and smiled. 'Are you terrified of him, my dear?'

'Me? Heavens, no, Miss MacFinn, and I'm sure you don't need to be, although I know you're not.'

'Well, bad news is never nice, is it? I suppose you want to take a look, Alexander?'

'Indeed I do; will you go with Florence?'

So his name is Alexander, reflected Florence, busy with buttons and hooks and eyes; a very nice name and suitable. Her thoughts seemed to dwell lovingly on Mr Fitzgibbon while she carried on a cheerful conversation calculated to soothe; knowing his name made her feel that she knew something about him at last.

Miss MacFinn was philosophical about having an operation. 'Of course, if you say so, Alexander, but is it sensible at my age?'

'Certainly it is and don't cast doubts on my surgery—I'll wager a hundred pounds that you'll be trotting around on your ninetieth birthday! Will you bet on that?'

Miss MacFinn thought for a moment. 'No, I just might lose my money. You can send me a very large bouquet of flowers instead.' She looked at him straight in the eye. 'Either way!' she added.

'I'll bring them myself.' He got up, smiling, and took her

hand. 'You'll go into the private wing as my special patient and no argument. I'll do it myself...'

'Good.' She looked at Florence, standing quietly by. 'It would be nice if this pretty creature would be there too...'

'I'll certainly arrange that.'

The next patient had been waiting for ten minutes or so; Florence showed him in and felt free to clear up the examination-room and get it ready once again, and after him there was only one more appointment and that was for a patient of some months, recovered from surgery and due for a check-up.

It was six o'clock before he had gone, and they began to clear up for the last time. Florence, on her way to the examination-room, was halted by Mr Fitzgibbon.

'I shall be obliged if you will make yourself available when I operate upon Miss MacFinn. I'll choose a day when Theatre Sister is off duty—you can scrub...'

When she didn't answer he added, 'Miss MacFinn liked you; we think she will need all the help she can get—even a whim satisfied.'

Florence said, 'Very well, sir,' and made for the examination-room once more, only to be stopped again.

'Get Miss Paton on the phone, will you?'

He was writing now and didn't look up.

Eleanor's voice spoke sharply in her ear. 'Yes?'

When Florence said, 'Mr Fitzgibbon wants to speak to you, Miss Paton,' she said even more sharply,

'Well, put him on, then, and don't waste my time.'

Florence handed him the receiver, her eyes sparkling with rage. She said unforgivably, 'And don't ever ask me to do that again, sir.' She swept away, and Mr Fitzgibbon, the receiver in his hand, unheeding of the voice issuing from it, grinned.

He waited until the voice paused for breath and then said quite mildly, 'I'm afraid I'll not be able to take you to the theatre, Eleanor. I'm still at my rooms and shall be for some time, and then I must go back to Colbert's.'

He listened patiently to the peevish voice and then said, 'There are any number of men only too anxious to take my place,' and with that he added, 'and I must hang up, Eleanor, or I shall be here all night.'

He was still at his desk when Florence and Mrs Keane wished him goodnight and left. They parted company on the pavement, and Florence walked slowly back to Mrs Twist's, a prey to worried thoughts. She had allowed her tongue to run away with itself again, and Mr Fitzgibbon would be justified in reprimanding her, and, if it happened that he was feeling bad-tempered, he might even give her the sack. She frowned as she opened Mrs Twist's gate, wondering why she spoke to him like that; she wouldn't have dreamed of addressing any of the patients or the consultants at Colbert's in such a fashion. She went soberly indoors, and presently sat down to sausages and mash and a pot of tea and, since Mrs Twist considered that she looked rather peaky and needed an hour or two in the air, she went obediently into the little garden and sat there, her knitting in her lap and Buster on the knitting. It was pleasant to sit there doing nothing, but a pity that her thoughts were so unsettling. 'I've cooked my goose,' she murmured to Buster, 'not that it matters, for now I have to decide whether I can bear to go on seeing him every day or whether it would be wiser to leave and never see him again. I think I'd better leave—I can say that Mother isn't so well. No, that won't do because he'll probably suggest arranging for her to be re-admitted or some such. I'll just say that she wants me at home…'

Buster rearranged the knitting to his liking and went to sleep, and Florence, closing her eyes, the better to solve her problem, went to sleep too.

CHAPTER SEVEN

FLORENCE WENT TO work in a fine muddle the next morning; uppermost in her head was the thought that she would spend the day, or most of it, in Mr Fitzgibbon's company, but this delightful prospect was overshadowed by the memory of her flash of temper on the previous day. 'One day, my dear girl,' she muttered, 'you'll go too far and get the sack, and have to go home and never see him again.' It was really very upsetting and she dawdled along, making up conversations in her head, all of which had a satisfactory conclusion as such conversations always did.

Mr Fitzgibbon, standing at his window, staring out into the quiet street, rattling the loose change in his pocket, watched her mooning along and wondered what she might be thinking. Nothing cheerful—that was evident. He smiled to himself, studying her neat fiery head and pretty face. She was wearing a cotton dress, one of thousands off the peg, but it was a restful pale green and suited her splendid shape, and she wore it elegantly. He turned away from the window a few moments before Florence instinctively raised her eyes to it as she always did just before she crossed the street. A minute later, when she arrived, he was sitting at his desk, reading his post.

Mrs Keane, coming in on Florence's heels, wished them both good morning and wanted to know with some asperity why Mr Fitzgibbon couldn't have waited for her to deal with his letters. 'For I'm sure I'm able to deal with them far more quickly—and tidily.'

Florence went away to get into her uniform, listening wistfully to the cheerful talk between Mrs Keane and her employer—she could hear him laughing now. He hadn't even smiled at her when she had wished him good morning. Perhaps she was going to get the sack…

However, the busy day came to an end without any mention of it, and at the end of the week she went home again, reluctantly because she wouldn't see Mr Fitzgibbon until Monday morning, but happy to have a day or two in the gentle peacefulness of Gussage Tollard.

The weekend went too fast, and every hour of it had been filled. There were gooseberries and strawberries to pick, currants and some early raspberries all growing higgledy-piggledy in the untidy kitchen garden, and flowers to cut for the church. Mrs Napier, almost her old self once more, was none the less glad to take her ease while Florence took over the cooking, dealt with a load of washing and ironing and went to the village to see how Miss Payne, who had been poorly, was feeling. Well enough to give Mrs Napier a helping hand once more, Florence was assured, to her relief. Now that she had a job she had enough money to pay Miss Payne's modest wage, and the small but necessary chores she did for her mother were worth every penny of it.

In the train, going back to London, Florence mulled over her brief stay. She had enjoyed every minute of it, excepting perhaps the conversation she had had with her mother that afternoon, sitting in the garden after lunch.

'You're not quite happy, are you, darling?' her mother had

remarked. 'Is this job too much for you? Is the bedsitter too awful?'

She had denied both vigorously, and Mrs Napier had persisted gently. 'Then it's Mr Fitzgibbon—isn't he kind to you, Florence? Does he work you too hard?'

'No, no,' Florence had said, 'he's very nice to work for, Mother, and it's such an interesting job...' She had been at some pains to give chapter and verse on this, and her mother had uttered a small sigh and said no more, but Florence felt uneasy. If her mother had noticed that something was troubling her, would Mr Fitzgibbon notice it too? It seemed unlikely.

An assumption borne out by his impersonal 'good morning' when he arrived the next day. He left again as soon as he had seen his post, to go out to his out-patients clinic, for he had no appointments until the afternoon, but before he went he put his head round the examination-room door, where Florence was tidying away the week's linen.

'I shall want you in Theatre tomorrow morning. I'll pick you up here at eight o'clock sharp. I shall operate upon Miss MacFinn—if you remember, she wanted to see you again and, as Theatre Sister is on holiday, it will be most convenient.'

He had gone before she could open her mouth.

'That'll make a nice change for you, dear,' said Mrs Keane.

They separated and spent a quiet morning, doing small chores, then sitting over their coffee and finally having their sandwich lunch, so that they were ready for him when Mr Fitzgibbon returned. There were several appointments and two of them stretched into twice their usual length; by five o'clock Florence was wishing the day were over. Outside the warm day was dwindling into what was going to be a lovely evening, but, despite the open windows, the consulting-rooms were close. She envied Mr Fitzgibbon, sitting back in his chair, giving his full attention to his patients and looking cool and at ease. So he should, she reflected grumpily, when I'm the one who's doing all the running around. When the last patient finally went she carried in his tea and made for the door.

'Not so fast, Florence. Before you go I'll sort out the instruments I shall want with me tomorrow morning. Take them with you and get them sterilised at Colbert's, will you?' He eyed her quiet face over his teacup. 'A pleasant evening ahead of you, I trust?'

'Very,' said Florence; there would be shepherd's pie for supper because it was Monday, and then she would wash her hair and sit in the tiny garden and knit. Even if anyone, and by that she meant Mr Fitzgibbon, were to ask her out that evening, she wouldn't go; she was tired and cross and rather unhappy too. Not that it mattered, of course, for he wouldn't do anything of the sort.

He didn't; he reached for the phone and presently, through the half-open door, she heard him asking Eleanor if they could meet that evening.

She left with Mrs Keane after exchanging polite good evenings. It hadn't been a good day.

It was another lovely morning. She walked round to the consulting-rooms and found the Rolls outside, with Mr Fitzgibbon standing in the doorway, talking to the porter. His 'good morning' was affable, but he wasted no time in small talk. At the hospital he handed her his instruments case and told her to go on up to the theatre block. 'I'll join you in half an hour,' he told her, and walked away towards the consultant's room.

Theatre was ready; the same little staff nurse was on duty and she knew the technician and the two other nurses. She got into her theatre smock and dealt with the instruments, checked that everything was as it should be and went to the anaesthetic-room. Miss MacFinn was there, lying on the trolley, having a drowsy conversation with Dr Sim, the anaesthetist, but when she saw Florence she smiled. 'Alexander promised you'd be here. Such a treat for sore eyes you are, my dear. I've just been talking to him.'

She closed her eyes and Florence gave her hand a squeeze. 'I'll see you later,' she promised, and went to scrub up.

Everything was quite ready as Mr Fitzgibbon came into the theatre. He cast a swift eye around him, waiting while his registrar and a houseman positioned themselves on the other side of the table, asked, 'Ready, Sister?' and bent to his work.

The morning was far advanced by the time he straight-ened his back for the last time, pronounced himself satisfied and, leaving his registrar to apply the dressing and oversee Miss MacFinn's transfer to the recovery-room, stripped off his gloves, allowed a nurse to help him out of his gown and went away.

Miss MacFinn in safe hands, Florence took off her gown and began to gather up the instruments. She didn't get very far; the theatre maid put a cautious head round the door. 'Sister, you're to go down to the office and have your coffee. Mr Fitzgibbon says so.'

The office was crowded, with the four men perched where they could, waiting for her to pour out. Mr Fitzgibbon gravely offered her Sister's chair, behind the desk, and went to lean his bulk against one wall. She sat down composedly, gave them their mugs in turn, handed round the biscuit tin and sipped her own drink, listening to the men talking about the case. It was rather nice to be back in the hospital, she mused; on the other hand, if she were here permanently, she would see very little of Mr Fitzgibbon. She brooded over this, unaware that they had stopped talking for the moment and were looking at her.

'Hey, Florence, daydreaming? How unkind, when there are four handsome men standing around—wanting more coffee…'

She went a delicate pink. 'Sorry, I was just thinking that it was nice to see you all again.'

She began filling mugs once more, and the registrar observed, 'Which encourages me to invite you out for a meal one evening—I've no money, of course, but we can go to that poky little Chinese place…'

'I remember—they kept looking at us through those bead

curtains. I'd like that, Dan.' She smiled at him; they had been out together once or twice in a friendly way; she knew that he was engaged to a girl—a children's nanny, living with a family in Switzerland—and that they planned to get married at the end of the year. Doubtless he wanted to talk about her, and Florence was a very good listener and always had been.

'Oh, good. I'll give you a ring.' He looked across to Mr Fitzgibbon, still lounging against the wall, looking thoughtful and faintly amused. 'Shall I check up on Miss MacFinn, sir?'

'No, I'll go myself, Dan. I'll take Florence back presently and come back here, do the ward-round and cast an eye on Miss MacFinn before I go, right?'

To Florence he said briskly, 'Be ready to leave here in half an hour.'

He went away and the other three men with him, leaving her to sit among the coffee-mugs and biscuit crumbs. She hadn't time to sit about, though; she went back to Theatre, saw to the instruments, checked that the theatre was ready for whatever might be coming to it next, and went away to change. Mr Fitzgibbon had said half an hour, and he wouldn't like to be kept waiting.

She got to the entrance hall a few minutes before he did, which pleased her mightily, for it seemed to her that she was always the one to be last. They got into the car without speaking, and he dropped her off at his rooms, bade her a brief goodbye and drove away. 'Home for lunch,' said Florence, sprinting up the stairs, intent on her sandwiches and tea.

There was one appointment at two o'clock and he was back at his desk five minutes before that. The patient was a middle-aged woman, quiet and composed. She did everything asked of her without demur, answered the questions put to her concisely, listened while Mr Fitzgibbon explained just why it would be necessary to have an operation, agreed to have it when arrangements could be made, thanked him nicely and went away.

Florence, putting a cup of coffee on his desk, remarked,

'What a brave woman; I do hope she has a nice husband or children to comfort her when she gets home.'

'Indeed, yes. I am going back to Colbert's, Florence; I should like you to come with me so that Miss MacFinn can see you. Don't bother to get out of your uniform. If I'm not back by half-past five you and Mrs Keane go home.' He glanced up at her. 'Go and drink your tea—I'm leaving in ten minutes. You can tidy up when you get back.'

'How?' asked Florence. 'How do I get back?'

'I'll bring you.'

She drank her tea in a few gulps, powdered her nose and tucked away a few strands of hair, and then joined him in the waiting-room, just in time to hear him telling Mrs Keane that he wouldn't be back until five or later and would she let anyone who phoned know this?

Eleanor, thought Florence, nipping smartly down the stairs ahead of him.

Miss MacFinn had come round from the anaesthetic and was doing nicely. She was enjoying a refreshing nap when Florence and Mr Fitzgibbon reached her room in the private wing, but within five minutes she had opened her eyes, taken a moment or two to focus them and then murmured in a thread of a voice, 'Admirably suited,' smiled faintly, and closed her eyes once more.

Florence, quite at a loss, glanced at Mr Fitzgibbon and saw that he was smiling, but within a few moments he had become the dignified consultant once again, giving low-voiced instructions to his registrar and then to Sister. That done, he turned to Florence. 'Most satisfactory,' he murmured. 'I'll take you back.'

So he drove her back to Wimpole Street and, beyond observing that Miss MacFinn had every chance of a good recovery, he had nothing else to say during the journey.

Mrs Keane, appraised of the brevity of the visit and Miss MacFinn's remark, looked thoughtful. It was strange, she reflected, that Mr Fitzgibbon treated Florence with nothing more than courteous reserve, but none the less sought her company. As pretty as a picture too, and a fine, big girl, just right for his own massive proportions, not in the least like that awful Miss Paton…

The telephone interrupted her interesting thoughts and, since she was sitting at her desk and Florence was standing by the phone, she said, 'Answer that, dear, will you? It'll be that man you rang about sharpening the surgical scissors; he said he'd ring back…'

It wasn't, it was Eleanor Paton, demanding to speak to Mr Fitzgibbon.

'He won't be back this afternoon,' said Florence politely. 'Would you like to leave a message?'

'Who's that speaking? Are you the woman with the red hair?'

Florence forgot that she was a vicar's daughter and ought to know better. 'Red hair? Brown curls, black eyes, five feet three inches tall, and slim.'

'You're new? She got the sack? Good. No, I won't leave a message…' Miss Paton hung up, and Florence replaced the receiver and looked defiantly at Mrs Keane.

'I didn't tell a fib,' she pointed out. 'If she liked to make what she wanted of it that's her business.'

Mrs Keane began to laugh. 'I'd love to see her face if ever she comes here,' she chortled.

'I wonder why she wants to see him? She sounded very cross; he arranged to see her yesterday evening—I got her on the phone for him. Do you suppose they quarrelled?'

'It must be hard to quarrel with him,' said Mrs Keane, 'it would be like butting one's head against a feather bed wrapped round a block of concrete.'

'Did he get on with Sister Brice?'

'Professionally, yes—but she wasn't his type.'

Florence couldn't stop herself from asking what his type might be.

'I don't think it's Eleanor—we'll have to wait and see.'

Perhaps, thought Florence, he had no idea himself, in which case he might remain single for the rest of his life and she would be able to go on working for him. It would be better than nothing, better than never seeing him again.

At five o'clock Mrs Keane tidied her desk. 'I should think we might go—I've got my in-laws coming to supper; I thought I'd do *coq au vin*...!'

'Then do go, Mrs Keane. I'm not in a hurry; I'll get ready to go and wait until half-past and lock up. It doesn't look as though he's coming back here.'

Mrs Keane went and Florence mooned around for another fifteen minutes. She was on the point of changing out of her uniform when the doorbell was rung. It wouldn't be Mr Fitzgibbon; he had his keys in his pocket—he'd been rattling them when they had been standing by Miss MacFinn's bedside. She opened the door: Eleanor was standing there, beating a tattoo with an impatient foot. She gave a gasp when she saw Florence. 'Why, you're still here—that other girl...' she pushed past Florence '...where is she?'

She turned to glare at Florence, standing by the still open door, saying nothing. 'It was you—there isn't another nurse.'

'I didn't say that there was,' Florence pointed out. 'I'm just locking up, and I'm afraid I must ask you to leave.'

Eleanor sat firmly down on the nearest chair. 'I intend to remain. I insist on remaining.'

They both had their backs to the door and Mr Fitzgibbon's quiet voice made them both start. He said, at his most bland, 'Go home, Florence; I'll lock up.' And when she went without a word to change, closing the door very quietly behind her, he said, 'Come into the consulting-room, Eleanor. I don't know why you've come; I think we have said all there is to say, don't you? And I'm a busy man.'

He opened the door of his consulting-room and he ushered her inside. 'That girl,' spat Eleanor. 'I phoned this afternoon;

she said, well, she led me to believe that she had left—she said she was dark-haired, small and slim…'

Florence, going silently to the waiting-room door, paused when she heard his bellow of laughter. They must have made it up, she thought unhappily.

She ate her supper and, feeling restless, got on a bus and got herself taken to Colbert's. The truck driver was still in hospital and she hadn't visited him for a week or more.

He was glad to see her. His wife had just gone home and he was sitting in a chair by his bed, doing the football pools. She pulled up another chair, offered the packet of chocolate biscuits she had brought with her, and sat for half an hour, listening with her full attention to his plans for the future. No good being a truck driver, was it? he reminded her cheerfully. He'd got a bit of compensation coming to him and he was going to open a greengrocer's shop. 'And yer know wot, miss? Mr Fitzgibbon 'ad a nice little place in the Mile End Road, side-entrance and all to a real classy flat over. Said 'e was glad ter 'ave it taken off 'is 'ands, too. No rent for a year, 'e says. 'Ome in a couple of days, though I'll 'ave ter come for physio and 'ave me leg fitted.' He grinned widely at her. 'Reckon 'm lucky. The missus isn't 'arf pleased.'

'Oh, I'm so very glad,' said Florence. 'I know you'll make a success of it. Give me the address, will you? I'll come and see you.'

She took the scrap of paper he handed her and got up. 'I must go. Do take care, won't you? And I will come and see you and your wife.'

He went to the ward door with her, proud of his prowess with his crutches, and she turned and waved goodbye before she turned the corner at the end of the corridor.

She was walking along an endless corridor on her way out when Dan came through a ward door. 'Hey there, I say, I've had some splendid news—Lucy's coming back. The family she's with is coming to London; a diplomatic posting-we'll be able to see quite a lot of each other. I have missed her…'

'What wonderful news, Dan; I'm so glad. Give her my love and tell her to give me a ring, if you can spare her—we could have a good gossip.' She smiled widely at Dan and he beamed back at her, a hand on her arm. It was unfortunate for Mr Fitzgibbon's peace of mind that he should be coming towards them; from where he was, they looked absorbed in each other.

He was very near when they became aware of him, and Dan said, 'Oh, hello, sir. Have you come in about that crushed chest, or did you want to see Miss MacFinn?'

'Both,' said Mr Fitzgibbon, 'Miss MacFinn first, I think.' He slowed his pace, waiting for Dan to join him and, when he did so, nodded to Florence, smiling blandly, his eyes cold. 'Sorry to interrupt,' he said pleasantly. 'Good evening, Florence.'

The two men went away and Florence loitered along the corridor, wondering what she had done now to make him look like that—coldly angry, and with her. After all, since she'd been a member of the nursing staff at the hospital, no one objected to her coming and going at odd hours, but he had looked at her as though she had no right to be there.

She went off back to Mrs Twist's, highly incensed at his manner.

Two days went by, Mr Fitzgibbon came and went, saw his patients, dictated his letters, and addressed Florence when necessary and not otherwise in an impersonal manner which chilled her to the very marrow.

By the time Friday came she was looking forward to going home; perhaps, away from the scene of her problems, she would be able to solve them. It was halfway through the afternoon when Mrs Keane was struck by a violent migraine. Mr Fitzgibbon was at Colbert's and there were no more patients for that day; they were getting ready to go home. Mrs Keane had been lying down on the examination-room couch, but she had got up to lock her desk before she left, and the phone rang at that moment. Florence, giving the kitchen a final scrutiny, heard Mrs Keane's voice.

'I'll be there at seven o'clock, sir,' she was saying, and, 'I'll bring it with me.'

She put down the receiver and sat down limply. 'Mr Fitzgibbon wants me to go his East End clinic with some vital notes he's left here…'

'Well, you can't,' said Florence very firmly. 'Tell me where to find them and where to go and I'll take them. And I'm getting a taxi for you this very minute. You're not fit to be on your feet.'

'Oh, but I must,' said Mrs Keane feebly.

'Pooh,' said Florence, 'there's no must about it. Where is this folder?'

'You'll miss your train.'

'I'm not going until the morning,' said Florence, thinking it was quite all right and very easy to tell fibs once you got into the bad habit of it.

'You really mean that? The folder is in the left-hand drawer of his desk. It's in a blue cover and it's marked "Confidential". You really don't mind going? I don't know what he'll say…'

Florence wasn't sure either, but all she said was, 'Well, he probably won't notice. Where is it exactly?'

Mrs Keane told her. 'Not a nice district, dear. When I've been I have always had a taxi there and back. On expenses, of course.'

Florence found the folder, locked everything up and put an arm round Mrs Keane, who had her eyes shut and was looking very pale. 'I'd better come with you,' she suggested, but Mrs Keane declared that she would be all right; all the same, when the taxi came Florence begged the driver to keep an eye on his passenger and give her an arm to her front door. The cabbie was elderly and delighted to see such a pretty, charming face at the end of a day of passengers who didn't bother to look at him, only snapped directions as they got in and paid him without a glance.

'Course I will, ducks; got a bad 'ead, 'as she? My old lady gets 'em too.'

Florence said that she was sorry to hear that, and if it hadn't been for a faint moan from Mrs Keane she might have enquired further. She gave him a last smile and waved as the taxi drew away from the kerb.

Mr Fitzgibbon had said seven o'clock, and it would take quite a time to cross London, for the traffic would still be heavy. She explained to Mrs Twist, who gave her a cup of tea and a bun and promised that there would be something in the fridge when she got back, and went to her room to change. Something severe and inconspicuous, she decided, going through her few dresses. The cotton jersey, she supposed, and got into it, subdued her hair into a tidy chignon, thrust her tired feet into sandals, picked up a small handbag she could safeguard if necessary and, with the folder safely in a plastic carrier-bag, went in search of a taxi.

It was a long drive through the City, its blocks of offices silent now, the streets quiet, and then into the lighted streets of the East End, the wholesale dress shops, take-away food shops, amusement arcades, boarded-up houses and here and there high-rise flats alien to their surroundings.

The cabbie turned round once to ask if she was sure she had the right address, 'For this ain't no place for a pretty girl like you, miss.'

She assured him that she had it right. 'It's all right, it's a clinic, and I know the people who work there.'

Anything less like a clinic would be hard to find, she reflected as she got out at last, paid the cabbie, assured him that she was quite safe and crossed the pavement to the half-open door. It was a corner house, its brickwork grimed, two of its three windows boarded up, the third covered with wire netting. She turned to smile reassuringly at the cabbie and pushed open the door. The hall was dark and smelled damp, and from one of several doors there was a subdued volume of sound and a crack of light around its ill-fitting door. Florence opened it and went in.

The room wasn't large, but it was empty of furniture, save for benches against its walls and rows of decrepit chairs taking up every inch of space. It was full of people, though, and those who hadn't got seats were standing against the walls. The babble of talk died down while everyone looked at her; only the noise of the continuous coughing from some of them continued.

'Lost yer way, love?' asked a cheerful stout woman with a small boy on her lap. 'Come ter see Doc?' And, when Florence nodded, 'Well, yer'll 'ave ter take yer turn, ducks, same as the rest of us.'

'I'm not here to see him,' said Florence matter-of-factly, 'I'm a nurse, and I've brought some papers he wants urgently.'

Several voices told her to go through the door at the end of the room, and a man lounging beside it opened it for her. She thanked him nicely and went through the door on a wave of onions and beer. The atmosphere on the other side of the door was quite a different matter. What fresh air there was in the Mile End Road was pouring in through a window high up in one wall, and the walls were distempered a cheerful pale yellow. The furniture was simple: a desk, a chair behind it and another before it, an examination couch, a cabinet housing the surgery equipment, and a large sink with a pile of towels beside it. Mr Fitzgibbon was bending over a small boy on the couch, Dan was standing opposite, and beside him was the child's mother, a pretty girl with greasy hair, a grubby T-shirt and torn denim trousers. The child was screaming and kicking, and Mr Fitzgibbon had a gentle hand on the small stomach, waiting patiently until he quietened. It was a pity that the girl broke into loud sobs, and when Dan put a soothing hand on her arm flung it off and added her own screams to the child's. Florence put the folder on the desk and joined the group round the couch.

'Now, now,' she said soothingly, and put an arm round the

girl's shoulders. 'Come and sit down here so that the doctors can take a look at your little boy. You can tell me all about it...'

She hardly noticed Dan's surprised stare but she couldn't fail to hear Mr Fitzgibbon's terse, 'What the devil—?'

'I'll tell you later,' she announced, and met eyes like cold steel with her own calm blue ones. 'I'll look after Mum,' she added kindly, 'while you get on with what you want to do.'

She led the girl to a chair by a desk in a corner of the room, ignoring his tight-lipped anger. He was probably thinking some very bad language, and most certainly he would have a great deal to say to her later on. But now there was the little matter of getting the girl to stop crying. Florence produced a clean handkerchief, begged her to mop her face, gave her a drink of water from the sink tap and enquired sympathetically as to what was wrong with the child.

The girl was vague; he'd been off colour, wouldn't eat, kept being sick and said his chest hurt him. 'So I brought him here,' she explained, 'seeing as how the doctor here seems to know his stuff.'

She sniffed forlornly, and Florence said, 'Oh, you're right there; he's a very clever man.'

'You his girlfriend?'

'No, no, I'm a nurse—I work for him.'

The girl eyed her with interest, her worries forgotten for the moment. 'Got a bit of a temper, hasn't he? Doesn't show, but you can tell.' She darted a glance at the little group by the couch; the little boy was quiet now, and it was Mr Fitzgibbon talking, making the child chuckle.

He turned his head presently. 'Since you are here, Sister, perhaps you will dress this little chap while I talk to his mother.' His manner was pleasant, but his voice was cold.

It seemed wise not to speak; Florence began to clothe the child in an assortment of garments, listening as best she could to Mr Fitzgibbon at his most soothing, persuading the girl to let him take the child into hospital. He explained cystic fibrosis very simply, enquired as to her circumstances and suggested that she should see the lady at the desk in the room adjoining, who would help her to sort things out. 'I'll get an ambulance,' he told her. 'You can go with Jimmy and then stay the night at the hospital if you wish to; if you want to come back home ask the lady for your fare. Have you any money?'

He sounded so kind that Florence felt the tears crowding her throat, and when Dan came over to see how she was getting on the smile she gave him was so lop-sided that he took a second look at her, but all he said was, 'I'll phone for an ambulance.'

Mother and child were borne away presently, and Dan said, 'I'll get in the next patient, shall I?'

Mr Fitzgibbon was at his desk, finishing a conversation with Colbert's about the child he had admitted. He put the receiver down and said, 'Not for a moment. Florence, I should like to know why you are here. I spoke to Mrs Keane on the phone…'

She sat down on the chair opposite him. 'Well, it's like this—she had the most awful migraine, so I put her in a taxi and sent her home and came instead of her.' She added in a motherly voice, 'And now I'm here I might as well stay and give a hand. You're bursting with rage, aren't you? But with all these people outside there isn't really time to give vent to it, is there?'

Dan gave a muffled laugh, which he turned into a prolonged cough, but Mr Fitzgibbon didn't smile. He was in a towering rage, all the worse for its being battened down with iron determination. He glanced at his watch. 'You came by taxi?'

She nodded.

'Is it waiting?'

'Heavens, no, that would cost a small fortune, and I was told to put it down to expenses.'

'In that case you had better stay and make yourself useful.' He got up. 'Let's have the next one, Dan.'

He ignored her for the rest of the long evening, but she had little time to worry about that. Wrapped around by a white pinny she found hanging behind the door, she dressed and undressed, applied plasters, redid bandages and cleared up after each patient. The majority of them were old patients who had come for a regular check-up, but nevertheless it was past ten o'clock by the time the last one went away. Florence, helped by the quiet little lady who had been doing the paperwork and attending to the patients' problems, tidied up the place, took off the pinny and followed her to the door, nodding to Dan as she went.

'Not so fast,' said Mr Fitzgibbon, still writing at his desk. 'Dan, go on ahead, will you, and write that child up for something, and make sure his mum's being looked after? I'll be along later.'

Dan hesitated. 'Shall I take Florence with me, sir?'

'I'll take her back to her lodgings.'

Florence advanced a step into the room. 'I shall catch a bus,' she said clearly.

'No, you won't.' He didn't look up. 'Off you go, Dan; I'll see Florence safely back.'

His registrar went with a sidelong smile for Florence and, since Mr Fitzgibbon showed no sign of being ready to leave, she sat down composedly on one of the few chairs in the room.

Presently he closed the folder he was writing in and put away his pen.

'You haven't had your supper?'

'No; Mrs Twist will have left something for me.'

He got up and crossed the room to stand in front of her, making her feel at a disadvantage, since she had to look up a long way to see his face. He put out a hand and hauled her gently to her feet and didn't let her hand go.

'I have been most unkind—will you forgive me?'

He sounded so kind that she had the greatest wish to throw herself on to his chest and have a good cry; instead she looked him in the eye. 'Yes, of course I will. I must have given you a surprise. Do you like to keep all this—' she waved her free hand around '—a secret?'

'As far as I can, yes. Dan knows, of course, and so do several of the local doctors who take it in turns to work here. I've never considered it suitable for women, though.'

'Oh, pooh,' said Florence. 'What about that nice little lady who was here?'

'Ah, yes, well, she's the local school-teacher, and perfectly safe.'

She gave her hand a tug, but he held it fast. 'Well, now I know about it, may I come and work here too? I should very much like to.'

'Why, Florence?'

She had no intention of telling him why; instead she said matter-of-factly, 'It's worthwhile, isn't it? And I've every evening…'

He lifted his eyebrows. 'Every evening? What about those evenings out with Dan?' He smiled faintly. 'A "poky little Chinese place".'

'That was years ago. I'm glad his fiancée is coming back so soon; she's a dear…'

She glanced at him and was surprised to see what amounted to amused satisfaction on his face. 'If you want to work here I see no reason why you shouldn't, but on the definite condition that I bring you and take you back, and that you stay here in the building. I won't have you roaming the streets…'

She said coldly, 'I'm not in the habit of roaming…' and remembered the unfortunate episode when she had looked for a short-cut to the bus. 'Oh, very well. How often do you come here?'

'Once a week.' He let her hand go, picked up his bag and opened the door. 'It's getting late.'

He stowed her into the car, parked in a scruffy yard behind the house. 'I'm surprised that it's still here,' observed Florence, and then added, 'no, I'm not; they depend on you, don't they?'

'To a certain extent—most of them either need to go into hospital or have just been discharged from it.'

The streets were quiet, and the homeward journey seemed much shorter than her taxi ride.

'Mrs Twist will be in bed?' asked Mr Fitzgibbon.

'Oh, yes, but I have a key.'

'In that case there is no need to disturb her. Mrs Crib will have a meal ready.'

Florence thought longingly of food. 'Well, that's all right for you, isn't it? If you'd just drop me off at the end of this street I can—'

'Don't be silly, Florence, you will eat your supper with me and I'll bring you back afterwards.'

'I don't think—!'

'Good.' He had turned into his street and stopped before his door.

He got out, went round the car and opened her door, and said, 'Out you get,' and, when she didn't budge, scooped her up and set her on her feet on the pavement. He held her for a moment and then bent and kissed her, took her by the arm, opened his street door and urged her inside.

Since she had no means of getting back to Mrs Twist's and there was a delicious aroma coming from the half-open baize door at the back of the hall, Florence, sternly suppressing delighted thoughts about the kiss, decided sensibly to stay for supper.

CHAPTER EIGHT

MR FITZGIBBON GAVE Florence a gentle push from behind. 'Straight through to the kitchen. The Cribs will be in bed, but everything will be ready.'

The kitchen was roomy, with an old-fashioned dresser laden with china dishes and plates, a scrubbed wooden table in the centre of the tiled floor, and an Aga stove taking up almost all of one wall. It was flanked by two Windsor armchairs with bright cushions, and between them was Monty, roused from sleep and pleased to see them, weaving round them, uttering whispered barks. Sharing her basket was a cat, stout and matronly, who yawned widely at them and then went to sleep again.

The table had been laid for one person and with the same niceness which would have graced an elegant dining-room. Mr Fitzgibbon opened a drawer and collected spoon and forks and knives, and carried them over to the table and set them tidily beside his own place. He fetched a glass from the dresser, too, and more plates. 'Sit down,' he invited. 'I have my supper here when I go to the clinic, otherwise the Cribs would wait up. You don't mind?'

She shook her head, feeling shy because Mr Fitzgibbon was

exhibiting yet another aspect of himself. Quite handy in the kitchen, she reflected, watching him ladle soup into two bowls and set them on the table. Excellent soup too, nothing out of a tin—home-made watercress soup with a blob of cream a-top and fresh brown crusty bread to go with it. After that there were chicken tartlets, kept warm in the oven, with jacket potatoes smothered in butter and a salad from the fridge. Florence forgot to be shy, ate her supper with a splendid appetite and made suitable small talk, all the while conscious of his kiss but trying not to think of it. They had their coffee presently, still sitting at the table, and he asked, 'You're going home for the weekend, Florence?'

'Yes, I promised Mother I would—we're going to make jam.' She glanced at the clock, a large old-fashioned one, hanging above the door. 'If it's convenient I'd like to go back to Mrs Twist's,' and then, by way of making conversation, she added, 'Are you going away for the weekend too?'

'Yes—like you, I'm going into the country.' He got up when she did and said, 'No, leave everything; I'll see to it when I get back.'

He drove her to her room and got out of the car and went with her to Mrs Twist's front door, took her key from her and unlocked it, gave her back her key and asked, 'Do we have to be careful of Buster?'

'No, he'll be upstairs with Mrs Twist. Thank you for a lovely supper, Mr Fitzgibbon, and…and…thank you for letting me come to your clinic each week.' She hesitated. 'But please don't think that I shall expect you to give me supper afterwards.'

'No, no, of course not, but this evening was exceptional, was it not?'

He opened the door and wished her goodnight with a casual friendliness, which for some reason annoyed her. She said 'Goodnight' quickly and went past him, but before he closed the door behind her he said, 'I do believe that we are making progress.' He shut the door before she could ask him what he meant.

Yes, there was a great deal to think about, she reflected as she got ready for bed, taking care to make no sound at all for fear of waking Mrs Twist. She got into bed and started to marshal her thoughts into sense, and went to sleep within minutes. In the morning the last evening's happenings were somehow put into their proper perspective: Mr Fitzgibbon had had every right to be surprised and annoyed at her arrival at the clinic, and common decency and good manners had forced him to take her back to his home for a meal. It was all quite explicable in the light of early morning, all except his kiss, which didn't quite fit in. She decided not to think about it any more.

She caught her train with a minute or so to spare, and sat quietly all the way to Sherborne, daydreaming; if it hadn't been for a child in the carriage excitedly pointing out the castle as they neared the little town she might have been carried on to Yeovil and beyond.

She had phoned her mother from the telephone box opposite Mrs Twist's house, and her father was on the platform waiting for her.

She drove the car back to Gussage Tollard, listening to her father's comments on the week and answering very circumspectly his queries as to her own week, and when they got home her mother, waiting with coffee and seed cake, asked the same questions, but rather more searchingly. Florence answered them all, leaving out as much as possible anything to do with Mr Fitzgibbon, something which her mother was quick to notice.

It was nice to be home; Florence pottered about the house, inspected the garden and then strolled down to the village to purchase one or two groceries her mother had forgotten.

There were several people in the shop, enjoying a gossip while they waited to be served. Florence knew them all and, after enquiring after their respective children, aged parents and whether the jam had set well, answered various enquiries as to her life in London.

'Nasty, smoky place,' observed one lady in house slippers and a printed pinny; she nodded her head wisely so that the row of curlers across her forehead nodded with it. 'No place for kids, I always say. There's Mrs Burge's youngest, went to live with his auntie and now he's in the hospital, having things done to his chest.' She beamed at Florence. 'Same as you worked in, Miss Florence—Colbert's; being looked after by a clever man, too…got a funny name—Fitz something, great big chap, she says, and ever so kind. He's got a house in Mells too; goes there at weekends…'

It was Florence's turn at the counter and she was glad of it; Mr Fitzgibbon's name, uttered so unexpectedly, had sent the colour into her cheeks and she was thankful to bend over the list in her hand.

Mrs Hoskins, serving, put a jar of Bovril on the counter and asked with a kindly curiosity, 'You'll know him, no doubt, Miss Florence? That's the smallest size Bovril I've got, tell your mother.'

'About a pound of Cheddar cheese,' said Florence and, since the village probably knew already that she worked for him but were far too nicely mannered to say so, she said, 'Well, yes, I work for him, you know. He's a very clever surgeon and marvellous with the children.'

There was a satisfied murmur from those around her, and the lady in the printed pinny looked pleased with herself. 'There, didn't I say so?' she wanted to know. 'And him living less than an hour away from here, too.'

Half an hour or so, reflected Florence silently, in that Rolls of his, and she asked for a bottle of cider vinegar, and, since he lived near by, he could quite easily give her a lift if he wanted to. Only he didn't want to.

She frowned so fiercely at the vinegar that Mrs Hoskins said hastily, 'That's the best make, Miss Florence; Mrs Napier won't have any of that nasty cheap stuff, and I won't sell it neither.'

Florence apologised quickly, adding that she had been trying to remember something or other she hadn't put on the list.

Which wasn't true, but it made a good excuse. She took her purchases home presently and then went into the garden, where she attacked the weeds with such ferocity that her mother, watching from the open drawing-room window, remarked to the Reverend Mr Napier, sitting beside her, that something had upset Florence. 'I wonder what it can be?' she mused. 'Of course, it's a great help—getting the weeding done.'

Her husband, without lifting his eyes from his newspaper, agreed with her.

One of the Sunday-school teachers was on holiday and Florence had volunteered to take her place with the toddlers' class, but first she intended going off for a walk with Higgins. She was up early on Sunday morning and, with Higgins panting happily at her heels, accompanied her father as far as the church, where he was to take the early service, and then went through the lych-gate, down the narrow lane that led to Mott's Farm, and turned off over the stile into the bridle-path, which would eventually bring her out on the other side of the village. It was a glorious morning and full of the country sounds she missed in London: there were birds singing, sheep bleating, a farm tractor starting up, prepared to make its ponderous way across a field lying fallow, and then the church clock striking the hour of eight. There was plenty of time; her father wouldn't be back until almost nine o'clock, and matins would be at eleven o'clock. She sat down on a fallen log and watched Higgins gallop clumsily from one clump of trees to the other hopeful of finding rabbits, thinking inevitably of Mr Fitzgibbon.

He was at that very moment sitting in her mother's kitchen, drinking tea, looking very much at his ease with Monty at his feet.

Mrs Napier, assembling eggs and bacon and mushrooms for breakfast, had greeted him with no surprise and a great deal of inward satisfaction; it was nice to know that her maternal instincts hadn't been at fault. Here, then, was the reason for her daughter's arduous gardening, her wish to go for long walks with Higgins, her animated conversations about her week at work without any mention of Mr Fitzgibbon. She offered him tea, remarked on the beauty of the morning and volunteered the information that Florence had taken Higgins for a walk. 'Her usual early-morning round when she is at home,' she explained casually, 'down the lane to Mott's Farm, only she goes over the stile and down the bridle-path. It brings her out at the other end of the village in nice time for breakfast.'

She smiled across the kitchen at her visitor. 'Have you come far? Not from London, surely?'

'No, I have a house at Mells—do you know it? It's not so very far from here.'

'A pretty village. Of course, you'll stay and have some breakfast, won't you?'

'That would be delightful. Mr Napier is in church?'

'Yes. He will be back just before nine o'clock. There's matins at eleven, and Florence is taking one of the Sunday-school classes.'

A smile touched the corners of his mouth. He put his mug down. 'Perhaps I could overtake Florence,' he suggested blandly.

'Easily—she doesn't hurry; Higgins likes to hunt for rabbits—he never finds any, but it makes him happy.'

After he had gone Mrs Napier stood for a few minutes, her hands idle over the mushrooms she was peeling, allowing herself a few moments of pleasant daydreaming. A splendid man, she reflected, but possibly proud and reserved and liking his own way, but, on the other hand, utterly dependable and sure of himself and what he wanted. She hoped fervently that he wanted Florence.

Mr Fitzgibbon had no difficulty in finding Florence; she was still sitting on the log, her thoughts miles away, and in any case Monty had seen Higgins and rushed to meet him so noisily that she looked round to see what was happening.

Mr Fitzgibbon, walking slowly towards her, had time to admire the sun glinting on her bronze hair and the faint freckles across the bridge of her nose; he admired the colour creeping up into her cheeks when she saw him too. Her rather faded blue cotton dress and old sandals on her bare feet seemed to him to be exactly right; she was as pretty as a picture; he would have thought the same if she had been wearing a potato sack, although he had at times had the violent urge to hang her around with pearls and jewels and drape her in the very latest of fashions. He controlled his thoughts with an iron will and walked towards her and wished her a casual good morning. 'Such a splendid morning,' he continued blandly, 'and Monty needed a walk.'

Florence eyed him warily. 'All the way from Mells?' and, at his lifted eyebrows, 'Mrs Burge's youngest; they were talking about him in the village shop yesterday and someone said that you lived there.'

He sat down beside her. 'Ah, yes—Billy Burge, a delightful small boy with the heart of a lion—he's a fibrocystic…' He went on smoothly into a detailed account of the child's illness. 'He's almost well enough to go to a convalescent home—it will have to be somewhere round about here so that his family can visit easily.' He glanced at his watch. 'May I join you? Your mother said nine o'clock breakfast—'

'You've been home?'

'I had the urge to explore,' he answered smoothly, 'and I remembered that you lived here.' It seemed that was all the explanation he had to offer.

She got to her feet, and Higgins and Monty bustled up, anxious to be on the move again. 'There's time for us to follow the path round the village; it comes out at the other end of the village by the school. It's not far.'

'I dare say I can manage it,' said Mr Fitzgibbon. He sounded so meek that she gave him a suspicious look, but he was looking away from her, his face devoid of what she had suspected was sarcasm. So they walked on, slipping presently into a comfortable conversation about the country around them, the village and its inhabitants, and the pleasures of the rural life. By the time they reached the vicarage Florence was feeling happier than she had been for some time, although she had no idea why that should be. She only knew, in her mind at least, that she thought of Mr Fitzgibbon as Alexander…

They ate their breakfast in the kitchen, sitting round the solid table with its white starched cloth and blue and white china, and Mr Fitzgibbon made a splendid meal and, very much to Florence's surprise, helped with the washing-up afterwards.

She wasn't sure if she was pleased or not when her father wanted to know if their guest would like to attend morning church.

'Oh, do,' said Mrs Napier, 'and come with us and have lunch here, or if you would rather you can lie about in the garden.'

He agreed very readily to go to church, and accepted his invitation to stay for lunch.

'Oh, good,' said Mrs Napier. 'When do you have to go back to London?'

'This evening—perhaps Florence would like to come back with me?'

He looked across the table at her, faintly smiling. 'It will save you the tiresome trip across town to Mrs Twist's, Florence.'

She said slowly, 'Well, yes, thank you. But don't you want to go to your home—I mean…?' She went a little pink. 'I didn't mean to be rude, but I don't want to spoil your day.'

'Oh, I don't think you'll do that. We can go there on our way back if you don't mind leaving a little earlier than usual.'

Even if she had wanted to refuse it would have been hard with her mother beaming at them both and her father observing that Sunday trains were always late and he had never liked her arriving in London late on Sunday evening.

Mr Fitzgibbon agreed quietly with him, and added blandly, 'That's settled, then. What do we do with the dogs—will they be all right while we are in church?'

'We leave Higgins in the conservatory; he's always quite happy. Monty will probably settle there too.' Mr Napier glanced at his watch. 'Florence, if you're going to take Sunday school you'd better get dressed, my dear.'

Florence went upstairs, feeling rather as though someone had taken the day away from her, rearranged it, and handed it back again. She took off the blue cotton and got into a short-sleeved crêpe dress in pale green, coiled her hair and did her face, found suitable shoes and stockings and went back downstairs, to find Mr Fitzgibbon in a tie and a beautifully tailored blazer. She frowned thoughtfully; she was sure that when he had joined her on the bridle-path he had been wearing an open-necked shirt and no tie. She caught his eye and found him smiling at her. It was a mocking smile, and it made her aware that he knew exactly what she had been thinking.

'I'll be off,' she told the room at large, and whisked herself away with a heightened colour.

Her class was large. Her father's congregation was large too, and there were a great many children in the village. She sat in the small village hall beside the church, telling them Bible stories and drawing on the blackboard to illustrate them, and at the appointed time she marshalled them into a straggling line and marched them into church to take part in the last few minutes of the service.

Mr Fitzgibbon watched her without appearing to do so, gently chivvying her restless brood into suitable quietness with an unselfconscious air which delighted him, and Mrs Napier, beside him, peeping up from under her Sunday hat, heaved a happy, hopeful sigh.

Back at the vicarage, Florence found a dozen reasons why she was unable to spend any time in Mr Fitzgibbon's company. There was the table to lay in the dining-room, the joint of beef, roasting in the oven, to inspect, its accompanying trimmings to deal with and the strawberry tart to arrange on a dish. She did all these things slowly, reluctant to join her parents and Mr

Fitzgibbon, sipping sherry in the drawing-room, bewildered by the way in which he had become, as it were, a friend of the family.

'Colossal cheek,' she muttered to Charlie Brown, curled up on a kitchen chair. He flicked a lazy tail by way of answer.

She had to go to the drawing-room eventually, where she drank her sherry rather faster than she should have done and then urged her father to come and carve the joint, aware that she was not being her usual calm self and unable to do anything about it. Once they were sitting at the table, she regained some of her usual serenity and indeed she began to enjoy herself. There was no doubt about it: Mr Fitzgibbon was a pleasant companion—his manners were beautiful, his conversation interesting, and his ability to listen to other people talking and not to interrupt was unequalled. The meal progressed in a delightful manner, and it wasn't until her mother was serving her mouth-watering fruit tart that Florence looked across the table at Mr Fitzgibbon and knew in a blinding instant that she really was in love with him. The knowledge left her with a slightly open mouth, pale cheeks, a tremendous bubbling excitement and a feeling of relief that now she knew why she had been feeling so cross and vaguely unhappy.

She also realised within seconds of this discovery that on no account must anyone know about it, so that she passed plates, offered cream and remarked on the flavour of the tart in a wooden voice so unlike her usual pretty one that her mother looked sharply at her and Mr Fitzgibbon lowered his lids to hide the gleam in his eyes, watching her face as her thoughts chased themselves across her mind.

Florence removed the plates and fetched the coffee, her feet not quite touching the ground, her head a jumble of thoughts, none of which made sense. An hour on her own would be nice, she thought, but in no way was she to get it; her father declared that he would wash up, and Mr Fitzgibbon offered to help, with the almost careless air of one who always washed up on a Sunday anyway, so she and her mother repaired to the garden to sit in the elderly deck-chairs with the dogs lolling beside them.

'Such a handy man,' observed Mrs Napier, 'but I dare say he does quite a lot for himself at home.'

'He has a butler and a cook, Mother—that's in his London house; I don't know about Mells. If it's a small cottage I dare say he has to look after himself.'

'Well, do let me know, my darling—you're going there first on the way back, aren't you?' She closed her eyes. 'We'll have that Victoria sponge for tea—I wonder what time he wants to go?'

'I have no idea,' said Florence snappily. 'I think perhaps I'll change my mind and stay here and go up on the train…'

'Just as you like, love,' said her mother soothingly, 'I'm sure he'll understand.'

Florence sat up. 'Mother, what do you mean?'

'Why, nothing, darling—just an idle remark.'

The two men went for a stroll when they had done their chores, taking the dogs with them, and Florence watched them go with mixed feelings. She felt shy of Mr Fitzgibbon and anxious to present her usual matter-of-fact manner towards him; on the other hand she wanted to spend as much time as possible in his company. Sitting there, with her mother dozing beside her, she tried to decide what she should do. It would be hard to maintain that manner towards him; on the other hand if it was too hard she would have to leave her job and go somewhere where she would never see him again. She was still worrying away at the problem when they came back, and she went indoors to get the tea. Mr Fitzgibbon followed her in presently to carry the tea-tray out into the garden, casually friendly and seemingly unnoticing of her hot cheeks and stilted replies to his undemanding remarks, so that presently she pulled herself together. After all, she reflected, she was the only one who would be affected by her feelings—no one else knew, nor would they ever know. Presently, when they had finished tea, he suggested that they might be going; she agreed with her usual calm manner and went upstairs to get her overnight bag, bade her mother and father goodbye, hugged Charlie Brown and Higgins and got into the car, to hang out of the window at the last minute to call that she would be home again the following weekend. Mindful of her companion, she added, 'I hope.'

Mr Fitzgibbon was at his most urbane as he drove back to Mells; Florence, filled with a mixture of uneasiness and excitement, found herself being soothed into her usual good sense by his reassuring if rambling remarks, none of them touching on anything personal. By the time they reached Mells she had got control of herself and told herself not to behave like a silly girl; it was a situation, she was sure, which occurred over and over again, and she would cope with it.

The first sight of the house took her breath. 'Oh, how can you bear to live in London?' she demanded. 'Just look at those roses…'

Mr Fitzgibbon said mildly, 'Yes, I'm very fond of it, although I like the house in Knightsbridge too. I have the best of both worlds, have I not?'

'Well, you have really worked hard for them,' said Florence, skipping out of the car, closely observed, did she but know it, by Nanny, peering out of the funny little latticed window by the front door.

Nanny went to open the door. This one was the one, then, she reflected with satisfaction, and a nice girl too—beautiful and the proper shape. Nanny had no time for young women like blades of grass. A nice wedding, she thought cosily, and children tumbling about the old house. She opened the door, looking pleased.

Mr Fitzgibbon saw the look and grinned to himself, but he introduced Florence with perfect gravity. 'I've some papers I need to pick up, Nanny—we've had a splendid tea, but perhaps you could find us some supper before we go?'

He watched Florence's face out of the corner of his eye and

saw delight, uncertainty and annoyance chase each other across it. 'It's only a couple of hours' drive—less—and I'm sure you would like to see the garden while you're here.'

'You leave it to me, Mr Alexander,' said Nanny briskly. 'A nice little chicken salad and one of my chocolate custards. In half an hour?'

'Splendid, Nanny—we ought to leave by nine o'clock at the latest.'

He turned to Florence, standing between them, feeling rather as though someone had put skates on her feet and given her a push. 'Well…' she began.

'Oh, good. Come along, then; there are some splendid roses at the side of the house, tea-roses, and some spectacular lilies—Casablanca; I put them in last year behind some Peruvian lilies.'

He led the way round the side of the house to where the garden stretched away to a magnificent red-brick wall, almost covered with wistaria, clematis and passion flower, a lawn of green velvet was edged by paths and wide herbaceous borders, bursting with summer flowers, and at the very end there was a circular bed of roses. Monty, trotting to and fro in great contentment, came and nuzzled her hand as she wandered along, very content, to admire the lilies and bend to smell the roses.

'Of course, you have a gardener?' she said presently.

'Oh, yes, but I potter around at the weekends and whenever I have an hour or so to spare.'

'Couldn't you commute?'

'I think it would be possible, but not just yet. Later, when I have a wife and family, perhaps.'

'Eleanor—Miss Paton is very pretty and wears lovely clothes…'

She had hardly been aware that she had spoken her thoughts out loud.

'Oh, quite charming,' agreed Mr Fitzgibbon placidly. 'You like clothes?'

'Well, yes, I do, but I don't have the time,' said Florence

crossly and, remembering to whom she was talking, 'and of course, I don't lead that kind of life.'

'You would like to do so?'

His voice was so casual that she answered without thinking. 'Certainly not. I'd be bored stiff.' She paused to examine a rose. 'That's a lovely Super Star. Do you prune in the autumn or in February?'

They strolled round the lovely garden, Monty at their heels, talking comfortably. I'm not just in love with him, thought Florence, I like him too.

Nanny called them in presently to a supper of cold chicken—a salad, and not just a few lettuce leaves and a tomato, but apples and nuts and grapes, mixed in with chicory and chopped-up mint. There were tiny new potatoes too and a home-made dressing. They drank iced lemonade, since Mr Fitzgibbon would be driving, and finished the meal with the chocolate custards Nanny had promised them.

'I should like to thank your nanny for such a lovely supper,' said Florence, 'but I don't know her name.'

'Nanny.'

'Yes, I know that, but I'm a stranger—it would be very ill-mannered to be so familiar with her.'

'Miss Betts. Run along to the kitchen while I see to Monty. We must go in ten minutes or so.' He opened the door for her. 'It's through that arched doorway by the stairs.'

Florence trod across the hall, wishing very much that she could have seen the rest of the house; the drawing-room was perfect, so was the dining-room, but there were three more doors leading from the hall. She opened the arched door and went down a few steps to another door and, since it was shut, she knocked.

Nanny's comfortable voice bade whoever it was to go in, so she lifted the old-fashioned latch. The kitchen was at the back of the house, a large low-ceilinged room, delightfully old-fashioned but, she suspected, having every labour-saving device that could be wished for. Nanny was standing at the table, picking over a bowl of red currants, but she looked up and smiled as Florence went in.

'I wanted to thank you for a lovely supper, Miss Betts,' said Florence. 'And I hope it didn't make a lot of extra work for you.'

'Lor, bless you, Miss Napier, not a bit of it, and it's a treat to see the food eaten. Times I could have cried seeing it being pecked over by Mr Alexander's guests. Here he is now, come for the currants; Mrs Crib likes to make a nice fruit tart and there's nothing like your own fruit.'

Florence, aware of Mr Fitzgibbon standing behind her, agreed with her and turned to go.

'And there's no call to say Miss Betts, Miss Napier—you call me Nanny, the way Mr Alexander does.' She smiled widely. 'I dare say we'll meet again.'

To which remark Florence murmured in a non-committal way, not wishing Mr Fitzgibbon to think that she was expecting to be asked to visit his house again.

They drove away presently with Monty on the back seat, leaning forward from time to time to breathe gently into the backs of their necks.

'I expect Monty likes being in the country,' observed Florence, intent on making small talk, and, when her companion made some brief reply, enlarged upon the subject at some length, anxious for some reason for there to be no silence.

When she paused for breath, however, Mr Fitzgibbon said gently, 'Don't try so hard, Florence; your silent company is contentment enough. And could you call me Alexander when we aren't working? I begin to dislike my own name, I hear it so frequently.'

Florence stared ahead of her. Of all the rude men… She drew a calming breath to damp down her feelings; if he wanted her silent then that was what he would get. She said stonily, 'Just as you like.' Nothing was going to make her say 'Alexander' after his remarks. Let him just wait until they were back at the consulting-rooms; if he didn't like being called Mr Fitzgibbon then she would address him as 'sir'.

'Don't sulk,' said Mr Fitzgibbon quietly. 'You have, as usual, got the wrong end of the stick.' He glanced at her cross profile. 'I fancy, however, it would be of no use putting matters right at the moment.'

They travelled some distance in silence until he said, 'I should like you to come to the hospital to see Miss MacFinn tomorrow morning. I've a round at nine o'clock; can you be ready by half-past eight or a little before that at the consulting-rooms? I only intend to look in on her for a few minutes—she has asked to see you again.'

'Very well,' said Florence. 'You have a patient at half-past eleven.'

'Yes, I'll see that you get back as soon as Miss MacFinn has had a word.' He stayed silent for a while and then said, 'I shan't see Mrs Keane before we go to Colbert's; will you ask her to change my appointments on Tuesday morning? I need to be free until one o'clock. Tell her to fit them in in the afternoon and early evening. We shall have to work late.'

'Very well,' said Florence again and looked out of the window. They didn't speak again until they reached Mrs Twist's front door, when she began a thank-you speech, uttered in a high voice quite unlike her usual quiet tones.

He cut her short. 'Oh, don't bother with that,' he begged her, 'you're as cross as two sticks, and I haven't the time to talk to you now.'

He had got out of the car as he spoke and opened her door. Florence got out haughtily, tripped up on the pavement and was set back on her feet with a, 'Tut, tut, pride goes before a fall,' as he took her arm and marched her to the door, unlocked it and, when she would have opened it, put a great hand over hers.

'I should like to think that I know the reason for your peevishness,' he observed blandly, 'but uncertainty forbids me from doing anything about it for the moment; you are like a weathercock being blown to every point of the compass.' He bent suddenly and kissed her quickly. 'Goodnight, Florence.'

He opened the door and shoved her gently into the little hallway beyond, and just as gently shut it behind her.

Florence stood very still and tried to make sense of being called a weathercock, but she had to give up almost at once, for Mrs Twist came out of her front parlour with Buster under one arm.

'I thought I heard a car,' she observed. 'Did you get a lift back? I'm just going to make a cup of tea; have one with me—I could do with a bit of company.'

So Florence stuffed Mr Fitzgibbon and his remarks to the back of her head and sat down on the sofa of Mrs Twist's three-piece, very uncomfortable and covered in cut moquette, and gave her an expunged version of her weekend, excusing herself at length with the plea that she had to be extra early at work in the morning. 'And I dare say you're nicely tired,' said Mrs Twist. 'You'll sleep like a log.'

A remark unfortunately not borne out by Florence, who spent an almost sleepless night, her muddled thoughts going round and round in her head, so that by the time she got up she had a dreadful headache and was no nearer to enlightenment as to Mr Fitzgibbon's remarks on the previous evening and, still more important, why he had kissed her.

CHAPTER NINE

FLORENCE LAY AWAKE for a long time and woke from a heavy sleep with no wish to get up and go to work. She had a sketchy breakfast and with an eye on the clock hurried to the consulting-rooms. She reached them at the same time as the Rolls whispered to a stop, and Mr Fitzgibbon thrust open a door, bade her good morning and begged that she should get in, at the same time remarking that she looked washed out. 'You're not sickening for something?' he wanted to know with what she considered to be heartless cheerfulness.

'Certainly not. I never felt better, Mr Fitzgibbon.'

'Alexander.'

'No...'

He was weaving in and out of the morning traffic. 'No? Ah, well, it will take time, I suppose, and you're still as cross as two sticks, aren't you? Is it due to lack of sleep? It's a good thing that we have a busy day ahead of us.'

There really wasn't an answer to this, and she sat silently until they reached Colbert's and there accompanied him to the lifts, very conscious of him standing beside her as they went up to the top floor.

Miss MacFinn was sitting in a well-cushioned chair by her bed, dwarfed by the necessary paraphernalia vital to her recovery. She greeted them with pleasure and bade them sit on the bed. 'Forbidden, I know,' she chuckled, 'but no one will dare say anything to you, Alexander. I hope this is a social visit?' She smiled at Florence. 'So nice to see you again, my dear; you're beautiful, you know, and it acts like a tonic…!'

Florence blushed and looked at her feet, and heard Mr Fitzgibbon's casual, 'Yes, she is, isn't she? And a splendid worker too. So often beauty is accompanied by a bird-brain.' He got up. 'I must just have a word with Sister; I'll be back presently and run an eye over you before I take Florence back.'

He sauntered away, and Miss MacFinn said, 'Does Alexander work you hard, my dear?'

'No—oh, no, the hours are sometimes irregular, but compared with running a ward it isn't hard at all.'

'He works too hard himself. I'm relieved to know that he intends to marry. It's time he settled down and raised a family.'

Florence, her hands clasped tightly in her lap, agreed quietly, 'I'm sure a wife would be a great asset to him; he's very well-known, isn't he? And I dare say he has any number of friends and a full social life.'

Miss MacFinn coughed. 'Well, dear, I'm not sure about that; he has many friends, but if by social life you mean dinner parties and dances and so on I think you may be mistaken, although I'm sure that, provided he had the right companion, he would enjoy these things.'

'Well, yes, I expect so.'

'Tell me, have you had a pleasant weekend? You live near Sherborne, don't you? A lovely part of the country. I had friends there…'

Mr Fitzgibbon came back presently and, when Florence would have got up, said, 'No, don't go, I shall only be a moment or two.' He sat down on the bed again. 'You're doing well,' he told his patient. 'I'm going to keep you here a little longer than usual, and then you can go to your sister's. I'll listen to your chest if I may… Very satisfactory. We must be off now; I'll be in to see you some time tomorrow.'

'Thank you, Alexander, and thank you, Florence, for coming too. Come and see me again, won't you?'

Florence said that she would. 'In the evening,' she suggested, 'if that's not too late?'

She bent and kissed the elderly cheek, and Miss MacFinn remarked, 'It really is most suitable,' which puzzled Florence and brought a reluctant smile to Mr Fitzgibbon's handsome visage.

The traffic was heavy now. He didn't speak as they drove back, only when they reached the consulting-rooms he reminded her to give Mrs Keane his message about his appointments for the following day.

He had gone to open the door for her and she got out carefully, not wishing to stumble again. She said quietly, 'Very well, sir.'

Then she gasped at his sudden, 'Oh, goodness, now it's sir, is it? Back to square one.'

She paused before she crossed the pavement. 'I don't know what you mean.'

'No? Then think about it, will you? And just as soon as I have the time we'll have a talk. There's a limit to my patience.'

She gave him a startled look—the blandness of his face matched the blandness of his voice, but his eyes were a hard grey from which she flinched. All the same, she might as well give as good as she was getting.

'In that case, Mr Fitzgibbon, let us hope that you will have a few minutes to spare at the earliest opportunity.'

She sailed ahead of him, her coppery head held high, ignoring whatever it was he rumbled in reply. Something rude, she had no doubt.

There were appointments booked until one o'clock and throughout the morning he treated her with a teeth-gritting civility that she did her best to return with a highly professional manner, which, while impressive, she found quite tiring. By the end of the morning she had made up her mind. She was not a particularly impulsive girl, but suddenly the prospect of working for him, seeing him each day and knowing that he didn't care two straws for her, wasn't to be borne. When he got back at two o'clock she gave him five minutes to get settled in his chair, and with an eye on the clock, since his first appointment was barely ten minutes away, she knocked on the door and walked in.

He was writing, but he looked up when she went in. 'Yes?' He glanced at his watch and Florence, who had weakened at the sight of him, bristled.

'I'll not take a moment, Mr Fitzgibbon. I should like to leave. After a month, of course, as we agreed.'

He put down his pen and sat back in his chair. Surprise gave way to a thoughtful look from under his lids, and his smile was full of charm, so that her heart thumped against her ribs and before she could stop herself she had taken a step towards him, brought to a halt, however, by his sudden laugh. 'Splendid; nothing could be better, Florence, and you have no need to stay for a month—I'll let you off that. Go at the end of the week—we will waive our agreement.'

It was the last thing she had expected to hear. 'But you won't have a nurse.'

'I have been interviewing several likely applicants. Mrs Bates, a widow lady, is ready to start work whenever I say so.'

He sat watching her. No doubt expecting me to burst into tears, thought Florence. Well, I won't. She said in a voice that wobbled only very slightly, 'Oh, good. In that case, there's no more to be said, is there?'

'No, not at the moment.' He smiled again. 'Ask Mrs Keane to come in, will you?'

In the waiting-room Mrs Keane looked up from her typewriter. 'Florence, whatever is the matter? You're as white as a ghost. Are you all right?'

'Yes, thank you. Mr Fitzgibbon would like you to go in, Mrs Keane.'

The door was barely closed behind that lady when the first patient arrived, which was a good thing, for Florence was at once caught up in her normal routine. As the afternoon wore on it became apparent that Mrs Keane knew nothing of her departure; Florence had expected Mr Fitzgibbon to tell her, since she was privy to his professional life. She waited until the last patient had been seen and he had left to go to Colbert's, and over a cup of tea broke her news.

'Whatever for?' asked Mrs Keane. 'I thought you were happy here…'

'Well, I like the work very much—that isn't why I'm leaving. In fact, I think Mr Fitzgibbon is glad that I am going; he didn't actually say so, but he knows of a nurse who will start on Monday.'

She looked at Mrs Keane with such sad blue eyes that Mrs Keane, normally the most unsentimental of women, felt a lump in her throat. 'I'm very sorry,' she said slowly, 'and surprised. I thought—well, never mind that now. Have another cup of tea and tell me if you have any plans.'

Florence shook her head. 'Not at the moment, but I'll get another job as soon as I can—not in London, though. I'd quite like to go abroad…'

Mrs Keane, who wasn't so old that she couldn't recognise unrequited love when she saw it, suggested New Zealand in an encouraging voice. 'And the world is so small these days that distance doesn't matter any more.'

She poured more tea. She was going to miss her usual bus home, but she wasn't going to leave Florence, usually such a calm, sensible girl, to mope. 'I heard a bit of gossip this morning. Those two women—Mrs Gregg and Lady Wells, one came early and the other didn't hurry away—they were talking about Eleanor Paton—remember her? She's about to marry the owner of several factories in the Midlands—rich, they said. All I can say is thank heaven she didn't get her claws into Mr Fitzgibbon. She tried hard enough, heaven knows, but of course he was never in love with her. She was fun to take around, I suppose, and he must get lonely.'

'I'm sure that he has no need to be,' said Florence with a snap. 'The world's his oyster, isn't it?'

Florence had got back some of her pretty colour and, judging by her last remark, was feeling belligerent. Mrs Keane, satisfied, got ready to go home. Tomorrow was another day and heaven only knew what it might bring forth.

As for Florence, she went back to Mrs Twist's, ate her supper after a fashion, told that good lady that she was leaving and counteracted a volley of questions by saying simply that she was needed at home. 'Since it's such short notice, Mrs Twist, I'll pay whatever you think is fair, since you'll hardly have time to let my room before I go.'

'As to that,' said Mrs Twist, 'I was thinking of having a bit of a holiday at my sister's. She lives in Margate and I can take Buster with me.' She pressed a second helping on Florence. 'In any case, you have been a good lodger and a nice young lady. I shall miss you.' Which, from Mrs Twist, was high praise indeed.

She had another bad night and went most unwillingly to work in the morning, unnecessarily so, since Mr Fitzgibbon's manner was exactly as it always was: remote courtesy, a few remarks about the weather and a reminder that she was expected at the East End clinic that evening. She muddled through her day, gobbled the tea Mrs Twist had ready for her and took a taxi to the Mile End Road, to find Dan already there, a room packed with patients and a lady in a severe hat taking the place of the gentle soul who usually sat at the desk.

'He's on his way,' Dan told her. 'I say, what's all this about you leaving?'

'Who told you?'

He looked vague. 'Bless me if I can remember—you know how these things get around.' He gave her a friendly smile; it didn't surprise him in the least that Mr Fitzgibbon intended to marry her; he had never said so, of course, but he had taken his devoted registrar aside and warned him that he intended taking a week's holiday and that he, Dan, would have to take over his hospital work while he was away.

Dan knew better than to ask questions, but he had remarked that he and his fiancée had hoped that Mr Fitzgibbon would come to the small party they were planning before they married. 'I shall ask Florence too,' he had added, 'she's an old friend of both of us.'

Mr Fitzgibbon had fixed him with a cold grey stare. 'Florence is leaving at the weekend,' he had said in a voice which had forbidden any further remarks. Dan, however, had eyes in his head and he had seen the way his chief looked at Florence. It was to be hoped that a week's holiday would settle the matter.

Mr Fitzgibbon came in then, greeted everyone much as usual, and they got down to work. It was a long evening and the lady in the hat lacked the smooth handling of the patients so that the clinic lasted longer than usual. When the last patient had gone Mr Fitzgibbon, sitting at his desk, writing, suggested that Dan should take Florence back. 'I shall be some time,' he pointed out, 'and there is no need for her to wait.'

He bade them a pleasant goodnight and returned to his writing.

It was on Friday evening, her packing done, everything left exactly as it should be at the consulting-rooms, that Florence got on a bus and took herself off to Colbert's. She had said that she would visit Miss MacFinn, and this was her last chance.

Miss MacFinn was looking almost as good as new again. She greeted Florence with pleasure and the news that she would be going to her sister's within the next day or so, adding that she would never be sufficiently grateful to Alexander for her recovery. 'The dear man,' she said warmly, 'I'm not surprised that he's so popular with his patients. He's such a good friend too, but I expect you've discovered that for yourself.'

'Yes, oh, yes; I've enjoyed working for him, but I'm leaving tomorrow. I—I'm needed at home.'

Miss MacFinn, who knew all about it anyway, said sympathetically, 'Your mother has been ill, hasn't she? And one's first duty is to one's parents. You will miss your work, though, won't you?'

Florence said steadily, 'Yes, very much. It's most fortunate that Mr Fitzgibbon has found someone to replace me. I—I've enjoyed the work.'

'Well, I'm sure Alexander is going to miss you.' Miss MacFinn smiled at the determinedly smiling face. 'And I dare say you will miss him, my dear.'

'It was a most interesting job,' said Florence, intent on giving nothing away.

She had already said goodbye to Mrs Keane and, although she had steeled herself to bid Mr Fitzgibbon a formal goodbye, he had forestalled her by leaving unexpectedly early for Colbert's, bidding her a cheerful farewell as he went. 'I'll give you a good reference if you need one,' he had paused at the doorway to tell her. 'I'm sure you'll find an excellent job to suit you.'

He hadn't even shaken hands, she remembered indignantly.

Mrs Keane, a silent spectator, had added her own rather more leisurely goodbyes. Being a loyal receptionist and a discreet woman, she had forborn from telling Florence that Mr Fitzgibbon had, with her help, rearranged his appointments so that he would be free for the whole of the next week. He hadn't said why, or where he was going but, as she pointed out to her husband, she hadn't been born yesterday.

'We shall certainly be asked to the wedding,' she told him happily. 'I shall need a new outfit…'

Florence went home on the early morning train, bidden farewell by a surprisingly tearful Mrs Twist, and if she had hoped against hope to see Mr Fitzgibbon before she went she was doomed to disappointment. She sat and stared out of the window at the countryside, seeing nothing of it, reviewing her future. She had brought the situation upon herself, and now she had no job and would never get Alexander Fitzgibbon out of her head or see him again. It didn't bear thinking about. She began resolutely to consider her assets: a month's pay in her pocket, a row of shining new saucepans in the kitchen at home and the washing-machine, and since she was to be home for the time being there would be no need of Miss Payne's services. She thought with longing of the elegant Italian sandals she had intended to buy, and then dismissed them and concentrated on what she should tell her parents. Perhaps she should have telephoned them, but explaining would have taken some time, and anyway what had she to explain? She got out at Sherborne and saw her father waiting for her.

He saw her case at once. 'Holidays, my dear? How delightful.'

'I've left my job, Father.' She had spoken matter-of-factly but when he looked at her face he made no comment other than a remark that her mother would be delighted. 'It's such a splendid time of year to be at home,' he went on gently as he stowed the case into the car and waited patiently while Higgins greeted her.

There was plenty to talk about as they drove home—village gossip, christenings, weddings and urgent repairs to the vicarage roof. She went into the house and found her mother in the kitchen, sitting at the table, shucking peas.

'There you are, darling,' said Mrs Napier. 'You didn't phone, so we knew you'd be home.' She darted a look at her daughter's pale face. 'You look tired, dear; perhaps you should ask for a holiday.'

'I didn't need to do that, Mother—I've left my job,' said Florence bleakly.

Mrs Napier emptied a pod before she spoke. 'If you weren't happy that was the right thing to do, Florence. It will be lovely to have you at home again.'

Florence sat down opposite her mother. 'Just until I find something else. I think I'd rather like to go right away, but I haven't had time to think about it properly.'

'Well, it's nice and quiet here,' observed her mother unworriedly. 'You can take your time deciding, and a few days' doing nothing won't do you any harm.' She smiled suddenly. 'It will be so nice to have you about the place, darling.'

Florence went round the table and kissed her mother's cheek. 'One day I'll tell you about it,' she promised, 'but not just yet.'

Presently she went up to her room and unpacked her case, arranged the photos and ornaments she had taken with her to London in their original places and got into a cotton dress. An afternoon's gardening would clear her head. To keep busy was vital, because she wouldn't have the chance to think about Alexander, and if she kept busy for long enough perhaps in time she would forget him altogether. She took the pins out of her hair and tied it back carelessly, and went downstairs again to help her mother get the lunch, a meal for which she had no appetite, although she pretended to enjoy it while she talked rather too brightly about the more amusing aspects of her work in Wimpole Street. When the dishes had been washed and she had settled her mother in a garden chair for a snooze, and seen her father off to the church to see one of the church wardens about something or other, she whistled to Higgins; a quick walk before getting down to the gardening seemed a good idea.

When she got back, half an hour later, Mr Fitzgibbon's Rolls-Royce was in the front drive and he was sitting on the grass by her mother's chair. Higgins pranced forward, delighted to see Monty lolling by her master, but Florence stood stock-still as he got slowly to his feet and walked towards her.

'Go away,' said Florence, wishing with all her treacherous heart that he would stay, and then, to make things clearer, she added, 'I don't want to speak to you and, if you want me to go back and work for you, I won't.'

'My dear girl, there is nothing further from my mind.' He looked amused. 'And certainly I am going away, but first I must bid your mother goodbye.'

Which he did, before whistling to Monty, who had gone to

have her ears rubbed by Florence, getting into his car and driving away with a casual wave of the hand.

'Well,' said Florence, bursting with rage and love and choked by a great lump of sadness, 'well, why did he come?'

'So kind,' said her mother presently. 'He hadn't forgotten that I had been ill and called to see if I had quite recovered.'

'Very civil of him,' agreed Florence in a colourless voice. She would telephone all the agencies she knew of on Monday and see if there were any jobs going a long way away. The other side of the world preferably.

With summer holidays in full swing and church-goers sparse, Florence found herself committed to taking the Sunday school the next morning. She was glad to do it—anything to fill the long, empty hours ahead of her. The class was a small one but unruly; she was kept fully occupied keeping law and order, marshalling the children into church for the last hymn and getting them sorted out at the end of the service. Several of them would have to be escorted to their homes in the village, and at the tail-end of the congregation she collected them ready for the short walk across the churchyard and down the village street.

Waiting for the six-year-old Kirk Pike to tie his shoe-lace, she glanced idly around her. The churchyard was peaceful, surrounded by trees and not in the least gloomy. Her father was walking along the path which would lead to the gate to the vicarage, and with him was Mr Fitzgibbon.

There was no mistaking that enormous frame. She watched until the two men disappeared from sight and then led the three small children that were in her care in the opposite direction, answering their questions with only part of her mind while she puzzled as to why he was there, talking to her father. Was he bent on getting her back to work in the consulting-rooms, and hoping to enlist her father's support? 'I'll never go back, never,' said Florence in a sudden loud voice that brought her small companions to a standstill.

She handed them over presently and walked back to the

vicarage, going cautiously in case she should encounter Mr Fitzgibbon.

However, he wasn't there; there was no sign of him or his car, and she wondered if she had imagined the whole thing. But her mind was put at rest once they sat down for dinner. 'I had an unexpected visitor after matins,' observed her father, 'Mr Fitzgibbon, on his way to a luncheon party. We had a most interesting talk. He is a man of wide interests and he's interested in medieval architecture. I was telling him about the squint hole and the parvise. He tells me that there is a splendid parvise in Mells church, with a stairs in excellent preservation. He kindly invited me to visit him when he is spending a few days at his home there so that I may see it for myself.'

'How nice,' said Florence rather inadequately.

Her mother sent her to Sherborne in the morning with a list of groceries that the village shop didn't stock, and Florence was glad to go. She would need notepaper and envelopes and any number of stamps if she was going to write to all the agencies listed in the *Nursing Times*. It was a glorious day; she put on the crêpe dress, thrust her feet into sandals and got out the car.

However leisurely she was, the shopping didn't take more than an hour or so. She had coffee in a pleasant café close to the abbey, and went back to the car. Another long walk in the afternoon, she decided, driving home through the narrow winding lanes, and after that she would start her letters. New Zealand would do, she had decided, or, failing that, Canada. They were both a long way from Mr Fitzgibbon.

She took her shopping into the house, to be met by her mother bearing a large cake, covered in foil on a plate.

'Oh, good, darling. Be an angel and run down to the village hall with this, will you? It's for the Mothers' Union tea and I promised a cake. I'd take it myself presently, but old Mrs Symes always likes to cut the cakes before we begin. I don't know why, I'm sure, but one must humour old age, I suppose.'

Florence put the shopping on the kitchen table and took the cake.

'It's a snack lunch,' said Mrs Napier. 'I'll have it ready by the time you get back.'

Carrying the cake in both hands, Florence went down the hall and out of the front door. Mr Fitzgibbon was sitting on the old wooden wheelbarrow no one had bothered to move from the colourful wilderness on the other side of the drive. He had a dog on either side of him, and all three got up and came towards her as she came to a halt. The dogs barked, but Mr Fitzgibbon didn't say a word.

'Why are you here?' asked Florence fiercely. Her heart was thundering away at a fine pace and her hands were shaking so much that the cake wobbled dangerously.

He took the cake from her. 'I'll tell you as we go,' said Mr Fitzgibbon in a gentle voice calculated to soothe the most agitated of hearts.

'I don't want—!' began Florence weakly.

'Now, now, let us have no more of this. I have a week's holiday, taken at great inconvenience to myself and my patients; I have wasted two days already, and I have no intention of wasting any more.'

They were walking towards the village street; already they had passed the first of the small houses at its end, and the village hall was in sight.

'Give me that cake,' said Florence wildly.

'My dear soul, you're not fit to carry anything—you're shaking like a leaf, and I hope that it's at the sight of me.'

Florence stood still, quite forgetting that she was in full view of anyone who might be in the village shop, let alone those idle enough to be sitting at their windows looking out. She said slowly, 'Of course it's at the sight of you, Alexander; it would be silly to deny it, wouldn't it? Only now I've told you will you please go away?'

'Certainly not. Why do you suppose I've taken this holiday?

Somehow the idea of proposing to you in my consulting-room didn't appeal, and on the infrequent occasions when we have been together somehow the right moment didn't occur.' He balanced the cake on one hand and took one of hers in the other. 'Will you marry me, Florence?'

She stared up at him and took a deep, glorious breath, but before she could utter they were hailed from a doorway.

'Miss Florence—is that your mother's cake? Let me have it here. I'm going to the hall now—it will save you a few steps.'

Florence wasn't listening, but Mr Fitzgibbon let her hand go and walked across the street and handed over the cake, and even spent a few moments in polite conversation before he went back to where she was still standing. He took her hand again and drew it under his arm. 'There's a little green bit between the school and the churchyard,' said Florence helpfully, and they walked there unhurriedly, watched by several ladies who had been peeping from the village shop and now crowded to the door to see what would happen next.

It was only a small green patch, but it was quiet. They stopped halfway along it, and Mr Fitzgibbon took her in his arms. 'I asked you to marry me, my darling, but before I ask you again I must tell you that I love you; I've been in love with you for some time now. Indeed, thinking about it—and I have been giving the matter a great deal of thought during the last few weeks—I believe that I loved you the moment I saw you hanging out of the window with a duster on your head.'

'But you never—never even hinted…'

'I have been so afraid that you might not love me; it wasn't until you came storming in declaring that you were going to leave that I thought that you might be a little in love with me. If you won't have me, my dearest heart, I think that I shall go into a monastery or emigrate to some far-flung spot.'

'Don't do that—don't ever go away,' said Florence urgently. 'I couldn't bear it. It took me quite a while to discover that I loved you, but I do and I shan't change.'

Mr Fitzgibbon swept her into his arms. 'I'll see that you don't.' He kissed her then, taking his time about it, and then he kissed her again.

The small green patch was no longer quiet; the village school had let its pupils out for their dinners, and a row of interested faces was watching them over the wall.

''E's kissing and cuddling our Miss Florence,' said a voice. Then there came a shrill, 'Hey, mister, will you get married?'

Mr Fitzgibbon lifted his head. 'That is our intention. Why not go home and tell everybody?'

Florence lifted her head from his shoulder. 'Alexander...'

'Say that again.'

'What? Alexander? Why?'

'It sounds nice...'

She smiled. 'Alexander, darling,' said Florence, and kissed him.

* * * * *

Never Say Goodbye

CHAPTER ONE

THE HOUSE, one of a row of similar Regency houses in an exclusive area of London, gave no hint from its sober exterior as to the magnificence of its entrance hall, with its imposing ceiling and rich carpet, nor even more to the equally imposing room, the door to which an impassive manservant was holding open. Isobel Barrington walked past him and, obedient to his request that she should take a seat, took one, waiting until he had closed the door soundlessly behind him before getting up again and beginning a slow prowl round the room. It was a very elegant room, with watered silk panelled walls, a marble fireplace and some intimidating armchairs of the French school, covered in tapestry. The rest of the furniture was Chippendale with nothing cosy about it, although she had to admit that it was charming. Not her kind of room, she decided with her usual good sense; it would do very well for people as elegant as itself; the kind who thought of Fortnum and Mason as their local grocer and understood every word of an Italian opera when they went to one.

She began to circle the room, looking at the profusion of portraits on its walls; gentlemen with unyielding faces in wigs and a variety of uniforms, all sharing the same handsome features; ladies, surprisingly enough, with scarcely a pretty face between them, although they were all sweet as to expression. Isobel, studying a young woman in an elaborate Edwardian dress, concluded that the men of the family had good looks enough and could afford to marry plain wives. 'Probably they were heiresses,' she told herself, and sat down again.

She might not match the room for elegance, but she shared a lack of good looks with the various ladies hanging on its walls. She was on the small side, with a neat figure and nice legs and a face which missed prettiness by reason of too wide a mouth and too thin a nose, although her skin was as clear as a child's and her blue eyes held a delightful twinkle upon occasion. She was dressed in a plain blue dress and looked as fresh and neat as anyone could wish. She put her purse on the small table beside her and relaxed against the chair's high back. When the door opened she sat up and then got to her feet with a calm air of assurance.

'Miss Barrington?' The man who spoke could have been any one of the gentlemen hanging on the walls; he had exactly the same good looks and forbidding expression, although his greying hair was cropped short and his clothes, exquisitely tailored, were very much in the modern fashion.

Isobel met his dark, impersonal stare with a steady look. 'Yes,' she said. 'And you are Dr Winter?'

He crossed the room and stopped before her, a very tall, largely built man in his thirties. He didn't answer her but observed coldly: 'The Agency assured me that they were sending a sensible, experienced nurse with a placid disposition.'

She eyed him with a gentle tolerance which made him frown. She said kindly: 'I'm a sensible woman and I have eight years' experience of nursing and I am of a placid disposition, if by that you mean that I don't take exception to rudeness or get uptight if things go a little wrong…' She added: 'May I sit down?'

The frown became thunderous. 'I beg your pardon, Nurse, please do take a chair…' He didn't sit himself, but began to wander about the room. Presently he said: 'You're not at all the kind of nurse I intended to take with me. Have you travelled?'

'No, but I've nursed in a variety of situations, some of them rather out of the ordinary way of things.'

'You're too young.' He stopped marching around the room and looked at her.

'I'm twenty-five—a sensible age, I should have thought.'

'Women at any age are not always sensible,' he observed bitterly.

Isobel studied him carefully. An ill-tempered man, she judged, but probably just and fair-minded with it, in all probability he was a kind husband and father. She said calmly: 'Then it really doesn't matter what age I am, does it?'

He smiled, and his face was transformed so that she could see that he could be quite charming if he wished. 'All the same—' he began and then stopped as the door opened and the manservant came in, murmured quietly and went away again.

'You must excuse me for a moment, Miss—er—Barrington. I shan't be more than a few minutes.'

She was left to contemplate the portraits of his ancestors on the walls, although she didn't pay much attention to them; she had too much to think about. It was a severe blow if he didn't give her the job…she needed it badly enough. When she had left hospital to take up agency nursing, she hadn't had her heart in it: she had loved her work as Male Surgical Ward Sister and her bedsitting room in the nurses' home and going home for her weekends off. However, when her only, younger brother Bobby had been given the chance of going to a public school and her mother had confided to her that there wasn't enough money to send him, she had given up her post, put her name down at a nursing agency and by dint of working without breaks between cases had earned enough to get Bobby started.

She didn't really enjoy it. It was a lonely life and she had far less free time; on the other hand, she could earn almost twice as much money and she had no need to pay for her food and room. And she wouldn't have to do it for ever. Bobby was a bright boy, he was almost certain to get a place in one of the universities in four or five years' time and then she would go back to hospital life once more. She should have liked to marry, of course, but she had no illusions about her looks, and although she could sew and cook and keep house she had never got to know a man well enough for him to appreciate these qualities. It was a regret that she kept well hidden, and it had helped to have a sense of humour and a placid nature as well as a strong determination to make the best of things.

She braced herself now for Dr Winter's refusal of her services, and when he came back into the room looking like a thundercloud, she gave an inward resigned sigh and turned a calm face to him.

'That was the nursing agency,' he said shortly. 'They wanted to know if I was satisfied with you for the job I had in mind, and when I said I'd expected someone older and more experienced they regretted that there was positively no one else on their books.' He cast her an exasperated look. 'I intend to leave England in two days' time, and there's no opportunity of finding someone else in forty-eight hours… I shall have to take you.'

'You won't regret it,' she assured him briskly. 'Perhaps you would tell me exactly what kind of case I'm to nurse.'

'An old lady crippled with arthritis. My old nurse, in fact.'

The idea of this self-assured giant of a man having a nanny, even being a small boy, struck Isobel as being faintly ludicrous, but the look that he bent upon her precluded even the faintest of smiles. He sat down at last in one of the Chippendale chairs, which creaked under his weight. 'She married a Pole and has lived in Gdansk since then. Her husband died last year and I've been trying since then to get a permit for her to return to England. I've now succeeded and intend to bring her back with me. You will understand that I shall require a nurse to accompany me; she's unable to do much for herself.'

'And when do we get back to England?' Isobel asked.

'I shall want your services only until such time as a suitable companion for her can be found.' He crossed one long leg over the other and the chair creaked again. 'We fly to Stockholm where we stay the night at a friend's flat and take the boat the following day to Gdansk, we shall probably be a couple of days there and return to Stockholm and from there fly back to England. A week should suffice.'

'Why are we not to fly straight to Gdansk? And straight back here again?'

'Mrs Olbinski is a sick woman; it's absolutely necessary that she should travel as easily as possible; we shall return by boat to Stockholm and spend at least a day there so that she can rest before we fly back here. And we spend a day in Stockholm so that the final arrangements for her can be made.'

He got up and wandered to the window and stood staring out. 'You have a passport?'

'No, but I can get one at the Post Office.'

He nodded. 'Well, this seems the best arrangement in the circumstances; not exactly as I would have wished, but I have no alternative, it seems.'

'You put it very clearly, Dr Winter,' said Isobel. Her pleasant voice was a little tart. 'Do you want to make the arrangements for the journey now, or notify the agency?'

'I'll contact the agency tomorrow.' He glanced at the watch on his wrist. 'I have an appointment shortly and can spare no more time. You will get your instructions, Miss—er—Barrington.'

She got to her feet. 'Very well, Dr Winter—and the name is Barrington, there's no *er* in front of it.' She gave him a vague smile and met his cold stare and walked to the door. 'You would like me to wear uniform, I expect?' And when he didn't answer, she said in patient explanation: 'It might help if you had any kind of difficulties with the authorities...'

'You're more astute than I'd thought, Miss Barrington.' He smiled thinly. 'That's exactly what I would wish you to do.'

He reached the door slightly ahead of her and opened it. 'Perhaps you would confine your luggage to one case? I'll fill in details during the flight.'

The manservant was hovering in the splendid hall. 'Oh, good,' said Isobel cheerfully. 'One wants to know something about a case before taking it on. Goodbye, Dr Winter.' She smiled kindly at him and made an exit as neat and unremarkable as herself.

She took a bus, a slow-moving journey of half an hour or more, back to her home—a small terraced house on the better side of Clapham Common. It looked exactly like the houses on either side of it, but in the narrow hall there was a difference. In place of the usual hallstand and telephone table there was a delicate wall table with rather a nice gilded mirror above it, and the small sitting room into which she hurried was furnished with what their neighbours referred to disparagingly as old bits and pieces, but which were, in fact, the remnants of furniture saved from the sale of her old home some ten years earlier. She never went into the little house without nostalgia for the comfortable village house she had been born and brought up in, but she never mentioned this; her mother, she felt sure, felt even worse about it than she did.

Her mother was sitting at the table, sewing, a small woman with brown hair a good deal darker than her daughter's, the same blue eyes and a pretty face. She looked up as Isobel went in and asked: 'Well, darling, did you get the job?'

Isobel took off her shoes and curled up in a chair opposite her mother. 'Yes, but it's only for a week or two, though. Dr Winter isn't too keen on me, but there wasn't anyone else. I'm to go to Poland with him to fetch back his old nanny.'

Her mother looked faintly alarmed. 'Poland? But isn't that…' she paused, 'well, eastern Europe?'

'He's got a permit for her to come to England to live. Her husband died last year and she's crippled with arthritis, that's why I'm to go with him; she'll need help with dressing and so on, I expect.'

'And this Dr Winter?'

'Very large and tall, unfriendly—to me at any rate, but then he expected someone older and impressive, I think. He's got a lovely house. I'm to be told all the details at the agency tomorrow and be ready to travel in two days—in uniform.'

Her mother got up. 'I'll get the tea. Is he elderly?'

Isobel thought. 'Well, no; he's a bit grey at the sides, but he's not bald or anything like that. I suppose he's getting on for forty.'

'Married?' asked her mother carelessly as she went to the door.

'I haven't an idea, but I should think so—I mean, I shouldn't think he would want to live in a great house like that on his own, would you?'

She followed her mother into the little kitchen and put on the kettle, and while it boiled went into the minute garden beyond. It was really no more than a patch of grass and a flower bed or two but it was full of colour and well kept. There was a tabby cat lying between the tulips and forget-me-nots. Isobel said: 'Hullo, Blossom,' and bent to inspect the small rose bushes she cherished when she was home. They were nicely in bud and she raised her voice to say to her mother, 'They'll be almost out by the time I get back. It's June next week.'

She spent her evening making a list of the things she would need to take with her; not many, and she hesitated over packing a light jacket and skirt. Dr Winter had said uniform, but surely if they were to stay in Stockholm for a day, she need not wear uniform, nor for that matter on the flight there. Perhaps the agency would be able to tell her.

The clerk at the agency was annoyingly vague, offering no opinion at all but supposing it didn't matter and handing Isobel a large envelope with the remark that she would probably find all she wanted to know inside it. Isobel annoyed the lady very much by sitting down and reading the contents through, for, as she pointed out in her sensible way, it would be silly to get all the way home and discover that some vital piece of information was missing.

There was nothing missing; her ticket, instructions on how to reach Heathrow and the hour at which she was to arrive and where she was to go when she got there, a reminder that she must bring a Visitor's Passport with her, a generous sum of money to pay for her expenses and a brief note, typed and signed T. Winter, telling her that she had no need to wear uniform until they left Stockholm. Isobel replaced everything in the envelope, wished the impatient lady behind the desk a pleasant day and went off to the Post Office for her passport. She had to have photos for it, of course. She went to the little box in a corner of the Post Office and had three instant photos taken; they were moderately like her, but they hardly did her pleasant features justice—besides, she looked surprised and her eyes were half shut. But since the clerk at the counter didn't take exception to them, she supposed they would do. Her mother, naturally enough, found them terrible; to her Isobel's unassuming face was beautiful.

She left home in plenty of time, carrying a small suitcase and a shoulder bag which held everything she might need for the journey. After deliberation she had worn a coffee-coloured pleated skirt, with its matching loose jacket and a thin cotton top in shrimp pink, and in her case she had packed a second top and a Liberty print blouse, and because she had been told at the agency that the Scandinavian countries could be cool even in May and June, she had packed a thick hooded cardigan she had bought with her Christmas money at Marks and Spencer.

She took the underground to Heathrow and then found her way to departure number two entrance and went to stand, as she had been told to, on the right side of the entrance. She was ten minutes early and she stood, not fidgeting at all, watching the taxis drawing up and their passengers getting out. She hadn't been there above five minutes when she was startled to hear Dr Winter's deep voice behind her.

'Good morning, Miss Barrington. We will see to the luggage first, if you will come with me.'

Her good morning was composed, a porter took her case and she went across to the weigh-in counter for their luggage to be taken care of, handed her ticket to the doctor and waited until the business had been completed, studying him while she did so.

He was undoubtedly a very good-looking man, and the kind of man, she fancied, who expected to get what he wanted with the least possible fuss. He looked in a better temper, she was relieved to see; it made him look a good deal younger and the tweed suit he was wearing, while just as elegantly cut as the formal grey one he had worn at her interview, had the effect of making him seem more approachable.

'Well, we'll go upstairs and have coffee while we wait for our flight.' He spoke pleasantly and Isobel didn't feel the need to answer, only climbed the stairs beside him, waited a few moments while he bought a handful of papers and magazines and went on up another flight of steps to the coffee lounge, where he sat her down, fetched their coffee and then handed her the *Daily Telegraph* and unfolded *The Times* for himself.

Isobel, who had slept badly and had a sketchy breakfast, drank her coffee, thankfully, sat back in her chair, folded the newspaper neatly and closed her eyes. She was almost asleep at once and the doctor, glancing up presently, blinked. He was by no means a conceited man, but he couldn't remember, offhand, any woman ever going to sleep in his company. He overlooked the fact that he had made no attempt to entertain her.

Isobel, while no beauty, looked charming when she slept, her mouth had opened very slightly and her lashes, golden-brown and very long, lay on her cheeks, making her look a good deal younger than her twenty-five years. Dr Winter frowned slightly and coughed. Isobel's eyes flew open and she sat up briskly. 'Time for us to go?' she enquired.

'No—no. I'm sorry if I disturbed you. I was surprised…'

She gave him her kind smile. 'Because I went to sleep. I'm

sure girls don't go to sleep when they're with you.' To make herself quite clear, she added: 'Nurses when you're lecturing them, you know. I expect you're married.'

His look was meant to freeze her bones, only she wasn't that kind of a girl. She returned his stare with twinkling eyes. 'You expect wrongly, Miss Barrington.' He looked down his patrician nose. 'Perhaps it would be better if I were to address you as Nurse.'

'Yes, Dr Winter.' The twinkle was so disconcerting that he looked away still frowning.

She had time to do the crossword puzzle before their flight was announced, leaving him to return to his reading.

She had a window seat on board and she was surprised to find that they were travelling first class, but pleased too, usually if she had to travel to a case, she was expected to use the cheapest way of getting there. She fastened her seat-belt and peered out of the window: it wasn't until they were airborne that she sat back in her seat.

'You've flown before?' asked Dr Winter. He didn't sound interested just polite, so she said that yes, once or twice, before turning her attention to the stewardess, who was explaining what they should all do in an emergency. And after that there was coffee and then lunch; and a very good one too, with a glass of white wine and coffee again. Isobel made a good meal, answered the doctor's occasional remarks politely and studied the booklet about Sweden offered for her perusal. A pity she wouldn't see more of the country, she thought, but she was lucky to have even a day in Stockholm; reading the tourist guide, there appeared to be a great deal to see.

There was someone waiting for them at the airport—a thickset man, very fair with level blue eyes and a calm face, leaning against a big Saab. He and Dr Winter greeted each other like old friends and when the doctor introduced Isobel, he took her hand in his large one and grinned at her. 'Janssen—Carl Janssen. It is a pleasure. We will go at once to my house and you will meet my wife Christina.'

He opened the car door and ushered her inside while Dr Winter got into the front seat. Isobel, who despite her placid nature had become a little chilled by his indifferent manner, felt more cheerful; Mr Janssen's friendly greeting had warmed her nicely. She made herself comfortable and watched the scenery.

It was beautiful. They were already approaching the city, which at first glance looked modern, but in the distance she could see a glimpse of water and there were a great many trees and parks. They slowed down as they neared the heart of the city and the streets became narrow and cobbled.

'This is Gamla Stan—the old town,' said Mr Janssen over one shoulder. 'We live here. It is quite the most beautiful part of Stockholm.'

He crossed a square: 'Look quickly—there is the old Royal Palace and Storkyrkan, our oldest church—you must pay it a visit.'

He swept the car into a labyrinth of narrow streets before she had had more than a glimpse, to stop and then turn into a narrow arched way between old houses. It opened on to a rectangular space filled with small gardens and ringed by old houses with a steeple roof and small windows and wrought iron balconies.

'This,' said Carl Janssen in a tone of deep satisfaction, 'is where we live.'

He opened the car door with a flourish and Isobel got out and looked around her. No one looking around them would have known that they were in the middle of a busy city. There was no one to be seen, although curtains blew at open windows and somewhere there was a baby crying and music. Between the high roofs she could see the thin steeple of a church and here and there in the gardens were lilacs, late blooming, and birds twittering in them.

'Heaven!' said Isobel.

Which earned her a pleased look from her host. 'Almost,' he agreed. 'But come in and meet Christina.'

He led the way between the little gardens to a small door and opened it. There was a steep staircase inside and Isobel, urged on by a friendly voice from above, climbed it. The girl at the top was about her own age, a big, fair-haired girl who took her hand as she reached the top and exclaimed: 'You are the nurse? Yes, my name is Christina.'

'Isobel.'

'That is pretty. Come in. Thomas, how wonderful to see you again!'

She flung her arms around the doctor's neck and kissed him warmly, and Isobel, standing back a little, thought how different he looked when he smiled like that. A pity he didn't do it more often. And discovering that his name was Thomas made him seem different.

Not that he was. He gave her a look which clearly was meant to keep her at a distance, said formally: 'Mr and Mrs Janssen are old friends of mine, Miss Barrington,' and stood aside politely so that she might walk into the narrow hallway.

It led to a roomy square hall from which doors led, presumably to the rest of the flat. Christina opened one of them and said gaily: 'Come in and sit, and we will have tea and then you shall see your rooms. Yours is the usual one, Thomas, and we have put Isobel in the corner room because from there she sees the garden below.'

She bustled round the large, comfortably furnished room, offering chairs, begging Isobel to take off her jacket, promising her that she should see the baby just as soon as he was awake. 'He is called Thomas, after this Thomas,' she laughed at Dr Winter, 'and we think that he is quite perfect!'

She went through another door to the kitchen and Carl started to talk about their trip. 'You have all the necessary papers?' he wanted to know. 'Without these there might be delays.' He smiled at Isobel. 'It is most sensible that you take Isobel with you, a good nurse may be most useful, especially as Mrs Olbinski is crippled.' He turned to Isobel. 'You are not nervous?'

'No, not at all—you mean because it's Poland? The Poles are friendly—they like us, though, don't they?'

'They are a most friendly people, and full of life.' He got up to help his wife with the tea tray and the talk centred upon Carl's work and where they intended to go for their summer holiday. 'We have a boat,' he told Isobel, 'and we sail a great deal on Lake Malaren and the Baltic. The islands offshore are beautiful and extend for miles—one can get lost among them.'

'You take little Thomas with you?'

'Of course. He is nine months old and a most easy baby.'

'You'll still be here when we get back?' Dr Winter asked casually.

'We go in three days' time, and if you are not back, but of course you will be, we will leave the key with our neighbours in the flat below. But you have ample time, even allowing for a day or so delay for one reason or another.' He looked at Dr Winter. 'She is well, your old nanny?'

'I telephoned last week—I'll ring again later if I may. She was very much looking forward to seeing us. And to coming home.'

'Well, you will stay as long as you wish to here,' declared Christina. 'Isobel, I will show you your room and when you have unpacked, come back here and we will talk some more.'

The room was charming, simply furnished, even a little austere, but there were flowers on a little table under the window and the gardens below with the old houses encircling them reminded Isobel of Hans Andersen's Fairy Tales. She looked at the plain pinewood bed with its checked duvet cover, and knew she was going to sleep soundly. It was a pity Dr Winter wasn't more friendly, but that was something which couldn't be helped. She had a shower, changed into a fresh blouse, did her face and hair and went back to the sitting room.

They ate in a tiny alcove off the sitting room after the baby had been fed and bathed and put to bed. The meal was typically Swedish, with a great dish of sprats, potatoes, onions and cream, which Carl translated as Janssen's Delight. This was followed by pancakes with jam, a great pot of coffee and Aquavit for the men.

The girls cleared the table, but once that was done, Isobel was amazed to see Dr Winter follow his friend into the splendidly equipped kitchen and shut the door.

'Thomas washes the dishes very well,' said Christina, and Isobel found herself faced with yet another aspect of the doctor which she hadn't even guessed at. Washing up, indeed! She wondered if the dignified manservant in London was aware of that and what he would have said.

She went to bed early, guessing that the other three might have things to talk about in which she had no part, and it wasn't until breakfast on the following morning that she learnt that Dr Winter had been unable to make his call; he had been told politely enough that there was no reply to the number he wanted. He was arguing the advantages of getting seats on the next flight to Gdansk when Carl said: 'Exactly what would be expected of you, Thomas. Keep to your plan and take the boat this evening,' and Dr Winter had stared at him for a long minute and then agreed.

'So that's settled,' said Christina. 'Thomas, you will take Isobel to see something of Stockholm, and when you come back I shall have made you the best *smörgasbörd* table you ever tasted.'

So presently Isobel found herself going under the archway, back into the narrow cobbled streets with Dr Winter beside her. He had raised no objection to accompanying her, neither had he shown any great enthusiasm.

'Do you want to go to the shops?' he asked her as they edged past a parked van and paused outside a small antique shop.

'No, thank you. I should like to see St George and the Dragon in the Storkyrkan, and the Riddarholmskyrkan, and then take a look at the lake. There won't be time to go inside the palace, but if it wouldn't bore you too much I should enjoy just walking through some of the older streets.'

He glanced at his watch. 'Then we'd better begin with St George,' was all he said.

He proved to be a good guide, for of course he had been before and knew the names of the various buildings and how to get from one place to the next without getting lost. And he waited patiently while she pottered round the churches, bought a few postcards with the money he offered before she realised that she would need to borrow some, and stood gazing at the lake. It was a bright morning, but cool, and she was glad of her jacket as she stood, trying to imagine what it must be like in the depths of winter.

'Have you been here in the winter?' she wanted to know.

'Oh, yes, several times. It's delightful. One needs to be able to ski and skate, of course.' He took it for granted that she could do neither of these things, and she saw no reason to correct him.

They had coffee at a small, crowded restaurant in one of the narrow paved streets, and she made no demur when he suggested that they should make their way back to the Janssens' flat. As they turned in under the arch once more, Dr Winter observed: 'One needs several days at least in order to see the best of Stockholm; there are some splendid museums if you're interested.'

'Well, yes, I am—and there's Millesgarden…all those statues—they're famous, aren't they? But I knew we couldn't have got there this morning.' She added hastily for fear he should take umbrage: 'Thank you very much for taking me round. I've enjoyed it enormously, it was most kind of you.'

They were standing outside the Janssens' door and it was very quiet and peaceful. He said harshly: 'No, it wasn't in the least kind, Miss Barrington. It never entered my head to take you sightseeing; I did it because Christina took it for granted that I would.'

Isobel opened the door. 'Well, I know that,' she said matter-of-factly.

After the *smörgasbörd*—a table weighted down with hot and cold dishes—the men went off together, leaving the girls to clear away, then put little Thomas into his pram and take him for a walk. They went through the narrow streets once more and came out by the water, finding plenty to talk about, although never once was Dr Winter mentioned.

The boat left in the early evening and after tea Isobel packed her case once more, said goodbye reluctantly enough, cheered by the thought that she would be back within the week, and went down to Carl's car.

The drive wasn't a long one, and once at the quay Isobel waited quietly while the two went off to see about their tickets, reappearing with a porter, and Carl then shook hands and dropped a friendly kiss on her cheek.

'We look forward to seeing you very soon, Isobel,' he told her. 'Even little Thomas will miss you.'

But not big Thomas, standing there, looking as impatient as good manners would allow.

The boat was large and comfortable. She had a splendid cabin with a small shower room and set about unpacking her uniform and hanging it up ready for their arrival in the morning. Dr Winter had handed her over to a stewardess with the suggestion that she should meet him in the restaurant once the ship had sailed—that meant an hour's time. She was ready long before then, and filled in the time reading the various leaflets she had collected about Gdansk and its harbour, Gdynia. They didn't tell her a great deal, but she studied them carefully. Once they were there, probably Dr Winter would have his hands full seeing to Mrs Olbinski's possessions and getting her to the ship, so she studied the map of those towns carefully too—one never knew.

He was waiting for her when she reached the restaurant, greeted her with the cool politeness she found so unnerving, and gave her a drink, and they dined presently—Swedish food, she was glad to discover; *kott bullarand* then fried boned herring and, once more, pancakes with jam. She didn't linger over their coffee and he didn't try and persuade her to stay. She wished him a cheerful goodnight and went back to her cabin, aware that he had been expecting her to ask any number of questions about the next day. In truth she had longed to do so, but had held her tongue. His opinion of her was already so low that she had no intention of making it lower. Let him tell her anything it was necessary for her to know. She fell asleep at once, rather pleased with herself.

CHAPTER TWO

ISOBEL WAS UP EARLY. She had slept well and now she was ready for her breakfast, but Dr Winter had suggested that they should meet in the restaurant at half past seven, and it was still only half past six. She rang, a shade apprehensively, for tea, then showered and dressed in her uniform and went on deck. They were close to land, she saw with a rising excitement, rather flat and wooded land with houses here and there. It was a pearly, still morning and chilly, and somehow London and home seemed a long way off. Isobel buttoned her navy gaberdine coat and wished she had put on her rather ugly nurse's blue felt hat. There wasn't any one else on deck and she started to walk along its length, to be confronted by Dr Winter coming out of a door.

His 'good morning' was polite and distant, and she was surprised when he fell into step beside her. 'I should perhaps mention,' he began casually, 'that there will probably be a delay in Mrs Olbinski's return. Carl told me there had been some trouble…' He didn't say what kind of trouble and Isobel didn't ask. She was surprised when he added: 'Are you a nervous person, Miss Barrington?'

She turned to face him. 'If you mean do I have hysterics and screaming fits if things go wrong, no. But if a situation got out of hand, I would probably behave like most women and scream for help.'

He said seriously: 'I must ask you not to do that; a calm, serene front is important.'

She started walking again. 'Is there something you should have told me before we left England?' she asked in a voice which she managed to keep calm.

'Certainly not, Miss Barrington. I must remind you merely that each country has its own laws. Mrs Olbinski's husband was unfortunately a dissident, so naturally they may be somewhat more strict...'

She stopped again and eyed him thoughtfully. 'You have got all the permits?' she asked.

'Of course. I'm only saying that because of her circumstances there may be some delay.' He frowned. 'We might as well go and have our breakfast.'

'Oh, good—I'm hungry. But before we go, where exactly are we now?'

'Coming into Gdynia, which is the port of Gdansk. Mrs Olbinski lives in the old town of Gdansk and you'll have a chance to see it.'

Isobel scanned the nearing coastline. 'Oh, good—Poland isn't a place I'm likely to come to again. Do they speak English?'

'A great many do, but I doubt if you'll have time to go sightseeing.'

She felt snubbed. Did he really think she would disappear the moment they landed, intent on enjoying herself? Her splendid appetite had had the edge taken off it.

Going through Customs took a good deal of time; she had to admire Dr Winter's calm patience in the face of the courteous questioning that went on at some length. When finally they were free to go, one of the officials apologised for the delay with the utmost politeness and the doctor waived the apologies with an equal politeness. As they got into the taxi he said: 'Sorry about that; understandably I had to give my reasons for our visit and they had to be checked.'

He told the driver where to go. 'There's nothing much to see here, but you'll find Gdansk interesting, I believe.'

They drove through a dock area which might have been anywhere in the world and presently came to Gdansk, where the taxi stopped before an enormous gateway, its centre arch opening into a wide paved street.

'This is where we walk,' observed Dr Winter, and got out.

He wasted no time in giving more than a glance at the enormous edifice before them but took her arm and walked her briskly through the archway and into the street beyond. It was a splendid sight, lined with Renaissance houses, many of them with small shops at street level. Isobel, going along a great deal faster than she wished, did her best to look everywhere at once and as they reached a square at the end of the street asked in a voice which demanded an answer. 'Is that the Town Hall we've just passed? And is that the Golden House I read about? And this fountain in the centre…?'

The doctor didn't pause in his walk. 'Miss Barrington, may I remind you that you're here for one purpose only; sightseeing is quite another matter.'

'If this is sightseeing then I'm a Dutchman,' declared Isobel roundly, 'and I only asked you a question!'

He looked at her, trotting along beside him, very sober in her uniform, and said harshly: 'If you remember, Miss Barrington, I said at the time of your interview that you weren't suitable.'

Unanswerable. They were going through another enormous gate with water beyond and warehouses on the opposite bank. But Dr Winter turned left, making his way along the busy street bordering the water, left again into a narrow street lined with lovely old houses. Half way down he stopped before an arched door and rang one of the many bells on the wall. To Isobel's surprise he turned to look at her. 'The city was in ruins after the last war. The Poles rebuilt it, brick by brick, many of them original, the rest so skilfully done that it's hard to detect the one from the other.' He then turned his back on her as the door opened, revealing a short narrow hall and a staircase beyond. 'Third floor,' he told her over his shoulder, and began to mount.

Isobel followed perforce, liking her surroundings very much; the wooden stairway, the small circular landings, the two solid wooden doors on each of these. On the third floor one of the doors was open. The doctor went in without hesitation, and Isobel, a little breathless, followed him.

The door opened on to a tiny vestibule with two doors and they stood open too. The doctor unhesitatingly went through the left-hand one, with Isobel so close on his heels that she almost overbalanced when he halted abruptly.

The room was small, nicely furnished and far too warm. The table in the centre of the room was polished to a high gloss and so were the chairs. The wooden floor shone with polish too and the curtains at the windows, although limp with age, were spotless. Isobel registered vaguely that the room looked bare before turning her attention to the old lady sitting in a chair whose tapestry was threadbare with age. She was a very small lady with bright bootbutton eyes, white hair strained back into a knob, and wearing a black dress covered by a cotton pinafore.

She said in a surprisingly strong voice, 'Mr Thomas…' She glanced at the small carved wooden clock on the mantelpiece. 'Punctual, I see. You always were as a little boy.' Her eyes darted to Isobel. 'And who is this?'

Dr Winter bent and kissed and hugged her gently. 'Hullo, Nanny. Nice to see you again. This is Nurse Barrington, I brought her along to give you a hand.'

Mrs Olbinski pushed her specs up her nose and stared at Isobel through them. 'H'm—rather small. Come here, young lady, so I can see you properly.'

Isobel did as she was asked. Old people said strange things sometimes, just as though one wasn't there, listening, but she didn't mind; probably she would do the same one day. 'How do you do?' she asked politely.

'Almost plain,' commented the old lady to no one in particular, 'but nice eyes and a nice smile too!' She bristled suddenly. 'Not that I need a nurse; I'm quite able to get around on my own…'

'Well, of course you are.' Isobel had never heard the doctor speak in such a soft, coaxing voice. 'I asked her to come for purely selfish reasons; there'll be people to see and so on, and I didn't want the worry of leaving you while I dealt with them.'

He had struck the right note. Nanny nodded in agreement. 'When do we leave?' she asked.

'By this evening's ferry, my dear. Have you packed?'

'There are still one or two things, Mr Thomas. I daresay this young lady will help me?'

'Of course, Mrs Olbinski—and my name is Isobel.'

'Now that's a good name, and one I've always liked. You can go into the kitchen and make the coffee, while I hear all the news.'

Isobel was in the minute kitchen, stealthily opening cupboards, looking for things, when she heard several pairs of feet coming up the stairs. The door wasn't quite shut, and she had no hesitation in going and standing as close to it as she could get. She didn't dare look round the door's edge, but she judged the feet to be either policemen or soldiers because of the hefty boots.

Soldiers. A rather nice voice, speaking excellent English, pointing out with regret that a final paper which was needed by Mrs Olbinski had not yet arrived. It was therefore necessary that she should stay until it did.

'And when will that be?' The doctor's voice sounded friendly, unhurried and not in the least put out.

'Tomorrow—the day following that at the latest. We deeply regret any inconvenience.'

'I quite understand that it is unavoidable and not of your making.' There was a short silence. 'I will get rooms for myself and the nurse I have brought with me at the Orbis Monopol. Mrs Olbinski will prefer to stay here, I expect.'

There was the faintest question in his voice.

'Of course, she will be perfectly all right, Dr Winter. As soon as the papers come, I will let you know so that you may complete your plans.'

The goodbyes sounded friendly enough—and why not? Isobel reasoned. The Poles and the English liked each other; whoever it was who had just gone had had a delightful voice… She wasn't quite quick enough at getting away from the door; she found the doctor's austere good looks within inches of her head. 'Next time you eavesdrop, young lady, control your breathing—you sounded like an overwrought female from an early Victorian novel.' He looked round the kitchen. 'Isn't the coffee ready yet?'

'No, it's not, and I wish someone would explain…'

'But there's nothing to explain. As you must know, anyone leaving the country must have their papers in order; Nanny's are not quite completed, that is all. You should be delighted; we shall have a day for sightseeing.'

She looked at him thoughtfully. 'Would you like me to stay here with Mrs Olbinski?'

He smiled for the first time, so nicely that she found herself almost liking him. 'That's very thoughtful of you, but there's no need. You shall enjoy the comfort of the best hotel here and tomorrow we'll take Nanny sightseeing; I daresay she'll be glad to say goodbye to as many places as possible; she hasn't had the opportunity, you see.'

The kettle boiled and Isobel poured the water into the enamel coffee pot she had found in one of the cupboards, set it on the tray with the cups and saucers off the shelf above the stove, and handed the doctor the tray. She smiled very faintly at the look of surprise as he took it. She didn't think he was a selfish man, merely one who had never had to fend for himself. Too clever, no doubt, with his splendid nose buried in books or people's insides while others ministered to his mundane wants.

Mrs Olbinski was sitting in her chair, looking impatient. 'You took a long time,' she observed tartly. 'I have always been under the impression that nurses are able to do everything anywhere at any time.' She sniffed: 'Not that I believe it for one moment.'

'Well, no, I shouldn't think you would, because that's a load of nonsense,' said Isobel forthrightly. 'I suppose we're trained to do some things others might not be able to do, but that's all—besides, this is a foreign land to me and your kitchen isn't quite the same.' She added hastily: 'Though it's charming and very cosy.'

Mrs Olbinski accepted her coffee and took a sip. 'The coffee isn't bad,' she conceded, 'and you seem a sensible young woman. Where did Mr Thomas find you?'

Isobel didn't look at the doctor, looming on the other side of the little dark table. 'Dr Winter asked an agency to send him a nurse,' she explained in a colourless voice. 'It was me or no one.'

Dr Winter made an impatient movement and she waited for him to say something, but he didn't, so she went on: 'It might make your journey a little easier if I give you a hand from time to time, just while Dr Winter sees to papers and passports and things…'

'You don't look very strong. Why do you keep saying Dr Winter in that fashion?'

Isobel sighed and went red as Dr Winter said repressively: 'Miss Barrington and I…' he stopped and began again. 'We've only recently met, Nanny.'

Nanny made a sound which sounded like Faugh! and then Phish! 'Well, I shall call her Isobel; it's a pretty name even if she isn't a pretty girl. And you can do the same, Mr Thomas, because you must be old enough to be her father. I'll have some more coffee.'

She took no notice of the doctor's remote annoyance but sat back comfortably in her chair. 'If we're to be here for another day, perhaps you'd take me to Oliwa; there'll be organ recitals in the afternoons now that it's summer, and I should dearly love to hear one before I go.'

Her old voice crumbled and the doctor said quickly: 'What a splendid idea, Nanny. I'll rent a car and we'll drive over there tomorrow—how about a quick look at Sopot as well?'

'Oh, I'd love that above all things—we used to go there in the summer…' She launched into a recital of her life while her husband had been alive, until Dr Winter interrupted her gently: 'Well, you shall see as much as possible, but in the meantime I think you might let Nurse… Isobel finish your packing, don't you?' He got up. 'Suppose I leave you for an hour while I see about a car and our rooms at the hotel?'

He stooped and picked her up out of her chair and carried her through the second door into a small bedroom. He paused on the threshold—and no wonder; there wasn't an inch of space, there were boxes, bundles and an old trunk taking up every available corner. Isobel cleared a pile of books off a chair, remarking comfortably: 'If you'll tell me what has to be done, I'll do it, Mrs Olbinski.'

'A sensible girl,' observed that lady succinctly. 'All this must go with me.'

Dr Winter was edging round the room looking at its contents. He said with gentle firmness: 'I'm afraid that you won't be allowed to take more than the clothing you're wearing and your most treasured possessions. No money, of course. Small stuff which will go into a suitase, or a well tied cardboard box.' He went to the door. 'I'll be back presently.'

Isobel took off her coat and hat. 'Men!' declared Mrs Olbinski pettishly. 'They're all alike, so quick to tell us of the unpleasant tasks they want done, and just as quick to go away until they're completed.' She darted a look at Isobel. 'But Mr Thomas is a good man, make no mistake, my dear—too clever, of course, with his head in his books and always working, never finding the time to get himself a wife and children.'

Isobel murmured politely, her mind occupied solely with the problem of how to pack a quart into a pint bottle—something, a great many things, would have to be discarded.

'What will you wear to travel in?' she asked. A question which led to a long discussion as to the merits of a shabby winter coat or an equally shabby raincoat. They settled on the coat, a weary felt hat to go with it, a dark dress, gloves and shoes, and Isobel hung them thankfully in the corner cupboard. Underclothes were quickly dealt with, largely because there were not many; and that left mounds of small bits and pieces, all of which Mrs Olbinski declared were vital to her future life in England. Isobel didn't say much, merely sorted family photos, a few trinkets, and a handful of small ornaments from the old scarves, ribbons, bits of lace and books. These she packed before going in search of something in which to put a few, at least, of the books.

She found a shopping basket in the kitchen and then patiently brought over Mrs Olbinski's remaining treasures so that she could decide which must be left behind. This took time too, but at last it was done, and Isobel suggested tentatively that there might be someone her companion knew who might be glad to have the remainder of the books and vases and clothes.

The old lady brightened. 'Go and knock on the door below, Isobel—there's a pleasant woman living there; she might be glad of these things since I'm not to be allowed to keep them.' She added crossly: 'Why doesn't Mr Thomas come back? He's doing nothing to help.'

Too true, thought Isobel, wrestling with the lady downstairs' valiant attempts to speak English. Signs and smiles and a few urgent tugs to an elderly arm did the trick at last; they went back upstairs together and Isobel left Mrs Olbinski to explain to her friend, who was so pleased with the arrangement that Isobel felt near to tears; how poor they must be, she thought, to be so glad with what were no more than clothes fit for the jumble. When she could get a word in edgeways she suggested that once Mrs Olbinski had gone, the lady might like to come back and collect the bedclothes and what food there was left. And that wasn't much—she had had a look. She had just ushered the delighted lady back to her own flat, deposited her new possessions in the sitting-room and wished her goodbye when the street door below opened. It could be anyone, it could be Dr Winter; she didn't wait to find out, but skipped upstairs once more to her charge.

It was Dr Winter, calm and unhurried and far too elegant for his surroundings. 'There you are,' declared Isobel, quite forgetting her place. 'Just nicely back when all the work is done!'

He chose to misunderstand her. 'Oh, splendid. I have rooms at the hotel and there's a car at the end of the street. I'm taking you out to lunch, Nanny, and since we have time on our hands, we'll take a short drive this afternoon.'

'I can't go like this!' The old lady was querulous; getting tired.

'If you wait a few minutes, I'll help Mrs Olbinski to put on her things,' suggested Isobel, and when he had gone, fetched the clothes from the cupboard and set about helping the old lady, wondering how she had managed in the lonely months since her husband's death, with her poor twisted hands and frail bent body. It took a little time, but the doctor made no comment when she called to him that they were ready. He picked up the old lady, reminded Isobel to lock the door behind them, and went down the narrow stairs. Once on the pavement they each took an arm, and made a slow painful progress to the car where the doctor set Mrs Olbinski in the seat beside his and bade Isobel get in the back. It was a small car and he looked out of place driving it.

The hotel was large and once Mrs Olbinski was comfortably settled with the doctor, Isobel was shown to her room, large and well furnished and with a shower room next door. She unpacked her case, did her face and hair and went downstairs again. It was, of course, a pity they couldn't return to Stockholm at once, but on the other hand it would be a golden opportunity to get even a glimpse of Gdansk. She looked forward to their promised outing with all the pleasure of a child.

They lunched presently in a stylish restaurant, half empty, for as the waiter told them, the summer season had barely started. The meal was wholly Polish—hot beet soup, crayfish, pork knuckle with horseradish sauce, followed by ices. Isobel enjoyed it all, and so, she noticed, did Mrs Olbinski.

They set off once lunch was finished, with the old lady quite excited now. They were to go to Sopot, a seaside resort only a few miles away and which she had known very well in earlier days. 'We went each year for our holiday here; there was a small hotel, quite near the Grand Orbis Hotel, and we would watch the people staying there in the evening, going in and out in their evening dress,' she sighed. 'Such a beautiful place!'

Very beautiful agreed Isobel, but almost deserted. They drove slowly about its streets; there were few people about and the shop windows looked almost empty, and at length they turned towards the sea and parked the car in a long avenue of trees. The sense of solitude was enhanced by the wide beach, quite deserted too, and the chilly grey of the Baltic beyond. 'We'll walk nearer so you can have a better view. Nanny will be all right and we can see her easily enough.'

There was a narrow concrete bridge crossing the sands, reached by a spiral staircase. It was a minute's walk away and Isobel ran up it ahead of the doctor to stand and admire the coast line stretching away on either side of her. 'This must be lovely on a warm summer's day,' she said, 'and with lots of people here.' She started to walk beside him towards the stairs at its other end. 'Where are all the people?' she wanted to know.

'The country is under martial law,' he reminded her. 'There's little money for holidays, and still less for food; I daresay tourists from other countries will come here when it's high summer.'

'It's very sad—your nanny must find it sad too.'

'She has her happy memories. We'll find somewhere for tea

and then drive along the coast. In Poland the main meal in a normal household is eaten about four o'clock, but we should be able to get tea or coffee and then have dinner at the hotel before taking Nanny back. You'll be good enough to help her to bed and leave everything at hand.'

They were walking back to the car across the path built on the sand.

'Wouldn't you like me to sleep there tonight?' asked Isobel. 'I'll be quite comfortable…'

'There's no need for that. You'll go to her after breakfast—I'll drive you there before going to check her papers—they may arrive by then.'

'Suppose they don't?'

'Then we'll spend another day here.'

They had coffee in a small café in the town and the owner pulled up a chair, delighted to air his English. He was a middle-aged man, with dark eyes and full of wry humour. They stayed quite a while, so that their drive along the coast wasn't as lengthy as Isobel had hoped, all the same she listened to Mrs Olbinski's titbits of information about the country around them and looked at houses and churches and old castles with all the zeal of a tourist.

They had dinner very soon after they got back to the hotel—soup again, grilled beef and dumplings and an ice. Dr Winter drank vodka, which Isobel prudently refused, although she did drink the beer he offered her. Nanny had vodka too, that and the good food and unexpected treat of a drive that afternoon had rendered her nicely sleepy. They took her back to her flat and the doctor waited while Isobel helped her to bed, tidying up afterwards and leaving coffee ready for the morning.

'You're a good girl,' declared Mrs Olbinski, when she went to say goodnight. 'How old are you?'

'Twenty-five, Mrs Olbinski.'

Nanny gave a chuckle. 'I shall be eighty in six weeks' time,' she declared. 'I'll have a proper birthday too with a cake and presents.'

Isobel and Dr Winter went back to the hotel in silence, only when they had gained the foyer did he bid her goodnight. 'Breakfast at half past eight, Nurse,' he reminded her, 'and afterwards we'll go immediately to Mrs Olbinski's flat.'

She didn't ask questions; there was no point, since she was sure that he wouldn't answer them. She went up to her room, had a shower, washed her hair and went to bed.

She woke early to a grey morning and the sound of early traffic in the street below. It was barely seven o'clock, a whole one and a half hours before she could go to breakfast, and she was wide awake and longing for a cup of tea. She went to peer out of the window and then on impulse, got dressed; there was still more than an hour to breakfast, she would explore a little, it would pass the time, and she had little hope of that meal being earlier if the doctor had said half past eight, then that was the time at which they would breakfast—not a minute sooner, not a minute later; she knew him well enough to know that. He would be a strict father, she mused, brushing her mousey hair, but kind and gentle. And why should I suppose that? she enquired of her neat reflection, he's never been either of those things to me. She pulled a childish face in the mirror, put on her coat and hat and left the room, locking the door carefully behind her.

There was a woman cleaning the corridor and a porter behind the reception desk in the foyer. Both of them replied to her good morning and the porter gave her a questioning look so that she said: 'I'm going for a short walk,' and smiled at him as she reached the big swing door.

Before she could open it, Dr Winter came in from outside, took her by the elbow and marched her back to the foyer.

'Where the hell do you think you're going?' he asked in a voice so harsh and so unlike his usual bland coolness that all Isobel could do was gape at him.

Presently she managed: 'Only going for a walk.'

'Going for a walk,' he mimicked mockingly. 'Of course you can speak Polish, know your way around Gdansk and have your passport with you, not to mention enough money for a taxi back if you should get lost.'

She said reasonably: 'I was only going a little way—close to the hotel, and you have no need to be so nasty about it, Dr Winter.'

She peered up into his angry face and saw that it was grey with fatigue and needed a shave. 'And where have you been?' she asked with disconcerting candour. 'You're cross and tired and you haven't shaved… Out all night?' She kept her pleasant voice low. 'At Mrs Olbinski's flat? She's ill?'

He shook his head. 'No, your eyes are too sharp, Nurse, and it's just my confounded luck to meet you…'

'There was a curfew.' She raised troubled eyes to meet his dark ones.

'Lifted half an hour since. I didn't like the idea of leaving Nanny alone.' And at her look: 'Oh, you were safe enough, the porter knew where I was; he's a friend of hers anyway, he promised to keep an eye on you.'

He didn't look angry any more, only faintly amused and impatient.

'And now, if you've finished your questioning, I'll have a shower and shave and join you for breakfast.' He caught her arm again. 'You'll oblige me by staying in your room until I come for you, and I'd like your promise on that.'

'I never heard such nonsense!' said Isobel impatiently. 'You've just said the curfew is over.'

'Your promise,' he insisted in a voice she didn't much like the sound of.

'Oh, very well.' She went with him up the stairs and when he took her key and opened her door, went past him without a word, only at the last minute she whizzed round and held out her hand.

Dr Winter put the key into it. He said softly: 'You are, after all, my responsibility until we're back in England.'

They breakfasted in a comfortable silence, broken only by polite requests to pass the salt, the toast or whatever. Dr Winter's face had lost its greyness; he was freshly shaved, impeccably dressed and very calm. Isobel, taking a quick peep, asked when she should go to Mrs Olbinski.

'We'll go together,' he told her, 'and while you're helping her to dress I'll go and see if her papers are in order. If so we can leave on the evening boat.'

Isobel had just coaxed Mrs Olbinski into the last of her garments when he returned to say that there would be no papers until the following morning. 'So we may as well spend the day sightseeing,' he finished. 'Where would you like to go, Nanny?'

'Oliwa,' she said at once, 'to listen to the organ recital—it's at twelve noon, I believe.'

They had coffee first in the hotel coffee room and then got into the car and drove the few miles to Oliwa. The Cathedral was magnificent—twelfth century, with Renaissance Baroque and Rococo added from time to time. The doctor parked the car and they began the slow progress to its entrance with Mrs Olbinski in the middle, insisting that she would rather die than be carried. The interior was splendid, with a high vaulted roof, painted with stars and hung with the Polish flag and with old-fashioned pews, already well filled. They found seats near the back, and presently the recital started with a disembodied voice explaining in English what music would be played and the history of the Cathedral, ending with the advice to turn round and look at the organ at the back of the Cathedral when the organist broke into particularly loud music. Isobel, with Mrs Olbinski's old hand in hers, only half listened. This was the real Poland, she thought, here in church, with the flag hanging on either side of the chancel and the quiet people sitting in the pews around her. The organ began then and she sat for half an hour, as still as a mouse, listening until the organist suddenly broke into a tremendous volume of sound. It was Dr Winter who leaned across Mrs Olbinski and touched her arm. 'Look behind you,' he said softly.

The organ, a massive eighteenth-century instrument, had come alive. The figures carved on it, angels with harps, trumpets, violins and flutes, were moving with the music, playing their instruments. The doctor's hand was still on her arm; she clutched it tightly and only when the music finally faded did she let it go, dropping it like a hot coal when she realised she had been clinging to it. 'So sorry,' she whispered, very pink, and was hardly reassured by his inscrutable face.

They went back to Gdansk for lunch, eating it at the Pod Wieza restaurant, and when they had finished, the doctor left them there, saying he would be back presently.

He was back within half an hour, during which time Isobel and Mrs Olbinski had had several cups of coffee and a good gossip. 'We can leave this evening,' he told them. He glanced at his watch. 'We'll go back to the hotel and get our things and pay the bill, then go to your place, Nanny. From there we can go down to the quay.'

Mrs Olbinski tried not to show her excitement but her old hands shook. 'You're sure, Mr Thomas? Everything's in order?'

'Yes, Nanny, we'll have you home in a couple of days now.' He smiled at her gently and took out a handkerchief and wiped her eyes for her. Oh, dear, thought Isobel; he is so nice when he's not being absolutely abominable!

Nice he might be to Nanny, but he allowed none of his finer feelings to show where Isobel was concerned. In businesslike tones he told her what had to be done, and she was kept busy, once they reached the old lady's rooms, parcelling up the things, which were to go to her neighbour, making tea for the three of them, and packing a small bag with essentials for the journey for both herself and Mrs Olbinski.

After tea the doctor took back the hired car, found a taxi and started on the slow business of loading Nanny and her few possessions into it. The old lady was fretful from excitement and tiredness by now and hindered every move. It was with a sigh of relief that Isobel saw the ferry at last, and even then she wasn't completely happy until they were actually stepping off the gangway on to the ship. Nanny was in tears again. She had, after all, lived in Poland for a long time and was leaving a life she had loved until the more recent years. Isobel coaxed her down to their cabin, got her undressed and into one of the bunks, and rang the bell for the stewardess. A large cheerful Swedish woman came at once; listening sympathetically she promised a light supper within the hour. Isobel unpacked the few things they needed for the night, talked Mrs Olbinski into a quiet frame of mind and when the supper came, sat down. Dr Winter hadn't said anything about her own meal and she wasn't sure if she wasn't supposed to have it in the cabin too. She was trying to decide what to do next when he knocked on the door and came in.

He enquired after Nanny's wellbeing and assured her that the stewardess would come the moment she was rung for, and invited Isobel with cold courtesy to join him at dinner. 'We'll go now and have a drink,' he concluded without giving her a chance to say anything.

So she followed him to the deck above, drank the sherry he invited her to have and sat down to dinner. He had little to say for himself, and she was glad of that; such a lot had happened in the last two days, she wanted to think about them.

However, over coffee he said suddenly: 'I think we may have to stay a couple of days in Stockholm,' and at her look of delight, added dryly: 'Not for sightseeing. Nanny is worn out and I'm not happy about continuing our journey until she has had a good rest.'

Isobel blushed. 'Yes, of course—she's been marvellous. It must have been pretty nerve-racking for her. I'll keep her in bed and get her to rest as much as possible.' She added: 'She won't like it.'

He passed his cup for more coffee. 'That's your business, Nurse. At least she likes you and will probably do as you ask.'

She said cheerfully: 'Let's hope so, I'll do my best, Dr Winter.' She put her cup down. 'Thank you for my dinner—I'm going back to the cabin now. I'll see that Mrs Olbinski is ready by the time we get to Stockholm—she can have her breakfast early and that will give us plenty of time.'

'You'll breakfast here?'

She said matter-of-factly: 'No, thanks, I'll have coffee and something when Mrs Olbinski does. Where are we to meet you in the morning?'

'I'll come for you.' He got up as she prepared to leave. 'Goodnight, Nurse.'

She gave him a friendly nod. 'Goodnight, Dr Winter.'

He didn't sit down again, but stood watching her neat figure as she threaded her way past the tables. If she had turned round she would have been surprised indeed to see that he was smiling.

CHAPTER THREE

MRS OLBINSKI SLEPT like a child, and like a child, woke early, so that there was ample time to help her dress after their coffee and rolls. By the time the docks were closing in on them they were both ready, so that when Dr Winter tapped on their door they were able to go with him without the smallest hitch.

It was a fine morning with a fresh breeze blowing from the Baltic, so that Mrs Olbinski shivered a little as Isobel helped her down the gangway with the doctor in front holding the old lady's hand—'Like a crab,' chortled Nanny, and allowed herself to be helped towards the Customs shed and the Passport office. There was a short delay while her papers were examined by one man, given to another to read and then handed back again, but her passport was stamped and the three of them made their slow progress to the waiting taxis. To Isobel's questioning look, the doctor said: 'No, Carl won't be here to meet us. We're going straight to their flat, although I rather fancy we shall have missed them by a couple of hours—they were going on holiday if you remember.'

The flat was empty when they reached it. Dr Winter carried Nanny up the stairs, took the door key from under the mat, and went inside. There was a note for him, and while Isobel saw to Mrs Olbinski, he read it, chuckling a good deal. 'That's all right,' he said at length, 'we may stay here as long as we wish.' He looked at the old lady with an apparently careless eye.

'Tired, my dear? How about bed for a while? Coffee first, though.'

Which was Isobel's cue, she supposed, to go into the splendid little kitchen and make it. When she got back the doctor was lying back in a chair with his eyes closed and Mrs Olbinski was snoring gently. He opened his eyes as she set the tray on the table and got up to fetch his coffee.

'Have your coffee, Isobel, then we'll wake her and get her to bed. I think it likely that we'll stay here for rather more than two days.' He paused. 'Why do you look so dumbfounded? I'd already said it was likely...'

'You called me Isobel.'

His eyebrows rose. 'Do you object? Since we're to be in each other's company for the next few days.'

'I don't mind in the least, Dr Winter.' She spoke in her usual matter-of-fact voice, and wondered what would happen if she called him Thomas. Probably he would explode. She smiled at the idea and he asked sharply: 'Why are you smiling?'

She said 'nothing' so firmly that it sounded almost true.

Mrs Olbinski wakened a few minutes later, declaring that she hadn't been to sleep, only shut her eyes; all the same, when she had drunk her coffee she went willingly enough with Isobel and allowed herself to be helped into her nightgown and settled in bed. She said rather fretfully: 'I haven't thanked Mr Thomas—whatever must he think of me? And I'm so grateful...it will be nice to be looked after.' She put out a hand and caught Isobel's. 'You're a dear child, Isobel, looking after a tiresome old woman who can't even remember to say thank you.'

'Hush now,' said Isobel, her pleasant voice gentle. 'You're tired and you've had a lot to do in the last day or so, I don't think Th... Dr Winter expects you to thank him until you're quite yourself again. If you have a good nap now, how about him coming here and having a cup of tea with you later on, then there'll be time to thank him properly.' She popped the elderly hand under the blanket. 'I'm sure he's tired too…all those papers…'

'It must have taken him months, and then that delay.' The old voice trembled. 'I thought just for a while that I wouldn't be able to come with you.'

'But everything turned out perfectly all right, didn't it?'

She went back to the sitting room once she was sure that Mrs Olbinski was asleep and found Dr Winter stretched out on the enormous sofa; he was snoring gently.

She collected the coffee cups soundlessly, bore them off to the kitchen and then went and sat down by the window. The garden below was charming; she spent some time admiring it and then, since the doctor showed no signs of waking, crept away to the kitchen to open cupboards and peer inside. Sooner or later, he would wake up and want a meal, it would help if she had some idea of what there was to cook. Soup for Nanny—that was easy; there was a row of tins, the wrappers illustrating their contents. In the freezer there was food in abundance, the only thing was that it was all wrapped and neatly labelled in Swedish. As soon as the doctor woke up she would ask him to go shopping. Thank heaven there were potatoes in plenty. She peeled some and set them on the stove ready to cook later on, then she sat down at the kitchen table and made a list of things to buy—too bad if the shops shut at noon; it was almost that already, and as far as she could remember there weren't many shops close by, only antique dealers and smart boutiques. The list grew alarmingly. She was doing her best to cut it down to a reasonable length when the doctor joined her.

Predictably he asked: 'Lunch?'

She eyed him severely. 'If you would be good enough to look in the freezer and tell me what's in all those packs, I can thaw something for this evening,' she told him. 'As for lunch—we need bread, milk and something to go on the bread. There's soup for Mrs Olbinski if she should wake.'

'My poor Isobel, left to wrestle with household problems while I take my ease!' He opened the freezer door and examined several packs. 'Chops,' he told her, and put them on the table, 'lamb chops. And I'll go out now and get what you need—we'd better have sandwiches.'

At the door he turned to look at her. 'Can you cook?'

'Yes—not Cordon Bleu, just plain cooking.'

'I see I have a treasure in you—nurse, companion to the elderly, excellent coffee maker, Girl Friday—oh, and a good plain cook…'

She went slowly red under his bland look and he made it worse by adding: 'Nothing personal intended, Isobel.'

There was no reason why she should mind so much, she told herself as she laid the kitchen table and found cups and saucers and plates, and then, because he wasn't back, she went along to the bedroom she had had before and did her hair and tidied herself. Perhaps now that they were back in Stockholm she could wear her own clothes again; she must remember to ask.

For a bachelor who, from her visit to his house, wasn't in the habit of doing the shopping, he had done very well—rolls and croissants, a plastic container with a delicious-looking salad of seafood, mushrooms and tomatoes, cheese and ham, fruit and a bottle of wine. Dr Winter laid them neatly on the table, took a roll and bit into it. 'I'll go out again when we've eaten and get whatever you want to cook for this evening. Make a list, will you?'

'Well, I have, but perhaps you'll think it's too much… There are the lamb chops, and I've got potatoes—if you got things for a salad and celery, I'll braise that, and if you like onions I could do Lyonnaise potatoes. I don't know if there's any rhubarb, if not apples will do, and I'll make a pie—we'll need some cream. I don't know the cheeses they sell here, but if you could get a little of several sorts; I found some crackers in the cupboard, and there's plenty of butter.'

She glanced up from her list and found him looking at her so intently that she said: 'Oh, is there something you don't like? I can easily alter it, it was just a rough idea…'

'It sounds marvellous, and if that's a rough idea I do hope I'm there when you really put your mind to it.' He smiled at her, not the usual cold smile he offered her, but a warm friendly grin. 'Who taught you to cook?' he asked.

'My mother.' She was cutting the rolls in half and buttering them.

'Have you brothers and sisters—a father?'

He was sitting on a chair, round the wrong way so that his arms rested along its back.

'A brother. My father died some years ago.' She would have liked to have talked to him about her family, but if she did she had no doubt that after a minute he would look faintly bored. She added rapidly: 'Would you like cheese in the rolls, or do I put this salad in them?'

'It's called *vastkustsallad*, it'll be easier to manage on plates.' He sighed gently. 'Our relationship is hardly a happy one, is it, Isobel?'

Her eyes flew to his face. 'But we haven't got a relationship, Dr Winter. I'm a nurse hired to help you with Mrs Olbinski—and you only hired me because there was no one else.' She spoke in her usual quiet friendly fashion, stating a fact without rancour.

He didn't answer but set about opening the wine, and she finished filling the rolls. 'I'll just look in on Mrs Olbinski, if she's awake she might like some soup.'

Nanny was sleeping deeply. Isobel went back to the kitchen and invited the doctor to his lunch. 'I hope you don't mind having it in here, just this once…'

He sat down opposite her, looming from his side of the table.

'You sound as though you imagine I never have eaten in a kitchen before.'

'Well, I don't suppose you do often, do you? You live in a very grand house.'

'My home, Isobel, and it happens to have a very pleasant kitchen. Will you try some of this salad, it's famous in these parts.'

She made coffee presently and over it he said: 'I have to go out this afternoon. I'll do your shopping first, though. You'll be all right here?'

'Yes, of course. Is there anything I ought to know about Mrs Olbinski?'

'Only that her heart isn't too good—I examined her when I was at her flat. There's very little to be done, I'm afraid—we'll keep her in bed for two days at least before we go back to England. She can get up if she wants to for an hour or so, but otherwise strict bed rest. Have you all you want for her?'

'I think so, thank you.' Isobel got up. 'I'll wash up. Do you mind if I get back into my other clothes?'

His cool look appraised her. 'Not in the least—wear whatever you like.' His tone implied that she could drape herself in a sack if she wanted to.

She stacked the dishes with a noiseless emphasis more telling than smashing plates. He was horrid, rude and thoughtless and always telling her what had to be done; it would do him good to do a few chores for himself!

Disconcerting therefore when he went to the sink and washed up.

She was heating some soup for Mrs Olbinski who had wakened feeling waspish, when he came back with the groceries. Then he unpacked them on to the kitchen table, enquired after the old lady, spent a few minutes with her and let himself out of the flat again. And all without more than a hullo and goodbye. But why should I care? she asked the kitchen at large as she was preparing an appetising snack for her patient.

Mrs Olbinski went back to sleep presently and Isobel went

into the sitting room and picked up a magazine. She couldn't understand a word of it, but the pictures were interesting. The doctor wasn't back by the time she decided to make tea. She would have liked a long hot bath and to have washed her hair and changed her skirt and top, but he'd left her in charge and supposing the phone rang or someone called or Mrs Olbinski wanted her? She drank her tea and went along to see how the old lady fared. She was still sleeping, but lightly now. Isobel crept around putting out clean clothes, fetching her own soap, clean towels and a brush and comb and in a little while, when Mrs Olbinski woke once more, she made fresh tea, found biscuits and then when the old lady had had her tea, set about her toilet. It was remarkable what a difference a fresh nightie, a wash with scented soap and a well brushed head did to improve matters. Mrs Olbinski, sitting up against comfortable pillows, smiled contentedly. 'Well, I must say I feel better for that,' she conceded, 'and I do believe I could eat a little supper presently. Where is Mr Thomas?'

'He's here, just got back,' said the doctor, coming down the hall and into her room. 'And what a sight for sore eyes, Nanny—you don't look a day over sixty, and pretty with it!'

'Don't you try and wheedle me, young man,' said Nanny severely, then smiled with pleasure. 'Where have you been?'

'Oh, doing this and that.' He put a parcel on the bed beside her. 'I saw this and somehow it looked like you. Go on, open it.'

There was a gossamer-fine wool stole inside, pink and pretty. He tossed it around the old lady's shoulders and stood back to admire the effect.

'Just right, wouldn't you say, Isobel?' he wanted to know.

'It's charming and suits Mrs Olbinski beautifully. Would you like tea, Dr Winter?'

'Tea? No, thanks, I had something…' He turned to look at her. 'You need some fresh air. I've arranged for the woman who comes here to help in the house to do the same for us. She'll be here in the morning and come again after lunch—you can be free for a couple of hours then. Why not go into the garden now for half an hour? I'll be here.'

Isobel thanked him quietly, got her coat and went down the stairs and into the quiet little garden. It was chilly now but peaceful; there were birds twittering and the sound of traffic, nicely muffled. There was a wooden bench under one of the lilac trees and she sat down, listening to the faint sounds coming from the old houses around her. They were faint because the walls were thick, but presently the windows began to glow with lights and there was a pleasant smell of something delicious cooking. It mingled with the lilacs and she sat sniffing appreciatively. When her half hour was up she went back indoors, hung her coat in the hall, and went straight to the kitchen. There was a light in Nanny's room and the door was half open. There was a light in the sitting room too, but she didn't go in.

The potatoes were on the boil, the onion was chopped and she was making the pastry for her pie when Dr Winter flung open the door.

'There you are,' he declared unnecessarily. 'You weren't in the garden—I imagined you getting lost in Stockholm. Why do you creep in and out so that no one knows where you are?' He sounded so angry that she paused in the rolling of the pastry to stare at him.

'But I've been in the garden,' she told him patiently. 'I came in at the end of half an hour—you said half an hour.' Her voice became very slightly shrill with annoyance. 'Do I have to report on and off duty, then?'

'Good God no! I thought...never mind what I thought. Nanny's asleep again. When you've done that come into the sitting room and have a drink.'

Isobel put her pie in the oven, put the potatoes to cool, found a frying pan and set everything ready for her promised *pommes Lyonnaises*. This done, she went into the sitting room. The doctor was standing with his hands in his pockets, staring out of the window, but he turned to look at her as she sat down. 'I thought you wanted to change your dress,' he observed.

She gave him a pitying look. 'I haven't had a chance,' she pointed out mildly.

'Ah, no, of course not. Stupid of me. Can dinner wait while you do whatever you want to do?'

'Yes, it can, if you don't mind it being half an hour later. And if you wouldn't mind going to Mrs Olbinski if she wants anything…'

He nodded and handed her a glass. 'Well, have your drink before you go.'

There was no reason why he should be eager for her society, even for five minutes. She had long ago accepted the fact that a quiet manner and a plain face held little attraction for a man, especially for Dr Winter, who presumably could pick and choose, bearing in mind the advantages of good looks, a splendid house and, presumably, an equally splendid job in the medical profession. Isobel drank the sherry rather too fast, murmured vaguely and went back to the kitchen where she rearranged her cooking and then went to her room, peeping in on Mrs Olbinski on the way.

She felt better after a shower. She would have liked time to wash her hair but that would have to wait; she brushed it smooth, made up her face in a moderate sort of way, put on the pleated skirt and the Liberty print blouse and went back to the sitting room.

'Supper will be about twenty minutes,' she announced from the door.

The doctor was at the window again, his back to the TV which he had switched on. He looked her up and down. He said: 'Ah, this is to be a special occasion, is it?' in a silky voice she didn't care about—there was, after all, no reason to mock her. She went to the kitchen, shut the door and put on the apron behind it.

The pie was baked. She took it from the oven and the fragrance of it brought the doctor into the kitchen. He eyed it with the same look which her younger brother would have bestowed on it. He said with an endearing boyishness: 'I like pie… I'm hungry.'

'Well, you shall have it, after the chops.' She was assembling the *pommes Lyonnaises* with small competent hands; the smell as she tossed the mixture into the hot oil in the pan caused the doctor to sniff appreciatively.

'I can't think why you haven't been snapped up by some discerning man,' he observed lightly. 'You may be a good nurse, but you appear to be a cook of the first water.'

'A good plain cook,' she reminded him gently, and laid a tray for Mrs Olbinski, not looking at him. He had sat himself on the edge of the table, and was eating a roll. 'That will take the edge off your appetite,' she warned him, and skimmed away to the dining alcove to lay the table. When she got back he had seen to the wine, found the glasses and wandered to the table with them, and since Mrs Olbinski's tray was ready, took it to her room while Isobel sat her up against her pillows.

The old lady inspected the contents of her tray with a sharp eye. 'It looks very nice,' she conceded. 'What's for pudding?'

Isobel told her. 'But if you'd rather, I'll make you a custard…'

'Certainly not!' declared Mrs Olbinski. 'I'm still young enough to enjoy a good fruit pie. Have you a light hand with pastry?'

'So they say,' said Isobel, and went away to dish up, leaving the doctor to pour a glass of wine for his charge.

She had a glass candle light in the centre of the table and a small nosegay of flowers on either side of it. The alcove glowed in its gentle light. Isobel began to carry in the dishes and Dr Winter, pouring the wine, observed in what she described to herself as his mocking voice: 'In any other circumstances this could be described as a romantic setting.'

'Well, we can soon change that,' said Isobel matter-of-factly, and whisked away the glass candle light from the table and switched on the bright overhead light above the table.

When she came back with the next lot of dishes she heard him say mildly: 'I didn't say I disliked it, Isobel.'

For such a serene girl the look she gave him was quite ferocious. 'No? Anyway, it wasn't my intention. Would you like your salad now or after the chops?'

'Oh, now, I think. I've annoyed you.' He waited until she had sat down and then sat down himself. The brilliant lighting did nothing to detract from his good looks; she wondered crossly what sort of adverse effect it was having upon her own unremarkable features. She said stiffly: 'Not in the least, Dr Winter,' and ate her salad in silence.

He followed her into the kitchen presently and carried in the dishes for her, then said in his mildest voice: 'If you would like to telephone anyone from here, you can do so easily. There's an extension in the hall and I'll get the number for you.'

'Oh, thank you, I'd love to. You—you don't know when we'll be back in England?'

'No, it depends largely on Nanny, but we shall be here for at least two days—I want her really fit. The delay in Gdansk shook her up a bit.'

Isobel passed him the dish of *pommes Lyonnaises* and he took a second helping. 'Did you expect that?' she asked.

'Yes, I hoped it could be avoided, but I wasn't surprised.'

'And not anxious that she wouldn't be allowed to leave?'

'Anxious? My dear girl, I was scared out of my wits!'

'You're joking!'

'No, although I have no intention of admitting that to anyone else. There is something else I must admit to you; you are, after all, most suitable, Isobel.' He got up from the table, fetched the candle light and set it between them and turned off the overhead lamp. 'I'm not being romantic,' he explained, 'merely offering my—well, no, let's say that I'm showing my appreciation.'

A remark she would have to think about later on. Now she

collected up the dishes and while he took them into the kitchen, went to see how Mrs Olbinski was getting on. She had eaten everything. 'Very well cooked,' she pronounced. 'I couldn't have done it better myself. Where's that pie?'

The pie was demolished and they washed up before they had their coffee, and by then it was time to settle Mrs Olbinski for the night. When Isobel went back to the sitting room it was to find Dr Winter deep in a book, so she wished him goodnight and went away again. He had got up when she went in, but he had kept his finger in the page as though he couldn't wait to get back to it, impatient to see her gone. I mustn't get so sensitive, she told herself, tumbling into bed. I daresay the book's far more interesting than I am. But he had enjoyed her cooking, on that pleasing thought she slept.

The next morning held no idle moments. There was Nanny to see to, and although the helper came after breakfast, there was lunch to prepare and a load of washing to put into the machine. The doctor took himself off after they had had coffee and he had taken a look at Mrs Olbinski. He would bring back bread and the groceries she needed, he told Isobel, and she watched him go with something like envy. It was a fine day and she longed for a chance to escape for a couple of hours; perhaps this afternoon while Mrs Olbinski had her nap, when it might be possible for her to go out if Helga was in the flat. She did her chores, got lunch, saw Helga off home with the promise that she would return at two o'clock, and sat down to wait for Dr Winter.

She had taken the opportunity of ringing her mother while he was out, and that lady, although delighted to hear from her, expressed no impatience when she said that she might be back a few days later than she had expected. 'The weather is dreadful here, darling,' said her mother comfortably, 'so stay as long as you can. It sounded a nice case—I hope it is, dear?'

'Yes, oh yes, Mother. I'll tell you all about it when I get back.'

Mrs Olbinski had called then and she had hung up.

They lunched off an omelette, light as thistledown, and rolls and cheese and fruit and another pot of coffee. 'When did Helga say she'd be back?' asked the doctor as he began washing up.

'Two o'clock.'

'Well, go and get Nanny settled and then fetch your jacket, you're due some time off.'

Isobel needed no second bidding. Fifteen minutes or so later she poked her nose round the sitting room door. Helga was there, talking in her peculiar English to Dr Winter. 'What time do you want me back?' asked Isobel.

The doctor nodded to Helga and came to the door. 'We'll be back about five o'clock; Helga knows just what to do and I've told Nanny where we're going.'

'We?'

'You'll see so much more if you're with someone who knows his way around,' said Dr Winter smugly.

'There's really no need...' began Isobel, regretting very much that there wasn't.

'I'm responsible for you while you're in my employ,' said the doctor blandly—a remark destined to banish any half-formed ideas in her head.

All the same the afternoon was a delight. They spent an hour wandering around the old town, and Isobel bought a Dala horse for her mother and a leather belt for her brother, borrowing the money from the doctor, and then, since he said that it was a shame not to get them while she had the chance, she bought some of the lovely coloured candles displayed in all the shops. It seemed logical to buy one or two candle holders to go with them.

'You'll keep a careful account, won't you?' asked Isobel.

'Every single *ore*,' promised Dr Winter.

They took a taxi and drove out to the Millesgarden. An absolute must, he explained; Milles was Sweden's famous modern sculptor and his work wasn't to be missed on any account. And he was right. The garden overlooked the Baltic and had been built in terraces, screened by silver birches and firs and flower beds, and the sculptures, cunningly arranged on the terraces, were each a work of art. Isobel, going slowly, stopping by each one, quite forgot the doctor patiently waiting beside her. Only when they reached the last terrace and she saw The Hand of God, did she put out a hand and clutch his sleeve.

'Oh, look—do look, isn't it marvellous? I've never seen anything like it. It's…there's no way of describing it…'

The doctor looked down at her animated face. It was astonishing that such a very ordinary face could become almost beautiful once its owner was aroused.

He said placidly: 'It is a marvellous work. Come and look at the fountain, and if you look up there you can see Milles' house and studio. We'll go back that way, but I expect you'd like to go to the last terrace and get a view of the Baltic.'

There were not many people about; it was a little early for tourists, he told her. In another month the roses would be out and it would be a good deal warmer.

'And in winter?' asked Isobel, staring up at Man and Pegasus, her eyes wide and her mouth a little open.

'If the snow's deep it makes sightseeing here rather tricky.'

'Oh, of course. Have you been in Stockholm in the winter?'

'That's when I prefer to come.' He was leading her up the stone steps towards Milles' house and the exit.

'Oh, skiing…'

'Yes.'

'Is it difficult?'

'No, not if you want to do it.' He looked at her small, neat figure. 'You should do well, I think.'

'Well, I don't suppose I'll get the chance to learn,' she observed matter-of-factly. 'I expect you want to get back to the flat.'

He looked amused. 'Do I? But tea first, I think.'

They took a taxi back to the centre of the city and had tea in a small and elegant tea room; the kind of tea Isobel so seldom had a chance to enjoy—thin china cups with lemon and mountainous cream cakes.

'Feel like a walk?' asked Dr Winter as they went back into the street. And when she nodded, he plunged into a complex of narrow lanes which eventually brought them out within a stone's throw of the flat. He waved aside her thanks as they entered the flat and went to speak to Helga, while Isobel went to her own room and then to Mrs Olbinski.

The old lady looked remarkably frail against her pillows, but she wanted to hear exactly where they had been and what they had done. Supper would have to be late, decided Isobel, embarking on a blow-by-blow account of their afternoon.

As it turned out, that didn't matter. When she eventually left Mrs Olbinski, she found the doctor in the sitting room, looking impatient.

'I shall be out to dinner,' he told her, in a cool remote voice quite at variance with his friendly manner during the afternoon. 'I've got a key, so go to bed and lock the door. I'll go and see Nanny before I go. How does she seem?'

She stifled her disappointment under a calm front. 'Tired, although she's been in bed almost all of today. Should I get her up for an hour or two, just for supper?'

He started for the door. 'I'll let you know. Give her a light meal and see she takes her tablets.'

Isobel went into the kitchen and looked in the cupboards and fridge. She had planned dinner in her mind—smoked salmon vol-au-vents, Swedish meat balls and stuffed cabbage rolls and an egg custard for afters. Now it need only be a light egg dish and probably soup and some fruit to finish with. The doctor came into the kitchen presently, ready to go out again. He had changed his clothes, she noticed, and had another shave. He gave a careless glance round the kitchen. 'Nanny's all right; not as spry as I could wish, but her pulse is stronger. If she's no worse tomorrow I'll get seats on a plane for the day after. Get her up by all means. If you want me urgently get this number.' He scribbled on the kitchen pad. 'Goodnight, Isobel.'

She wished him goodnight in a bright voice and busied herself at once getting out bowls and eggs, butter and a can of soup. Only when she heard the door close did she put everything down and go along to Mrs Olbinski. For some reason she didn't want to be alone with her thoughts.

The evening seemed very long. Mrs Olbinski didn't want to get up for her supper; Isobel washed her and made her bed, turned on the TV for her and went to make an omelette and a warm drink. It wasn't until much later, when the old lady had dozed off, that she went back into the kitchen to get her own meal. To cook for one was absurd, so she boiled an egg, found a roll and butter and sat at the kitchen table with a magazine, and then because the TV was still in Mrs Olbinski's room and she didn't want to disturb her, she took herself off to bed. She stayed awake for a long time, but Dr Winter hadn't returned by the time she went to sleep.

Rather to her surprise, he offered to take her sightseeing again the next morning, but as she pointed out, even with Helga there, she had the ironing to do and Mrs Olbinski to care for.

He didn't appear to mind whether she accepted or not, merely told her to take an hour off after lunch. 'I'll go along and get seats on an afternoon flight for tomorrow,' he told her. 'Nanny is no worse—no better either, but I think we'd better get her home. Helga will be here at two o'clock and you can safely leave her then.'

Isobel spent a busy morning, what with her patient, who was rather fretful, the ironing, and the preparation of the evening meal. By the time the doctor came back she had rolls and butter, cheese and cold meat on the table and a mouthwatering salad.

The doctor was politely friendly as they ate, helped her clear the dishes ready for Helga to wash presently and then went along to talk to Mrs Olbinski. He didn't stay long; Isobel made the old lady comfortable for her nap, promised she would be back within the hour, and fetched her jacket. Helga was already in the kitchen and the doctor was in the sitting room, but she reached the little hall and he joined her, opened the door and went down the stairs with her. Just for a few moments she thought that he intended accompanying her on her walk, but as they reached the archway to the road he said casually: 'Well, have a pleasant hour, Isobel,' and turned away in the direction of Storkyrkan. She had intended to pay the church another visit, but now she went briskly in the other direction, hoping she looked as though she knew where she was going. She was quickly lost, of course, but there were always the tall church spires to guide her. She pottered through the charming cobbled streets, peering in the windows of the small expensive antique shops, jewellers and boutiques, but after half an hour she made her way back to the great church and spent the remainder of her free time there, wandering up and down its splendid wide aisles and standing to stare at the fifteenth-century statue of St George and the Dragon. She stayed so long that she had to hurry back to the flat and got there just in time to answer Mrs Olbinski's fretful voice demanding tea.

She had a cup with the old lady and stayed to chat with her for a little while, and then because she was still fretful, wrapped her in her pink stole and helped her to the kitchen. She settled her there in a well cushioned chair, wrapped a blanket round her knees, and started to get things ready for their evening meal. Dr Winter found them there presently, Isobel busy with the vol-au-vents and Mrs Olbinski with a bowl and an egg whisk, preparing the eggs for the custard.

Mrs Olbinski stayed up for dinner, sitting between them in the dining alcove, her peevishness forgotten, telling them tales of her life in Poland, and when the doctor suggested at last that she should go to bed, she went happily enough and fell asleep at once, like a small child.

The doctor had almost finished the washing-up by the time Isobel got back to the kitchen. She made more coffee and carried it through to the sitting room, where she listened quietly to his plans for the next day and since he showed no desire for conversation, she wished him goodnight and went to bed. There was, after all, she told herself reasonably, no earthly reason why he should want her company; she was there to look after Mrs Olbinski and he had no interest in her beyond the fact that she was a nurse, there to do a job for him. She speculated if things might have been different—if she had been blue-eyed and pretty and a clever talker—and studying her commonplace reflection in the dressing table glass thought that it was very likely they would. She nodded to herself as she brushed her hair. 'This time next week, he'll have forgotten you.' She said it very firmly.

The flight left at two o'clock from Arlanda Airport, thirty-eight kilometres from the city. Isobel spent a busy morning getting Mrs Olbinski up and dressed, preparing an early lunch for them all, packing their few things and helping Helga to tidy the flat. A taxi took them there, and since there was time to spare, Isobel and Mrs Olbinski were settled in the bar, given coffee and a handful of papers and magazines while the doctor went off to see about their luggage. He didn't come back until their flight was called, and this time he had a wheelchair with him. Mrs Olbinski, half asleep, made no objection to being put into it, and once at the plane, he carried her up the steps, settled her in a window seat, told Isobel to sit beside her and settled himself on the other side of the aisle. He must be relieved to have the business finished, thought Isobel, watching him unfold *The Times*. He had become aloof since they had left the flat, as though he was looking forward to seeing the last of her, and he had answered her vaguely when she had asked if he required her services once they got to his house. There would be servants enough to help Mrs Olbinski; she began to speculate on how to get herself home as quickly as possible.

Of course he might dismiss her at Heathrow, but that was unlikely; she felt sure he would at least ascertain that she could get home as easily as possible. If she could telephone her mother before she left his house and catch a bus…he might even allow her the taxi fare. She would go along to the agency in the morning in the hope that he had paid promptly, and see about another case, that would give her the rest of the day to see to her clothes and tell her mother all her news. She would have gone on for some time making plans, only Mrs Olbinski, who had dropped off again, awoke and wanted tea, and while she had it, wanted to know how soon it would be before they were home. 'Because I'm tired,' she said in a rather thin voice. 'Everything's happened so quickly and I shall feel so strange… I'm so glad you'll be there, Isobel.'

It seemed hardly the time to say that that wasn't very likely. Isobel edged the conversation round to the old lady's memories of life in Poland, and hoped that the awkward moment was over.

It seemed as though it was. They landed presently, and throughout the business of getting themselves out of the plane, in and out of Customs, finding a porter, and collecting luggage, scarcely a word was spoken. The doctor, as usual, had everything in hand. There was no hitch, and they were outside on the pavement in no time at all and before Isobel had time to wonder what happened next, a dark blue Rolls-Royce crept to a halt beside them. The driver got out, exchanged a few words with Dr Winter, helped the porter stow the luggage and disappeared. The doctor lifted Mrs Olbinski into the back seat, nodded to Isobel to get in beside her and took the wheel. He hadn't spoken except to ask if Nanny was comfortable and it was difficult to shout questions at his back. Isobel settled back in luxury. When they reached his house she would find out exactly what he expected of her, and at the same time point out, in the most reasonable manner possible, that he might have had the good manners to keep her informed beforehand. He was a tiresome man, she mused silently, far too sure of himself. She paused—well, being sure of himself had helped in Poland, she supposed, and once or twice he had been quite friendly. It was a waste of time thinking about him anyway, so she turned her attention to Mrs Olbinski who, now that they were approaching London, was getting excited.

CHAPTER FOUR

DR WINTER'S HOUSEHOLD apparently ran on oiled wheels. The glossy front door was opened as the car drew up before it and the same impassive manservant came down the steps, greeted Dr Winter with a warmth which lightened his solemn features to a surprising extent, and opened the door for her to get out. Isobel found herself going into the house behind the doctor with Mrs Olbinski in his arms and, once there, following him through a massive mahogany door into a long room with windows at both ends; it was an elegant room; she hoped that she would have time to look round it properly before she went, but just for the moment her patient was her main concern. The terrible hat had to be lifted from a tired elderly head, the shabby coat carefully removed and their owner settled in a comfortable chair.

'I'd like a cup of tea,' declared Nanny in a thready voice, and the doctor nodded to a stout cosy woman who had hurried to meet them as they entered the room. 'For all of us,' he added.

But when it came, he refused his, went to a sofa table against one of the walls and poured himself a whisky, before sitting down in a wingback chair by the empty fireplace. He raised his glass to the old lady. 'Welcome home, Nanny,' he said. 'Tomorrow we'll celebrate together, but it's been a long day; how about early bed and a nice supper on a tray?' He glanced at Isobel. 'Ah, yes—and you, Isobel…'

He was interrupted by the door being flung open and a light laughing voice exclaiming, 'It's all right, Gibson, I know my way,' and a girl came in—tall, slim, dramatically dark, wearing clothes Isobel had studied in the glossy magazines with a strong envy.

She ran across the room on preposterous heels and flung herself at Dr Winter. 'Thomas—why didn't you let me know you would be back? There's this party this evening and I've been so miserable thinking you wouldn't be here to take me—now you can.' She flung her arms round his neck and kissed him. 'Where've you been?'

She unwound herself and glanced at Nanny and Isobel sitting side by side, each very upright in her chair. 'Who ever are these people?'

He took her arm. 'Come and meet my old nanny, Mrs Olbinski, who's coming to live with me, and this is Miss Barrington, a nurse who's been looking after her. He smiled at Nanny. 'This is Miss Ella Stokes, Nanny—Isobel.'

Miss Stokes smiled tepidly at Nanny and coldly at Isobel. 'The party is at half past eight—we can eat afterwards, though.'

'I'm afraid not, Ella. We've just this minute got back. You'll have to find someone else. That should be easy enough.'

'Of course it's easy,' said Miss Stokes pettishly, 'but I want you, Thomas.'

'I'm flattered but adamant, darling. I'll give you lunch tomorrow instead.' He sounded amused, but he also sounded as though he meant what he said.

'Oh, all right, but I simply must talk to you—just for a few minutes, please, Thomas?'

'How could I refuse that?' he asked, laughing. 'But wait a minute while I get Nanny upstairs.' He picked up the old lady, looked at Isobel and said: 'Nurse—if you will come too?' and led the way out of the room.

Nanny's room was on the first floor, large, airy and convenient. 'You'll find all you want,' Dr Winter said, setting her down on a chair near the bed. 'If you need anything, ring the bell and Mrs Gibson will come.' He bent to kiss the old lady. 'I'll look in later,' he promised her, and had reached the door by the time Isobel had caught up with him.

'Dr Winter,' her tone was quite decidedly fierce, 'I should like to know…'

He stopped to look at her. 'Ah—of course, Isobel, you want to know where your room is. Mrs Gibson will show you.'

'I didn't know that I was staying for the night here. And do you want to see me before I go in the morning?'

He was staring at her now with a kind of impatient amusement. 'Go? But am I not still employing you? I wasn't aware that I'd mentioned you leaving.'

'No, nor have you, but when you interviewed me you said that you would require my services only until such time as you had a suitable companion for Mrs Olbinski. Well, you have. Mrs Gibson and she are old friends.'

He said coolly: 'Mrs Gibson is also my housekeeper.'

'That's as may be. I may be only in your temporary employ, Dr Winter, but I merit some of your consideration—I've been wholly in the dark…'

'Oh dear, oh dear!' His cool eyes were sparkling with amusement now. 'I see that I must beg pardon. If I ask you nicely will you be kind enough to stay the night, and in the morning we must have a talk. You have another case waiting, perhaps?'

It was a temptation to say yes, but Isobel shook her head.

'In that case…' he smiled at her with sudden charm, 'we'll see each other tomorrow.'

He had gone, along the gallery and then down the staircase, and she heard him answering Ella's laughing voice. Which was no reason why she should feel so forlorn.

But she shook the feeling off as Mrs Gibson came trotting along to join her. 'I've put you in the room next to Nanny's, Nurse dear. There's a bathroom between you, but if you keep the doors open you'll be able to hear if she wants anything.' She bustled ahead and opened a door, ushering Isobel into a charming room, all pale colours and pretty light shades and a carpet to lose one's feet in. 'What an adventure!' went on Mrs Gibson, bent on a nice chat. 'We was all worried when Mr Thomas went off like he did, all secret like, as you might say, though we're that pleased to have Nanny back with us—twenty years she's bin gone, but it don't seem that long. Were you frightened, Nurse?'

Isobel reflected. 'Not frightened, though it was a little alarming when we were told that Nanny couldn't leave at once. But Dr Winter knew just what to do.'

She had taken off her jacket and was tidying herself before the triple mirror on the delicate rosewood table between the windows.

'You can be sure of that,' agreed Mrs Gibson happily, 'always knows what to do, does our Mr Thomas.'

Isobel agreed silently, adding the rider that it would be nice if he would share his plans with others from time to time. Like that time he disappeared for the night at Gdansk—just suppose she had wanted him during the night, or she'd fallen down and broken a leg…the possibilities of disaster were endless. She spent quite a few minutes exploring them, rather forgetful of Mrs Gibson, standing near, watching her.

'Well, if you've got all you want, Nurse, I'll pop along and see if the doctor wants his dinner at home—that Miss Stokes is always fussing him to take her somewhere or other—he needs a quiet evening at home, if you ask me. There'll be dinner in half an hour, Nurse. You'll want to get Nanny into her bed first. When you're ready, just ring the bell and someone will be up with her supper, and I'll come along and have a chat with her so you can have your dinner in peace.'

Isobel had Mrs Olbinski comfortably settled in bed within

twenty minutes with a supper tray on the bed table before her, which left her ten minutes in which to get ready for her own meal. It seemed unlikely that the doctor would be joining her; all the same, she changed her blouse, made up her face and did her hair and then went, rather nervously, downstairs.

Gibson was hovering in the hall and his impassive face was very smiling. He opened a door and ushered her into a small room—well, compared to the room she had already been in—it seemed small, it was cosily furnished with glazed chintz covers on the easy chairs and two sofas, one on each side of the fireplace, and the colours were nicely muted. She hadn't expected the doctor to be there, and when he turned round to look at her she said in a surprised voice: 'Oh, you are here!'

'Where else should I be?' he wanted to know. 'This is my home.'

She felt her face glow under his amused look. 'Well, yes, I know that!' she told him patiently, 'but I thought you'd be out with—with Miss Stokes.' And since he went on looking at her and didn't utter a word: 'The party, you know...'

'I seem to remember telling her I wouldn't be going...'

'Oh, I know that, I heard you, but I didn't think you meant it.' Isobel added by way of explanation: 'She's so very pretty.'

'If you knew me better, Isobel, you would know that if I say something I mean it.'

'Always?'

'Always. Would you care for a glass of sherry before we have dinner?'

'Well—thank you, yes. But I don't think I should stay away too long—Mrs Olbinski...'

He interrupted her: 'Mrs Gibson is with her, and they'll have a nice cosy gossip about the old days. It would be most unkind of you to disturb them.'

So Isobel drank her sherry and then crossed the hall with him to the dining room, where amidst its subdued splendour and under the watchful eye of Gibson she ate her dinner; artichoke soup, sole Véronique, *steak au poivre* and a delicious trifle for dessert. She was hungry and ate with a good appetite, drinking the wine poured into her glass and making polite conversation with the doctor. She longed to ask him if she was to leave in the morning, although she was sure she would be going. Mrs Olbinski didn't need a nurse any more and there seemed enough staff in the house to attend to her small wants. As they got up from the table she said: 'I should like to phone my mother, if you don't mind.'

'Of course. There's a telephone in the sitting room across the hall and you won't be disturbed. It will, of course, be useless for you to give any details of your departure from here until we've had our little talk tomorrow, but I'm sure you want to let your mother know you're back in London.'

He opened the door for her and ushered her inside, then left her with a quiet goodnight.

Her mother, although delighted to hear from her, didn't seem to mind that she might not be home for a day or two. 'Although I'm pretty sure I'll be leaving some time tomorrow,' said Isobel, 'only Dr Winter's being pigheaded about telling me.'

'Ah, yes—you did tell me that he wasn't keen on engaging you in the first place. Has he been tiresome?'

Isobel thought about that. 'Well, no, not really. Look, love, I'll give you a ring tomorrow morning and let you know what time I'll get home.'

She was so certain in her own mind that she would be leaving once she had seen the doctor that she had packed her case when she got up on the next morning, although she didn't say anything to Mrs Olbinski when she went along to her room to help her dress and see that she ate her breakfast. And it was almost lunchtime, and she was fuming at the delay, before Mrs Gibson came sailing upstairs to say that the doctor was home and would she be good enough to join him in the study.

His 'good morning' was casual and his apology perfunctory but she was prepared to forgive all that until he added carelessly: 'I should have come straight here, I know, but Ella wanted to see me.'

Isobel said she quite understood, in such a frosty voice that he looked at her sharply, then proceeded to leave her speechless with: 'I phoned the agency this morning—I've engaged you for another week.'

Isobel found her breath again. 'I expected to leave today—this morning,' she told him in a voice, which, despite her anger, came out very calmly. 'You are, if I may say so, Dr Winter, a very inconsiderate employer.'

He looked interested. 'Am I? I can't think why. After all, nursing is your job, surely it doesn't matter overmuch who or where you nurse? I'd better pay you, hadn't I? The agency reminded me...and you have to have a free day—two, I believe, but perhaps you could manage with one?'

'It seems I have very little choice, but I really must have time to go home and get some more clothes.'

He looked surprised. 'Oh, must you? The ones you're wearing seem quite adequate. But you know best. You can go now if you like—well, after lunch, and be back here for lunch tomorrow. I shall be out, and I'd be happier about Nanny if you are here.'

He sat down at his desk and opened his cheque book, barely glancing at her as he said: 'Do sit down, Isobel.'

She wanted to argue with him, but she couldn't find the right words. She sat rather primly and looked around her. The room was of a pleasant size, its walls lined with bookshelves, the chairs leather-covered and large. There was a table under the window with a chair pulled up to it, its surface scattered with books and papers, and another small table with a reading lamp kept company with an easy chair in a corner. The desk took up a good deal of one wall; it was piled high with papers, books and pamphlets. Isobel longed to tidy it up and wondered what would happen if she did—the doctor would probably go spare. She pictured Mrs Gibson tiptoeing round with a feather duster, not disturbing a single sheet of paper.

She glanced at the doctor and found him staring at her. She went a guilty red and he said: 'You should learn to hide your thoughts, Isobel; you long to organise my desk, don't you?' and when she nodded: 'Well, you're not going to.' He got up and came and stood in front of her so that she had to tilt her head back to see his face. 'Here's a cheque for your first week—I'm told that the correct thing is for me to pay them, but if I did so I daresay you might have to wait a couple of weeks for your fee, which seems hardly fair. Don't, whatever you do, give them any of that money, I'll settle with them separately. How is Nanny?' he added.

'Very comfortable. She's up and dressed and Mrs Gibson is with her while I'm here.'

He nodded. 'I'll get her downstairs into the small sitting room so that anyone passing through the hall can keep an eye on her. Do you suppose she'd be up to getting some clothes in a couple of days? When you get back tomorrow, perhaps? Gibson can drive you and get her in and out of the shops.' He studied his nails thoughtfully. 'She'd better go somewhere they'll have all she needs, then she can sit quietly and choose everything from her chair.' He wandered off across the room to look out of the window. 'Better still, how about you getting a selection of things for her to choose from? Pretty dresses and so forth.' He sounded vague and Isobel smiled a little. He turned round to look at her. 'She's unlikely to go out in the foreseeable future, but get her a coat and a hat just the same.'

He didn't explain further, but she didn't need to be told, she said quietly: 'Very well, I'll get her measurements and shop when I get back tomorrow.'

'You'd better go to Harrods—I've got an account there. I'll give them a ring presently. Go to the Accounts Department and say who you are. Now shall we have lunch? I've got a busy afternoon before me.'

Just as though she had been hindering him! Isobel thought indignantly.

She got home much sooner than she expected. They had eaten lunch with a minimum of talk, and that concerning Nanny, and after making sure that her patient had all she needed and that Mrs Gibson knew what to do in an emergency, Isobel hurried out of the house. Gibson was standing on the steps and there was a Daimler Sovereign parked at the kerb. He said, 'Good afternoon, Nurse,' just as though he hadn't been serving her lunch not an hour since, took her case from her and opened the car door. 'Dr Winter asked me to drive you to your home. Where would that be, Nurse?'

'Clapham Common—the far side, twenty-four, Jordan Street, and thank you, Gibson.'

'A pleasure, Nurse. I'll fetch you tomorrow at noon, if that suits you?'

A mere figure of speech, of course. Dr Winter would have said noon and noon it would be, whether it suited her or not. 'That would do very well,' she said pleasantly; after all, she shouldn't look a gift horse in the mouth.

Her mother was coming out of the house as Gibson stopped before its door, but she put the key straight back in the lock and opened the door again. 'Darling, how lovely!' She came down the path and smiled at Gibson and when Isobel introduced him offered a hand. 'You have no idea what an awkward journey it is from your part of the world to ours,' she commented chattily. 'Can I offer you tea before you go back?'

Gibson's boot face had become quite human. 'Thank you, no, ma'am, I have to get back at once. I'll be here at noon tomorrow to drive you back, Nurse.'

He got out of the car and carried Isobel's case to the door, wished them good day and drove off.

'Goodness me,' observed Mrs Barrington, 'he's like something out of another world—I mean, you just don't meet people like that any more; they wear jeans and long hair and call you love.'

'Dr Winter has got a house full of people just like Gibson,' said Isobel, and hugged her mother. 'I'm to stay there another week, and I've got my first week's cheque—I'm supposed to wait and get it from the agency, but Dr Winter bends rules when they don't suit him.' She picked up her case. 'I'll dump this lot in my room and we'll do the shopping. I've got twenty-four hours off to get some more clothes, and I must get my uniforms washed ready for the next case…'

'That will give me something to do when you've gone again, darling. I haven't much shopping, let's get it done and then have an early tea and a good gossip. I'm longing to hear about your trip and the old lady…' Mrs Barrington was longing to hear about Dr Winter too, but she was too cunning to say so. A few questions carefully put, later on…

She didn't glean much, though. Isobel, accustomed to telling her mother almost everything concerning her own doings, found herself quite unable to talk about the doctor. She admitted that he was good-looking, quite young, presumably comfortably off, devoted to his old nanny and living in some style, but these sparse titbits were all that Mrs Barrington was offered. She was left frustrated and intrigued; Isobel was being remarkably reticent. She reflected that Isobel would be there for another week—a lot could happen in a week. Mrs Barrington's daydreams might be farfetched and absurd, but she was a devoted mother; Isobel would make a specially splendid wife and Dr Winter was unmarried, surely their rather unusual journey to Gdansk had provided just the right background for romance?

Luckily for her she wasn't there when Isobel met Dr Winter on her return the next day. He was coming down the stairs as she entered the house and growled out a greeting from a face as black as thunder. Isobel wasn't to know that Nanny had been reading him a lecture, blandly ignoring the fact that he was a grown man and not the small boy she had looked after so lovingly. It was time that he married, she had told him in no uncertain terms—'And not that pert miss who came upstairs unasked to see me while she was waiting for you to come home yesterday afternoon,' Nanny breathed fire. 'She called me Nanny, the saucebox!'

The doctor had preserved a calm manner, but he had had a tiring busy morning at the hospital and it was years since anyone had even made a timid attempt to query his lifestyle or what he did and why. He had cut the old lady politely short and with the excuse that he had work to do, had made for his study, only to meet Isobel's placid gaze as he reached the bottom of the staircase. The calm enquiry in her look incensed him even more and he snapped: 'You're late!'

Isobel might be unassuming in appearance, but a loud cross voice and beetle brows left her unmoved. 'No, I'm not,' she spoke in the soothing voice she would have used towards a difficult patient or a grumpy child. 'You said noon, Dr Winter.'

There was a magnificent grandfather clock at the foot of the stairs. It wheezed obligingly and began a ponderous striking; it took some time to get to the last of the twelve chimes. 'You see?' observed Isobel kindly. 'I daresay you've had a busy morning.'

'My God,' said Dr Winter, 'you're as bad as Nanny!' He disappeared into his study and shut the door with a restrained slam. Isobel went on up the stairs to her room and then along to see how Mrs Olbinski fared.

The old lady was glad to see her. 'I've been a bit lonely, as you might say,' she observed, 'not but what it's a pleasure to have old friends round me but you've got a way with you, I suppose. I'll have my lunch now you're back and I've made a list of the clothes Mr Thomas says I'm to have, only you'll need to measure me.' She looked sideways at Isobel. 'In a temper, he is, just because I told him not to marry that silly young woman…' A slow tear trickled down one cheek, and Isobel wiped it away gently and put an arm round the thin shoulders.

'I wondered why he was cross when I came in,' she remarked matter-of-factly. 'But I'm sure he'll have forgotten all about it in no time at all. Look, how about measuring you before lunch, then I'll go down and see what there is for you. Do you fancy anything special?'

'A nice little lamb chop with a bit of mashed potato and one of Mrs Gibson's jelly creams. It's not like him to be angry. Perhaps I shouldn't have come here… I'm going to be a nuisance to him.' Another tear had to be wiped away.

'Now that's nonsense and you know it, Mrs Olbinski.' Isobel dropped a kiss on her patient's cheek and busied herself with notebook and pen and the tape measure Mrs Olbinski had in her handbag, and presently in the excitement of being measured for new clothes and weighing the advantages of navy blue against brown, Mrs Olbinski cheered up.

Lunch was at one o'clock. Isobel saw her patient comfortably settled at a small table with her lunch before her and went downstairs to the dining room. She felt sure she would be on her own. Dr Winter was in no mood for company, but he was there, standing in front of his fireplace with his hands in his pockets and an expressionless face. Still cross, she decided, and took her place wordlessly.

There was no conversation with the soup. He was behaving like a small spoilt boy, and she found it surprisingly pathetic. She said cheerfully: 'My mother was very glad to see me; it was kind of you to send me home in the car and fetch me back as well.'

'I'm delighted to hear it.' He waved away the pudding Gibson was offering. 'You'll excuse me, I have a busy afternoon ahead of me. Take a taxi to Harrods and return in one, Isobel.'

She said cheerfully: 'Oh, but the walk will do me good…'

'Be so good as to do as I ask. You'll be reimbursed.'

She started indignantly: 'Well, I had no intention…' but he had gone.

Even if she had wanted to, she had no chance to disobey him. Gibson had a taxi waiting for her when she came downstairs to leave the house, and to tell the truth, she was glad to have one back, she had so many boxes and parcels. The amount of money she had spent made her feel quite faint, although she was well within the limit Dr Winter had set—indeed, the saleslady, knowing this, had tried hard to sell her a fur-lined raincoat, assuring her that it would be a most useful garment for an elderly lady.

'She's not very active,' observed Isobel, and eyed the garment with envy. Dr Winter's bride would be a lucky young woman; if he didn't cavil at a few hundred pounds for his old nanny, he certainly wouldn't begrudge his wife a magnificent wardrobe.

She was back at the house by five o'clock, which just went to show, she reflected, that if one had sufficient money, one could buy all one wanted in a couple of hours if necessary.

Gibson, ever on the alert, fetched in her parcels from the taxi and carried them upstairs. 'I don't suppose you had time for tea, Nurse?' he asked.

'Well, no, Gibson, I didn't, but it's rather late…'

'Not at all, Nurse, it shall be brought up to Nanny's room.'

She gave him a grateful smile. 'That's very kind of you, Gibson. I'm sorry to give you the trouble.'

'If I may say so, Nurse, you're no trouble to myself or anyone else working here.'

Isobel flung off her jacket and hurried to Nanny's room, to find that lady in a ferment of excitement. They spent the next hour or more unwrapping things and trying them on. 'You said navy blue or brown,' said Isobel, 'but when I saw this dress I knew it would suit you.' She held up a fine wool dress in a paisley pattern of soft blues and deep red. 'Isn't it pretty? And these slippers—so soft, and don't you love the little bows on them? You'll have to get up every day, Mrs Olbinski, so you can wear all these pretty things.' She rummaged among the piles of tissue paper. 'And I bought this hat, although they said if you didn't like it I could return it. It matches the coat very well.' She popped a smart matronly velvet toque on her patient's head and handed her a mirror. 'Isn't it smashing?'

'Oh, decidedly,' said Dr Winter from the door. 'We'll have to take you out in that, Nanny, it deserves a larger audience than two.' He came into the room and bent to kiss her cheek. 'Has Isobel chosen well? Is there anything you still need?'

The old lady caught his hand and held it tightly. 'Mr Thomas, you've given me everything I've ever wanted—all these lovely clothes and living in your beautiful house and having this dear child to look after me.'

'You looked after me for a good many years, Nanny,' he reminded her cheerfully. 'Would you like to come down to dinner this evening? It's a chance to wear that new dress.'

So Isobel dressed Mrs Olbinski up in the new dress, put on the pretty slippers, arranged her hair nicely and led her to the wall mirror to have a look.

'Well, I never—I am smart, aren't I?' declared Nanny. She turned to Isobel. 'A lot of trouble it must have been for you, child.' She paused. 'You can call me Nanny.'

'Oh, may I? You wouldn't think it too familiar? I mean, I hardly know you or anyone here, and I'll be gone in a few days, you know.'

Nanny gave her a sharp look. 'Yes, well, I suppose there's those that might need you more than I do. I'll be sorry to see you go, though. And not only me will be sorry. Now sit me down somewhere, dear, and go and pretty yourself up.'

Isobel spent five precious minutes deciding whether to wear the Marks and Spencer cotton voile new for the summer or a cream linen dress of impeccable taste which did nothing for her except to make her look older than she was and douse her mousey hair to even greater mousiness. She decided on the linen; it seemed suitable for her status in the household and no one was likely to give her a second glance.

She was mistaken there. The doctor looked at her several times, wondering why she had made no attempt to make the most of her not unattractive person. She looked like a strict governess or a frightfully efficient personal assistant to some executive; all she needed was a pair of specs. She looked up once and caught him staring at her and put up a questing hand to tidy her hair, looking faintly questioning, and because he was essentially a kind man he said: 'You look very nice, Isobel,' and watched her pinken with pleasure. Poor girl, he mused, sipping his whisky, she's had to put up with quite a lot during the last week. He laid himself out to be pleasant, making Nanny laugh and Isobel smile widely, and felt relief when Gibson appeared in the doorway to say that dinner was served.

There was a commotion in the hall as he spoke and Ella Stokes darted past him to fling herself at the doctor.

'Thomas, you beast!' she shrilled. 'You wouldn't take me out this evening, so I've come to see for myself what's stopping you.' She glanced at Mrs Olbinski and Isobel and dismissed them; there was nothing about either of them, in her opinion, to prevent him leaving them alone for the evening. She put up a hand and straightened his tie and he frowned a little. 'Look, I dressed up specially for you,' she wheedled. 'It's new—do you like it?'

She twirled round, and expensive chiffon and silk floated beguilingly round her. 'We'll have to go somewhere quiet because you haven't changed, but there's a little Italian place…'

Dr Winter took her hand very gently from his tie. 'Sorry, Ella, we're having a little celebration dinner in honour of Nanny.'

She pouted prettily. 'Oh, Nanny wouldn't mind—would you, Nanny?' she asked over her shoulder, to be met by one of Nanny's glacial stares, perfected after years of dealing with naughty children. Ella wilted a little but recovered enough to add: 'You've got Nurse—it is Nurse, isn't it?—to keep you company.'

'But I mind, Ella,' said the doctor quietly, 'and I'm having my dinner here in my own house because I want to.'

Ella's pretty face was ugly with rage for a moment, but the next instant her smile was as sweet as ever. 'OK, darling Thomas, so you'd better invite me to join you. I'm not going home to eat something on a tray in a brand new dress that's cost the earth.'

It was impossible to tell if Dr Winter was pleased or not. Isobel, sitting quietly on the fringe of things, couldn't even begin to guess. She finished her drink and watched Ella skilfully take over the conversation. She could be very amusing, and whether the doctor was pleased that she was there or not, she had him laughing long before Gibson came for the second time to say that dinner was served.

She was the life and soul of the evening after that, praising the food, toasting Nanny, who stared back at her with eyes like pebbles, ignoring Isobel completely except to remark unforgivably: 'You shouldn't wear that colour, you know—it makes you a complete non-person, no colour—you haven't much anyway, have you? I suppose being in that dreary uniform stunts any dress sense you might have.'

Isobel said nothing, although her head teemed with rude words. It was Dr Winter who answered for her. 'You're quite wrong, Ella,' he declared. 'I thought how nice Isobel looked. I should imagine that her taste is excellent.'

'There are some,' began Nanny weightily, 'who have no taste in clothes but enough money to go to a shop where they'll be fitted out right. And we don't all need to dress like peacocks and flaunt our bosoms to catch a man's eye.'

Isobel, who had been feeling like crying, found herself stifling a giggle but a glance at the doctor's face told her that for once she was seeing him out of his depth. She said in her calm way: 'Clothes are a fascinating topic, aren't they? and some of them are so lovely—I could have spent a fortune in Harrods…'

Ella turned her blue eyes on her. 'Harrods? Isn't Marks and Spencer more in your line?'

'Oh, yes,' said Isobel, still calm, 'I was getting some things for Mrs Olbinski. We couldn't bring back much with us, you see.'

'Oh, that boring trip!' declared Ella. She turned a ravishing smile on Dr Winter. 'You're really rather a darling, rescuing people from dreary places.'

'I wouldn't call Poland dreary even under present conditions, as a matter of fact, we had a couple of very pleasant days there, didn't we, Nanny?'

He went on from there talking about this and that, keeping away from personal matters, but for Mrs Olbinski the evening was spoilt, and for Isobel too, although she told herself that it didn't matter in the least what the wretched girl said. She would probably never see her again, only it would be a great pity if Ella married Dr Winter. She was a clever young woman, used to getting her own way. Nanny would be out of the house and into some old people's home before the doctor would know what was happening.

It was a good thing that shortly after dinner Mrs Olbinski declared that she was tired and wanted to go to bed, so that Isobel naturally enough went with her, wishing Ella goodnight as she went upstairs behind the doctor carrying Nanny. Before he left them he invited Isobel to join them again once Nanny was settled. Her refusal was pleasant and firm; the less she saw of the horrid creature downstairs the better.

Nanny wasn't all that tired; she had a great deal to say about ill-bred young women who should know better. 'The impertinence of her!' she fumed in her peevish old voice. 'Inviting herself to dinner for all the world as though she was one of the family! What Mr Thomas sees in her I do not know.' Her voice came muffled by the nightgown Isobel was drawing over her head. 'And don't you listen to a word she says, Isobel—you look like a lady in that dress, and very nice you were when she was so rude. You might have come from my nursery.' Which remark Isobel recognised as the greatest compliment.

'I had a nanny when I was small,' she told her companion. 'She left to get married when I went to school; she lives in Australia and she still writes to me.'

Mrs Olbinski nodded. 'You're a lady, that I can see—knew it the moment I clapped eyes on you. Fallen on hard times, have you?'

Isobel tucked her into her bed and then sat down on its edge.

'Well, yes. My father died ten years ago and we had to leave my home. We live at Clapham Common, a little terraced house, and my mother is quite wonderful about it. I've got a brother too—he's at school and very clever. He'll go on to university…'

'And that's why you're a nurse.' Nanny patted her hand gently. 'Wouldn't you rather be in a hospital?'

'Yes, of course, but private nursing is well paid, you see.' She added cheerfully, 'It's interesting too, I never know what sort of case I shall get next.' She bent and kissed an elderly cheek. 'Now you're going to sleep. I'm going to bed too. Goodnight, Nanny.'

She was eating a solitary breakfast the next morning when Dr Winter came into the dining room. He didn't bother with a 'good morning'. 'I'm sorry about yesterday evening; Ella doesn't mean half the things she says—she's an only child, and spoilt…'

'Please don't apologise, Dr Winter. It didn't matter a bit, although I think Nanny was a bit upset, that's because she's got a bit out of touch during the last few years—I mean, people don't behave as they did ten years ago.'

'Perhaps not. Can you suggest anything to make her feel better about it?'

'It would be nice if she could go for a quiet drive now and again—if you could spare Gibson to drive. She's longing to wear her new clothes. She told me that she had a niece living at Peckham Rye.'

'A splendid idea. Of course she can go whenever she wants—we'll manage without Gibson for an hour or two.'

Isobel looked down at her plate. 'I can drive,' she told him quite quietly.

He pulled out a chair and sat down and poured himself some coffee.

'Another of your accomplishments, Isobel? Could you tackle the traffic in town?'

'Yes, I think so.' She wasn't going to tell him that she had often driven her mother up to London after her father had died. She hadn't driven much since, of course, but she wasn't nervous.

'Good, you can have the Sovereign tomorrow afternoon.'

She thanked him quietly, pleasantly surprised that he hadn't heaped her with warnings and doubts as to whether she was capable of driving or not. At least he trusted her; a nice warm glow crept under her ribs and she smiled at nothing in particular. Just for a moment she looked pretty, and the doctor, getting up to go, paused to take another look. She wasn't to be compared with Ella or any of the other young women she supposed he knew, but she was a great deal more restful.

CHAPTER FIVE

THE NEXT FEW days were rather fun. Isobel settled Nanny, dressed in her finery, in the back of the car, got into the driver's seat and once she had gained Vauxhall Bridge, tooled it down the Camberwell Road to Peckham. Of course once she left the main road, she got lost amongst the narrow rows of small brick houses, all exactly alike, but finally she arrived and rang the bell of a similar house, its tiny front garden filled with gnomes and small shrubs struggling to survive. There had been no time to let Nanny's niece know of their coming, so when the door was flung open by a young man in his shirt sleeves, Isobel said baldly: 'Good afternoon, I've brought Mrs Olbinski to visit her niece.'

For a moment he started and stared at her in utter surprise. 'Aunty Ethel…here? How did she get here, then?'

'Dr Winter fetched her from Poland.'

He smiled then. 'Well, I'll be jiggered—wait till I tell Ma!' He suited the action to the word and bellowed over his shoulder, 'Where is she, then?'

'In the car. She can't walk very well—if you could carry her inside…?'

And from then on it was excited greetings, endless cups of strong tea, neighbours popping in and a glass of port all round to mark the occasion.

It was difficult to prise Nanny loose from her family, and only then with the promise that they would come again the next day—'and we'll have a proper tea for you, Aunty, and Nurse here.'

It was obvious to Isobel that this was to be the pattern of their days until she left, and since the doctor made no objection, she drove each afternoon to Peckham Rye and after a splendid tea and endless talk, drove back again. By the time the doctor got back in the evening, Nanny was once more in her dressing gown, sitting in her easy chair, waiting for her supper.

It made a long day, not that there was much to do, but Nanny liked to talk, which slowed up dressing and meals considerably, so that Isobel had little time alone. In the evenings when she would have loved an hour or so to herself, she had dinner with Dr Winter, who while not talking overmuch, expected her presence at his table. He asked about Nanny, of course, and visited her each day, but seemed preoccupied, Isobel thought, not exactly worried, but weighing the pros and cons about something or other. Perhaps he was worried about a patient; if it hadn't been for his austere expression she might have been tempted to ask. It wasn't until her week was half over that he observed during the soup: 'Well, you haven't much to say for yourself, have you?'

Tired, she thought, and peevish with it. She said soothingly, 'It seemed to me that you didn't want to talk, so I didn't. And if you'd rather be alone do say so. I don't mind a bit having my dinner somewhere else—I could always have a tray with Nanny; she likes company…'

'Meaning that I don't.' He sounded savage.

'Certainly not,' she said reasonably. 'And if you stopped to think, you'd realise what a silly thing to say that was.'

He looked at her with interest. 'And what exactly do you mean by that, Isobel?'

'Well, you come back from a day's work, glad to get away from patients and hospitals and illness; the last person you want to see is someone who reminds you of all those things…'

'So what do you suggest I do?' His smile was mocking and amused.

She ignored that. 'Go out to dinner, or have someone to dine with you—someone like Miss Ella Stokes.'

'And she'll guarantee me a delightful evening?' His voice was silky.

'I should think so; she's so very pretty and she makes you laugh…'

'And you don't?'

Isobel shook her head. 'No.' She added thoughtfully, 'Not that kind of laughing.'

He didn't answer that. Presently he said: 'I spoke to Carl on the phone today—they send you their love. They hope they'll see you again one day.'

'I liked them; I'd love to see them again, but of course I'm not likely to.'

He raised his eyebrows. 'Do you not care to travel, Isobel?'

'Well, of course I do, but I don't get many chances; I shan't forget these last two weeks.'

He examined the dish of vegetables being offered to him and didn't look at her. 'Neither shall I.' And when Gibson had left the room: 'Have you a boyfriend, Isobel?'

The question was so unexpected that she just sat and goggled at him until presently she managed: 'No, I've never had one. I'm not likely to either.'

'Why not?'

'I'm plain,' she pointed out patiently, 'you can see that for yourself. Even if I weren't I don't have much chance to meet people—men…'

Gibson came back into the room to clear the plates and hand the pudding, and when he had gone again she said composedly: 'If I'm to leave here on the day after tomorrow, would you mind if I telephoned the agency in the morning? So that if there's another case I can take it at once.'

'Why not give yourself a few days' break?' he asked perfunctorily.

'This case has been a very easy one, Dr Winter—I don't need a break.'

'You don't mind if we have our coffee here? I have some work to do. You take the next case that comes along, never mind where it is?'

'Well, yes.'

'So very soon Nanny will become a vague memory.'

She handed him his cup. 'No, she won't. I like Nanny very much, I'm going to miss her and I'll not forget her.'

'But you'll forget me?' he asked blandly.

'You haven't been my patient, Dr Winter.'

'You haven't answered my question, Isobel.' He gave her a small mocking smile, but she didn't smile back at him. Of course she wouldn't forget him; he was going to be with her for the rest of her life, in her dreams, beneath her eyelids when she closed her eyes, reflected in every mirror, his voice in her ear—and what a time to discover that! With him sitting opposite her, watching her like a hawk—and how could she have been in love with him and never known it until that moment?

She looked at him steadily, her face composed. 'No, I shan't forget you, Dr Winter. We shared quite an exciting week—at least, it was exciting for me.'

He nodded unsmiling. 'I think I might say the same. It only remains for me to thank you for your help, Isobel. And now, if you'll excuse me…'

She got up too, said goodnight quietly and went up to her room. It was a little too soon to settle Nanny for the night and she was glad of half an hour to herself.

It was going to be difficult, going away knowing that she would never see him again, but it was something she would have to face up to. She had had schoolgirl crushes, even supposed herself in love with a young houseman at the hospital where she had trained, but she knew that she loved Thomas Winter with a depth of feeling that wasn't going to be dismissed lightly. Even if she never set eyes on him again, it would make no difference to her love. It was just as well, she reminded herself sensibly, that he didn't like her very much.

Nanny was tired and a bit crotchety, so Isobel drew up a chair to the bed, picked up the book the old lady had been reading, and offered to read to her until she felt sleepy. It was a simple romantic story in which the girl was quite obviously going to marry the man before the last page, and Nanny listened avidly, so that when Isobel paused before the final chapter she was told in no uncertain terms to read that too.

'I'll sleep better if I know the pair of them are to wed,' declared Nanny.

So Isobel read on, glad that the final chapter was a short one. She read the satisfactory finish with a faint wistfulness; real life wasn't like that, at least not for her. But Nanny gave a happy sigh. 'That's how it should be,' she declared, 'a nice happy ending for each and every soul in love. And it's time you were wed, Isobel.'

'Isobel is wedded to her work,' said Dr Winter from the door, 'and you aren't asleep, Nanny. Why?'

Isobel laid the book down and got to her feet. 'I'll come back presently,' she murmured, and made for the door, to be turned back by a firm hand.

'No need, I've only come to say goodnight to Nanny, and you may as well stay and hear what I have to say.'

He went and sat on the old lady's bed and picked up a knotted hand. 'I'm going away for a couple of days,' he told her, 'but I'll be back the day after tomorrow—in the late evening. Isobel is leaving us that morning, but Mrs Gibson will look after you, my dear, and Gibson will take you for a drive in the afternoon.'

Nanny looked into his face. 'You're very good to me, Mr Thomas, and it's lovely to be among old friends.' She gave a little cough. 'I'm sorry Isobel's going, but of course she has other patients, I daresay.' She presented a cheek for his kiss. 'I'll see you in two days' time, then.'

He got up and went to the door; his 'goodnight, Isobel', was impersonal and he didn't look at her for more than a second. When he had gone she went over to the bed and saw at once that Nanny was crying.

'But the doctor will be back in no time at all,' she comforted her, and Nanny said quite fiercely: 'That's not why I'm crying, my dear.' She dried her eyes. 'I'm going to sleep now, so you can say goodnight.'

Isobel went to bed too and hardly slept a wink, and just as she was dropping off wearily at six o'clock, Nanny called.

'I'm parched for a nice cup of tea,' she said. 'I know it's early, but would it be bothering you to boil a kettle—you could have a cup with me.'

So Isobel crept downstairs, the house silent around her, and went along to the kitchen and made tea. She was carrying the tray across the hall when the study door opened and Dr Winter came out, so that she stopped rather suddenly and cried: 'My goodness, you gave me a fright!' And then: 'It's tea for Nanny.'

'Hasn't she slept?'

'Oh yes.'

His eyes searched her face, rather pale from sleeplessness and wreathed around by a cloud of mousy hair. 'But you haven't.'

She wondered why he was there, shaved and dressed ready for the day, and then remembered that he was going away. If she hadn't come down for the tea she would never have seen him. 'You're going away,' she said. 'You weren't going to say goodbye.' She added matter-of-factly: 'Of course, there's no earthly reason why you should. I hope you have a—a nice time.'

He didn't answer her but took the tray and set it on a nearby table. 'You feel I should have wished you goodbye, Isobel? By all means let us do the thing properly, then.'

He caught her close and kissed her hard, set her free and said blandly: 'I didn't expect to see you again, Isobel.'

He stood looking at her for a moment, her face puffy from a bad night, her hair wild, her sensible dressing gown bundled on anyhow, then he picked up the tray and put it into her hands once more, and all the while she stood speechless. It was only when he said in an offhand way, 'That tea will get cold', that she scuttled away and up the stairs, almost falling over her own feet in her hurry to get away from him as quickly as possible. He had thought so little of her that he had intended leaving without a word of goodbye, and yet he had kissed her in such a fashion—it had amused him to do so, perhaps, and he would forget all about it within an hour, whereas she would have to remember it for the rest of her life.

The day, begun so early, seemed to be twice its usual length. Isobel took Nanny to Peckham Rye, played cards with her until she was ready for bed and then went to bed herself. She had packed her few things, received her wages; an envelope with her name scrawled upon it in Dr Winter's fierce handwriting and nothing but a cheque inside, and telephoned her mother to expect her during the next afternoon. There was nothing more to be done now; fate couldn't be altered.

Gibson drove her back home, assuring her that it had been the doctor's orders that he should do so, and Isobel was glad of it for what with Nanny's tearful goodbyes, and Mrs Gibson's regretful farewell, not to mention those of the housemaid, the daily help and the old man who did odd jobs and kept the small, delightfully colourful garden behind the house in apple-pie order, she was feeling tearful herself. And at the house even Gibson's controlled features relaxed as he wished her goodbye. 'We shall all miss you, Nurse,' he assured her. 'It's been a pleasure to have you in the house.'

She smiled mistily at him. 'Oh, Gibson, I've been so happy there!'

Her mother opened the front door then and she shot inside,

afraid that she would blot her copybook by bursting into tears in the street.

Her mother kissed her, ignored her watery looks and said briskly: 'I've just made the tea. I expect you made some good friends at Dr Winter's, didn't you? What an unusual case it was, going all that way to fetch Mrs Olbinski. I hope Dr Winter thanked you properly.'

Isobel sat down in one of the shabby armchairs. She remembered vividly how he had kissed her and went a little pale. She said: 'Oh, yes. He's away from home now.' She mustered a smile. 'I shall miss Nanny—she had such a sharp tongue, but she was an old dear. I've been paid too—we'll go to the bank tomorrow and then I'll go along to the agency…'

Mrs Barrington poured the tea. 'Not even one day off, darling? You do need time to relax, you know.'

'Well, I thought I'd have tomorrow free; get my clothes sorted out and wash the smalls, and I'll take you out to lunch.'

'That will be lovely, darling, and now tell me all about your trip—I've always wanted to go to Stockholm…'

The agency, when Isobel called the next day, were able to offer her a new case on the following day—a well known film actress, the agency lady told her, and mentioned a name Isobel had never heard of, suffering most regrettably from mumps.

'You've had them, of course?' asked the agency lady, fixing Isobel with a sharp eye, and relaxed when she said she had. 'It shouldn't be a long case, Miss Barrington—you'll be expected to live in, of course. She has a studio flat somewhere off the Brompton Road.' She smiled frostily. 'Dr Winter was very satisfied with your services. I can't say that we were altogether pleased with the way in which he handled the financial side of it, but he's too valuable a client to argue with.' The smile was switched off. 'You will take the case, Miss Barrington?'

'Oh, yes,' said Isobel; a film actress, even with mumps, might help to take her mind off Thomas Winter.

It hadn't helped at all, Isobel admitted as she got wearily into bed at the end of her first day at Miranda le Creux's flat. If her own small shabby home had seemed cramped after the doctor's spacious home, Miranda's seemed even worse. Not that it was small—the rooms were large and lofty—but stuffed so full of flounced dressing tables, over-stuffed chairs, white rugs thick and shaggy enough to lose one's feet in, extravagantly draped curtains half covering net ruffles over the windows, and blown-up photos of Miranda in every conceivable position, that there was hardly room to turn round. Isobel discovered her patient lying in a king-size bed with a brocade headboard and a fur coverlet. Probably a very pretty girl, if the photos were to be believed, but just now with swollen jaws which turned her into a caricature of herself. Isobel felt instant sympathy, cooled, however, by her reception.

'There you are!' exclaimed Miss le Creux. 'I hope you know your work. I've never felt so ill in all my life, and Dr Martin actually dared to laugh at me this morning! It's vital that I get well quickly—I've landed a super modelling job in Cyprus. You'll have to do something about it.'

'I expect the doctor will have you well soon enough—mumps make you feel rotten, but they're soon over.' Isobel spoke with a calm certainty and her patient muttered, 'Oh, well, you'd better be right. You're not to let anyone in to see me. Nurse, there's a daily maid, Winnie—I've given her something to keep her mouth shut; and don't you dare tell anyone either.'

'I'm not in the habit of discussing my patients, Miss le Creux,' said Isobel gently. 'And now, since Doctor Martin is coming later on this morning, suppose you have a bath while I make the bed and tidy up?'

She had never known a patient make such a fuss. It wasn't as if Miss le Creux had a high temperature or a sore throat. Isobel thought of Nanny, tied in knots with arthritis and never complaining, and naturally her thoughts went straight to Thomas Winter; she thought of him lovingly and sadly, wondering what he would be doing and whether he had spared a single thought for her since she had left his house. She was sure he hadn't.

Miss le Creux shrieking from the bathroom brought her unhappy thoughts to a halt, and the rest of her day was taken up completely with ministering to that young lady's wants. She didn't need a nurse, Isobel decided sleepily as she climbed into her bed in the over-furnished room next to her patient's, but if she chose to have one and pay for it, that was her business. Isobel flung one of the fat frilled pillows on to the floor, her last waking thought predictably of Dr Winter. He would have had the mumps, she decided; he led the kind of well-ordered life which wouldn't tolerate anything likely to disrupt its smooth passage. He must have been a dear little boy. She wished she had asked Nanny about him, but that would have been a gross impertinence. Perhaps it was as well that she didn't know too much about him, she might forget him all the sooner.

As the slow week crawled towards its end, she wondered just how long it took to forget someone you loved—well, forget wasn't the right word; she would never forget him, but somehow or other she had to push him out of sight at the back of her mind. Only he wouldn't go. He popped up at the oddest times, especially when Miss le Creux was being extra tiresome and she found herself longing to drop everything and leave the flat. She couldn't do that, of course. Bobby's school fees loomed on the horizon, and they were an ever-present spur to work, but she longed foolishly for the weeks to roll back, so that she might find herself in Dr Winter's house, looking at the portraits on the walls and then watching the door open as he came into the elegant room.

It was half way through the second week before Dr Martin assured his patient that there was no reason at all which should prevent her getting out into the fresh air and resuming a normal life. 'You're not ill, young lady,' he boomed at her. 'The sooner you go out and about, the sooner your face will resume its normal proportions.' A remark which sent Miss le Creux to the nearest mirror to give her lovely, empty face a close examination.

'Do I sag?' she demanded of Isobel. 'What did he mean? I won't have my career ruined!'

Isobel paused in her endless tidying after her patient had dragged herself out of her bed. 'You look perfectly all right to me,' she said tartly. 'I can think of lots of actresses, famous ones, who aren't in the least pretty. I don't know what you're worrying about.'

'Of course you don't,' snapped Miss le Creux, 'how could you possibly? You're so plain you don't need to worry about your face at all. But I suppose that doesn't matter to you—nurses are supposed to be wedded to their work, aren't they?' She gave a little titter and turned back to the mirror. 'I must say you've been quite nice; I suppose I must take Dr Martin's advice and get around a bit. Your week's up in two days, isn't it? You might as well go tomorrow. I suppose I settle up with the agency?'

'Yes, I'm afraid they'll expect you to pay for the full week even if I leave a day earlier.'

Miss le Creux turned astonished blue eyes on her. 'Like hell they will! But I shouldn't worry, my boyfriend will see to all that anyway. Do I have to tip you?'

'No,' said Isobel stonily. Miranda le Creux might be very pretty, she might even be talented, but she had what Isobel's mother would have called no background. True, most patients gave their nurse some small gift when they left, but it was given with gratitude and accepted in the spirit in which it was given, and it certainly wasn't expected. She suddenly wanted to leave as soon as possible and be sent to a case where she really had to nurse someone who needed nursing. She went along to the kitchen to ask Winnie for her patient's morning coffee, her heart so full of longing for Thomas Winter that her chest felt as though it might burst. It was lovely to go down the stairs of the block of flats where Miranda le Creux lived and through the entrance door into the street and know that she was free of the tiresome girl and her dreadful flat. Isobel nipped smartly to the nearest bus stop and set off for home. She would have to ring the agency when she got there and tell them she had left and find out about another case, but at least she would have the rest of the day, perhaps longer.

Her mother was in the garden, hanging up the washing with Blossom gavotting round her feet. She put the clothes pegs down at once as soon as she saw Isobel and said happily: 'Hullo darling, are you back for good, or is this a day off?'

'For good, thank heavens.' Isobel whisked Blossom on to her shoulder. 'Gosh, it's nice to be here!'

'We'll have coffee—oh, there's a parcel for you—quite a small one. It came three days ago, but you said not to send anything on…'

It was quite small, square and neatly wrapped, and her name and address were typed on a label. Isobel turned it over several times and then unwrapped it slowly. The box inside was leather, and when she opened it there was an amber necklace carefully coiled inside on the velvet. There was a card inside written in Dr Winter's fierce hand. 'To Isobel, with my thanks.' It was signed T. W.

'How charming,' observed Mrs Barrington, peering over Isobel's shoulder. 'The necklace, I mean—and what a businesslike little note.'

'Well, he didn't like me very much, Mother,' said Isobel soberly.

'So why this really lovely amber necklace?'

Isobel touched it with a gentle finger. The day they had taken Nanny out for a drive they had stopped in Sopot and looked in a small shop tucked away in one of the side streets. The necklace had been in its window and she had admired it. And he had bought it, but perhaps not for her; she would never know that. 'I must write and thank him,' she said quietly, and closed the box, then because she knew that her mother was looking at her thoughtfully, added brightly: 'Amber's very common in

Poland, you know. I believe you can buy it in most of the Baltic countries. It will look very nice with that brown dress…'

'It'll look lovely with your blue—I should wear it, darling, not put it away in a drawer.'

So Isobel put on the blue dress and the amber necklace and that evening composed a stiff little note of thanks. She had no idea that it would be so hard to write to someone you loved who didn't love you, without letting them see how she felt. It reached the doctor the following morning, and he read it several times with an inscrutable face and then put it carefully in his pocket.

There was another case for Isobel when she rang the agency—an elderly man living in Hampstead; a heart failure, too ill to be moved, and perhaps she wouldn't mind going along that evening, suggested the agency lady. A car would be sent for her at nine o'clock. Isobel hesitated; she had planned to have a day at home and was on the point of saying so when the voice at the other end said: 'It'll be a very short case, Miss Barrington—perhaps only a day or possibly two at the most.'

So she packed her case once more and when an elderly chauffeur-driven car drew up outside the front door, she said goodbye to her mother and got in. The chauffeur was elderly too, and since she had got in beside him, he was willing to talk, so by the time that they had reached the house, she knew that her patient was over eighty, a widower with a scattered family, a faithful but elderly housekeeper, the chauffeur and a couple of daily helps. 'So we're all at sixes and sevens,' said the chauffeur, 'Mrs Wills not being that young any more, as you might say, and the two women who come in not knowing what to do. Doctor said we'd have to have a nurse straight away. Did you count on staying up all night, miss?'

'No, but I can,' said Isobel bracingly. 'I'm just back from an easy case and I'm not tired.' She peered out. 'Is this it?'

They had entered a short drive and stopped before a massive Edwardian brick villa, very ugly and very solid. Isobel got out of the car and mounted the wide steps to its massive front door.

Twelve hours later she was going down them again. The agency lady had been right; the case had been a very short one.

'Bed for you, darling,' said her mother when she walked into her home, blue eyes wide in a face white with a sleepless night. 'And what's more,' went on Mrs Barrington, 'you're having a day off tomorrow.' She added cunningly: 'The garden wants weeding and the kitchen curtains need washing, and you know I can't get at them.'

It was pleasant to be home, pottering around the house and tiny garden, playing with Blossom, and since it was a lovely warm day, taking down the kitchen curtains, washing and ironing them, and as there was time before tea, climbing rather precariously on to the stepladder to hang them up again. She was half way through this task when her mother called from the chair by the sitting room window.

'Do we know anyone with a Rolls-Royce, darling?'

Isobel stretched across the window to insert a hook. 'Only that friend of Father's, years ago—Mr… Oh, lord, Dr Winter's got one!' She stuck in another hook and raised her voice so that her mother would hear her in the other room. 'But he's the last person to come here.' She leaned over a little further and inserted the last hook, and then in sudden panic cried, 'Mother, if it's him, I'm not here…'

Too late, of course. He was at the kitchen door, making the little room smaller than it already was. She perched on the top step, watching him, not speaking for the simple reason that her heart was thumping so madly that breathing had become difficult.

He didn't waste time over social niceties. 'Nanny's got bronchitis, she wants you to look after her.'

Isobel forgot about being shy. 'Oh, the poor dear, is she bad? And just as she was doing so nicely too…' She looked at him properly then; she hadn't gone higher than his tie when he had come in. He looked stern and angry as well and his eyes were like granite; she thought it very likely that he had come against his will because Nanny had insisted. She said kindly in her gentle voice, 'I'm indeed sorry to hear about Nanny, but I can't come, you know; I go where the agency sends me and I'm only just back from a case. I'm sure if you phone them they'll have a nurse free…'

He gave her a thin smile. 'My dear Isobel, you underestimate me. I have already arranged with the agency that you'll return with me this evening.'

Her eyes grew round. 'The arrogance of it!' she declared. 'I may refuse a case, you know, Dr Winter, and I'm doing just that!' Her voice spiralled into a squeak as he reached up and lifted her off the steps and set her down gently, his hands still on her shoulders.

'You won't do that,' his voice was quiet, 'you're a kind girl, and gentle. I'm sorry if I've made you angry, but Nanny is ill, and I haven't brought her all this way to see her slip through my fingers.'

Isobel, very conscious of his hands, conscious too that for him this was a handsome apology, smiled at him. 'I'll need half an hour to collect my things. Do you want me to come with you or shall I come later?'

Before he could reply Mrs Barrington spoke from the door where she had been shamelessly eavesdropping. 'While you get your things together I'll make tea—you'll have a cup, Dr Winter, and one of the scones Isobel made this morning?'

He dropped his hands from Isobel's shoulders. 'Indeed I will, Mrs Barrington. Your daughter's cooking was one of the high spots of our trip.'

'Then come into the sitting-room,' invited Mrs Barrington, 'and I'll put the kettle on. How long will Isobel be with you?'

He opened his mouth to say something and then bit it back. 'A week, two perhaps,' he said suavely. 'It's hard to tell at this stage. Nanny is elderly and tired.'

Isobel had gone, he sat on the edge of the kitchen table while Mrs Barrington filled the kettle and put it on the old-fashioned gas stove. The scones were on a plate on the table and he took one and ate it.

'Exquisite,' he said, and took another, and Mrs Barrington, her back to him, putting cups and saucers on a tray, said: 'Yes, it's eighteenth-century Bow, it belonged to my mother.'

'Actually,' said the doctor, and his voice sounded surprisingly young, 'I was talking about the scones, not the plate.'

Mrs Barrington turned round to look at him. She said softly: 'She's such a dear girl.'

He stared back at her, his dark eyes gleaming. 'Yes, I've discovered that, Mrs Barrington.'

They were embarked on their tea, chatting cosily, by the time Isobel got downstairs again. 'I've packed enough for a week,' she said to no one in particular, and looked with surprise at the almost empty plate.

'I had no lunch,' said the doctor meekly.

They left shortly afterwards, Isobel very neat in uniform; she was wearing the amber necklace under it. She didn't think that the slight bulge it made showed.

'I have to go out as soon as I get back home,' said Dr Winter, 'so listen carefully now so that I don't have to say it all over again.' He embarked on a brief résumé of Nanny's illness, her treatment, medicines, diet and condition. When he'd finished he asked briefly: 'Well, have you got all that? I'll leave a phone number where I can be reached if you're worried, but don't do that unless you have to.'

He didn't seem the same man who had sat not half an hour since discussing the beauties of Coalport china with her mother, devouring her scones like a hungry wolf. He was abstracted now, coolly impersonal, his voice as cool as his manner. She wondered where he was going that evening that could be so important that she was only to phone him in a dire emergency. That beastly girl, probably. Isobel turned her head away and stared out of the window. She had been silly to come, opening a wound that hadn't yet begun to heal.

But she forgot that when she saw Nanny. The old lady was sitting up high against her pillows. She looked small and frail and very tired, but she smiled when she saw Isobel and took her small capable hand and put it to her cheek.

'You naughty old thing,' said Isobel softly, 'but don't worry, we'll have you well again in no time. Just let me go along to my room for a moment, then we'll spend a cosy evening together and you'll eat your supper and go to sleep.'

'I can't sleep,' said Nanny peevishly.

'Yes, you can. I'll sit here until you do.'

The old eyes peered at her. 'You will?' She stopped to cough. 'I'm not scared, only...'

'I know, Nanny, and if you wake in the night, one squeak from you and I'll be here—I'm only in the next room with the door open.'

Dr Winter came in then; he had changed into a dinner jacket and her heart almost stopped at the sight of him. No man had any right to be as good-looking as he was. She gave him a chilly look. 'If you're going to be here for a moment, Dr Winter, I'll go and see Mrs Gibson about Nanny's supper...'

She didn't wait for his answer and when she got back he was on the point of leaving. 'I'm already late,' he told her austerely, just as though it were her fault.

There was a lot to do for Nanny. The attack had come on dreadfully suddenly, and although Mrs Gibson had done her best, Nanny had been fretful and difficult. It would be a day or two before the antibiotics would take effect, in the meantime it was just a question of good nursing—a ceaseless round of cool drinks, pillows shaken, sheets smoothed, bedbaths and nourishment taken however unwillingly. Isobel settled her patient for the night finally and with Mrs Gibson taking her place for half an hour, had her supper, bathed, got into her nightie and dressing gown and went back to Nanny's room. The old lady was indeed poorly, but once she could be got to sleep it would help matters. Isobel listened to Mrs Gibson's whispered offer of a tray of sandwiches and a thermos in case she was kept up late, wished her goodnight and turned her attention to Nanny.

The old lady was wide awake, feverish and inclined to talk a lot. So Isobel pulled up a chair close to the bed, took a hand in hers, and listened while Nanny rambled on about her life in Poland. 'Such a waste, if I've come all this way home—I might just as well have stayed in Gdansk and saved Mr Thomas the trouble.'

'You're wrong there,' said Isobel. 'The doctor—Mr Thomas is lonely, I think. He really needs you, Nanny…'

'What he needs,' said Nanny weakly, 'is a wife and children.'

'Then he'd need you even more.' Isobel turned a pillow deftly. 'You simply have to get well as quickly as possible, Nanny.'

'Yes, dear, I'll do my best.'

'Well, that's more like it. I'm going to give you your antibiotic and a warm drink and then you're going to close your eyes, Nanny, and I promise I'll stay here until you're asleep. If you wake in the night you only have to call.'

It didn't take long, with Nanny settled against her pillows, her eyes resolutely shut, Isobel made a note of her temperature—down a little, she was glad to see—made sure that she had everything handy for the night and sat down again, tucking the old hands on the coverlet into her own. She reckoned she would be there for an hour or so yet; Nanny, despite her cough medicine, was coughing a lot. But presently she nodded off into a light doze, only to wake in a little while and ask querulously what the time was. 'And you ought to be in bed,' she added.

'I've had a lazy day at home and I'm not a bit tired. Go to sleep again, Nanny dear. You're going to feel better in the morning.'

So Nanny dozed off again and this time she slept through Mrs Gibson's soundless entrance with a tray and her whispered: 'You'll be all right, Nurse? The doctor said we'd best get to bed early—we were up most of the night and it's been a long day.'

'I'm fine, Mrs Gibson. Have a good sleep, and goodnight.'

The house was very quiet. Presumably Gibson had gone to his bed too and the doctor would let himself in. Mrs Gibson had left the door open and Isobel could see the faint glow of a light in the hall. She stifled a yawn and decided to wait another half hour and make sure that Nanny was sleeping properly.

Before the half hour was up, Nanny had roused again, demanding a drink, wanting to know the time once more, complaining of being hot. Isobel dealt with everything with quiet speed, persuaded Nanny to have another pill, assured her that she would sleep again, and sat down once more.

'Hold my hand,' said Nanny and this time she slept deeply. Isobel waited a little while; it was almost one o'clock and she longed for her bed. She was on the point of loosening the old lady's hand from hers when she heard the faint sound of the door being shut downstairs. Dr Winter was home again. Presently she heard him coming upstairs. He trod quietly, but he was a big man and the stairs creaked a little. He came just as quietly into the room, went straight to beside the bed and looked at Nanny and then at Isobel, sitting there with her hair hanging round her face, and that pinched with tiredness. 'Go to bed!' His whisper was so harsh that she stared at him, wondering what she had done to make him angry.

'Nanny has only just gone to sleep,' she whispered back. 'I promised I'd stay with her until she slept.' She nodded towards the notes on the side table. 'Her temp's down, so is her pulse.'

'Good. Now do as I say. Goodnight!' His whisper was worse than a loud angry voice, the furious look he turned on her made her insides cold. She got up from her chair and went out of the room without a word. In the morning she would ask him what was wrong. She tumbled into bed and was asleep in an instant.

CHAPTER SIX

ISOBEL WAS UP again soon after five o'clock, dealing with Nanny's cough, giving her a hot drink, more medicine, sponging her face and hands. She went away to dress when Mrs Gibson came, and have a quick breakfast before setting about getting her patient comfortable again. The old lady was sitting up, looking decidedly brighter when Dr Winter arrived. He bade Isobel a brief good morning, examined Nanny, pronounced her to be progressing nicely, rang the bell and when Gibson answered it, requested that Mrs Gibson should come to the room, and when that good lady had presented herself, asked her to keep Nanny company for a short time. 'And you, Isobel, will come to my study, if you would be so good.'

She followed him without a word; at least she would have the opportunity to ask him why he had been so angry in the early hours of that morning. He opened the study door for her and she went past him and at his invitation sat down. He sat himself behind his desk, and before he could speak, she plunged in, anxious to get it over with.

'I made you angry last night,' she said levelly, 'and I think I should be told why; if it's something I've done wrong, I'm sorry, though I can't for the life of me think what it could be...' She added in a reasonable voice: 'I expect that's why you wanted to see me.'

'I wanted to see you, but for a different reason—to apologise for speaking as I did last night. I wasn't angry with you, Isobel, but with myself for leaving you here in my house, to all intents and purposes alone with a sick old woman when you should have been asleep in your bed.'

'Oh, that's quite wrong,' said Isobel bracingly. 'That's what I'm here for—I'm used to sitting up till all hours and I don't mind being alone. Why, you might just as well blame yourself for leaving the maids to wash up after you've had a meal. You pay them for doing it, they work for you. Well, you pay me and I work for you too.' She smiled a little and her eyes twinkled. 'It's no good keeping a dog and barking yourself, you know.'

He laughed then. 'I've never met a girl with so much common sense,' he told her, a remark which she hoped was a compliment, although no girl wanted to be complimented on common sense; a pretty face or lovely eyes or beautiful hair, but what did common sense ever do for a girl?

She got to her feet. 'Oh, well, if that's all, I'll get back to Nanny.'

The doctor stood up too. 'I've arranged with Mrs Gibson to be with Nanny for two hours each afternoon so that you may go out if you wish, and I shall be at home for the next few nights, so there'll be no need for you to sit with Nanny once you've settled her for the night. I'll look in on her from time to time and call you if necessary.'

Isobel shook her head. 'That won't do at all,' she observed calmly. 'You work all day like the rest of us.'

He went to the door and opened it. 'You will allow me to arrange things as I wish, Isobel.' She had heard that silky tone before; she didn't dispute it now. She said quietly: 'Yes, of course, Dr Winter,' and slipped past him, back to Nanny's room.

There wasn't much improvement in Nanny during the day,

but Isobel hadn't expected it. It was enough that she was holding her own and not getting worse. 'You're getting better,' Isobel encouraged her. 'Another day or two and I expect Dr Winter will let your niece come and see you.'

The old lady brightened at the prospect. 'Now that would be fine. I'd like to show her how grand I am—it's a pity my poor Stan isn't alive to see me too.'

'Wouldn't he be glad to see you living here with all your old friends?' observed Isobel cheerfully. 'Now, what do you fancy for lunch?'

The day wore on and when the doctor came home he went straight to Nanny's room. 'You're better,' he said at once, and after he'd gone over her chest and pronounced an improvement: 'You went out, Isobel?'

'Yes, thank you. It was a lovely afternoon, I went along to the park.'

He nodded. 'Good. Take the car if you want to go to your home, although it would be better for you if you took some exercise.'

She gave him a limpid look. Her days were hardly idle; to sit with her feet up in the sun would do nicely. She said: 'Yes, Dr Winter,' in a mild voice which caused him to give her one of his hard stares.

'I shall be home for dinner, I hope you'll join me, Isobel.'

She went downstairs presently, still in uniform, her hair very neat under the white cap, wishing with all her heart that she was in billowing silk and her hair in one of those artless styles which took hours to achieve. She would, of course, need another face to go with that, in which case, she told herself sensibly, she might just as well keep the one she'd got.

She had come downstairs quietly, but the doctor had the ears of a hawk. 'In here,' he called from the drawing-room, and as she pushed open the door which was ajar: 'Have a drink, Isobel, I'm sure you've earned it. Try some Madeira and tell me if you like it.'

She sat down composedly on a small armchair and sipped her wine. 'It's very…' she paused and finished lamely: 'nice.' And when he didn't remark on that: 'Have you had a busy day, Dr Winter?'

'Very. I had quite a backlog, but I'm almost through it. I want to be free for the weekend. I shall be away.' He was watching her carefully. 'I'm going down to Ella's home in Sussex.'

Isobel's heart gave a great leap and stopped, then went on again very fast, but her face remained serene. 'Sussex is a charming county,' she offered pleasantly.

'Not your part of the world, though?' asked the doctor idly.

'Oh, no.' The Madeira was loosening her cautious tongue. 'But Berkshire is beautiful too.'

'Isn't that rather depending on which part of the county you're in? Can't say that I care for Reading…'

'Oh, we lived miles from there,' said Isobel. 'Hinton Bassett—it's a beautiful village and so quiet once the tourists have gone. We lived…' She stopped, aware suddenly that she was talking about herself and probably boring him.

'You lived?' prompted her companion.

'In the village,' she mumbled, and added: 'I think Madeira is a little strong.'

'You don't like it? Let me give you some sherry…'

She said hastily: 'Oh, no, thank you, I've almost finished it anyway.'

Dinner was a pleasant enough meal. Isobel, in her efforts to be nothing more than the nurse sent to help out for a week or so, leaned over backwards to be just that, and the doctor, wickedly plying her with his best claret, enjoyed himself very much, and when after they had had their coffee she excused herself on the grounds that Nanny would need to be tucked up for the night, he watched her go with real regret, wondering how he could possibly have found her rather dull when they had first met.

The days slipped away in a gentle routine, with Nanny improving slowly but steadily. Isobel spent her afternoons in

Kensington Gardens or peering in the windows of the smart boutiques, and once, when it was raining, in Harrods, prowling from one department to another, pretending that she could buy whatever she fancied. She got so carried away that she was very nearly late back.

Dr Winter she saw only briefly during the day, although each evening they had dinner together. She wished, a little wistfully, that he would invite her to stay after that meal and talk, for they had plenty to talk about at table, but he never did, getting up at once when she said she should go back to Nanny, opening the door for her and wishing her goodnight so smartly that she could only feel he was glad to see the back of her.

On Friday she asked Gibson if she was to have dinner downstairs. 'For the doctor will be away, won't he, and it seems a great waste to lay the table just for me. I could easily have a tray in the little room at the back of the hall.'

Gibson's features had relaxed in a smile. 'That wouldn't do, Nurse. Dr Winter would wish you to have your meals exactly as though he were here too.' He added: 'He'll be going about six o'clock, Nurse.'

The doctor had been to see Nanny in the morning. She was making real progress now and sitting out of bed for several hours, but she was tired and crotchety with it, and Isobel was hard put to it to keep her happy during the day. She was reading aloud to her patient when the doctor came home just after five o'clock. She stopped when he came in, put a finger in the page and waited patiently while he talked to Nanny, looked at her progress chart and then said: 'How would you like visitors tomorrow, Nanny?' He glanced at Isobel. 'A good idea, don't you think, Isobel? Nanny's niece could come to tea and stay for half an hour, and if she's not too tired, then one or two of the rest of her family can come—but only one at a time to start with.' He didn't wait for an answer but went away, to reappear after half an hour, dressed for the evening. 'Isobel, come downstairs, will you, I'll give you a number to ring if you should want me for any reason, and change the medicine too, I think.'

She followed him downstairs and into his study. 'Sit down,' he told her, and sat down himself to write on a pad. 'Now listen,' he began, 'I think we might make one or two changes…'

He was interrupted: the door was flung open and Ella came in, a vision in a sky blue suede skirt and a silk shirt, its sleeves carelessly rolled up, its buttons undone to what Isobel considered to be a quite indecent level, not that the effect wasn't devastating…

'Darling!' cried the vision. 'You're ready and I haven't had a minute to change, so I've brought everything with me, and I'll slip upstairs and dress now. Shall I use your room?'

'Certainly not.' It was impossible to tell from the doctor's manner if he was annoyed or not. 'Use one of the guest rooms—and be quiet, Nanny's resting and I don't want her disturbed.'

Ella wrinkled her nose at him. 'You grumpy old thing! I'm glad I'm not one of your patients.' She allowed her lovely eyes to rest on Isobel for a moment. 'Hullo, you back again?' She didn't waste time on her, though, but smiled enchantingly at the doctor, blew him a kiss and danced out of the room.

There was a brief silence after she had gone and then the doctor went on with what he had been saying just as though there had been no interruption. 'And I'll be back late on Sunday night—please leave a message on the hall table if there's anything worrying you.' He smiled briefly. 'That's all, thank you, Isobel.'

She went back to Nanny and found the old lady sitting up in bed, very peevish. 'That young madam's here, rattling around, banging doors, and I can hear the bath water somewhere…'

'It's not for long, Nanny. Miss Stokes is changing before they leave.'

'She'd better not come in here,' declared Nanny crossly, and added, 'Baggage!'

'Shall I read to you for a bit?' asked Isobel. 'It's too early to get your supper, isn't it? Or there's that show you like on the TV.'

'You read to me, my dear, you've got a nice soothing voice.'

So Isobel read—another simple love story with a happy ending; Nanny never tired of them. She had been reading for half an hour when the door was thrust open and Ella came in. This time she was in pink taffeta, with a long tight bodice and a very short full skirt. Her hair was piled up on top of her head and a pink scarf was twisted round it, and her shoes were mere scraps of gold kid on four-inch heels. 'How do I look?' she wanted to know, 'it's a bit *avant-garde*, but at least everyone will notice me.'

'You're not decent,' said Nanny with a snap.

'It's very unusual,' said Isobel mildly, anxious for Nanny not to get all worked up, 'but would you mind going away? Mrs Olbinski isn't allowed visitors.'

Ella shrugged. 'You make a fine pair!' her voice was a little shrill. 'I say, I've left my things in your room, will you go and pack them up? I'll have to take them with me.'

'No, I will not pack your things, Miss Stokes. I'm Mrs Olbinski's nurse, not your maid—and will you please go?' Isobel added gently: 'And leave my room tidy, won't you.'

Just for a moment she thought that Ella was going to hit her, but she turned on her ridiculous heels and went out, banging the door shut; even then Isobel could hear her raging as she went down the stairs. It was five minutes or more before Mrs Gibson poked her head round the door.

'I've tidied your room, Nurse—Miss Stokes had no reason to use it, there are rooms enough and to spare—messed up the bathroom too. I got Edith to get her things together and take them down to her. They've gone now.' She glanced at Nanny. 'Shall I see about a nice supper for Nanny?'

'Thank you, Mrs Gibson.' Isobel smiled and spoke with her usual calm, although her hands were shaking. She hadn't met anyone quite like Ella Stokes before, and her mild nature had erupted into a fine temper she was struggling to subdue. She asked: 'Did the doctor hear any of the—the fuss here?'

Mrs Gibson shook her head. 'He was in the study telephoning. He only came into the hall as Miss Stokes went shouting downstairs, but she'd done that so often he didn't take much notice, only asked her to hush up.'

Nanny was sitting very upright against her pillows. 'It ought to have been you, Isobel…'

'Me, Nanny?'

'Yes, instead of that trumpery creature—going off for the weekend with Mr Thomas, I mean; he doesn't know a dear sweet girl when he sees her.' She nodded her head vigorously. 'A fine pair you'd make, and you're good for him too, especially when he gets a bit uppity.'

'Nanny, whatever are you talking about? Dr Winter and I haven't a thing in common…'

Nanny chuckled. 'You mark my words. Things aren't always what they seem, and as for that saucebox, she'll find there's many a slip 'twixt cup and lip.'

Having delivered herself of these wise if unoriginal remarks, Nanny consented to lie back against her pillows once more, leaving Isobel to go down to the kitchen for her supper tray, her thoughts far away, whizzing down to Sussex, imagining Thomas and his Ella talking together. Ella would be witty and amusing and Thomas would laugh, something he so seldom did with herself. She sighed, received the creamed chicken Nanny fancied and bore it back upstairs to her patient. After supper she telephoned Nanny's niece and arranged to get her to come to tea on the next afternoon. 'Just for half an hour and a cup of tea,' she advised. 'Nanny's still not very well, but she'd love to see you.'

And that done, she went down to her solitary dinner. She had very little appetite, but Gibson seemed determined that she should enjoy the various dishes Mrs Gibson had prepared, so she ate her way obediently through seafood pancakes, lamb cutlets and an assortment of vegetables and a rich chocolate pudding which Gibson assured her had been made especially for her, seeing that she had enjoyed the last one Mrs Gibson had made.

'And I've put the coffee tray in the drawing room, Nurse,' he informed her. 'Nanny's quite comfortable and you can drink it in peace.'

The weekend passed peacefully enough. Nanny's niece, rendered tongue-tied by the magnificence of the doctor's house, hardly spoke above a whisper and agreed eagerly to a return visit on the next day, and as for Nanny, she thoroughly enjoyed the visits, pointing out the great comfort with which she was being surrounded, describing the food, eulogising the doctor and, when she wasn't in the room, Isobel.

Her cough was almost gone, although she was tired out as a result of it and would take some time before she felt herself again. All the same, Isobel was content with her progress. Another week, she thought, and her services wouldn't be required any more.

She had settled Nanny for the night, had had her own dinner and was sitting in the drawing room with the coffee tray when the door opened and Dr Winter walked in.

Isobel put down her coffee cup, a delicate Sèvres trifle which tinkled against its saucer because her hand was shaking. 'Oh,' she said, 'you're not coming back until very late this evening,' and then blushed because it had been such a stupid thing to say.

'So I had thought, but circumstances dictated otherwise.' He went and sat down in the winged chair opposite hers and Gibson came noiselessly in with a tray of sandwiches and fresh coffee. He looked hungry, thought Isobel—no, not hungry, tired and, under the tiredness, angry. She said in her pleasant way, 'You're tired, I expect. I was going up to see if Nanny was all right anyway.'

But before she could get to her feet he said: 'No, don't go. I'm in no mood for talking, but you're restful.'

So she sat and watched him wolfing his sandwiches, but only

when he lifted the now empty coffee pot to refill his cup did she say: 'You'd like more coffee—I'll ring,' and did so without waiting for him to reply. He didn't speak until he'd emptied most of the second pot too, and by then his face had resumed its habitual bland expression.

'I think Nanny is well enough to have a change of air; I'd like you to go with her, Isobel.'

She hadn't been expecting anything like that, and she looked up in surprise without speaking, waiting for him to explain.

'Do you know Suffolk at all? No? I have a cottage at Orford—it's a few miles from the sea—a smallish place and delightful at this time of year. Mrs Cobb, who lives nearby, will look after you and I'll arrange for a wheelchair for Nanny. You won't be bored. Yachts come in and go out to the North Sea, there's plenty to see.' He gave her a long look. 'Two weeks, Isobel?'

She said quietly: 'Yes, of course, Dr Winter.'

He nodded. 'Good. I'm thinking of having a holiday myself—perhaps you would stay here for another few weeks after you get back. I know there won't be much for you to do, but Nanny has taken a fancy to you and I want someone here with her.'

She said again: 'Very well, but I'd be glad if you could arrange for someone to take over once in a while so that I can go home. My brother starts his holidays soon, we hadn't planned to go away'—when had they ever had the money to go away?—'but we usually go somewhere for the day…'

'That will be arranged.' And then with sudden brusqueness: 'Don't let me keep you up.'

She wished him goodnight quietly, not much liking her summary dismissal but reasonable enough to realise that he was worried about something and most likely wanted to be alone. In any case, she pointed out to herself in her usual sensible manner, he had never sought her company; he had only asked her to stay so that he could tell her his plans for Nanny. In due course, she supposed, she would be told the details.

But not from him. It was Nanny, all agog after his visit to her the next morning, who supplied them.

'Many's the time I've been there,' she told an avidly listening Isobel. 'Each summer I'd take Mr Thomas down in June and his mother and father would come down later. Very nice it was too.'

'A cottage?' asked Isobel.

'Well, as you might say, there's cottages and cottages. Merman Cottage is bigger than most, I daresay. Mr Thomas says he'll arrange for the little sitting room downstairs to be fitted for me to make it easy. You don't mind coming with me?'

'I think it sounds great fun.'

'Well, I hope you'll stay for a few weeks yet. I know I'm better, but it's nice to have you around, so I told Mr Thomas, especially as he's going on holiday himself when we get back. The Far East he says, he wants to get right away.'

Probably with Ella, thought Isobel miserably.

Her mother, when she told her, was delighted, and made light of the fact that Isobel would probably not be home to see much of Bobby. 'You won't be gone all that time,' she pointed out, 'and his holidays are endless in the summer—besides, it's a good job, darling, and you won't have to go to that beastly agency every week or so. You go and enjoy yourself. I'm sure Dr Winter will arrange something so that you can see Bobby—a day off before you go or something…'

But the days slipped by and nothing was said. Nanny was up and dressed now, although still not quite herself, and soon the date was fixed for their departure. Isobel, picking over her scanty wardrobe for suitable clothes to take with her, since she wasn't to wear uniform, began to worry. Bobby would be home within the next day or so, and since the doctor never seemed to be at home, and when he was he was either in a hurry to go out, or went straight to his study and shut the door, she had managed only once to ask him if she might have a free day before they went to Orford.

He had frowned, glancing up only briefly from the letter he

was reading. 'I said I would arrange something,' he told her, 'and I will do so.' But here it was on the eve of departure and not a word said. She had packed for Nanny and was busy piling clothes neatly into her own case when she put down the skirt she was folding and marched downstairs, only to find him actually at the door on his way out. His 'Yes?' was hardly encouraging, and then before she had managed to get a word out, 'I haven't forgotten, Isobel.' He was through the door and had shut it firmly while she was still staring at him.

And after that she wasn't going to say another word. She phoned her mother briefly in the morning to say that she wouldn't be home for a week or so and then went to get Nanny ready for their journey.

They were to be driven there and she had supposed Gibson was to do that, but when she followed the doctor with Nanny in his arms down the staircase and into the hall it was to find the Rolls at the door, their luggage in the boot and Gibson standing holding the door for them to get in. Nanny was stowed on to the back seat, wrapped around with rugs and cushions, but when Isobel prepared to get in beside her the doctor said: 'In front with me, Isobel.'

She got in, her temper ruffled enough for her to say tartly: 'You probably consider it a waste of time, Dr Winter, but "would you" or "will you" and the occasional "please" would be appreciated.' She shot him a severe look, at the same time loving him so fiercely that she was hard put to it not to tell him so.

He gave a crack of laughter. 'You sound just like Nanny used to! Are you going to disapprove of me for the whole trip?' He sighed over-loudly. 'And I was looking forward to a pleasant run too.'

'I have no wish to spoil your pleasure,' declared Isobel. 'How long does it last—this journey?'

'About ninety miles. We'll stop on the way for lunch—Nanny will need a break. We'll stop in Dedham at the Tolbooth and be in Orford well before tea. I have to be back in town this evening, but half an hour should suffice to settle you both in.'

He was working his way eastwards out of London, going smoothly at a steady pace. 'I'll put you in the picture as we go along,' he said presently, 'that'll save some time when we get there.'

Isobel turned round to see if Nanny was all right. 'She's asleep,' she said, and added encouragingly: 'Yes, Dr Winter?'

'I've arranged for the bank to let you have money if and when you need it. Mrs Cobb will see to the shopping and so on and her husband keeps the garden tidy. All you have to do is to keep Nanny happy and encourage her to get out and about as much as possible. I know quite a few people there and they know Nanny, so you'll get the occasional caller. I've arranged with Mrs Cobb to stay with Nanny for an hour each afternoon so you can get out on your own. I hope you won't feel tied down.'

She was surprised. 'Me? Tied down? Why should I be? It'll be like having a summer holiday.' And then, mindful of Bobby, 'But I would like to know how long we're to be there, please?'

'I'll let you know that in a week's time, Isobel.'

They were clear of the suburbs now, on their way to Chelmsford, then Colchester and a few miles further on the Tolbooth Restaurant.

Any qualms Isobel had had about getting Nanny into the restaurant were put at rest as soon as the car was parked before its door. She might have been sure that Dr Winter, having master-minded their trip to Poland, wasn't to be deterred in such a small matter. They were expected. He carried the old lady to the powder room with Isobel in close attendance, then settled them at a corner table near the door, and all done with a minimum of fuss. Nanny, very pleased with herself in her new hat and coat, ate a good lunch and did most of the talking with an occasional encouraging word from the doctor, while Isobel sat almost silent, depressed by the thought that after today she would see almost nothing more of Thomas; they would return to London and he would go away immediately and she would never see him again. The prospect took away her appetite.

They reached Orford in mid-afternoon, looking its delightful best, with the sun shining on its charming cottages, boats moored at the quayside and the stretches of grass between the houses. They drove up Market Hill and into Pump Street and stopped before an ivy-covered brick-built house. The doctor had called it a cottage, and so had Nanny, but to Isobel's mind it was a fair-sized house, with wide sash windows and a stout white-painted front door. It was separated from the street by a narrow pavement with painted railings and tubs of geraniums on either side of the very short path, and it had an air of being lived in, which seemed surprising, since the doctor had given her to believe that it was a country retreat and nothing more.

The door opened as he got out of the car. A large, bony woman came out to meet him, then poked her head into the car to shake Nanny by the hand. 'And this'll be Nurse,' she exclaimed cheerfully. 'Come on in, I've got a kettle on the boil.'

There was a lovely tea waiting for them; scones and farm butter, cream and jam and a large fruit cake which they ate in the sitting room, a roomy apartment overlooking the street, furnished most comfortably, its open hearth ready laid with logs against the first autumn chills, still some months away. And when they had had their tea, Nanny was shown to her room just across the small square hall, and then Isobel had a look at the dining room and the kitchen with its Aga and old-fashioned wooden table and chairs and a tabby cat snoozing before the stove. It would be fun to cook on that, thought Isobel, and had her unspoken thought answered by the doctor.

'Mrs Cobb will be in each day to do the housework and washing—could you manage the cooking, Isobel?'

'Oh, yes!' She gave him a smile of pure pleasure. 'What a lovely house!'

He nodded absently; it was obvious that he was in a hurry to be gone. Indeed, Mrs Cobb had taken her upstairs, leaving him and Nanny in the sitting room, and when she got down again it was to find Nanny alone.

'Mr Thomas asked me to say goodbye—he wanted to get back.'

'Yes, of course,' said Isobel, 'he did tell me that he had to go out this evening. Nanny, I've got such a pretty room, you have no idea. I think we're going to be very comfortable here, don't you?' She made sure that the old lady was comfortable and declared her intention of unpacking for both of them and having a little talk with Mrs Cobb. The unpacking was quickly done and it took only a short time for her and Mrs Cobb to come to a comfortable understanding about housework and shopping. 'And that reminds me, Nurse,' said Mrs Cobb, 'I almost forgot, there's a wheelchair in the cupboard under the stairs—it came the other day—so that Nanny can get about a bit, I daresay. Very thoughtful of the doctor to remember.'

And very thoughtless of him not to have mentioned it to her, thought Isobel, still smarting from the manner in which he had gone off without so much as a wave of the hand.

There was plenty of food in the house. When Mrs Cobb had gone with the promise to be back at nine o'clock the next morning, Isobel cooked supper for them both, helped Nanny to bed and went upstairs to bath and get ready for her own bed, but before that she went round the rooms again. Besides the sitting room and the dining room there was a small room cosily furnished and with a small desk under the window, and beyond the kitchen there were some large cupboards, an old-fashioned scullery where there was a washing machine and a tumble-dryer and a door leading into a small very pretty garden with a high brick wall around it. There was another door too, at the end of the hall, opposite the front door. Isobel locked it carefully and went upstairs again. She had been surprised to find that there were five bedrooms, two quite small, and a splendidly appointed bathroom as well as the shower room tucked away behind the room Nanny was to use as a bedroom. And the rooms were furnished with great taste and no thought of expense. She went to her own room and undressed slowly, had a leisurely bath, then went down to see if Nanny was already asleep. She was. Isobel left a lamp on in the hall and the door open and started for the stairs. She was within reach of the telephone when it rang, and she snatched it up quickly for fear of waking Nanny. The doctor's voice asked: 'Were you waiting for me to ring? Such promptness!'

'Nanny has just gone to sleep and I happened to be by the phone,' said Isobel coldly. Why should she be civil to the wretch when he hadn't even the good manners to say goodbye?

'Is everything all right? You have all you want?' and when she muttered yes: 'Good. I'll leave you to go to bed. Goodnight, Isobel.' He'd rung off before she could say a word.

Beyond wondering wistfully what Thomas was doing, she was too tired to think much, and in the morning her common sense had returned: There was no reason at all why he should have wished her goodbye. She was, after all, Nanny's nurse and as such had no share in his life. She got up and looked out of the window at the lovely morning and the quiet village and the sparkle of water beyond the quay, determined not to think about him.

There was plenty to fill their days. With Nanny in her wheelchair and Isobel pushing it, they explored the village street by street, went down to the quay to watch the yachts going in and out, took a look at the church of St Bartholomew and each day went back to a sparkling house, the day's shopping laid out on the kitchen table and Mrs Cobb's cheery 'Bye-bye' as she went off home for her dinner.

Nanny liked to eat in the evening and so did Isobel. She made salads and little cheesy dishes for lunch and they drank home-made lemonade before Nanny took her afternoon nap. Mrs Cobb was back by half past two and with Nanny still dozing, Isobel was free to go out if she wished to. There were a few shops where she bought their small necessities and spent pleasant minutes choosing paperbacks for Nanny, but once her small chores were done, she made her way down to the quay again and sat watching the busy scene. Each day seemed better than the last, and towards the end of the week they abandoned their afternoon walk and spent the hour before tea in the garden, Nanny with her chair shielded from the sun by an old-fashioned tussore silk parasol Isobel had unearthed from a cupboard and Isobel in a bikini, barefooted and with her hair hanging round her shoulders, lying on the grass, reading aloud.

It was Saturday and they had been there a week. Mrs Cobb had gone home and wouldn't come again until Monday and Isobel had baked a cake to have for their tea, prepared lamb cutlets for their supper, and wheeled Nanny into the shade of the plum tree in the garden. It was hot enough to lie and do nothing, but Nanny wanted to be read to. Isobel opened the book—another of the romances Nanny liked so much—and began to read.

She finished a chapter and turned the page, then glanced up to see if Nanny had gone to sleep, to find her staring at the house behind them smiling widely.

Isobel rolled over to have a look too. Standing in the open doorway were her mother and Bobby, smiling widely too. She was on her feet in a flash, hurling herself first at her mother and then her brother. 'How did you get here—how did you come? When do you…' She stopped as she caught sight of Thomas Winter coming through the hall from the open front door.

'You brought them!' she cried, and went to meet him. 'Oh, how very kind of you! I'll never be able to thank you enough. It's such a heavenly surprise to see you—all of you,' she added hastily. 'If I'd known I would have had a lovely tea waiting for you.'

He had put down the cases he was carrying and stood, very elegant in slacks and an open-necked shirt, looking down at her. He said: 'Hullo, Isobel, how well you look.' His smile made her glow all over and she remembered then that her hair was in a hopeless mess and she was in a bikini, which made her cheeks glow too.

She said shyly: 'It's too hot to take Nanny out in the afternoons, so we sit in the garden. I'll go and put on a dress.'

'Don't bother as far as I'm concerned, you'll do very nicely as you are.'

He was laughing at her now, so she said coldly: 'I'll just introduce my mother and Bobby to Nanny and go and get the tea.' And she went back into the garden, hearing him chuckle as she went.

There was no need to introduce anyone, they were already the best of friends. 'We're here for a week, darling, Thomas invited us, and he'll fetch us back next Saturday. Can you manage with the two of us extra?'

'Oh, Mother, of course! How absolutely super—I can't believe it! Look, I'm just going to get into a sundress, then we'll have tea and I'll get the rooms ready.'

'No need,' said the doctor's voice from behind her. 'I telephoned Mrs Cobb in the week and she's made up the beds and seen to the rooms.' He sauntered over to Nanny and bent to kiss her. 'Why not take your mother upstairs to her room before tea?' he suggested. 'Bobby and I will keep an eye on Nanny.' He glanced briefly at Isobel. 'I thought your mother might like the room overlooking the garden, and Bobby can have the small one next to you.'

'There's not time to talk,' said Isobel, bustling her parent upstairs. 'I must get into some clothes and get your tea—thank heavens I made a cake and some scones.'

She whisked away, tore into a sundress and sandals, brushed out her hair and raced downstairs. They were still in the garden. She went into the kitchen and began to pile cups and saucers and plates on to a tray. They could have tea out of doors, thank goodness. While she buttered scones she reorganised supper; the chops wouldn't do; she'd cook macaroni cheese and several vegetables and a fruit pie and cream. She got the cake from its tin and cut a few slices, and the doctor, who had just come in, leaned over and helped himself.

'That is nice,' he observed, studying the sundress—last year's and faded, but a pretty mixture of greens. 'The bikini was nice too.' He took a huge mouthful of cake. 'You've not lost your touch with the cooking. I expect you're working out frantic alternatives for supper tonight, but you need only cater for four, I'm going back after tea.'

He took another bite and watched through half closed eyes as telltale disappointment clouded her face. She was spooning jam from a pot into a little dish and didn't look up. 'Oh, isn't that rather a long journey all in one day? There's still a bedroom and I can cook for five just as easily as four. Besides, it is your home…'

'I'm flattered by your concern, Isobel, but it's an easy ride from here—and besides, I have to be back this evening. And now tell me, is everything going well with Nanny?'

He carried the tray out presently and they all sat about on the grass, and just for a while Isobel was completely happy. Thomas was here, sitting right beside her, and he would be back in a week's time to fetch her mother and Bobby, so she would see him again quite soon. She was a little silent savouring her happiness, but as everyone else was talking nineteen to the dozen, it wasn't noticeable, at least only to her mother's eye, and the doctor, who had his own reasons for watching her.

He went directly after tea and they all crowded to the front door to see him off, Nanny in her chair too. He kissed Nanny and Mrs Barrington, shook Bobby's hand, then came to where Isobel was standing. 'Why not?' he asked no one in particular, and kissed her too.

CHAPTER SEVEN

THE COTTAGE SEEMED a great deal larger once the doctor had gone, and somehow empty, but Isobel had no time to brood about that. There was Nanny to see to, supper to get, and between those a chance to talk to her mother and Bobby, although he was off in no time at all to take a look at the quay.

'So kind of Thomas,' said Mrs Barrington, 'though I can't think what put the idea into his head. He just turned up one evening and suggested it, said that you'd had no days off and this was to make up for it. Very generous of him when you think about it, inviting Bobby too.'

'What did you do with Blossom?' asked Isobel.

'That nice Cat Protection Society I sell flags for have taken her as a boarder. Thomas offered to have her at his home, but his housekeeper has got a cat and kittens and they might not have got on.'

Isobel finished laying the table and stood back to admire the effect. 'I think I'm to stay for another week or so when we get back,' she said carefully. 'Dr Winter wants to go on holiday—somewhere remote.'

Her mother followed her into the kitchen. 'Natural enough, I suppose, after all that…'

'All what?'

Her mother gave her a wide-eyed innocent look. 'Darling, if he hasn't told you, I certainly can't.'

'You seem on very friendly terms,' said Isobel tartly.

Her mother ignored the tartness. 'Oh, but we are, and he and Bobby get on very well, isn't that nice?'

Isobel opened the oven door and took a look at the macaroni cheese. 'Very,' she said.

The weather stayed warm, hot and dry, so that each day they were able to stroll down to the quay, visit the few shops or just sit in the garden. Of course Bobby spent only a little time with them; sea fishing was one of his hobbies and here he could fish from dawn to dusk, and after the first day he made friends with one or two of the boat owners and went off with them, down to the Ness and out to sea, coming back with fish for the next day's dinner. And extra company certainly did Nanny good. She and Mrs Barrington sat happily discussing everything under the sun while Isobel gave Mrs Cobb a hand round the house or got the meals. There was really nothing to do for Nanny now; she was walking just a little with the aid of a stick and provided there was someone to help her round the house when they got back, Isobel could see no reason why she should stay. It would be better, she decided, if she were to go as soon as possible now—get a job, if possible, miles away where there was no chance of seeing Thomas ever again or being anywhere where she might be reminded of him. Perhaps there would be a chance to tell him so when he came at the weekend.

It was a long week despite her well filled days, but Saturday came at last with a message at breakfast time that the doctor would be with them for lunch. Bobby had answered the phone, and when his mother asked if he had been told if they were going back that day or not, he looked vague and said that he hadn't thought of asking.

'Boys!' sighed Mrs Barrington resignedly, and went back to pack their cases. 'Because I'm sure Thomas will want to get back so that he can spend Sunday with all those friends of his.'

But that was no reason why they shouldn't have a splendid lunch, a kind of culinary farewell, Isobel decided. She popped out to the shops and came back with fresh salmon and a few extra ingredients to augment the salad. It would have to be an apricot flan for pudding; there had been fresh apricots at the greengrocers, and she had bought extra cream; she could make the pastry while the salmon mousse was setting. Bobby had already seen to the potatoes before he had escaped to the quay and she had all the morning.

Her mother and Nanny were in the garden and Mrs Cobb was upstairs making beds. Isobel shut herself in the kitchen and got to work.

The mousse was setting nicely, the salad was made and the potatoes were in their saucepan and the ladies had had their coffee. Isobel was arranging apricots in the flan case when the kitchen door opened behind her.

'There's nothing for you to eat,' she said, not bothering to turn round. 'If you're as famished as all that you'll find biscuits in the tin in the cupboard.' She added, wheedling: 'Bobby, be a darling and put those two bottles of white wine in the fridge, before you get at those biscuits.'

'I'll be a darling and uncork the wine,' said the doctor from the kitchen door, 'but I haven't come all this way just to eat biscuits.'

She spun round to look at him. 'Oh!' she said breathlessly. 'You're early.'

'A cold welcome and dry biscuits,' said the doctor. 'For two pins I won't see to the wine.'

'Oh, I'm sorry—I thought you were Bobby and I didn't think you'd get here for another hour and I was going to have everything quite ready for you. I expect you want to get back again as soon as possible.' Isobel arranged the last of the fruit and popped the flan into the oven. 'Mother has packed.'

'Glad to be going?' he asked blandly.

'Of course not—they've loved every single minute.'

'I'm glad to hear it. I planned to stay until tomorrow tea time—if that's not too late for your mother and Bobby.'

'Oh, no, they'll be glad.' She beamed at him, so happy that she forgot to hide her feelings. 'Mother's in the garden and Bobby's down at the quay—he's made so many friends...if you like to go into the garden I'll bring you some coffee and a slice of cake.'

'I'll have it here. I like watching you cook. A woman's place is in the home, so I've been told, though I can't call to mind many young women who do that these days.'

He came and sat on the table and ate the best part of the cake she had made for tea; luckily she had made a second one, thinking it would keep nicely for later in the week. He drank all the coffee there was in the pot, too, and then with a careless remark that he would take his case up to his room, he strolled away. Isobel heard him then in the garden, and when she peeped out, he was lying stretched out at the ladies' feet, presumably asleep. She put the finishing touches to the salad, laid another place at the table and ran upstairs to tidy herself. She uttered a moan of horror when she saw herself in the mirror; hair all over the place, no make-up left after all that cooking in the warm kitchen, and an elderly cotton dress she wore only for cooking and housework.

She changed into the blue cotton dress, the one she had worn the first time she had seen Thomas, did her hair with great neatness and made up her face as best she could; she was so brown now that her powder didn't match, so she applied lipstick and left her face to shine.

The doctor had taken drinks out into the garden, sherry for Nanny and Mrs Barrington, a soft drink for Bobby, who had just turned up, and beer for himself, and when Isobel joined them, 'I'm not going to ask you what you want,' he told her. 'I got you a Dubonnet with lots of ice and lemon.'

It sounded somehow as though they had had drinks together so often that he knew exactly what she liked. She thanked him composedly and sat down, avoiding her mother's thoughtful eye.

Lunch went down well, and afterwards the doctor and Bobby washed up and the went off to fish, which gave Isobel the chance to make another cake, cut a plateful of sandwiches, settle Nanny for a nap and then sit in the garden with her mother.

'I suppose you'll be back next weekend?' her mother asked casually.

'I think so. Dr Winter's going away as soon as we get back, isn't he? Now Nanny's so much better I should be able to get home for an afternoon now and again.'

'That'll be nice, dear. Let's hope that the next case is as interesting as this one.'

Isobel didn't look at her mother. 'Yes, I thought I'd get right away if there's anything going—out of London.'

'What a good idea,' agreed her parent cheerfully. 'Do you want any help with supper, darling?'

'No, thanks—luckily there were half a dozen lamb cutlets in the freezer, peas and broad beans and mint sauce, and there are some prawns. I'll make prawn cocktails for starters and fresh fruit salad and cream for dessert. Will that do?'

'Admirably. What a blessing that you can cook, dear. We aren't going until after lunch tomorrow, are we?'

'No, but I'd planned roast pork anyway. We shall eat it all at one go, but I can get something else for the two of us in the week. And I'll make a trifle later on.'

'We do keep you busy, but it's nice that Thomas enjoys his food. Has he got a good cook?'

'Mrs Gibson the housekeeper cooks; she's super too.'

'A well run household, I've no doubt,' observed Mrs Barrington.

The men came back presently with a dozen mackerel which

they insisted on cleaning before tea, sternly advised by Isobel to leave the kitchen spotless when they had finished. 'Tartar!' said Thomas, grinning at her. 'You're as bad as a nagging wife!'

Only if I were your wife, I wouldn't nag you, promised Isobel silently.

The weekend went too fast. In no time at all Isobel was standing at the door of the cottage with Nanny standing bravely beside her, leaning on her stick, waving them all goodbye. The doctor was coming to fetch them during the week, probably at tea time, and she had been told to be ready to leave on Wednesday unless he telephoned otherwise. He had told her quite casually just before they left and all she could say was: 'Very well, we'll be waiting for you. Shall I tell Mrs Cobb and pay any bills?'

For some reason he had smiled then. 'Yes, do that. How indispensable you've made yourself, Isobel—I don't know what we're going to do without you.'

She hadn't answered him because she couldn't think of what to say. Something lighthearted if only she could have thought of it, instead of wanting to burst into tears. He had turned away to kiss Nanny and then waved a careless hand at her as he got into the car. She had ignored all that and made some bright remark to her mother, sitting in splendour on the back seat. Nanny had waved, but Isobel's hands felt glued to her sides.

The doctor returned on Wednesday, just as he had said he would, at tea time. Isobel and Nanny were both ready to leave, so it was just a question of putting the kettle on and fetching down their bags. Mrs Cobb had been bidden goodbye with the promise of instructions from Dr Winter at a later date, small bills had been paid and meticulously accounted for by Isobel, together with the remainder of the money she had had for housekeeping expenses. There was nothing left to do but to greet him politely when he arrived and give him his tea.

Isobel, now that it was time to go, didn't want to leave. The cottage had begun to seem like home and she had made a few friends here and there and there had been time to dream a little; impossible dreams, of course, but very comforting. Nanny was sorry to be leaving too, but not too much so. Once back in London she would have her niece and her family to visit and Mrs Gibson with whom to gossip. She plied the doctor with questions over tea and he answered her patiently. He looked tired, Isobel thought, and a holiday would do him the world of good. She wondered if Ella would be going with him, or if not Ella, someone else. She wished for the hundredth time that she knew more about him.

She cleared away presently and washed up the tea things and left everything tidy: Mrs Cobb would be in the following morning to put the place to rights, but Isobel whisked round the cottage making sure that everything was just so while Nanny was being got into the car, and then got in herself and waited while Thomas locked the door. They drove back to London very fast and none of them had much to say. Nanny was tired by the time they arrived back and Isobel, accompanied by a solicitous Mrs Gibson, bore her off to bed, stood over her while she ate the delicious supper prepared for her and then went to her room to unpack her bag and tidy herself. Not quite sure what was expected of her, she went downstairs presently, to be met by Gibson in the hall.

'Dinner's ready for you in the dining room, Nurse,' he informed her, 'and Dr Winter wished me to say that he will see you in the morning.'

A not very satisfactory ending to their return.

Nanny was up and dressed and sipping her mid-morning coffee by the time Isobel was sent for by the doctor. He had gone out very early, Gibson had told her—some emergency at the hospital, and now he had come back briefly before going to his rooms to see his morning patients.

So he would be tired and possibly ill-tempered as well as hungry. Isobel crossed the hall and went into his study.

If he was any of these things, he didn't show it. He was as

immaculate as he always was, his face bland, a tray of coffee at his elbow. His good morning was pleasant as he waved her to a chair. 'I'm sorry we've had no opportunity to talk—I've got about five minutes to spare now, though. I'd be glad if you'd stay until Sunday, Isobel. I shall be leaving quite early in the morning, so you'll be free to go as soon as you wish after that. Nanny has made a splendid recovery and Mrs Gibson feels she'll be able to manage with some extra daily help. I'll let the agency know, and leave a cheque for you…'

'The agency usually…' began Isobel.

'Yes, but I prefer to pay you myself, just as I did the first time. It only remains for me to thank you once more. Nanny and I are most grateful to you for all you've done.'

He was a stranger, polite and distant and withdrawn. Isobel stood up. 'Nanny has been a wonderful patient. I hope you'll have a very good holiday, Dr Winter. Shall I see you again before you leave?'

'Well, I shall be out this evening and I have guests coming to dinner on Saturday, but I daresay we'll have the chance to say goodbye before Sunday.' And as she went to the door, 'Take the car if you want to run Nanny over to see her niece.'

Isobel said thank you in her quiet voice and closed the door silently behind her. It seemed likely that whatever he said she wasn't going to see him again. She wouldn't allow herself to think about it, but went back to Nanny and began at once to embark on plans to drive over to Peckham.

But she did see him once more, on the following evening, coming up the stairs two at a time towards her as she was on her way down to get Nanny's supper tray. She summoned a normal voice and wished him a good evening, and was surprised when he stopped beside her. 'There's something I've been meaning to ask you. Why don't you want me to see that you wear the amber necklace? You wear it—I've seen it under your dress.'

He put out a hand and gently tapped its slight bulge.

Isobel looked round for inspiration and found none. After

a minute she said: 'It reminds me of Poland.' She blushed as she said it and then stared at him surprised when he said with a kind of angry impatience:

'I need nothing to remind me of Poland—or, for that matter, of you.'

He bent his head suddenly and kissed her hard, then went on upstairs without another word. She didn't see him before she left. People came to the house that evening, she could hear them from her room where she had asked, very firmly, if she might have her dinner. The doctor had been angry when she had refused to join him and his guests at table; if he hadn't been so coldly annoyed she would have explained that she had nothing suitable to wear, that she knew none of his friends, that she would feel like a fish out of water. As it was, she gave no explanation at all, and he had agreed in a tight-lipped fashion. She thought of that as she ate her solitary meal and listened to the muted sounds of people enjoying themselves downstairs.

She took care not to go down in the morning until she heard the unmistakable sounds of his departure, and since saying goodbye was a painful business, she made as short work as possible of her goodbyes, and with the cautious promise that provided she wasn't working, she would come and see Nanny whenever she could, she got into the car beside Gibson and was driven home.

The little house looked closed and forlorn as Gibson pulled up in front of it, and Isobel could see Blossom peering through the sitting room window, looking disconsolate. Gibson put down her case at the door and she urged him not to wait. 'My mother's out, I expect,' she told him. 'Besides, it's your day off and I've taken up too much of your time already.' She shook his hand and thanked him and watched him drive away before opening the door, setting her case in the hall and going into the sitting room.

Blossom came rushing at her, mewing unhappily, and Isobel picked her up and carried her through to the kitchen and fed her, then she opened the back door so that she could go into the garden. Her mother must have gone out unexpectedly, as although she hadn't known exactly when Isobel was coming home, she had known it would be Sunday; besides, she didn't go out on Sunday except to church, and it was too early for that.

She lugged her case upstairs, put it in her room and then, not knowing quite why she did it, pushed open the door of her mother's bedroom on the other side of the tiny landing. Mrs Barrington was lying on the floor by the bed. She was in her nightdress and dressing gown and there was a broken cup and saucer and a still damp patch of tea on the floor beside her.

Isobel's heart seemed to stop for a moment, then she knelt down and took her mother's pulse; faint but fairly steady. It was obvious that her mother was unconscious and she could see no sign of injury. She put a pillow under her head, covered her with her quilt from the bed and flew to the phone.

Her mother's doctor was away for the weekend, and his stand-in was out on a case. Isobel left an urgent message, wishing with all her heart that Thomas had been somewhere where she could have got hold of him. That he would have come at once she never doubted, but wishing the impossible wasn't going to help matters; she went back to her mother and began to examine her methodically, just as though she were a patient brought into Casualty. Her pulse was stronger and there was a tinge of colour in her face, although she made no response to Isobel's voice or touch.

'CVA,' said Isobel out loud. 'Not too bad, thank God, at least I think so. I wish that doctor would come…'

She heard the car draw up as she said it and went to let him in. He was a stranger, a small mild man who introduced himself as Dr Watts and wasted no time in small talk. Nor did Isobel; she took about two minutes to lay the facts before him and then led him upstairs.

She had been right. Her mother had had a stroke—not, thank heaven, a serious one. They got her back into bed and when he suggested that she should go to hospital, Isobel heard the reluctance in his voice.

'I'm a trained nurse, between cases,' she told him. 'I can nurse Mother here just as well as if she went to hospital—probably better, because it's only a question of care and feeding and patience, isn't it? Is it a thrombosis or haemorrhage, do you think?'

'I'm not sure at this stage. As soon as your mother regains consciousness we shall be able to see if she has any paralysis. I'll telephone Dr Martin in the morning, but I'll be round again this evening to see how she is.' He looked at Isobel anxiously. 'You're sure you can manage?'

'Quite sure, Doctor.'

And manage she did, through the first few anxious days when her mother became conscious again, and although unable to speak clearly and use her right arm and leg, demonstrated quite clearly that she was going to get better. Then there were the long tedious days of feeding and nursing and getting in and out of bed to sit in a chair by the window, the careful exercises, the doctor's visits and above all the constantly cheerful face and voice.

Isobel never faltered, at least not in front of her mother or Dr Martin, and at night she was so tired that she couldn't put two thoughts together before she was almost asleep. But those two thoughts were always the same—a longing for Thomas and sheer terror as to the future. She wasn't earning; her mother's small pension was just enough to pay the rent and maintenance of the little house once the food was paid for; her earnings had covered Bobby's fees, his clothes and their meagre comforts. Now she was digging into the money put aside for those, and the nightmare of not having the school fees for the next term was something she went to bed with every night.

That it was silly to wish for Thomas was something she acknowledged; it was like wanting the moon or the stars. After the first week or so she managed to douse the very thought of him. She had found time to write to Nanny, making light of her mother's illness but making it the reason for her not visiting the old lady, and she had a letter back almost at once, full of little titbits of news, although the doctor wasn't mentioned. Quite clearly Nanny had no inkling of the severity of Mrs Barrington's illness, for she wrote quite cheerfully that Isobel must be looking forward to another case. 'And mind you come and see us all when you have the time,' the letter ended.

Mrs Barrington was as mettlesome as her daughter. Not for one moment did she allow herself to despair; the only thing which worried her was the fact that Isobel was tied to the house, day in, day out. True, she tore out to the local shops once or twice a week and spent an hour in the garden every afternoon, while her mother had her rest, playing with Blossom and pottering among the roses, cutting the tiny lawn and trimming the hedge. None of the neighbours had called, but she hadn't expected them to. London, she had learned a long while ago, could be a lonely place. In the village where she had lived everyone knew everyone else, at least by sight, and to pass anyone without a greeting was unheard-of, and as for being ill, neighbours would be round within the hour with offers of help. During her brief spells of doing nothing Isobel began to think seriously of ways and means of getting out of London. It would be difficult, probably impossible, but there might be a way...

In the meantime she pressed on with the task of getting her mother back to her usual self once more. A masseuse came twice a week and on the other days Isobel contrived to be her substitute, and now that her mother was sitting for a good deal of the day in a chair, she was going to do more and more for herself. All the same, progress was slow even if steady, and Isobel, worried sick about the lack of money and how she was going to manage during the next few months until her mother was on her feet again, got thin and pale, and her looks, never remarkable, suffered. Only her eyes kept their deep blue, looking much too large in her peaky face. Dr Martin came twice a week now, declaring himself well satisfied with his patient's progress, urging Isobel to take more exercise. 'Get someone in to sit with your mother,' he suggested. 'I'd send the practice nurse, only she's up to her eyes with this whooping cough epidemic.' He hurried to the door, a busy man. 'I'll be in at the end of the week—let's see, it's just over three weeks, isn't it? Your mother has done very well—she's a wonderful woman, and you are a splendid nurse. You must turn a room downstairs into a bedroom, Isobel, so that your mother can try to get around the house. She's doing well with the zimmer.'

To all of which Isobel cheerfully agreed, and once he had gone, sat down to ponder the problem of getting a bed downstairs into the poky little dining room, rearranging the furniture and conveying her mother downstairs. As for the holiday, she didn't dare think of that.

She was up early next morning, tidying the house, seeing to her mother, getting breakfast. Dr Martin wouldn't be coming for two days, which gave her time to get her mother downstairs. She knew exactly what she had to do, and once her mother was settled in her chair, the bell by her good hand, her book propped up so that she could read, Isobel went into the dining room. Luckily there wasn't a great deal of furniture in it; a rather nice gate-leg table, four chairs and a graceful mahogany sideboard. The sideboard would have to stay, the table and chairs must somehow be fitted into the sitting room. She had decided to bring her own small bed downstairs; it was easier to move than Bobby's, and she could sleep there while he was away at school. The thought reminded her that in about ten weeks' time his fees would be due and she had already dipped into her savings. She brushed it aside; first things first.

She had heaved the table into the hall, lifted the chairs on top of it and squeezed her way round them to get back into the dining room, when the front door bell rang. It wasn't the day to pay the milkman or the baker, it could be the man for the rent, a day early. Isobel squeezed her way back again and opened the door.

Dr Winter stood on the doorstep, filling the entire doorway. She goggled up at him, the instant delight which filled her considerably damped down by the thought that she wasn't dressed for the occasion. An elderly cotton dress, a plastic pinny with 'All hands on deck' printed across its front, her hair, not at its best, tied back anyhow with a bit of ribbon. She opened her mouth closed it and then opened it again to utter: 'Oh, dear!'

But Thomas had seen the delight, although he gave no sign, only sighed inwardly. Here was a situation which would need instant and careful handling.

His 'good morning' was pleasantly bland, and since she had no choice but to invite him Isobel bade him enter. A difficult business, she realised, too late. The table and chairs, and the doctor with her squashed in between them, made an awkward situation. She stayed where she was and waited for him to speak.

'I've come to see your mother—I've had a chat with Dr Martin and he has no objection. Perhaps there's something I can do… I'm very sorry to hear that she's been ill, but he tells me she's making a wonderful recovery.' His keen eyes took in her neglected hair and shining nose and the dreadful pinny. 'Due largely to your nursing, I'm told.'

She didn't answer; for one thing she was so happy despite her untidy person, that she had lost her voice. Miracles happened, after all; for what other reason could there be for Thomas to come out of the blue like this when she had imagined him to be in some exotic place miles away?

'If I might see her?' prompted the doctor gently. 'Are you spring-cleaning?'

Isobel found her voice. 'No, just getting the room ready for Mother—Dr Martin thought it would be a good thing to get her downstairs now that she's well—well, not quite walking, but on her feet, at any rate.' She squeezed past him. 'If you could manage past the table.'

It was a silly thing to say, his massive bulk couldn't possibly get through such a small space. He lifted the chairs down and moved the table back into the dining room and professed himself ready to follow her upstairs.

He had, Isobel had to admit, a splendid bedside manner. He greeted Mrs Barrington like an old friend, shook her hand, professed himself delighted to see how well she was recovering and then suggested that, since Dr Martin had no objection, he might be allowed to examine her. Then he listened without a trace of impatience while Mrs Barrington explained how she had become ill and how frightened she had been and how determined to get well again. She still spoke slowly with slightly slurred speech, but her eyes were alive and alert. She owed her recovery to Isobel, she told him. 'More than three weeks, and the child has hardly been outside the door, and no help either.'

The doctor nodded sympathetically. 'Well, let's get you on the bed and take a look, shall we?'

He took a long time, with Isobel, having shed the pinny, once more a nurse. 'You know, you're almost there, Mrs Barrington. A few weeks' intense physiotherapy and some speech therapy and you'll be as good as new. I have beds in a small private hospital near my home, I want you to go there for a little while. Would you agree if I arrange it?'

He was looking at her and smiling, although he shot a lightning glance at Isobel, whose face betrayed her thoughts only too plainly; he sighed again behind imperturbable features. 'You must be tired now—suppose you have a short nap on your bed while Isobel and I get the matter settled?'

Isobel tucked her mother under the eiderdown and led the way downstairs to the sitting room. She offered him a shabby but elegant wingback chair and shut the door behind her.

'Well, Isobel?' asked the doctor without waste of time.

She sat down rather primly in a small balloon-backed chair facing him.

'I don't understand,' she said in a voice which shook a little despite her calm face. 'How did you find out about Mother's illness? And why did you come here? And before we settle anything, there's one thing you must understand. I'm deeply grateful for your offer to take Mother into your hospital—and why you had to say so, I can't think—but it's quite impossible. I'm not working for the moment, my mother's pension is small and she has no capital. There are Bobby's school fees to consider…'

'I take it that you pay those?' interpolated the doctor quietly.

'Well, yes, I do, but the thing is I've had to take some of the money to—to buy one or two things Mother had to have…' She paused. 'And there's no one I can borrow money from to pay for her fees, you must understand that—we haven't any family, no one at all, just the three of us.' She sounded suddenly fierce. 'And up until now we've managed very well and shall again. I know it will take longer for Mother to get well, but when the masseuse came the first time she showed me what to do, and I can help her walk…'

The doctor sat back in his chair and stretched out his long legs with the air of a man who had all the time in the world. 'Isobel, have you looked at yourself lately?' And when she didn't answer: 'Before your mother is fully recovered you'll be flat on your face. You're too thin, you're tired to death, probably you don't eat enough or take much exercise. Oh, I know you are on your feet all day, but that's not the same thing. And I wasn't aware that the question of fees had arisen. I consider your mother to be a friend, and as such she will be treated without any charges.'

'You're very kind,' said Isobel stiffly, 'but I won't accept charity…'

'No? You would allow your mother to remain just a little slow in her speech, just a little paralysed, just to be a little bit tired for the rest of her life so that you may justify a pig-headed pride? I'm disappointed in you, Isobel.'

She looked down at her hands, folded neatly on her lap, and could scarcely see them for tears. 'But I haven't any money,' she muttered. 'You must try and understand—we rent this house, the furniture's nice, but it wouldn't fetch enough—besides, Mother must have a home and these things are all she has left. Even if I asked you to lend me the money, I wouldn't be able to pay you back for years…'

'It's very simple, Isobel.' His voice was quiet, placid even. 'Your pride against your mother's recovery. And what is money compared with good health and life? Your mother's health, Isobel.' His voice was suddenly harsh. 'And I wasn't aware that I'd asked any fees.'

She still didn't look up. 'Could you really get her quite well again?'

'Yes.'

'And would you keep an account of—of what it will cost so that I can repay you when I can?'

The doctor examined his carefully trimmed nails. 'Certainly I will.' He added casually: 'Have you made serious inroads into Bobby's school fees?'

She forgot for the moment that she had no intention of telling him about her difficulties. 'Yes, but if I can go back to work soon I can pay it back. I can earn a lot more if I do night duty or go without my days off or look after a mental patient.'

'Just at the moment you aren't fit to look after anyone, not even yourself, Isobel.'

She looked up then, her eyes wide with apprehension, but before she could utter, he went on: 'I'll make arrangements for your mother to go to the hospital—' he mentioned a clinic by name— 'this afternoon.' He frowned. 'Surely there's someone you can go and stay with for a few days?'

She shook her head. 'Besides, there's Blossom.'

'You will come back with me, Isobel, and Blossom shall come with you, and you'll do nothing at all for at least two days. After that you can find yourself another case.'

He looked around the little room. 'You can't stay here alone.'

'Oh, but I…'

'I must ask you not to argue, Isobel. I got back from the Caribbean this morning early and I have a touch of jet lag. Now go and pack a few things for your mother and be ready to leave here in an hour's time.'

She said fiercely, 'Yes, but that's all very well—how did you know…?'

'I have ways of finding out. Now be a good girl and do as I ask.' He stood up, towering above her head, and she got up too. She said with belated politeness, 'I hope you had a good holiday.'

He was at the door but he turned round to answer her. 'I've just spent two weeks with Ella,' he said.

It was silly to cry, she dried her eyes and went upstairs and began to pack a bag for her mother, embarking on a cheerful conversation about a rosy future, which, however much it cheered Mrs Barrington, held no comfort for her.

The doctor was as good as his word. Precisely on the hour the Rolls drew up before the front door. He got out and rang the bell, not noticing the twitching lace curtains in the houses on either side of him, and when Isobel opened the door he wasted no time, but lifted her mother into the car, put the luggage in the boot, Blossom in her basket on the back seat, shut the front door briskly and urged Isobel to get in beside him. He had barely spoken, and Isobel was glad of that; her head was full of the small problems of their sudden departure. Had she given the milkman sufficient warning? Had she double locked the back door? She had turned off the electricity; should she have done the same for the water? She had turned off the gas too, and taken everything perishable—and that wasn't much—round to the surly woman who lived next door. She had phoned the landlord and promised to send on the rent. She closed her eyes for a moment and didn't see the doctor's sharp glance. She had changed into her blue dress and done her hair and looked as neat as she usually did, only she was a bit too thin and pale.

And that was the opinion Mrs Gibson was quick to offer when she saw her. 'You're to come right upstairs with me, Nurse, doctor's orders, and go to bed. I'll bring you a nice lunch, presently. You shall see Nanny later, he says, but first you're to sleep.'

Isobel, in the room she had had previously, felt like bursting into tears again. 'Oh, please, Mrs Gibson, may I have a bath first? I'll be quick…'

So she had a bath and washed her hair, then got into bed and ate the delicious lunch Mrs Gibson brought up, and when the tray had been taken away she lay back on her pillows, thinking about the day's happenings.

Her mother wasn't far away. The clinic was a fairly small one in an elegant street not five minutes' walk from Thomas's house. She had been taken to a charming room on the ground floor and the Matron had listened to the doctor with the air of someone who wouldn't wish to vex him in any way, and Isobel, standing in the background, couldn't help but see that his air of authority carried a good deal of weight. She had bidden her mother goodbye and felt reassured to see her parent remarkably cheerful and happy. 'And you'll have a few days' rest, darling,' her mother had said, 'and you deserve every minute of them.'

And now here she was, tucked up in her bed in this delightful room with Blossom asleep on her feet, and she really must set her mind to making some sort of plan for the future. She closed her eyes the better to think, and was sleeping in the instant. The doctor, coming up to visit her, stood in the doorway, smiling a little. Lying in bed with her hair loose around her sleeping face, her gentle mouth slightly open, she looked surprisingly pretty.

CHAPTER EIGHT

ISOBEL WAS SITTING up in bed eating an enormous breakfast when Thomas knocked and walked in. His 'good morning' was as impersonal as a family doctor's and his glance even more so. 'Slept well?' he wanted to know. 'Get up if you feel like it, if you don't stay in bed, but be in bed by nine o'clock.'

'When can I see Mother?' She had a slice of toast, laden with butter and marmalade in her hand, ready to bite into.

'Not today.' He gave her a reassuring smile. 'I'll be seeing her later on, I'll let you know how she is. Tomorrow, if you feel really rested, there's no reason why you shouldn't see her.'

'It's very kind of you to have me here, but I'll go home after I've seen Mother, if you don't mind. I can get a case straight away, somewhere where I can go home each evening—because of Blossom, you know.'

He gave her a hard look. 'Just as you like, Isobel. But I beg you to allow your mother to stay where she is until her cure is complete. Are you all right for money?'

Isobel went a slow red. 'I can fetch Mother's pension at the end of the week.'

He nodded. 'I must be off, I've got a full day. Please remember what I've said. Mrs Gibson will get you anything you want.'

Everything but you, dear Thomas, thought Isobel, watching him go.

She got up presently and went along to see Nanny, now in a room of her own downstairs. They had coffee together and then Isobel went to the kitchen to talk to Gibson and his wife, a placid Blossom draped over one shoulder. She had her lunch with Nanny and after lunch, just as she was being urged to go and rest on her bed until tea time, the doctor rang.

'Your mother is fine,' he told her without preamble. 'She's had her therapy and settled in nicely. She sends her love. I hope you're doing exactly as I said?'

'Yes, Dr Winter, and thank you for letting me know about Mother.'

'Will you be good enough to tell Gibson I shan't be home for dinner?' His 'goodbye' was brisk and he hung up at once.

Obediently Isobel went to bed at nine o'clock after a leisurely session at the dressing table. A good sleep and a lazy day had worked wonders, but she longed for a row of expensive creams and lotions to turn her into instant prettiness. As it was, she slapped on most of a pot of night cream someone had given her for Christmas, brushed her hair, and got into her bed, where she sat doing terrifying sums in the notebook she always carried with her. The fees at the nursing home would be astronomical, not to mention speech therapy and physio, and she was determined to pay back every penny. If she got a job right away—night duty for preference—and she was very careful, her mother's pension would be untouched and could be saved together with most of her earnings. All the same, at a rough guess, it was going to take years to pay back the doctor. The slow tears dripped down her cheeks and she didn't bother to wipe them away, there were plenty more ready to follow them. She put the notebook down and closed her eyes.

The doctor, coming in at one o'clock in the morning, paused

in the corridor when he saw the light under her door, and when no one answered his knock, he went in. He stood for quite some time in the open doorway, looking at Isobel, fast asleep, her face shiny with cream, runnelled by tear stains, her hair tousled. Blossom was curled up on her feet and the notebook lay where she had put it down. The doctor crossed the room soundlessly and picked it up and studied it at his leisure, his face expressionless, then he put it back again, tickled Blossom's matronly chin, and went away. It was difficult to find a greater contrast between two girls—the lovely spoilt expensive young woman he had spent the evening with, and Isobel's unremarkable, shiny visage, and yet it was her face which was uppermost in his mind; had been for some time now, he had to admit. He went downstairs again, and into his study, to bury his handsome head in a pile of medical journals; reading them might clear his head of the ridiculous ideas invading it.

Isobel got up as soon as she had had breakfast, which Mrs Gibson had insisted on bringing her in bed. 'And I'm to tell you from the doctor that he has to be away until late this evening, but that you're to visit your mother when you wish and you're to ask Gibson to drive you back home. He said to tell you he's sure that you'll get another case very quickly and you're to get in touch with him if the need arises. Oh, and I almost forgot, Dr Martin—is that the name?—will let you know how your mother is progressing. There, I think I've remembered everything.' She beamed at Isobel. 'Now you eat your breakfast—and why don't you stay another day or two? Nanny loves to have you here, and you're not a scrap of trouble.'

Isobel summoned a smile. 'You're all so kind, Mrs Gibson, but I really must get back to work. I've had a really good rest and I feel as fit as a prize-fighter. I'll go and see Mother—and may I leave Blossom with Nanny while I'm gone? I'll be back before lunch and perhaps Gibson would be kind enough to take me home then?'

'You'll have your lunch here, Nurse dear, and no nonsense, and Gibson shall take you home when you've eaten it.'

Isobel was dressed and sitting at the pretty dressing table doing the best she could with her face when there was a knock on the door. Mrs Gibson with coffee, she had no doubt, or a message from Nanny to have it with her. It was neither. It was Ella Stokes, stunning in a suede skirt and a sheer silk blouse with nothing but flesh beneath it. Her hair was tossed into a carefully untidy mop and she had one of those shoulder bags which cost the earth slung over one shoulder. Isobel, eyeing all this, was struck dumb with surprise and envy, but before she could find her tongue, Ella spoke.

'Hullo,' she said, and smiled widely. 'I say, I came to say how sorry I was to hear about your mother—what rotten luck for her, and for you; you can't work, of course. She's getting better, though, isn't she? Trust Thomas for that; he enjoys pulling people back from the brink—oh, sorry, I shouldn't have said that—and he's so stinking rich that he'll not even notice the expense. You won't need to pay him back. Besides, I put in a good word for you and said you'd never be able to afford to, and he owes you a good turn after all you've done for Nanny.'

She sat down on the bed and Isobel said in a colourless voice, 'That was kind of you, but I don't need any help, thank you, and I prefer to manage my own affairs. The doctor knows that.'

Ella's tinkly laugh rang out. 'Oh, I know that too—what was it he called you? Prickly—he meant it nicely, of course.'

'Of course,' Isobel agreed gently. 'Why have you come here to see me?'

Ella's eyes widened. 'Why, to say how sorry I am, of course.' She got up and strolled to the door. 'I told Thomas I'd come; he's so good to the people who work for him, and I intend to be the same. Goodbye, Isobel.'

Isobel stared at her reflection in the triple mirror; it stared back at her, pale with rage and misery. She supposed that it was natural enough for a man to confide in the girl he was going to marry, and she had no right to mind that, but he need not have called her prickly or discussed her finances… Once again she sought fruitlessly for some means whereby she could pay the hospital fees. There were none.

She packed everything, so that she would be able to leave as soon as she had had lunch, took Blossom down to Nanny's room, and walked round to the clinic.

Her mother was up and dressed, walking up and down the corridor outside her room, a stick in one hand, the physiotherapist beside her. She was delighted to see Isobel and full of praise for the clinic. 'I'll be home in no time at all,' she told Isobel in her slurred voice. 'They're so kind and helpful and I know I'm going to get quite better. And you look rested, darling. Are you going home soon?'

'Today, Mother. I'll try and get a case not too far away and I'll let you know as soon as I'm settled with one. I'll take Blossom with me and only go somewhere where I can come home each day.'

'Dear Thomas,' said Mrs Barrington, 'how kind he's been! He came to see me yesterday and he's coming again this evening. He says I've responded so well that it will only be two or three weeks. I'm so grateful, and to you, darling, for all you've done for me.' The physiotherapist had walked a little apart. 'We are all right for money, aren't we?'

'Yes, Mother,' said Isobel steadily. 'There's nothing to worry about at all, all you have to do is get quite well.' She kissed her mother's cheek. 'Goodbye, love, I'll be along to see you as soon as I can, and I'll telephone tomorrow.'

At least her mother was going to be all right, she reflected as she walked back to the doctor's house, and that was all that mattered.

Home looked small and shabby and unwelcoming. Gibson had put her case in the hall for her, bade her a goodbye in a voice which held regret—the same regret Mrs Gibson and Nanny had shown. She had left a polite note for the doctor, a bread-and-butter letter which betrayed none of her true feelings, and now here she was, back in the little terraced house once more. She let Blossom into the back garden, put on a load of washing and made a pot of tea and presently telephoned the agency.

The agency lady was inclined to be huffy. Isobel had been one of the most reliable members, ready to take on anything at a moment's notice, and sick mother or no, she had been away all of three weeks. But the urgency in Isobel's voice melted the huffiness a little. She said severely: 'If you'll wait a moment I will see what I have in my files. You say it must be night duty and living out?'

She had exactly the right case on her files; she had already offered it to two other nurses who had refused it, but she had no intention of letting Isobel know that. 'It just so happens,' she said with the right amount of hesitancy, 'that there is a case—came in this morning.' She added mendaciously: 'Night duty, seven nights a week and live out. An elderly widow recovering from pneumonia and suffering from insomnia. She dislikes sleeping tablets and although she has living-in staff, she doesn't want their night's rest disturbed.' She added to clinch the matter: 'The pay is good; night duty seven nights a week—I know it's not acceptable, but it should be a short case.'

Isobel was doing sums on the back of an envelope. The money would be beyond her wildest dreams, and it really didn't matter what kind of patient she had, the thing was to get back on to a financial even keel once more.

'I'll take it,' she said. 'And am I wanted tonight?'

The agency lady heaved a sigh of relief that Isobel didn't hear. 'If possible. Here's the address, very handy for you.' She read out a house number and a street in Chelsea, very near the Embankment. 'You can get a bus across Battersea Bridge. The hours are half past eight until half past eight with half an hour for a meal during the night.' She added cautiously: 'There's no mention of breakfast, but I should suppose they would give you something before you leave each morning.'

It was nice to have something to do; it took her mind off Thomas and her mother. She hung out the washing, made up the bed, nipped smartly to the local shops and stocked up food for herself and Blossom, then returned to attend to the little cat's needs, cook a quick meal for herself and change into uniform. With Blossom safely in her basket, the doors and windows securely shut and the washing brought in, Isobel left the house. She had allowed herself time enough to reach the destination, but it was important to get there punctually on her first evening; she might have to wait for a bus, or not find the street at once.

As it turned out, a bus came along just as she reached the bus stop and she found the street without any difficulty. The house was half way down a terrace of Edwardian red brick houses, substantial, ugly and much sought after. Isobel turned on her heel with a good fifteen minutes to spare and walked back to the Embankment, to present herself, exactly on time, when those minutes were up.

A neat maid opened the door, wearing, most unusually, a black dress and a white apron and cap. She looked pleased to see Isobel and ushered her into a small room leading off the hall. 'If you'd wait a moment, Nurse, I'll tell Madam.'

The room was stuffy and far too full of furniture. Isobel found herself comparing it with the room she had first been interviewed in at Thomas's house and shook her head impatiently. To forget him was going to be impossible, but to encourage thoughts of him was just plain stupid. She stared at a glass case housing three stuffed birds until the door opened and an elderly man came in.

He said rather pompously: 'Nurse Barrington? I'm Dr Snow, Mrs Dalton's physician. I was informed of your coming and wished to see you to give you some idea of her illness.'

He took up a stand before the empty fireplace and cleared his throat. 'She is a sensitive lady, Nurse, and must be treated with great consideration. Her pneumonia is now resolved—antibiotics, of course—but she's always had a great fear of illness and can't believe that she can recover so swiftly. She worries unduly, refuses sleeping tablets as she feels they'll harm her, and as a consequence, sleeps very little. Her domestic staff have done their best but are hardly suitable…' He paused to look at Isobel as though he wasn't sure if she were suitable either. Apparently she was, for he went on: 'She must be kept content, you understand? There's very little nursing care needed; she's able to walk about, take baths and so on, but she requires a good deal of attention.'

He moved away from the fireplace to look out of the window. 'You're prepared to work for seven nights a week? Mrs Dalton dislikes the idea of different faces.'

'Quite prepared, Dr Snow. But I would like to make it clear to my patient that I must leave punctually every morning. If I'm to work each night there can be no question of staying later than half past eight in the morning.'

'Er—oh, yes, I'm sure there can be no objection to that. Now, if you're ready, we'll go to Mrs Dalton.' He added, more pompous than ever, 'I'm a busy man, Nurse Barrington.'

She didn't like him, and she had a horrid feeling that she wasn't going to like her patient either. And she was quite right: Mrs Dalton was sitting up in bed, a large, too fat woman in an unsuitable satin and lace nightgown. There were books and magazines strewn on the elaborate silk coverlet, and a box of chocolates, and a bottle of wine and glasses on a tray on the bedside table. The room was far too warm and smelled strongly of French perfume.

Isobel advanced to the bedside with Dr Snow and was introduced briefly. Mrs Dalton nodded at her, not smiling, her pale eyes screwed up in slow scrutiny. 'You're to come for seven nights a week,' she said.

'Yes, Mrs Dalton, but I've just told Dr Snow that since I'm to be here each night, I must leave punctually in the mornings.'

'I may not be ready for you to go exactly at half past eight.'

'In that case I might suggest that you get a day nurse to relieve me, Mrs Dalton.' Isobel heard Dr Snow's hissing indrawn breath.

'The very idea, when the house is crawling with servants! But I suppose I must agree, although I think it's very inconsiderate of you.' Her pale eyes swivelled to the doctor. 'You'll come tomorrow?'

'Of course, Mrs Dalton; mid-morning, as usual. And now I'll wish you a good night; I'm sure you'll sleep now that you have someone with you. I look forward to hearing better things of you in the morning.'

He didn't bother to say goodnight to Isobel but said loftily: 'I'll see myself out.'

Mrs Dalton, Isobel quickly discovered, was going to be a handful. She had met her kind before, of course, but on a hospital ward where the pithy remarks of the other patients did much to stop the constant complaints and demands. But there weren't any other patients with Mrs Dalton; she was able to keep up a string of complaints and self-pitying remarks and there was no one to stop her. It wasn't nursing, thought Isobel, it was pandering to a selfish woman who wasn't ill any more and who could have quite well done everything for herself. It was almost midnight when Mrs Dalton professed herself ready to try to sleep. 'And you will remain in the room, Nurse, I am sure to wake and need your attention.'

Isobel arranged a chair as far from the bed as possible, set a shaded lamp on a small table nearby and went to the door. 'I'll just go down to the kitchen and see if someone has left a meal for me,' she said calmly. 'I expect you'd rather I had it before you settle for the night.'

Mrs Dalton shot up in bed. 'But I can't be left! I'm ill, I insist…'

Isobel paused at the door. 'I was assured at the agency that I was to work for eleven and a half hours each night with a half hour meal break.' She added gently, 'The hours are very long, Mrs Dalton. I'm not supposed to work more than ten hours a night.'

'Well, I suppose you'd better go down and see,' said Mrs Dalton sulkily. 'I gave no orders, you'll have to find things for yourself.'

There was no need; someone had put a tray ready on the kitchen table, nicely laid out with cold meat and a salad under a glass cover, rolls and butter and a little dish of trifle. There was a thermos jug of coffee too. Isobel sat down thankfully, ate her supper, cleared the tray away tidily and went back upstairs with three minutes to spare. Mrs Dalton was awake.

'Well,' she said, 'I hope you haven't taken too much…'

'A tray had been made ready for me, Mrs Dalton—I don't know by whom. Is there anything else you would like me to do before I turn out your light?'

It was the first of a sequence of difficult nights; Mrs Dalton might be paying big fees, but she expected an awful lot in return. By the end of a week Isobel was almost on her knees, only the thought of the money she simply had to have kept her going. There had been no sign of Thomas; he had probably relegated her to the back of his busy mind, to be remembered in due course when her mother was cured. She was aware that this was an ungenerous attitude, but at least it propped up her pride.

She visited her mother twice during that week, going straight from a hasty breakfast, because she knew that once she had done the chores at home, attended to Blossom's wants and done any shopping, she simply would not have the energy to sustain a bright and cheerful conversation with her mother. As it was, she became almost as pale and thin as she had been while she had been nursing her mother.

It was in the early days of the second week that she acquired another responsibility—a miserably thin and tattered dog which she had found tied to the door of a derelict house on her way home. She had spent a fruitless hour knocking on the neighbouring doors trying to find its owner, but no one wanted to know, and in the end she had gone to the police station where a kindly police sergeant had advised her to give the little beast house room and he would let her know if the owner turned up. 'And that's not likely,' he told her. 'More than likely they did a flit and didn't want to be bothered with the creature. Not much to look at, is he?'

He certainly wasn't; a half-starved mixture of countless breeds with a long wispy tail and a pointed foxy face, his matted black coat sorely in need of attention. Isobel took him home, bathed and fed him, introduced him to Blossom, fed him again and settled him down on an old blanket. He was going to be a nuisance, but he needed a home, and his gratitude was pathetic. Within three days he was a firm friend of Blossom, and showed a flattering devotion towards Isobel.

'Heaven knows what Mother will say when she comes home!' Isobel told him. She had christened him Friday because that was the day on which she had found him, and bought him a collar and lead and a metal tag with his name and address on it. He went to the shops with her and had a quick gambol on the Common in the mornings; not an ideal life, she knew, remembering the long walks she had taken with two dogs which her father had owned years ago, but better than being left to starve on the end of a rope. He was company for Blossom, who after the first rather wary friendliness was now a devoted companion.

At the end of the second week, Dr Snow told her that her services wouldn't be required beyond another week. She felt inclined to point out that her services hadn't really been required in the first place, but discretion held her tongue for her. She had, after all, earned every penny of her money but it had been worth it, she had almost put all of it back into the bank towards Bobby's school fees.

She had taken Friday for his walk, tidied the house and was putting on the kettle for a cup of tea before she went to bed, when the door bell rang. Thomas was on the doorstep, carrying his bag and seemingly unaware of the twitching curtains on either side. He went past her into the tiny hall. 'Tell me, Isobel, do your neighbours watch your every movement? And why in heaven's name, if they want to be curious, don't they have a good look and not just peep round the curtains?' He put his bag down. 'I've taken care to look the part; I wouldn't want them to get ideas about your love life.' He smiled at her. 'My bag makes me instantly respectable.'

She led the way into the sitting room. 'You've come about Mother?'

'No, you. I hear you're working a twelve-hour night seven days a week. That's too much, Isobel. You look…well, never mind how you look, but obviously it's doing you no good at all.'

'How did you know?' she asked.

'Your mother mentioned Dr Snow's name; I happen to have a slight acquaintance with him. You'll give the case up, Isobel.'

There was nothing she wanted to do more, but the arrogance of it put her back up. 'I will not! Besides, I'm to leave at the end of the week.' She added bitterly: 'I don't know why Mrs Dalton needed a nurse in the first place. How is Mother?'

'Making excellent progress—a star patient. Another week and she'll be fit for discharge with an occasional check-up. I recommend a holiday and a return to normal life.'

Isobel stared up at him, all her careful calculations knocked for six. Holidays cost money; she would have to borrow the school fees once again. The doctor, watching her face, knew exactly what she was thinking. He said smoothly: 'We'll worry about that when the time comes, Isobel.' His eye fell upon Friday, who had wrapped himself round Blossom in her basket. 'What on earth have you dredged up there?'

'He was tied to the door of an empty house and no one wanted him. He's company for Blossom…'

'And suppose your next case is one where you have to live in?'

'I'll worry about that when the time comes,' she told him gently.

He said quite violently: 'No, you won't, by God! I'll take him home with me. I've been steeling myself to get another dog ever since old Prince died. Friday seems a fitting substitute and Blossom can come along too for company.' He glanced at the pair of them. 'They'll be splendid company for Nanny while I'm away from home.'

'You're going away?' Isobel hadn't meant to ask, but the words had slipped out.

He gave her a long considered look. 'Only to my consulting rooms or the hospitals where I have beds. Why should I go away?'

She was tired; too tired to think properly any more. 'Well, on your honeymoon…'

He said smoothly, 'Someone's been talking out of turn.'

'Oh, no—I mean it wasn't servants' gossip, and anyway, none of the people who work for you would do that, and Ella didn't actually say so—but when people get married they have a honeymoon, don't they?'

His eyes were dark flint. If she had been looking at him she would have seen how angry he was. 'It is the normal procedure, yes. Did she tell you where we were going?'

'No, of course not—she didn't actually mention going away with you, only that—that you were kind and considerate to everyone who worked for you and she intended to be the same.'

'And on the strength of that remark, you've come to the conclusion that Ella and I are getting married?'

'Well, you've just been away on holiday with her—and you spent the weekend…oh, that was weeks ago; you did, didn't you?'

He said silkily: 'Oh, yes Isobel, indeed I did. I had no idea you took such an interest in my private life.'

She looked at him without speaking and then because she could think of nothing to say that would help matters—for of what use would it be if she were to say: 'Yes Thomas, I take an interest in you because I love you, even though you're in love with Ella, whom I detest wholeheartedly,' she asked in a polite voice: 'Would you like a cup of coffee or tea? I was just going to make one.'

'No,' said Thomas, and he sounded goaded. 'If you would fetch a lead for Friday and put Blossom in her basket I'll take them with me.' And when she had done that: 'I thought, erroneously it seems, that we'd become friends, Isobel. I know it seemed unlikely at first, but you've grown on me, we seem to have done a lot together. You're a remarkably restful woman, you know.'

She bent over Blossom, not looking up. 'And a good plain cook,' she muttered, and had Blossom's basket snatched from her. 'You have no intention of allowing me to forget that, have you?' he said harshly.

She looked at him dumbly and went past him into the hall to open the front door. What with both of them, Blossom's basket and Friday dancing with excitement, there was hardly room to move.

'I'll see you're kept informed of your mother's progress,' said Thomas, sounding like Dr Winter at his most urbane. 'She should be at the clinic for at least two more weeks, so you can safely take a case outside London.' He looked over her head at the shabby wallpaper. 'Let Dr Martin know if you can't get back here, and we will arrange something. I'll take care of these two.'

'Thank you very much, Dr Winter, I'm very grateful,' said Isobel, addressing the vast expanse of waistcoat inches from her face. 'Goodbye.'

She opened the door. 'Never say goodbye,' he said softly, and kissed her hard.

The little house was very quiet after he had gone. Without the animals she was going to be lonely, but it was much better for them to stay at Thomas's house until her mother was home again and there was someone home all day. She made her tea and went to bed, to lie awake and plan. She would go and see her mother in the morning, tell her that after this week she might not be able to visit her for a while, and somehow, by hook or by crook, she would have to get a case as far away from London as she could. The agency was well known, they often had cases from the provinces, Scotland even. A week or two in some remote place would help her to forget Thomas, or at least come to terms with the situation. She fell asleep at last, quite worn out by sorrow so deep it made sensible thinking an impossibility.

Her mother, when she saw her in the morning, was remarkably cheerful. She was walking alone now, with a stick to give her security, and her speech was almost normal again. She was quite unconcerned about the future and Isobel didn't do more than touch lightly on it. 'I thought I'd get a case outside London, Mother,' she explained, 'now that you're so much better and in such good hands. Mrs Dalton's been a bit trying and I'll look for something easier.'

Her mother looked at her pale unhappy face. 'Yes, darling, do that. I'm quite all right here, and you can phone. It must be lonely at home.'

Isobel was to leave Mrs Dalton on the Saturday. On Friday morning she went to the agency and found, just for once, the agency lady in an unexpectedly friendly frame of mind.

'Funny you should come in,' she said chattily. 'There's a case at Penn—that's a village just off the M40 near High Wycombe, not all that way away but real country. A six-year-old boy with severe measles. His mother is expecting a baby very shortly and can't nurse him. There's an old nanny there at present, but she can't cope. It wouldn't be a long case, I'm afraid, but the conditions sound pleasant and they're a young family.'

'I don't leave Mrs Dalton until tomorrow morning,' said Isobel.

'That's all right. If you could manage to get down there on Sunday morning—that would give you twenty-four hours.'

It would be a scramble, thought Isobel, but it sounded just what she wanted. 'I'll take the case. How do I get there?'

'If you phone this number they'll come and pick you up.'

'Well, that's a change, and thank you. Would you mind posting on my fees? I'll need some money while I'm there.'

Mrs Dalton chose to behave really badly for her last night. There was nothing wrong with her at all, but somehow or other she contrived to stay awake, demanding drinks, her bed to be remade, her face sponged, more drinks, until finally she slept. She was still sound asleep at half past eight, and Isobel had no mind to wake her in order to take an insincere farewell of her. She drank a welcome cup of tea in the kitchen and left a polite message for her erstwhile patient with Cook, then she went home.

There was a lot to do—fresh uniform to pack, her mother to phone, and her new patient's mother, Mrs Denning, to give her details of exactly how to find her. This done, she washed her hair, ate several slices of bread and butter and fell into bed. She was up again in the evening; there was still her newly washed things to iron, the house to tidy and another phone call, this time to Gibson to enquire about Blossom and Friday.

Both very well and happy, he reported, and uttered the hope that they would be seeing her soon. She longed to ask after Thomas too, but there was no way of doing that. She sent her love to Nanny and hung up.

She was to be fetched between nine o'clock and half past in the morning. She got a sketchy supper, had a bath and went to bed and slept all night, although she hadn't expected to—her head was too full of Thomas.

A good night's sleep worked wonders. She was up and dressed and looking almost her usual calm self when the car arrived—an Aston Martin, driven by a youngish man with a craggy face, who got out and looked uncertainly at the miserable little row of houses. Isobel opened the door and wished him good morning and, with the least possible fuss, got herself into the car. The pavement was hardly the place to introduce themselves; the curtains were twitching like mad, and besides, Mr Denning looked uneasy.

'I'm afraid people like to see what's going on around here,' she explained, and when he laughed, she laughed with him. He was nice, she decided as they drove out of London, going westwards towards the M40. If his wife was nice too, and the little boy, she was indeed in luck.

She heard a lot about Peter, the boy, as they went. 'He's a high-spirited lad,' explained Mr Denning with fatherly pride, 'and he's too much for Nanny—actually she stopped being a nanny some years ago and does the housekeeping, but someone had to look after him. He's very spotty.'

'In bed?'

'I'm afraid so—he's been running a high temperature. He's only been ill for four or five days.'

Mr Denning turned off the motorway and took a country road, and presently reached Penn. It was a charming village, and Isobel sighed happily at the sight of the village green with its pond, and the lovely old cottages round it. The Dennings lived at the far end of the village in a low, rambling red brick house with a large, rather untidy garden, and when he stopped in front of the door it was flung open to allow several dogs to rush out, followed by a pretty woman, who embraced her husband and then turned to Isobel. 'Gosh, am I glad to see you!' she said happily. 'And Nanny will be even gladder. Peter doesn't like being in bed, you see, but he's not very well, she says. Presently, when you've got your breath, perhaps you'd take a look at him. The doctor's coming later this morning.'

Isobel was led inside, through a wide rather untidy hall, and up the stairs to a pretty room overlooking the garden at the back of the house. 'You unpack,' urged Mrs Denning, 'and come down when you've finished—we have to fix things like time off and so on, don't we?! We'll have coffee and then you can go and meet Peter. I'm not allowed near him because of this.' She patted herself gently. 'Only two weeks to go, and we do hope it's a girl!'

Left to herself, Isobel emptied her case, tidied her already neat hair and went downstairs. The sitting room was lovely, full of comfortable chairs, strewn with the Sunday papers and sleeping cats and dogs.

'We're not very tidy,' said Mrs Denning without being apologetic. 'Have some coffee and let's get down to this question of time off. We thought…' She stopped and looked out of the long windows behind Isobel, who would have liked to turn round and look too, only she was too polite.

'There you are!' cried Mrs Denning. 'I suppose you left the car at the front and came round the garden. You're just in time for coffee. And here's Nurse… I can't call you Nurse, what's your name?'

'Isobel,' said Thomas, and came round the back of her chair.

CHAPTER NINE

ISOBEL SHOT ROUND to face him, powerless to prevent the delight surging over her face or the colour flooding it, but her voice was commendably calm if a trifle high as she wished him good morning.

He crossed the room and kissed Mrs Denning's cheek. 'Molly, my dear, as beautiful as ever. How is my godson?'

'Covered in blotches and as cross as two sticks. I don't envy Isobel one little bit.'

'Isobel can cope with most things. Are you going to give me a cup of coffee? Jack's just coming, he's putting the car away.'

'They've only just got here, poor Isobel doesn't know a thing about us or Peter.' Mrs Denning poured coffee and Thomas took a cup over to Isobel before taking his own to an outsize chair between the two of them.

'Isobel and I will go and see Peter together, I can tell her all she needs to know then. Let's see, it's his fourth day, isn't it? I'll go over him just to make sure everything is OK.'

So far Isobel hadn't spoken a word, although she didn't feel out of things. The atmosphere in the room was friendly and when Mr Denning came in and poured himself a cup of coffee and sat down close to her she relaxed nicely under his casual charm, but once she and Thomas were on their own, going upstairs to visit the invalid, it was a different matter. She stopped at the head of the stairs and turned to look at him. 'I didn't know Peter was a patient of yours, Dr Winter—I would have refused the case if I'd known...'

He leaned back against the banisters, his hands in his pockets, studying her face. 'I do believe you would, too. Too late now, it's this way.'

He led her down a short passage at the back of the house. 'I saw your mother quite late yesterday evening, she really is doing splendidly. How very fortunate that Bobby has gone straight from school to stay with friends.'

'Yes, it's funny how things turn out—one worries, and there's really no need.'

The doctor grunted, then opened a door and stood aside for her to go into the room, which was large and light and airy, the walls hung with posters and with a bed facing the window. The small boy in it looked suspiciously at her and then whooped with joy.

'Uncle Thomas! I want to get up—say I can! Nanny says no, but she's not a doctor.'

His godfather strolled across the room and leaned over the end of the bed. 'Nanny's quite right, you can't get up until your temperature goes down. Isobel's come to look after you and give Nanny a rest—she's going to phone me each day, and when she says you have no more fever, then you may get up, not before. Now lie down, there's a good chap, while I take a look.'

Peter allowed Isobel to give a hand, studying her the while. 'You look nice,' he decided finally. 'You're not very pretty, but your mouth turns up and your eyes twinkle. Will you get angry with me?'

'I don't suppose so,' said Isobel. 'I've got a young brother of my own, you see, and I don't suppose you'll do anything outrageous.'

She sat him up and laid him down, took his temperature and finally made him comfortable against his pillows once more.

'It's very dull in bed,' complained Peter.

'Then we'll have to find something to do to pass the time, won't we?' She smiled at him; even covered in red blotches he was endearing.

The doctor put his stethoscope away and wandered over to the window. 'Provided you do exactly what Isobel tells you to do, you'll be out of bed in five or six days, just nice time to see the baby when he or she arrives.'

'I don't really want a brother or sister, Uncle Thomas…'

'Oh, yes, you do—think how nice it will be to have someone to keep an eye on and boss around a bit—an elder brother is very important in a family, you know.' He strolled back from the window. 'I'll be down again in a day or two; look after Isobel, won't you? She's a stranger in these parts. Isobel, come outside while I give you some instructions.'

In the corridor outside he asked: 'Which is your room? This one?' He nodded towards the half open door of the room next to Peter's and when she nodded: 'Good, we'll get things settled, shall we?'

They sat side by side on the bed while he wrote out the routine she was to follow. 'And you must give me a ring if you're in the least worried—young Peter is a favourite of mine.' He turned to look at her. 'You don't look too good yourself—get out as much as you can. Molly knows about time off and so on. You may have to skip your day off this week, though, but they'll make it up to you.' He got up, so she stood up too and, because she felt shy and angry with him too, said the first thing that entered her head. 'How are Blossom and Friday? Did they settle down?'

'Very well—they're being hopelessly spoilt by everyone in the house. They're doing Nanny a lot of good, she's becoming quite active.'

Isobel edged to the door and out into the corridor. 'Please

give her my love. I'll—I'll go back to Peter if there's nothing more you want to tell me.'

He smiled faintly. 'My dear Isobel, there's a great deal I want to tell you, but not just now.' He opened Peter's door and she went past him and he closed it behind her without another word.

Peter was a handful, but compared with Mrs Dalton he was sheer heaven. She lost no time in establishing the routine Thomas had laid down, and while she obeyed it to the letter, she found plenty of time to amuse the small boy. Reading was out of the question for him, conjunctivitis was a real danger with severe measles, so she read to him by the hour and when he was bored with that, they made Plasticine models together. She had found two recorders in the nursery adjoining his room, and they played easy tunes together, making a lot of mistakes and rolling around laughing at themselves.

Isobel had been nervous of meeting Nanny, but she soon discovered that the poor dear was only too glad to have a lively boy taken off her hands, although she did sit with him while Isobel took her few hours off each day.

She didn't see much of Mr Denning, who roared away in his car quite early each morning, and roared back home again after tea, but she got to know Mrs Denning quite well—the soul of good nature, anxious that Isobel should be comfortable and happy. They lunched together each day after Isobel had divested herself of the white overall she wore over her uniform while she was with Peter. Strict isolation, Thomas had said, so strict it was.

She hadn't heard any more from him and although Mrs Denning talked about him frequently, she never said anything that gave Isobel an inkling as to what he was doing or where he was.

Probably married by now, thought Isobel miserably. How strange life was, she thought, lying awake in her pretty room. There she had been, bent on getting away from London, putting as many miles between her and Thomas as she could, and what happened? He turned up again. In a romantic novel, of course, the hero would have arranged the whole thing, but unfortunately this wasn't a romantic novel, just unkind fate playing a dirty trick on her. If she hadn't been so miserably unhappy she would have enjoyed herself in the Dennings' house. They were kindness itself. She had time to herself each day, Nanny was a splendid cook and little Peter liked her. The days were fine and warm too, and she began to acquire a pleasant roundness and pink cheeks. It was the kind of case every nurse hoped to get and so seldom did, and unfortunately it wouldn't last. Peter was very much better, the rash was fading and the complications which might have turned a childish illness into something serious hadn't materialised. She would be leaving in another week at the latest; there was no risk of infection now and once he was up and about his mother would be able to cope with him. He had a large garden to play in, dogs to keep him company; another week—maybe less. Isobel went down to breakfast the next morning quite sure that either Mr or Mrs Denning would tell her, ever so nicely, that they wouldn't be needing her for more than another few days.

She was right, of course, although it wasn't they who told her. It was Thomas, dropping in on the Saturday afternoon, to lie on the lawn behind the house, half asleep between his host and hostess. After a while he had heaved himself to his feet and gone upstairs to see his patient and Isobel.

'You're a fraud,' he told his godson. 'Tomorrow you're going to get up for an hour or so, and in a couple of days you can go into the garden, but only if Isobel says you may, understand?' He turned to Isobel. 'You're out of a job as from next Saturday, Isobel.'

'Yes—well, I expected to be, Peter's made such good progress.' She didn't quite meet his eye. 'And really it will be most convenient. I'll be home to look after Bobby…'

'You won't be taking another case?' Thomas's voice was bland.

'Of course I will, only I'll try to get one where I can live at home.'

'Perhaps I can be of help?'

She said gravely, 'You're very kind, but there's no need. I shan't find it difficult to get another case. Shall I see you before I go?'

He said easily: 'Oh, I daresay!'

'We've said goodbye so many times and then we meet again—it's strange.'

'Very strange,' he agreed blandly. He turned to look out of the window so that she didn't see the gleam in his eyes. 'But of course, I don't say goodbye, Isobel.'

She felt sick at the idea of never seeing him again. She said a little wildly, 'I saw a photo of Ella Stokes in the *Tatler*; she's very beautiful.'

If he was surprised at the sudden change of topic he didn't show it. 'Ella? No, she's not beautiful; stunning, pretty eye-catching if you like. Beauty is something quite different.' He added: 'Do you admire her so much?'

'She's all the things you say.'

'And a great deal more besides. She'll be a very expensive wife—it costs a lot to look like that.'

Isobel said in a strained little voice: 'Well, it won't matter, will it? Someone, I can't remember who it was, told me you had a great deal of money.'

When he spoke his voice was dangerously silky. 'And I suppose this person told you also that Ella and I were to be married?'

'Oh, no—' She hesitated, anxious to say the right thing. 'Well, yes—you see, it was Ella who told me you were rich and she said you were very good to everyone who worked for you and she was going to be like you—very good to everyone too.'

'Did she mention the date of our wedding?' asked Thomas with interest. He looked as though he was enjoying himself.

'No, but why would she tell me, Dr Winter?'

'I can think of several good reasons.' He turned back from the window. 'Have you had a day off this week?'

'No, but I didn't particularly want one. I'm not overworked, you know, and Mr and Mrs Denning are so kind to me. I've been out each afternoon.'

'Good,' he nodded. 'You look better. What's worrying you, Isobel?'

The question was unexpected and she stood staring at him, trying to think of an answer that might satisfy him. She came up with, 'Nothing,' which was of no use at all.

She could see that he wasn't going to leave it there. She was saved from a ruthless questioning by Mr Denning, poking his head round the door to announce that tea was ready and they were having it in the garden—something to which Peter took instant exception, demanding to go into the garden for his tea as well. 'I'll have my tea with you, Peter,' declared Isobel, only too glad to have time to collect herself before another bout of questions from Thomas. But in this she was thwarted.

'That'll upset Nanny,' said Thomas instantly. 'She's been looking forward to having tea with you, I heard her say so. There's jam sponge and she made it specially for you.'

'Oh, well,' said Peter, 'OK, but you won't be long, will you, Isobel?'

'No, love. We'll have a game of Ludo before bedtime.'

Tea was under the mulberry tree at the back of the house—sandwiches, cake and shortbread and scones. 'Nanny's a superb cook,' said Mrs Denning.

'So is Isobel—we fed like fighting cocks when we were in Oslo, and she did all the cooking at Orford.'

Mrs Denning beamed at Isobel. 'My dear, you never said…'

'Isobel is too modest about her perfections,' said Thomas, his mouth full of cake.

He went again before dinner, pleading an engagement in town. He kissed Mrs Denning, thumped Mr Denning on the shoulder and nodded casually to Isobel. To her, 'Goodbye, Dr Winter,' he didn't even bother to reply.

She devoted herself to young Peter for the whole evening, playing one game after another, and then went down to dinner, very bright-eyed and flushed, alternately falling silent and then bursting into conversation. Mrs Denning watched her pretending to eat and, when Isobel wasn't looking, winked at her husband. When Isobel had gone upstairs she said: 'I do hope Thomas knows what he's doing.'

'My love,' said Mr Denning, 'I've known Thomas for a very long time, I've never known him to fall flat on his face, and he won't now.'

'Yes, dear, I'm sure you're right, only I can't help feeling that they're at cross purposes, as it were.'

Her husband considered. 'Isobel is the kind of girl who'll think up all sorts of good reasons why she shouldn't marry a rich man, for a start. She has to be convinced that money is of no importance at all when you're in love. She also has to discover for herself that Thomas isn't and never has been in love with Ella, because he isn't going to tell her—indeed, she may have said something to make him hesitate to do so just for the moment. I think we have to have patience, darling.'

'But she's leaving at the end of the week,' said Mrs Denning fiercely.

Mr Denning picked up his newspaper and hid behind it. 'Yes, dear.'

It was Thursday before Mrs Denning found herself alone with Isobel. Young Peter, up and about and under Isobel's motherly eye, meant that she spent a good deal of time in the garden with him, playing croquet, strolling round tossing a ball, and on the one wet day they had, spending it in the nursery playing endless games of Ludo and sharing the delights of his electric train set. But on Thursday he had been invited to the kitchen to sit with Nanny while she made a batch of cakes, and Mrs Denning, drifting into the living room and seeing her chance, said at once: 'Let's have tea early, we'll go in the garden, shall we? We can have a nice gossip.'

They drank their tea and then ate the fairy cakes Nanny made so well, and talked about clothes and babies and children, and by easy stages through holidays and travel abroad, to Isobel's stay in Sweden and, finally, to Thomas.

'We've known him for ever,' said Mrs Denning. 'Quite brilliant, of course, and works far too hard. Everyone likes him, though he can show a nasty side if he feels like it. I'm so glad he finally finished with Ella—nasty little piece! He's been going off her for months, but she knew how to stick like a limpet, cooking up excuses for him to go to her parents for the weekend, pretending they were ill. I think he was amused at first, and then he got angry. He'd agreed to go to Italy with several friends and somehow or other Ella got herself invited. She did herself a bad turn, actually, because he loathed every minute of it. Of course, we've all known that he'd never marry her, but she was amusing and I suppose he was lonely. He's just been waiting for the right girl to come along.'

'And has she?' asked Isobel in a very small voice.

'Oh yes.'

Isobel, who had hated Ella wholeheartedly ever since she had first met her, formed an instant and strong antipathy towards this unknown creature. She would be blonde, of course—Thomas had admired Ella, hadn't he, and she was blonde… she would be a raving beauty, of course, because she couldn't imagine him falling for anything less than that, and she would have lovely clothes…

Mrs Denning, reading her thoughts accurately, said complacently: 'She's not at all like Ella.' She waited for this to sink in, then, 'We're going to miss you, Isobel—you've been so good, not taking days off and managing Peter so well. I'm sure without you he'd still be in bed with all those complications Thomas kept on about. Are you going to take a little holiday before your next case? Is your mother home yet?'

'No, but I imagine she soon will be, it's wonderful the way she's got better so quickly.' A holiday would be lovely, she thought, somewhere quiet with nothing much to do all day, while her mother got used to living normally again.

She packed her things the next day, played a final game of croquet with Peter, exchanged goodbyes with Nanny because she was leaving quite early in the morning and phoned the agency. No, there was nothing, said the agency lady. She was so sorry, but doubtless if Isobel liked to telephone on Monday there would be something in. Which in a way was nice, as she could have two days at home to see to the garden and her clothes and dust and Hoover. She wondered fleetingly why Mr Denning was so firm about her leaving directly after breakfast. She hadn't liked to ask, because probably they had plans of their own for later in the day. At least he was going to drive her to the station.

It was a beautiful morning when she woke up, and still early. She bathed and dressed, drank her morning tea and packed the last of her things. Mr Denning was a dear, but fanatical about punctuality so she went silently down to the kitchen where a housemaid was beginning on the breakfast and had hers sitting at the kitchen table. That way she'd have more time to say goodbye to Peter. She had already bidden Mrs Denning goodbye the night before and now she went back upstairs to Peter's room. He was awake, doing a jigsaw puzzle in bed.

'I wish you weren't going,' he said the moment she went in. 'I won't have anyone to play with.'

Isobel sat herself on the bed. 'Of course you will! Your mother can play with you now and soon you'll have the baby to keep an eye on, and you'll be going to school in a few weeks. My brother loves school and I'm sure you will too.' She held out a hand. 'So we'll say goodbye for now, shall we? We've had great fun together, haven't we?'

She got up from the bed as Mr Denning came in. 'Ready,

Isobel?' His eyes fell on his small son's unhappy face. 'Cheer up, old man, we'll see Isobel again.'

'Really we will?'

'Promise.'

Peter sat up in bed and flung his arms round Isobel's neck. 'Oh, I'm so glad! You're quite the nicest person after Mummy that I know.'

Isobel gave him a rather lopsided smile. 'Well, that's super, Peter.' She kissed the top of his head. 'So I won't say goodbye.'

'That's what Uncle Thomas said to you.'

It was funny how the man cropped up, just when she was trying hard to forget him. She followed Mr Denning downstairs and out of the front door.

Thomas was there, leaning against the Rolls' bonnet, whistling to himself. Isobel stopped at the sight of him and then walked on, for the simple reason that Mr Denning had given her a friendly poke between the shoulder blades.

'Morning,' said Thomas. 'Is this all the luggage?'

'Mr Denning's taking me to the station…' began Isobel in a voice that quavered.

'Well, that was the idea, but I happen to be around and it'll save him getting the car out.' Thomas opened the door and she turned to Mr Denning, all ready to ask questions, only he kissed her quickly and somehow or other she found herself in the car with Thomas, after a brief exchange with his friend, sitting beside her.

'Lovely day,' observed Thomas, and took the car out of the drive and into the lane.

'Delightful,' agreed Isobel, once more her sensible self and lapsed into silence. It wasn't until they reached the M40 and turned on to it that she spoke again. 'We're going the wrong way,' she pointed out.

'No, we're not.' His tone defied her to argue the point, but presently she tried again. 'Are you taking me to another case?'

She turned to look at his profile. 'When I phoned the agency there wasn't anything.'

'I know. I asked the woman to say that.'

'You *what*? But I need another job… You can't do things like that!'

'I can, and I do when it suits me. We'll talk about it later.'

'Now,' said Isobel very crossly and then subsided at his even: 'I said later, Isobel.'

'Well, I don't want to talk to you anyway,' she declared with a volte-face which brought a smile to his mouth, and she closed her eyes and pretended to go to sleep. She didn't sleep, of course, her head was seething with a wild medley of ideas which made no sense, and since she couldn't make head or tail of them she opened her eyes again.

They were racing down the M40, going beyond Oxford, a stretch of road she knew well; they would be coming to the exit for Lechlade soon. She gave a little gasp when Thomas slowed the car and turned off the motorway and turned the car again at the familiar signpost pointing down a narrow country road. Hinton Bassett six miles…

Isobel sat upright with a jerk. 'We used to live in Hinton Bassett!'

'I know.' He was maddeningly placid. 'Priory House—the people who bought it from your mother sold it to me a few weeks ago. Your mother is there, and Nanny is keeping her company for a week or so.'

She said in a very small voice: 'Are you going to live there? Mrs Denning said you'd met the right girl.'

'Have I not just said that your mother is living there, and will continue to do so for a great many years yet? I have a fondness for my future mother-in-law, but I don't want to live in her house when I have two perfectly good homes of my own.'

'Your *mother-in-law*?' Isobel's voice was squeaky with a rush of feelings.

'That's what I said.' He added softly, 'My darling girl.'

'Are you—are you asking me to marry you?' asked Isobel.

They were going slowly through the village and Thomas slowed the car to a stop outside the local stores and post office. He looked around him at the small bustle of a Saturday morning. Several people had paused to look at the car; it wasn't every day that Rolls-Royces actually stopped in their midst. He turned in his seat and looked at Isobel and began to smile. 'Not the best place in the world to propose,' he observed. 'Just think, in years to come when our children want to know how their parents became engaged I shall be forced to say "outside a grocer's shop". No romance, my dear love, and I thought you were romantic!'

'Oh, but I am—if I say yes now, could we drive on and stop somewhere quiet, and you can ask me again?'

Thomas didn't answer her, only smiled with such tenderness that her insides melted, and then he started the car again. He stopped at the top of the gentle hill through the village at a spot where if one craned one's neck one could see the tall brick chimneys of Priory House half way down the valley beyond. He got out of the car and went round and opened Isobel's door. She fell into his arms and he held her close.

'For the second time of asking,' he said, 'but first things first,' and he bent to kiss her happy face.

* * * * *

The Chain Of Destiny

CHAPTER ONE

THE ROSE BRICKS of the gracious old manor house shone warmly in the late August sunshine, and the small groups of people walking towards it paused to admire the pleasant sight; it wasn't one of the great country houses but it was early Tudor, still occupied by the descendants of the man who had built it and well worth a pleasant drive through the Wiltshire countryside on a bright afternoon.

There were still ten minutes before the door, solid wood in its stone archway, would be opened, and the visitors strolled around, studying the latticed windows and black and white plasterwork which presented a picture of enduring peace.

Appearances could be deceptive; behind its serene front there was a good deal of activity. The family had retired to their private wing, leaving a number of people to organise the afternoon. Mr Toms, the estate steward, was in charge; a small wiry man, familiar with the house down to its last creaking floorboard, he was counting small change into a box on the table just inside the door, ready for the vicar's wife, who would be issuing tickets. And disposed around the large square entrance hall stood the guides: Miss Smythe, the church school teacher, tall and thin with a ringing voice which allowed no tourist to dawdle or lose interest; Mrs Coffin, who ran the village stores and post office, and lastly Suzannah Lightfoot, whose aunt lived in the front lodge, offered to her for her lifetime after years of devoted duty to the family's great-aunt, who had lived to a great age and been something of a trial to them all. The family were seldom all there any more; the house was lived in by a peppery old uncle and his niece, a young woman of twenty-five or so, whose parents were living in America where her father had a diplomatic post. In the meantime the house was kept in good shape—helped by the modest number of visitors who came at weekends—ready for when the younger members of the family should return.

Mr Toms was frowning and tut-tutting. He had omitted to bring a spare roll of tickets with him, and there were barely five minutes before the door would be opened. He beckoned to Suzannah, gave her hurried directions and sent her off with an urgent wave of the hand.

She knew the old house well; two years ago she had been taken on as one of the house guides and, since she couldn't leave her aunt for any length of time, the small job suited her well enough. True, there was little money to be had from it, but what there was served to pay for her scant wardrobe and a few extras for her aunt, and she was a girl who made the best of what she had. Not that that was much.

She nipped up the worn treads of the oak staircase and along a wide corridor leading to the wing where the family lived and where Mr Toms had his office. It meant going through the picture gallery with its rows of paintings and dark oak wall tables and beautifully carved Jacobean chairs, isolated by crimson ropes, which she dusted twice a week. It was a gallery she loved, but she didn't waste time on it now, opening a little door in the panelled wall and hurrying along a small passage to Mr Toms' office. The roll of tickets was on his desk, so she picked it up closed the door behind her and started back again, a rather small girl with no pretentions to beauty, although her grey eyes were large and clear and her mouth, rather on the large side, curved up at its corners very sweetly. Her figure was pretty, but hardly showed to its best advantage in the checked cotton blouse and plain dark skirt; all the same, she was as neat as a new pin and her hair, richly red and shining, was tied back in a ponytail. She whisked through the door in the wall, closing it behind her, and then stopped short. Halfway down the gallery a man stood studying one of the portraits on the wall, and as she looked he began to stroll towards her. He was a large man, and tall, and certainly not in his first youth, for his hair was silvered at the temples and he had an air of assurance; he was also well-dressed in a casual way.

Probably sneaked in ahead of the rest, decided Suzannah, advancing towards him. She said politely, 'I'm sure you aren't aware that this part of the house is private? If you will come with me, I'll show you where the entrance is and you can join up with a guided party.'

He had come to a halt before her, studying her down his high-bridged nose with eyes as cold as blue ice. She bore this scrutiny with equanimity, although she went rather pink under it, especially when he asked indifferently, 'And what makes you think that I wish to be guided?'

She answered with tart politeness, 'It says very clearly at the door that visitors must take a guided tour, so perhaps you would come with me?'

'Are you a guide?'

'Yes.' She led the way through the gallery, paused at the end of the corridor to make sure that he was still behind her, and went down the staircase, where she left him with a firm, 'You may join any of the guided groups—you'll need a ticket.'

She turned away, but he put out a large, well-kept hand and took her gently by the elbow. 'Tell me,' he said softly, 'are you the local schoolteacher, or, if not that, the vicar's daughter?'

Suzannah lifted his hand off her arm and said with dignity,

'You are a very rude man.' She added with a tolerant matter-of-factness, 'Such a pity.'

The first of the visitors were being admitted; she handed over the tickets to the vicar's wife and went to stand in her appointed place to the left of the massive carved table in the centre of the hall. One by one she was joined by sightseers; each guide took from six to twelve visitors at a time, and today, with the summer holidays nearly over, there were fewer tourists; another month and the house would be closed for the winter. Suzannah, waiting patiently for the last of her group, allowed herself to worry about getting a job to take her through the months until the house opened again at Easter.

The guides were setting off, each on her own itinerary, and Suzannah counted heads, wished everyone a good afternoon and led the way out of the hall into the panelled dining-room, closely followed by an elderly couple, a stout man in a cloth cap, a thin lady in a hard felt hat, a pair of teenagers carrying a transistor radio and, last but by no means least, a tired-looking young woman carrying a fretful baby. Suzannah smelled trouble ahead, either from the baby or the transistor radio, but they had paid their money and they expected value for it. She exchanged a sympathetic smile with the young woman and took her stand by the table in the centre of the room. She laid a loving hand on its age-old patina. 'Elizabethan,' she began in her lovely clear voice, 'the carving is beautiful, and you will notice the bulbous legs, reflecting the clothes of that period; the oak cupboard is a court cupboard of the same period…' Her listeners crowded around as she pointed out the great silver salt-cellar, the engraved silver tankards and the silver sweetmeat boxes arranged on it. By the time they had reached the two-tiered chimneypiece they were beginning to show a faint interest and, much encouraged, she urged them to view the ceiling. 'Strapwork,' she recited, 'with a central motif of the ship of the Jacobean period. The same ship is carved above the door we are about to go through.'

Heads were lowered obediently as she led the way to the door, opened it and stood beside it to make sure that everyone went through. The last one was the man from the picture gallery, who despite his great size had managed to join the tail end of the group without her seeing him.

She gave him a chilly look as he went past her.

The dining-room led into the drawing-room, rather more William and Mary than Elizabethan, and here there was a good deal more to see. Suzannah went from the side-table with barley-sugar legs—these called forth a joke from the man in the cloth cap—to a Charles the Second armchair in walnut and cane, and a Gibbons chimneypiece. She loved the room and would have lingered in it, but her group were only vaguely interested, although they obediently followed her from one portrait to the next, commenting upon the opulent charms of the ladies in them and making outspoken remarks about the gentlemen's wigs, and all the while the man from the gallery wandered around on his own, but never so far that she felt that she must beg him to keep up with everyone else. A tiresome person, she reflected, leading her party across a handsome inner hall and into the ballroom.

It was here that the three guides met and passed each other and here, naturally enough, that the laggards wandered off with the wrong lot. Today there was the added complication of the baby beginning to cry. Its thin whimper gradually gathered strength until it was a piercing scream. Suzannah, gathering her little party together to move out of the ballroom and into the library, waited until the woman passed her.

'Look, why don't you sit down for a minute while I talk? We always allow a few extra minutes in the library, there's a lot to see.'

The woman looked very tired and pale. 'You don't mind?' she whispered and, rather to Suzannah's astonishment, handed her the baby.

It stopped crying at once, stared up at her with large blue

eyes and sank into instant sleep. No one seemed to have noticed; she tucked the infant firmly against her shoulder and made her way from one visitor to the next, answering questions and pointing out the massive bookcases, the library steps and the enormous painting on one wall depicting the ancestor of the present owner, sitting on his charger, and staring in a noble fashion into the middle distance.

An eye on her watch told her that she was a little behind schedule; she nipped smartly to where the woman was sitting and handed back the baby and turned away to collect up the others. The man from the gallery was leaning nonchalantly against one wall, his hands in his pockets, watching her and smiling. It wasn't a nice smile, she thought, and to her annoyance she blushed.

There was only the inner staircase, the state bedroom and the boudoir to visit now. They straggled up the staircase, not really listening to her careful description of its wrought-iron balustrade, nor were they interested in the coffered ceiling, but the bedroom they enjoyed, admiring the great four-poster with its brocade hangings, and the silver jug and ewer on the little oak table with the silver mirror hanging above it. And the boudoir was admired as much and at even greater length, for it was furnished at a later period, with hanging cabinets, a chaise-longue, and some pretty shield-back armchairs. But at length she was able to collect everyone and lead them back down the main staircase to the hall, trying to ignore the man who, most annoyingly, wandered along at his own pace and, when they reached the hall, disappeared completely.

'And good riddance,' muttered Suzannah, wishing everyone goodbye.

The next group was already forming, a quite different kettle of fish, she saw at once: a donnish-looking elderly gentleman accompanied by a staid wife, and two stout ladies carrying books on antiques. It was nice to have an attentive audience, and she enjoyed herself, although just once or twice she found herself wishing that the strange man had been there too. But there was no sign of him. She escorted two more groups round the house before the door was finally shut and, after doing a round to make sure that everything was as it should be, and checking the takings with the vicar's wife, she walked down the drive, took a short-cut through the dense shrubbery half-way down its length, and reached the small grass clearing enclosed by a plain iron fence. She stood alongside the gate, a handsome edifice of wrought iron between two stone pillars, lichen-encrusted and topped by griffons. The lodge was a picturesque cottage, built for outward effect, and quite charming with its small latticed windows, miniature gabled roof and tall, twisted chimneys. Inside, the rooms were poky and dark, and the plumbing was in need of modernisation. All the same, it had been home to Suzannah for several years now, ever since her parents had died in a motoring accident while she was at boarding-school. Aunt Mabel had just retired and had offered her a home at once, and Suzannah had left the school and her hopes of a university and gone to live with her. Any vague ideas she had had about her future were squashed within a few months when her aunt became ill and it was found that she had a cerebral tumour. Inoperable, they had said, and sent her home again under the care of her doctor and with instructions to Suzannah not to tell her aunt what ailed her.

There was a small pension, plus Suzannah's small earnings to live on, and the cottage was rent-free; they managed very well, and the tumour, slow-growing, seemed quiescent except for the headaches it caused. Suzannah, now twenty-two, had accepted her life sensibly, thankful that her aunt was still able to potter around and take pleasure from their quiet way of living, and if sometimes she regretted the future she had planned for herself, she never gave a sign that it was so. Only now, as she opened the door, she was wondering how she could best find a job which would allow her to be with her aunt for most of the day. But nothing of her worries showed as she went inside. The door opened directly on to the sitting-room, simply furnished but comfortable with a door leading to the small kitchen beyond. Another door in the wall opened on to the narrow stairs which led to the two bedrooms above; a narrow shower-room and toilet had been built on behind the kitchen when her aunt had gone there to live, and beyond that there was the garden where between them they grew vegetables and flowers, which Suzannah heaped into buckets and boxes and left at the gate in the hope that the visitors might buy them. Which they very often did, but now the summer was beginning to fade there was little to sell.

Her aunt was sitting in her chair with her cat, Horace, on her lap. She turned her head and smiled at Suzannah as she went in; she had a nice smile, which made her lined face looked years younger.

'There you are, dear. Did you have a busy afternoon?'

'Just busy enough to make it interesting,' said Suzannah cheerfully. Her eye fell on the table. 'You haven't had tea?'

Her aunt looked apologetic. 'Well, dear, I did get up to make a cup, but I had to sit down again. It's so silly, but I'm a little dizzy…'

Suzannah whisked across to her chair. 'Only dizzy?' she asked gently. 'No headache?'

'No, dear, just a dull, heavy feeling. I'd love a cup of tea.'

They had their tea and presently her aunt dozed off, which left Suzannah free to get their supper, feed Horace and shut up the few hens at the end of the garden. Supper was cooked and the table laid before her aunt awoke and sat down at the table. But she ate very little and presently said that she would go to bed.

'You're still dizzy?' asked Suzannah. 'I'll come up with you, Aunty, and if you're not better in the morning I'll get Dr Warren to call. Perhaps your tablets are too strong.'

She stayed upstairs until her aunt had fallen asleep and then cleared away their supper, laid the table for breakfast, settled

Horace for the night and took herself off to bed, worried about her aunt. True, she had been known to have dizzy spells before, but they were over quickly, and this evening her aunt had looked ill and pale.

She crossed the tiny landing and made sure that her aunt was asleep before she got into bed herself. It took her a long time to go to sleep, and when she did she dreamed of her aunt and, inexplicably, of the man in the picture gallery.

It was a crisp, bright morning when she got up. She hung out of her small window to admire the trees beyond the meadow at the back of the cottage. She put on her dressing-gown and crossed the landing, to find her aunt wide awake.

She was still very pale, Suzannah saw uneasily, but all the same she said cheerfully, 'Did you have a good night, Aunty? I'll get you a cup of tea…'

Her aunt peered at her. 'Not tea, dear, I don't feel quite the thing—it's so silly to feel giddy when I'm lying in bed, isn't it?'

She began to sit up in bed and then with a muttered, 'Oh, dear', slid back against her pillows. 'Such a bad headache,' she whispered, 'and I feel so sick.'

Suzannah fetched a bowl, made her aunt comfortable and murmured in a reassuring way and when, surprisingly, her aunt went suddenly to sleep, she leapt down the stairs to the phone, a modern blessing which had been installed when her aunt had first become ill. It was barely seven o'clock, but she had no hesitation in ringing Dr Warren; he had told her to do just that if he was needed, and she wasn't a girl to panic and call him for something trivial.

His quiet voice assured her that he would be with her in ten minutes before he hung up.

He was as good as his word, and by then her aunt was deeply asleep. 'More than sleep,' he told her, 'a coma, but not very deep as yet.' He looked at the small figure standing before him. 'Your aunt is too ill to move. Do you think you can manage?'

'Yes, of course—if you'll tell me what I have to do?'

'Very little.' He explained what needed to be done. 'And I'll get the district nurse to pop in later on.' He hesitated. 'I've an old friend staying with me for a couple of days—he's a friend of the Davinishes at the manor, too—he's a brain surgeon—I'd like him to take a look at your aunt, there might be something…'

'Oh, please—if there's anything at all… You see, she's been quite well for months and it's been hard to remember that she's ill. She's been getting slower and more tired, but never like this.' She shivered and the doctor patted her shoulder.

'Get yourself dressed and have some breakfast, I'll be back in an hour or two and see what can be done.'

He was as good as his word; she barely had the time to dress, bathe her sleeping aunt's face and hands and straighten the bed, feed a disgruntled Horace and make herself some tea before he was back, this time with his friend and colleague. The man from the picture gallery, coming quietly into the cottage, greeting her gravely and giving no sign at all that he had already met her.

But in any case Suzannah was too worried to give much thought to that; she led the way upstairs and stood quietly by while he examined her aunt with unhurried care and then trod downstairs again where he conferred quietly with Dr Warren. When they had finished Dr Warren called Suzannah from the kitchen, where she had been making coffee.

'Professor Bowers-Bentinck thinks that the wisest course for us to follow is to let your aunt remain here. There is no point in taking her to hospital; she is gravely ill—you do understand that, don't you? There is nothing to be done, my dear, and let us be thankful that she has slipped into a coma and will remain so…'

Suzannah gave a gulp. 'Until she dies?'

'Yes, Suzannah. Believe me, if there was the faintest hope of saving her by surgery, the professor would operate. I'm sorry.'

'How long?'

'A day—a few hours. I shall ask the district nurse to come here as soon as she has done her round. You will need help.'

All this while the professor had stood quietly by the window, looking out on to the little strip of grass and the flower border which separated the lodge from the drive. Now he turned to face her.

'I am so sorry, Miss Lightfoot, I wish that I could help, but Dr Warren is quite right, there is nothing to be done.'

He sounded so kind that she felt tears prick her eyes. It was hard to equate this calm, impersonal man with the hard-eyed, tiresome creature who had been in the picture gallery. She said in a small voice which she strove to keep steady, 'Thank you, I quite understand. It was good of you to come.' After a moment added, 'Aunty will sleep? She won't wake and feel frightened?'

'She won't wake again,' he told her gently.

She nodded her untidy red head. 'I'll fetch the coffee.'

They drank it, sitting in the small room, the two men talking about nothing in particular, covering her silence, and presently the professor got to his feet and went back upstairs. When he came down again, the two men went away, getting into Dr Warren's elderly car with a final warning that she was to telephone and that Nurse Bennett would be with her directly.

Nurse Bennett had been the district nurse for years; the very sight of her comfortable form getting out of her little car was reassuring. She had known Miss Lightfoot for a long time and Suzannah for almost as long. She put her bag down on the sitting-room table and said cheerfully, 'Well, love, we've known this would happen—it doesn't make it any easier for you, but it's a gentle passing for your aunty, and we'd all wish for that, wouldn't we, after all she's done for others.'

Suzannah had a good cry on to her companion's plump shoulder and felt better for it. 'I'll make a pot of tea while you go upstairs,' she said in a watery voice, and managed a smile.

Miss Lightfoot slipped away as she slept, and by then it was late in the evening and Dr Warren had been once more. He had liked his patient and felt sorry for her niece. 'Nurse Bennett will stay here tonight,' he told Suzannah, 'and I'll deal with everything.'

He went back home and his wife asked him what would happen to Suzannah. 'She's a sensible girl', he observed. 'That's a nice little house and I dare say she'll find work; she's a clever girl, you know, should have gone to a university by rights. I dare say they'll give her a helping hand at the manor house.'

The professor had already left to keep an appointment; Dr Warren picked up the phone and left a message for him.

Almost the entire village went to the funeral. Miss Lightfoot had been liked by everyone, and Suzannah, going home to an empty little house, felt comforted by their kindness. She had refused several offers of hospitality; it would only be putting off the moment when she would be alone with Horace. She had been unhappy before when her parents had died, and she knew that the unhappiness would pass, and pass more quickly if she faced up to it and carried on with her life as usual. She cooked her supper, fed Horace, saw to the hens and went to bed, and if she cried a little before she slept, she told herself it was only because she was tired after a long and trying day.

It was hard at first and time hung heavy on her hands, for she had been doing more and more for her aunt during the past few months. She turned out cupboards and drawers, gardened for hours at a stretch, and in the evenings sat at the table, pondering ways and means. Her aunt had left only a very little money, for she had been supplementing her pension from her small capital. Suzannah had a few pounds saved, but she would have to find work as soon as possible. There had been a rumour in the village that Miss Smythe had asked for an assistant to help her in the school; Suzannah had had a good education, a clutch of A-levels and could have had a place in a university. Much cheered with the idea, she went to bed a week or so after her aunt's death, determined to go and see Miss Smythe in the morning.

She was up early to find that the postman had already been—several letters which she skimmed through and laid on one side to answer later; the last one was from the manor house and rather surprised her—a formal note asking her to call there that morning.

She read it a second time; perhaps there was a job for her there? She got dressed and had breakfast, tidied the little house and walked up the drive and round the side of the house to the door which the staff used. She met Mr Toms as she was going through the flagstoned passage which would lead her to the stairs and the private wing. She had always got on well with him, but now he showed no wish to stop and pass the time of day; indeed, he muttered that he was already late and barely paused to wish her good morning, which surprised her very much.

Grimm the butler answered the door when she pressed the discreetly hidden bell by the door at the top of the staircase. He bade her good morning, ushering her into a small ante-room, and then he went away, to return in a few minutes and ask her to go with him.

She had expected to see old Sir William, but there was no sign of him in the study into which she was ushered. Only his niece, a girl a little older than Suzannah, sat behind the desk. Suzannah had met her on several occasions and hadn't liked her; she liked her even less now as she went on writing, leaving Suzannah to stand in the middle of the room. She looked up finally and Suzannah thought what a pretty girl she was, tall and dark with regular features and blue eyes and always beautifully dressed. She said now, 'Oh, hello. Uncle isn't well enough to see anyone, so I've taken over for a time. I won't keep you long. I expect you've heard that there is an assistant teacher coming to live here to give Miss Smythe a hand. She'll start after half-term, in a couple of weeks' time, so we shall want the lodge for her to live in.'

It was the very last thing Suzannah had expected to hear. She was sensible enough to know that sooner or later she would have to leave the lodge unless she could get a job connected with the manor house, and somehow she had believed that old

Sir William would have agreed to her applying for the post of teacher or at least allowed her to have stayed on and continued to work as a guide.

She said in a carefully controlled voice. 'I had hoped to apply for that post…'

'Well, it's been filled, and don't expect to find a job here. Sir William has been far too easygoing; I'm cutting down on the staff. But you're able to shift for yourself, I suppose?' She gave Suzannah a cold smile. 'I consider that we've more than paid our debt to your aunt; there's no reason why we should have to go on paying it to you.' She pulled some papers towards her. 'Well, that's settled, isn't it? I don't know what you intend doing with your aunt's furniture—sell it to the schoolteacher if you like, only the lodge must be empty of your possessions in two weeks. Goodbye, Suzannah.'

Suzannah didn't answer, she walked out of the room and closed the door very gently behind her. It was like a bad dream, only it wasn't a dream, it was reality, and presently when she could think straight she would come to terms with it. Without thinking, she took the long way round to the front door, through the picture gallery, and half-way along it found herself face to face with Professor Bowers-Bentinck. She would have walked past him, but he put out a hand and stopped her, staring down at her pale, pinched face.

'Well, well, Miss Lightfoot, so we meet once more—there must be a magnet which draws us…' He had spoken lightly, but when she looked up at him with her lovely grey eyes full of hurt and puzzlement, he asked, 'What's wrong? You're not ill?'

She didn't answer, only pulled her arm away and ran from him, out of the gallery and down the staircase, through the front door and down the drive. She would have to be alone for a while to pull herself together and then think what was best to do. Fleetingly she wondered why the professor was at the manor house, and then she remembered that old Sir William wasn't well. And anyway, what did it matter?

Back at the lodge, she sat down at the kitchen table with Horace on her lap and tried to think clearly. Two weeks wasn't long, but if she was sensible it would be time enough. She fetched pencil and paper and began to write down all the things which would have to be done.

The professor stood for a moment, watching Suzannah's flying figure, then he shrugged his huge shoulders and went back to the private wing, opened the door of the study and strolled in.

The girl at the desk looked up and smiled charmingly at him.

'Phoebe, I have just met that small red-haired girl who works as a guide here, with a face like skimmed milk and tragic eyes…'

The girl shrugged. 'Oh, she's that woman's niece—the one who died and lived at the lodge. The new assistant teacher will have to live there, so I've arranged for the girl to move out.'

He leaned against the wall, looking at her without expression. 'Oh? Has she somewhere to go?'

'How should I know, Guy? She's young and quite clever, so I've heard; she'll find something to do.'

'No family, no money?'

'How on earth should I know? Uncle William has been far too soft with these people.'

'So you have turned her loose into the world?'

The girl frowned. 'Well, why not? I want that lodge and there's no work for her as a guide—I've got rid of that woman from the post office, too. Miss Smythe can manage on her own, and if we get more visitors in the summer I'll get casual help.'

'Does your uncle know about this?' he spoke casually.

'Good heavens, no! He's too old to be bothered. I'll write to Father and let him know when I've got time.'

'And he will approve?'

She shrugged and laughed. 'It wouldn't matter if he didn't—he's on the other side of the world.' She pushed back her chair and smiled charmingly. 'Let's talk about something else, Guy—how about driving me over to Hungerford and giving me lunch?'

'Impossible, I'm afraid, Phoebe. I have to be back in town this afternoon.' He strolled back to the door. 'I came to see your uncle before I left.'

'You're not going? I counted on you staying for a few days…' She got up and crossed the room to him. 'You don't mean that?'

He had opened the door. 'My dear girl, you tend to forget that I work for a living.'

'You don't need to,' she retorted.

'Agreed, but it's my life.' He made no move to respond when she kissed his cheek.

'We'll see each other?' she asked.

'Undoubtedly, my dear.' He had gone, shutting the door behind him.

He went back to Dr Warren's house, made his farewells, threw his bag into the boot of the Bentley and drove away. But not very far. At the main gates of the manor house he stopped, got out and knocked on the lodge door. There was no answer, so he lifted the latch and walked in.

Suzannah was sitting at the table, neatly writing down what needed to be done if she were to leave in two weeks—the list was long and when she had finished it she began on another list of possible jobs she might be able to do. It seemed to her, looking at it, that all she was fit for was to be a governess—and were there such people nowadays? Or a mother's help, or find work in a hotel or large house as a domestic worker. Whichever way she looked at it, the list was depressing.

She looked up and saw him standing in the doorway, and for some reason she wanted to burst into tears at the sight of him. She said in a slightly thickened voice, 'Oh, do go away…'

Despite her best efforts, two large tears rolled down her cheeks.

'I'll go when I'm ready,' he told her coolly, 'and don't, for pity's sake, start weeping. It's a waste of time.'

She glared at him and wiped a hand across her cheeks like a child. She wasn't sure why he seemed to be part and parcel of the morning's miserable happening; she only knew that at that moment she didn't like him.

He pulled out a chair and sat down opposite her, stretching out his long legs before him. 'You have to leave here?'

'Yes.' She blew her nose and sat up very straight. 'Now, if you would go away, I have a great deal to do.'

He sat looking at her for a few moments, frowning a little, then shrugged his shoulders. 'Miss Davinish tells me that you have no job. Perhaps I could have helped in some way,' his blue eyes were cold, 'but it seems that I was mistaken.' He got to his feet. 'I'll bid you good day, young lady.'

He went away as quietly as he had come, and she heard his car drive away.

CHAPTER TWO

SUZANNAH DID HER best to shake off the feeling that the not very solid ground beneath her had been cut from under her feet. She might not like the professor, but he had offered to help her and she badly needed help, and like a fool she had turned his offer down; she hadn't even thanked him for it, either. A pity he hadn't had the patience to stay a little longer until her good sense had taken over from her stupid bout of weeping. She winced at the thought of the cold scorn in his eyes. And yet he had been so kind when Aunt Mabel had been ill…

As for the professor, he drove back to London, saw a handful of patients at his consulting rooms, performed a delicate and difficult brain operation at the hospital and returned to his elegant home in a backwater of Belgravia to eat his dinner and then go to his study to catch up on his post. But he made slow work of it. Suzannah's red hair, crowning her white, cross face, kept superimposing itself upon his letters. He cast them down at length and reached for the telephone as it began to ring. It was Phoebe at her most charming, and she had the knack of making him laugh. They talked at some length and he half promised to spend the next weekend at the manor house. As he put the phone down, he told himself that it was to be hoped that Suzannah would be gone.

He spoke so forcefully that Henry, his long-haired dachshund, sitting under his desk, half asleep, came out to see what was the matter.

He had a long list the next day, and when it was over he sat in sister's office, drinking coffee and taking great bites out of the sandwiches she had sent for, listening courteously to her rather tart observations on lack of staff, not enough money and when was she to have the instruments she had ordered weeks ago?

'I'll see what I can do,' he told her. 'We need another staff nurse, don't we? We didn't get a replacement for Mrs Webb when she left. You're working at full stretch, aren't you, Sister?'

She gave him a grateful look. Sister Ash was in her fifties, a splendid theatre sister and, although she had a junior sister to take over when she was off duty, she was hard-pressed. Just like Professor Bowers-Bentinck to think of that, she reflected; such a nice man, always calm, almost placid when he was operating, and with such lovely manners. She thanked him and presently he went off to the intensive care unit to take a look at his patient. It was as he was strolling to the entrance, giving last minute instructions to his registrar, Ned Blake, that he stopped dead.

'Of course,' he murmured. 'Why didn't I think of it before?'

'A change in treatment?' asked Ned.

'No, no, my dear chap—nothing to do with our patient. Keep on as I suggest, will you? I'll be in the earliest I can in the morning, and give me a ring if you're worried.' He nodded goodbye and went out to his car and drove home, where he went straight to his study, sat in his chair for five minutes or more, deep in thought, and then picked up the phone.

The voice which answered him was elderly but brisk. 'Guy, dear boy, how nice to hear your voice; it would be nicer still to see you...'

He talked for a few minutes and the voice said cosily, 'Well, dear, what exactly do you want us to do?'

The Professor told her.

Suzannah spent several days packing up the contents of the cottage. There was little of value: a few pieces of jewellery which her aunt had possessed, one or two pieces of silver, a nice Coalport tea service… She put them into cardboard boxes and carried them down to the post office, where Mrs Coffin stowed them away safely in an attic. The new assistant teacher had called to see her too, and had been delighted to buy the furniture, which was old-fashioned but well-kept. Everything else Suzannah had promised to various people in the village. And, this done, she set to, writing replies to every likely job she could find advertised which could offer her a roof over her head. Several of her letters weren't answered, and those who did stated categorically that no pets were allowed. It was a blow, but she had no intention of abandoning Horace, so she wrote out an advertisement offering her services in any domestic capacity provided she might have a room of her own and Horace might be with her, and took it down to the post office.

Mrs Coffin, behind the counter, weighing out oatmeal for a beady-eyed old lady, greeted her with some excitement. 'Don't you go posting that letter, m'dear, not if it's a job—there's something in the local paper this morning…' She dealt with the old lady and then invited Suzannah to join her behind the counter. 'Just you look at that, love.' She folded the paper and pointed at the situations vacant column. 'Just up your street.'

Suzannah, with Mrs Coffin breathing gustily down her neck, obediently read. A competent, educated person was required for a period of two or three months to sort and index old family documents. An adequate salary would be paid and there was the use of a small flatlet. Pets not objected to. Good references were essential. Application in the first instance to be made in own handwriting. A box number followed.

'Well,' declared Suzannah and drew a great breath. 'Do you suppose it's real?'

'Course it is, m'dear. Now you just go into the room at the back and write a letter, and it'll go with the noon post.' Mrs Coffin rummaged through a shelf of stationery behind her. 'Here, take this paper, it's best quality and it will help to make a good impression.'

'References…'

'You can nip round to the vicar and Dr Warren when you've written it. You just sit yourself down and write.'

The dear soul pushed Suzannah into the little room at the back of the shop and pulled out a chair, and, since she had nothing to lose, she wrote.

Three days went by and, though she had made up her mind not to depend too much on a reply, she was disappointed to hear nothing. She got up early on the fourth morning and wrote out her own advertisement once more, and was putting it into an envelope when the postman pushed several letters through the letterbox. There were still outstanding matters arising from her aunt's death and, trivial though they were, she had dealt with them carefully; she leafed through the little bundle to discover most of them were receipts of the small debts she had paid, but the last letter was addressed in a spidery hand on thick notepaper and bore the Marlborough postmark.

Suzannah opened it slowly. The letter inside was brief and written in the same spidery hand, informing her that her application had been received and, since her references were satisfactory, would she be good enough to go to the above address for an interview in two days time? Her expenses would be paid. The letter was signed by Editha Manbrook, an elderly lady from the look of her handwriting, which, while elegant in style, was decidedly wavery.

Suzannah studied the address on the letter: Ramsbourne House, Ramsbourne St Michael. A village, if she remembered rightly, between Marlborough and Avebury. She could get a bus to Marlborough and probably a local bus to the village, which was only a few miles further on.

She went to Mrs Coffin's shop after breakfast, told her the good news and posted her reply, and then hurried back to the lodge to worry over her wardrobe. There wasn't all that much to worry about. It would have to be her tweed suit, no longer new, but with a good press it would pass muster; it was grey herringbone and did nothing to improve her looks, but on the other hand she considered that it made her look sober and serious, two attributes which would surely count when it came to selecting a candidate for the job? There was a grey beret to go with the suit, and a pair of wellbrushed black shoes and her good leather handbag and gloves. She tried them all on to make sure that they looked all right, with Horace for an audience.

The appointment was for two o'clock; she had an early lunch, told Horace to be good while she was away, and caught the bus to Marlborough. There was a local bus going to Avebury several times a day and she caught it without trouble, arriving at Ramsbourne St Michael with time enough to enquire where Ramsbourne House was and then walk for ten minutes or so to the big gates at the end of a country lane.

The drive was a short one, running in a semicircle between shrubs, and it opened out before a pleasant Regency house, painted white and with wide sash-windows. The drive disappeared round one side, but Suzannah went to the canopied porch and rang the bell.

An elderly maid opened the door and Suzannah said, 'Perhaps I shouldn't have come to this door—I've come for an appointment about a job…'

The woman smiled and ushered her inside. 'That's right, miss, I'll show you where you can wait.'

She opened a door to one side of the entrance hall and Suzannah went past her into a pleasant room with wide windows overlooking the side of the house. She paused only for a moment, and then sat down in the nearest chair.

She hoped that her surprise hadn't shown too clearly upon her face; it had been foolish of her to suppose that she would be the only person after the job. She murmured a rather belated good afternoon and took a surreptitious stock of the other occupants of the room. There were four of them, and each of them had the look of a woman who was skilled at her work and knew it. One of them said loudly now, 'There is no mention of shorthand and typing, but I imagine it will be an absolute must for this kind of job.' The others agreed and Suzannah's heart sank into her shoes. Her journey was a waste of time; she could have put her advertisement in the paper three days ago and perhaps by now she would have had some replies; time was running out… She checked her thoughts; fussing wasn't going to help. She watched the other young women go in one after another until she sat alone, and presently the last one came out and gave her a cursory nod. 'You can go in.'

So Suzannah knocked on the door at the end of the room and went in. The room was large, opulently furnished in an old-fashioned style and very warm. Two old ladies sat on either side of a bright fire and neither spoke as she crossed the room over the polished wood floor towards them. When she was near enough she wished them a good afternoon in her quiet voice and stood patiently while they took a good look at her.

One of the old ladies took up her letter and read it. 'Suzannah Lightfoot? A pretty name. What do you know about cataloguing and indexing documents?'

'Nothing—that is, I have never done it before, but I think it must be largely a matter of common sense and patience. I'm interested in old books and papers, and I know I would very much like the work, but I can't do shorthand nor can I type.'

The second old lady said thoughtfully. 'From your references I see that you had a place offered you at Bristol University reading English Literature. You didn't mention that in your reply to my advertisement.' And when Suzannah didn't answer, 'Modesty is always refreshing. We think that you will be very suitable for the post. The salary we offer is by no means large; indeed, we were left with the impression that it is quite inadequate when it was mentioned to our other applicants. But there is a small flatlet where you may live while you are here.'

'I have a well-behaved cat,' said Suzannah.

'We have no objection to your pet, but perhaps you may object to the salary we offer.' She mentioned a sum which, while modest, was a good deal more than Suzannah had hoped for.

She said quickly, 'I'm quite satisfied with that, thank you, Miss Manbrook.'

'Then we shall expect you—let me see—in four days' time? I think it best if we send the car for you, since you will have luggage and your cat. We have your address, have we not?' She glanced at the other lady. 'You agree, Amelia?' and when that lady nodded, 'Then you will be good enough to press the bell; you will wish to see the flat.'

The same elderly maid answered it and led Suzannah away, back across the hall down a passage and out of a side door. The small courtyard outside was encircled with outbuildings: a garage with a flat above it, store-rooms and what could have been a stable, now empty. At the end of these there was a small door which her companion opened. There was a tiny hall leading to a quite large room with a cooking alcove in one corner and an open door leading to a small bathroom. There were windows back and front and a small Victorian fireplace. It was nicely furnished and carpeted and, although the front window looked out upon the courtyard and the side of the house, the view from the back window was delightful.

'Oh, how very nice,' said Suzannah, and beamed at her companion. 'Would you tell me your name?'

'Parsons, miss. And you've no call to be nervous; there's the cook's flat over the garage and the rest of us have got rooms on this side of the house.'

Her rather severe face broke into a smile. 'I was hoping it

would be you, miss—didn't take a fancy to any of the other young women.'

'Why, thank you, Parsons. I'm quite sure I'm going to be very happy here. When I come in four days' time will you tell me where to go for meals and at what time?'

'It'll be Mr Snow to tell you that, miss—the butler, it's his day off but he'll be here when you come.'

'You've been very kind. Now I must go back and pack my things. Miss Manbrook…'

'Lady Manbrook, Miss.'

'Oh, I didn't know. She didn't mention when I would be fetched.'

'Mr Snow will let you know.'

'Oh, good.' At the door, on the point of leaving, she asked, 'And the other lady?'

'That's Lady Manbrook's sister, miss, Mrs van Beuck; they're both widowed.'

'Thank you, Parsons.' Suzannah glanced at her watch. 'I must catch my bus.' They wished each other goodbye and she went off down the drive and along the lane and found that she would have to wait ten minutes or so for a bus, which gave her the chance to think over her afternoon and dwell on the delights of the little flat.

Her friends in the village were glad when she told them her news. Mrs Coffin gave her an old cat basket for Horace, Dr Warren and his wife gave her a pretty eiderdown, and Miss Smythe presented her with a red geranium in a pot. Suzannah bade them all goodbye, cleaned the lodge ready for its new occupant, packed the last of her possessions and, obedient to Mr Snow's letter, stood ready and waiting by ten o'clock in the morning, Horace restless but resigned beside her in his basket.

It was a pity there was no one to see her leave, thought Suzannah, for the car which arrived was an elderly, beautifully maintained Daimler. The driver was a short, thick-set man, with grey hair, very smart in his dark grey uniform.

He replied in a friendly way to her good morning and added, 'Croft's the name, miss. I'll just put everything in the boot.' He eyed Horace, peering at him through the little window of his basket. 'You've got a cat there? He can go on the back seat.'

His wife was housekeeper for Lady Manbrook, he informed Suzannah as they drove; they had been there for twenty-five years and most of the staff had been there almost as long. 'I hope you like a quiet life, miss,' he observed, 'for there's nothing to do of an evening. Got a telly, have you?'

'No, I haven't, but I have got a little radio and I like reading. I'll be quite happy; I've lived in the country for some time and I like it.'

'Of course, there's guests from time to time, but mostly it's just the two ladies.'

She had been a little nervous of meeting Mr Snow, but she need not have been. True, he was very dignified and smiled seldom, but she felt that he approved of her. She was handed the key of her new home, her luggage and Horace were deposited in it and she was requested to present herself in half an hour in the front hall, when she would be taken to Lady Manbrook.

Half an hour wasn't long in which to get settled in; Horace, set free and allowed to roam round the room, ate the snack she got for him and settled down on the window-sill beside the geranium, and she made herself a cup of coffee, tidied her already neat person and went across to the house.

The two old ladies didn't look as though they had moved since she had last seen them, only they wore different dresses. The butler ushered her in and Lady Manbrook said, 'Come and sit down, Miss Lightfoot. Snow, please bring coffee; we will lunch half an hour later than usual, that will give Miss Lightfoot time to unpack her things.'

Snow trod quietly away and Suzannah waited to see what was to happen next.

'When we have had coffee Snow will show you to the room where you will work,' said Lady Manbrook. 'The papers and diaries are in one of the attics; he will accompany you there and you may decide which of them you wish to begin work upon.'

'Some of them are most interesting, so I am told,' remarked Mrs van Beuck.

'Do you want to see any of them before I start?' asked Suzannah. 'There is nothing private…?'

'I think not; if there is, I feel sure that you will inform me. All I require is that they should be put in some kind of order, and when that is done, I should like you to read them carefully and index them.'

'Are there many papers?'

'I have been told that there are two or three trunks. These things do tend to accumulate,' added Lady Manbrook vaguely. 'Ah, here is coffee. Be good enough to pour, Miss Lightfoot. We lunch at half-past one; you will, of course, join us.'

Suzannah thanked her nicely, drank her coffee and excused herself. If she looked sharp about it, she could unpack and get settled in, feed Horace properly and introduce him to his surroundings before then. And in the afternoon she would make a start on the contents of the attic. She found Snow waiting for her in the hall and they climbed the staircase at the back of the hall to the floor above, opened a door in a wall and climbed to the next floor and then once more mounted a very narrow, twisting staircase to the attics. Snow opened a door with a flourish and she went in. There were several attics, running the length of the house, connected by open archways, all well lit by dormer windows. The trunks were in the second, large and old-fashioned, made of leather and strapped tightly. They undid one of them between them and Suzannah got down on her knees to inspect the contents. There was no sort of order: bundles of letters, foolscap sheets tied with string, a number of what appeared to be diaries all jostled themselves together. It would be hard to know where to begin, she decided.

'Lady Manbrook said that you would show me where I could work, Mr Snow, but I think I shall have to do the sorting here.

There's plenty of room and the light's good. When I've got things in a bit of order I can carry them to wherever I've to work and start the indexing.'

'Just as you say, miss. I will arrange for a small table and chair to be brought here, and anything else that you may require. I must say there appears to be a good deal of work involved.'

'Yes, I think so, too,' said Suzannah cheerfully, 'but I'm sure it will be interesting.' They went back down the little stairs and he showed her a room, very light and airy with a wide table and comfortable chair and an open hearth, in which, he pointed out, a fire would be lit while she was working there.

Her own little room seemed very small when she reached it, but decidedly cosy; it already looked like home, too, with the geranium on the window-sill and Horace curled up on one of the chairs. She unpacked her few things, fed him and took him outside for a short time and then tidied herself and went back to the house for lunch—a meal eaten in some state in a large, heavily furnished dining-room with a great deal of white damask and silver. After an initial shyness Suzannah began to enjoy herself; the two old ladies were charming, keeping up a gentle flow of conversation calculated to put her at her ease. She left them after they had had their coffee, took a quick look to see if Horace was comfortable, and then repaired to the attics.

It seemed at first glance a formidable task, but not a dull one. She opened the first trunk…

She was completely absorbed when Snow tapped on the door and brought her a tea-tray. She sat back on her heels and said apologetically, 'Oh, Mr Snow, I could have come down—I didn't know.' She smiled at him. 'I got rather carried away.'

He surveyed the neat rows of piled-up papers, old dance programmes, newspaper cuttings and the like. 'Indeed, miss, I can well understand that. It is no trouble to bring you a tea-tray. Dinner is at eight o'clock; the ladies go to dress just after seven o'clock.'

'Oh, but surely I'm not to dine with them?'

'Indeed you are, miss. They quite understand that you would not wish to join them for tea and interrupt your work, and breakfast is taken by the ladies in their beds. Your breakfast will be served in the morning-room at eight o'clock.'

'Thank you, Mr Snow.'

'And if you will not find it presumptuous, miss, you should address me as Snow.'

'Oh, but the maid who showed me to my room called you Mr Snow.'

'And quite rightly; I am in charge of the staff here and head of the domestics, but you, miss, are employed by Lady Manbrook.'

She said in her sensible way, 'Oh, I see, thank you for telling me. I'll try not to give any of you any extra work.'

'If I may say so, miss, it is a pleasure to have some one young in the house.'

He made his stately way out of the room, leaving her to enjoy tiny sandwiches, hot buttered toast and fairy cakes as light as air.

By seven o'clock she had the trunk empty, its contents extending in piles half-way across the attic floor. Tomorrow she would go through each pile and arrange the contents according to the dates, dealing with the newspaper cuttings first, for it seemed to her that they would be the easiest. There were two more trunks; she would have to sort them in the same way and then add the piles together. Weeks of work, if she was to index them too.

She went downstairs and through the side door to her flat, fed Horace and took him for a brief stroll, then came back to switch on the lights and draw the curtains. A fire had been laid ready to light in the small grate and she put a match to it, put the fireguard in front of it and went to take a bath and dress. She had nothing really suitable for dinner, only a dark brown dress in fine wool, very plain and at least two years old, or a grey pinafore dress with a white silk blouse. She got into the brown, promising herself that with her first pay packet she would buy something suitable for dining in the splendour of Lady Manbrook's dining-room. She took pains with her face, brushed her tawny head until it shone like copper, and went back to the house to be met by Snow.

'The ladies expect you to join them in the drawing-room,' he offered, and led the way.

Suzannah saw at a glance that her brown dress was woefully inadequate, but she didn't allow it to worry her; she sat down to enjoy her sherry and take her sensible part in the conversation. And dinner, although somewhat more lengthy than lunch, was just as pleasant. She excused herself shortly afterwards, wished the two ladies goodnight and went back to her room. The fire was burning nicely and Horace was sitting before it, the picture of a contented cat. Suzannah too uttered a sigh of contentment, made a cup of tea from the selection of beverages she had found in the tiny cupboard in the kitchen corner, and went to bed. The room was warm and the firelight comforting, and she curled up and went to sleep within minutes, with Horace beside her.

Within a few days she had found her feet. She had little time to herself but that didn't matter overmuch; no one had suggested the hours she should work, so she arranged her own; from nine o'clock in the morning until lunchtime, and then work again without a pause until the seven o'clock gong. Horace, that most amenable of cats, was quite happy to have a walk in the morning after breakfast, another few minutes after lunch and then a more leisurely stroll in the evening. Snow had offered scraps from the kitchen: tasty morsels of chicken, ends off the joints and fish; and she had arranged to have milk left at her door from the local farm. Life might be busy, but it was pleasant, and she had no idle moments in which to repine. When the opportunity occurred, she would have to ask about having a half-day a week so that she could shop in Marlborough for her bits and pieces.

She thought that probably she was going about her task in a very unprofessional way but, be that as it may, she had made headway. The piles of letters, cuttings and old photographs were beginning to take shape and make sense.

Some of them were very old indeed; letters written in spidery hands, crossed and recrossed, invoices and bills, dressmaker's accounts and any number of receipts and recipes. She began to deal with these, getting them roughly into date order, separating them into heaps. It was slow work but she was methodical and very patient. She was able to tell Lady Manbrook that the last of the trunks had been emptied by the end of her first week; it had seemed a good opportunity to ask about her working hours, but before she could touch on the subject Mrs van Beuck observed, 'You will accompany us to church, my dear? The rector preaches an excellent sermon. You will come in the car with us, of course; it will be at the front door at half-past ten precisely.'

She looked across at her sister, who smiled and nodded. 'We have discussed the matter,' she said, 'and we would prefer to call you by your Christian name if you have no objection?'

'Oh, I'd like you to. No one calls me Miss Lightfoot—well, almost no one.' She had a brief memory of Professor Bowers-Bentinck's cold voice uttering her name with what seemed to her to be mocking deliberation. And after that it hardly seemed the moment to bring up the matter of her free time. It was, after all, only a week since she had started work, and she was happy in her little flat and everyone was kind to her; even Snow, who could look so austere, had unbent sufficiently to save the best morsels for Horace. There was, of course, the little matter of when she would be paid. She had a little money, but it wouldn't last for ever. Perhaps Lady Manbrook intended to pay her when she had finished her work, but that would be a month or six weeks away, or even longer. There was no use worrying about it; she went back to the attic with the careful notes she had made to show Lady Manbrook and then made her way back to the flat to get ready for dinner.

She would have enjoyed the walk to church in the morning but, since she had been expected to accompany the ladies, she got into the old-fashioned car with them and was borne in some state to the village church. The family pew was at the front and the church was comfortably full; she was conscious of curious glances as she followed the two ladies down the aisle. After the service, as they made their stately progress to the church porch, she was introduced to the rector and a number of elderly people who made vague, kind enquiries about her without really wanting to know, so that she was able to murmur politely without telling them anything.

At lunch she made another effort to talk about her free time; indeed, she got as far as, 'I was wondering about my hours of work…' only to be interrupted by Lady Manbrook with a kindly, 'We have no intention of interfering, Suzannah. It is, I'm sure, most interesting and you enjoy it, do you not? And I must say that what you have told us about it, has whetted our appetites to know more about your finds. Perhaps you would take tea with us this afternoon and bring down those old dance programmes you were telling us about? We have tea at four o'clock, and it would be most amusing to go through them.'

'I haven't got them in order yet, Lady Manbrook…'

'You are so quick and efficient that I'm sure you can get them sorted out before tea.' The old lady smiled at her very kindly, so that Suzannah stifled a sigh and agreed.

So when she had fed Horace and taken him for his short trot, she went back to the attic once more. It was a lovely day, and a walk would have been very satisfying; she made up her mind to talk to Lady Manbrook when she went downstairs for tea.

She was on her knees, carefully sorting the old-fashioned dance programmes with their little pencils attached into tidy piles; most of them were late nineteenth century and charming, and she lingered over some of them, trying to imagine the owners, picturing the quadrilles and polkas and waltzes they must have danced and their elaborate dresses. She was so absorbed that she didn't hear the door open, but a slight sound made her turn her head.

Professor Bowers-Bentinck was standing there, leaning against the wall watching her.

'Well, well, this is a pleasant surprise.' His voice had a silkiness she didn't much like.

'A surprise,' she amended in her sensible way, 'but I don't know about it being pleasant.'

'An outspoken young lady,' he commented, 'but I should feel flattered that you remember me.'

She was still kneeling, a handful of programmes in her hand, looking at him. She said matter-of-factly, 'Well, I'd be silly if I didn't—you're much larger than most men, for a start, and you must know you're good-looking; besides that, you came to see Aunt Mabel.'

'Such an abundance of compliments,' he murmured.

'They're not meant to be,' said Suzannah prosaically, 'just facts.' She had a sudden alarming thought. 'Lady Manbrook—she's not ill? Or Mrs van Beuck? They were all right at lunch.' She sprang to her feet. 'Is that why you are here?'

'Both ladies are in splendid health', he assured her. He eyed her coldly. 'You are very untidy and dusty.'

'Of course I am, it's dusty work, and I have to get down on to the floor—there's more room, and anyway, I can't see that it matters to you.'

'It doesn't. Tell me, why do I find you here? How did you find this job?'

'It was advertised. I've been here a week, and I'm very happy.' She looked at him uncertainly. 'Do you mind telling me why you're here?'

'I've come to tea.'

Her lovely eyes grew round. 'Have you really? How extraordinary that we should meet again…'

'Yes, isn't it? You don't object?'

'Object? Why should I? I mean, one is always bumping into people in unexpected places.'

'How true.' He eyed her frowningly. 'Had you not better finish and wash your hands and tidy your hair? It's almost four o'clock.'

She dusted her skirt and gave him a tolerant glance. 'Don't worry, I'll make myself presentable. I usually have my tea up here on a tray.' She added kindly, 'You don't need to fuss.'

His voice was as cold as his eyes. 'I'm not in the habit of fussing—what a tiresome girl you are.' He went through the door, closing it behind him, leaving her to gather up the programmes and then leave the attic after him. Undoubtedly a bad-tempered man, she reflected, and because of that to be pitied.

She told Horace all about him while she brushed her bright hair into smoothness, ready for tea.

CHAPTER THREE

THE DRAWING ROOM looked charming as she went in; the lamps were lit and the firelight flickered on the walls and twinkled on the silver muffin dish on the tea-table. The two ladies were sitting in their usual chairs, and lounging in an outsize armchair was the professor, looking very much at home.

An old friend, she wondered, or the family doctor? Quite obviously someone who knew the old ladies well.

He got to his feet as she crossed the room and drew forward a small armchair for her, and Lady Manbrook said, 'Our nephew tells us that he has met you previously, Suzannah, so there is no need to introduce you. I see that you have the dance programmes we were discussing with you; when we have had tea you must show them to us.'

Suzannah murmured a reply. Of course, now that she saw the three of them together there was no mistaking the relationship—those high-bridged, self assured noses, the cool blue stare from heavy-lidded eyes. She sat composedly, drinking tea from paper-thin china and nibbling at minuscule cucumber sandwiches, and allowed her imagination to have full rein. The professor would live in London, because undoubtedly that was where a man of his ability would work, but he was friends—close friends, probably—with Phoebe Davinish. He would be spending the weekend with her, and had dropped in to say hello to his aunts.

She was brought up short by his voice, rather too smooth for her liking, wanting to know if she was enjoying her work.

'Very much, thank you,' she told him.

'And how long do you suppose it will take you to finish it?' he continued.

'I'm not sure. Everything is sorted into dated piles, but I think that is the easiest part; you see, the letters and cuttings are about a great many people—they'll have to be sorted out.'

'There is no hurry,' declared Mrs van Beuck. 'You seem to have accomplished a great deal in a week…'

'Even on a Sunday,' murmured the professor. 'Do you prefer to have a free day in the week?'

'Me?' Suzannah spoke sharply, with a fine disregard for grammar. 'I'm very happy—'

He cut her short. 'I'm sure you are; nevertheless, you should have time to yourself. I cannot imagine that my aunts will mind if you take a week or so longer with your sorting and indexing; I am equally sure that they would wish you to enjoy a certain amount of time to yourself.'

Lady Manbrook was looking quite upset. 'My dear child, how thoughtless of us—of course you must have some hours to yourself. What do you suggest, Guy?'

He didn't even look at Suzannah to see what she thought about it, which annoyed her. 'Oh, a day off each week—most office workers and shop assistants have two days—and set hours of work each day; nine until lunchtime, and then four hours' work between two o'clock and dinnertime, to suit herself.'

Just as though I'm not here, thought Suzannah crossly. She shot him a speaking glance and met his cold eyes. 'You are agreeable to that?' he wanted to know.

It was tempting to tell him that she wasn't agreeable at all, but Lady Manbrook was still looking upset so she said in a colourless voice. 'Thank you, Professor, yes, that will do very well,' and then, because she felt peevish, 'So kind of you to bother,' she added waspishly.

'I'm not a particularly kind man,' he observed, 'but I hope that I am a just one.'

Maybe he was; he was also rude. She picked up the dance programmes and asked if the ladies would like to see them.

The next hour passed quickly, with the ladies exclaiming over the charming little cards with their coloured pencils attached by still bright cords, most of them filled by scrawled initials, one or two woefully half-empty. 'That would be Emily Wolferton,' declared Lady Manbrook. 'Such a haughty piece.' She tossed the card down and added with satisfaction, 'I always had partners,' and her sister echoed,

'And so did I. Here's one—Phoebe's grandmother—a nasty, ill-tempered girl she was too, always wanting something she hadn't.' She looked across at the professor, sitting impassively doing nothing. 'I hope Phoebe isn't ill-tempered, Guy?'

'Oh, never, just as long as she gets what she wants,' he replied idly.

'And of course, she gets it,' observed Mrs van Beuck. 'William Davinish is too old to want any more than peace and quiet at all costs.'

He made no reply to this, but said presently, 'Perhaps Suzannah would like an hour or two to herself before dinner.' He glanced at his watch. 'I must go presently...'

'So soon, dear?' asked Lady Manbrook.

He looked at Suzannah. 'I'm dining with Phoebe.'

Suzannah got up, excused herself with nice manners and made for the door. The professor had it open before she reached it. He couldn't get rid of her fast enough, it seemed, but he spoke as she went past him.

'A pity we had no time to talk.'

She gave him a thoughtful look. 'Is it? I can't think of anything we would want to talk about, Professor.'

She didn't much like his smile. He said softly in a silky tone. 'You may be mouselike despite that hair of yours, but your tongue, like a mouse's tooth, is sharp.' He opened the door. 'Goodnight, Suzannah.'

She mumbled goodnight as she whisked past him.

He stood at the open door watching her disappear across the hall, and the look on his face made Lady Manbrook say, 'Such a nice girl, Guy, so neat and tidy and hard-working.'

He smiled at his aunt and wondered what Suzannah would say to that; no girl, however self-effacing, would consider that a compliment. He shrugged huge shoulders, impatient with himself for his unwilling interest. It had been easy enough to arrange this job for her with his aunts; he had done that, he reflected, out of pity and because he considered that she had been unfairly treated by Phoebe. He had no reason to feel interest in her future; he had made it possible for her to have a couple of months' respite, and in that time she could decide what she wanted to do. She would have to earn her living. He strolled back to his chair and sat for another hour or so listening to his aunts' gentle chatter.

Suzannah bounced into her little flat, fed Horace, lit the fire and got her coat, all the while muttering and grumbling to Horace, who ate his supper in a single-minded fashion and didn't bother to answer.

'He's a very rude man,' declared Suzannah. 'I think he dislikes me very much—it's most unfortunate that we had to meet again.' She tugged her coat-belt tight in a ruthless fashion, scooped up Horace and went outside. Horace, during the previous week, had indicated in a positive fashion just where he preferred to take his walk. She followed him across the yard, along the back drive and then circled the grounds of the house, which brought them to the front gates. There was never anything about at that time of the evening; Horace meandered along, stopping to savour a few blades of grass as he went. They were on the last leg of their walk, rounding the curve of the drive back to the courtyard, when the Bentley swooped silently round the corner, to brake sharply within a foot of Horace.

The professor poked his handsome head out of the car window. He said testily, 'For heaven's sake—must you stroll around in the dusk without a light? I could have killed that cat.'

However, Suzannah had Horace, shocked and indignant, clasped firmly against her. 'This,' she pointed out in a voice squeaky with fright and rage, 'is a private drive. I wasn't to know that you would come tearing round the corner at ninety miles an hour!'

He laughed. 'Thirty at the most. And I'm a good driver. But let it be a lesson to you in the future.' He withdrew his head and drove on, leaving her very cross indeed.

Safely in her room again, she looked at the clock. It was time for her to get ready for Sunday supper. She went into the tiny bathroom and began to clean her teeth. 'I hope I never see the beastly man again,' she told Horace through a mouthful of toothpaste.

The second week slid away pleasantly enough; the old ladies seemed to have taken their nephew's suggestions to heart, for she was narrowly questioned each day as to whether she had worked for longer hours than he had suggested, and when Saturday came she was told to take the day off.

Something she was glad enough to do; the dance programmes had been dealt with and neatly catalogued and she was well into the newspaper cuttings; much harder work but even more interesting, although tiring too. Besides, she had two weeks' pay in her pocket and the desire to spend some of it was very great. There wasn't enough for a dress, but she was handy with her needle; material for a skirt and wool for a sweater would leave money over for her to save. She hadn't forgotten the future; indeed, she lay awake at night sometimes worrying about it, but there was still four weeks' work, and if she limited her spending to a pair of shoes and small necessities she would have enough to tide her over until she could get another job. She would have to start looking in the situations vacant columns before she left, of course. In the meantime she settled Horace, got into her tweed suit and caught the bus into Marlborough.

She found what she wanted: a fine green wool for the skirt and green knitting wool to match it—the jumper pattern was intricate and boasted a pattern of small flowers in a number of colours—but she was a good knitter and there was time enough in her free time to work at it. She had a frugal lunch in a little café away from the main street and caught an early bus back.

Back in her flat, she lit the fire, fed Horace, and got her tea. She had brought crumpets back with her; with the curtains drawn and the lamp by the fireplace alight, she sat down contentedly munching and drinking tea. How nice the simple pleasures of life were, she observed to Horace, and licked her buttery fingers.

There was still plenty of time before dinner. She tidied away the tea things, made up the fire and spread her material on the floor and cut out her skirt. She would have to sew it by hand, but that didn't worry her; she tacked it together, tried it on in front of the small bedroom looking-glass and then got ready to go over to the house.

There was no sign of the professor during the next week, but then she hadn't expected to see him and certainly no one mentioned him. She worked away at the press cuttings, sewed her skirt in her free time and took a brisk walk each day. A dull week, but its very dullness gave her a sense of security. She went to Marlborough again on her free day, but she spent very little of her pay; the future was beginning to loom. Another three weeks and she would be finished. There were only the letters and diaries to sort and read now, and the cataloguing, now that she had made sense of the muddle, presented no difficulties. Next week, she promised herself, she would decide what was to be done. Hopefully, she would get a good reference from Lady Manbrook and a study of the domestic situations in *The Lady* seemed hopeful. She treated herself to tea in a modest café and caught the bus back.

The letters, when she began on them, were fascinating. The contents were, for the most part, innocuous enough; accounts of morning calls, tea parties and dances with descriptions of the clothes worn by the writer's friends, some of them a trifle tart. But a packet of envelopes tied with ribbon Suzannah opened with some hesitation and then tied them up again. The top letter began 'My dearest love', and to read further would have been as bad as eavesdropping. She took the bundle, and another one like it, down to the drawing-room before dinner that evening and gave them to Lady Manbrook, who looked through them, murmuring from time to time. 'Great-Aunt Alicia,' she said finally, 'and Great-Uncle Humbert—before they became engaged. How very interesting. But you did quite right to give them to me, Suzannah; if there are any more of these letters, will you fasten them together—put them into an envelope, perhaps?—and write "Private" on it. I scarcely feel that they were meant for any eyes, but those for whom they were intended. Are there many more?'

'I don't think so, Lady Manbrook, but there are several in another language—it looks a little like German…'

'Dutch,' said Mrs van Beuck promptly. 'Are they written or typed, my dear?'

'Typed, for the most part.'

'Marriage settlements when I married dear Everard. Dear me, such a long time ago.'

Suzannah wasn't sure what to say; she knew nothing about marriage settlements, and Mrs van Beuck was looking sad. 'We went together to the family solicitor,' she ruminated. 'I had a lovely hat—grey tulle with pink roses,' a remark which led to the two ladies talking at some length about long-forgotten toilettes. Suzannah sat between them an appreciative audience, until they went in to dinner.

It was as they drank their coffee afterwards that Lady Manbrook said, 'We shall miss you, Suzannah; you have worked so hard and I am sure you have made a splendid job of arranging those tiresome papers. Do you have any plans?'

'Not at present, Lady Manbrook. I think that I shall be finished in three weeks; the cataloguing will take a good deal of time, but I've almost finished looking through the letters and I left those until last.'

'I'm sure you will find something nice to do,' observed Mrs van Beuck comfortably. 'It must be very quiet for you here.'

'I've been very happy here, and I love the country.' Suzannah excused herself presently and went to her flat, feeling anxious. It seemed to her that the two ladies were eager for her to finish, although they hadn't said so. She sat down by the fire with Horace on her lap and studied the situations vacant column in the local paper; several pubs wanted barmaids, but even if she had known something about the work she doubted if anyone would consider her suitable; barmaids were usually pretty and buxom, and she was neither. There was a job for a home help to live in; five children in the family, must love dogs, be cheerful and prepared to assist a handicapped granny when needed; salary negotiable. Suzannah wasn't quite sure what that meant, but she had a nasty feeling that she would come off second-best in negotiations of any kind. She folded the paper tidily and decided to go to the domestic agency in Marlborough on her next day off.

It was almost the end of another week and she was sitting in the room Snow had made ready for her, carefully cataloging the last of the dance programmes, when the professor walked in.

'Still at it?' he wanted to know, and went to stand in front of the small fire, effectively cutting off its warmth.

Suzannah looked up from her work. 'Good afternoon, Professor Bowers-Bentinck,' she said pointedly, and waited for him to speak.

'If it will take the disapproving look off your face, good afternoon to you too, Suzannah. Almost finished?'

Here was another one anxious for her to be gone. She said carefully, 'Very nearly, I'm going as fast as I can...'

'Good. Have you another job to go to?'

'I have several likely...' She caught his hard blue eyes boring into her. 'Well,' she went on, 'I haven't really, but I've applied to three.'

'Any money?'

She went rather pink. 'Really, Professor, I hardly think that's your business.'

'I asked you if you had any money, Suzannah. I can see no reason why you shouldn't answer my question.'

'No, I don't suppose you can.' She drew a deep breath. 'But let me tell you something. I'm not in your employ; you were kind enough when Aunt Mabel died, although probably that was bedside manner—I imagine you can put that on and take it off again whenever you want to—but I won't be patronised...'

Her calm voice had become a little shrill; she took another steadying breath and added, 'If you don't mind, I'd like to get on with my work...'

She had been annoyed with him; she was even more annoyed now when he strolled away, closing the door gently behind him.

There was no sign of him when she joined the two old ladies in the drawing-room that evening.

'Such a pity that Guy had to go back to his consulting rooms,' observed Mrs van Beuck. 'The dear boy works far too hard; it amazes me where these people come from.' And at Suzannah's puzzled look, 'People with brain tumours, my dear. And of course dear Guy is so clever, he knows exactly what to do...' She drew a sharp breath. 'My dear child, I am so sorry, for the moment I forgot that your aunt...'

Suzannah said composedly, 'It's quite all right, Mrs van Bueck, there was nothing to be done for my aunt; Professor Bowers-Bentinck examined her most carefully and was kindness itself.'

Quite a different man to the visitor she had had that afternoon. She supposed that she must annoy him in some way, certainly he needled her into being rude. Aunt Mabel would have been vexed; so, too, would her two companions if they could hear her!

She sat listening with half an ear to the two ladies' gentle chatter. 'I cannot believe that the dear boy will be thirty-five next week,' observed Lady Manbrook. 'It seems only the other day he and his dear parents were here on a visit—while he was at Marlborough, was it not? Such a pity they haven't lived to see him achieve fame in the medical world. And so modest, too; never an unkind word.'

Obviously, thought Suzannah, there was a side to the professor which she had failed to discover.

And not likely to either; another week went by with no sign of him—and why should there be? she argued to herself. He was a busy man and his work kept him in London. She was almost at the end of her cataloguing by now; another four or five days and she would be finished. She was too honest to spin it out for a few more days, but she was sorely tempted, for she had had no replies to the advertisements she had answered.

She resisted the temptation, arranged the last of the letters in a neat pile beside everything else and went to tell Lady Manbrook that four more days' work would suffice to tidy everything away once more.

That lady looked surprised. 'Already, my dear? How very quick you have been. You will need a day or so to clear up your own things, of course, and make arrangements. Croft will drive you back…' She paused. 'Where to, Suzannah? Is not someone living in your former home?'

'Mrs Coffin will give me a room until I go to another job, Lady Manbrook.'

'Ah, yes, of course. I'm sure you must be much in demand.'

Suzannah hoped that she would be, too. But the last day came with nothing in the post for her, so she stowed Horace in his basket, packed the geranium carefully, wished the two old ladies goodbye, made her farewells in the kitchen and then got into the car beside Croft. Mrs Coffin had sent her a cheerful letter, happily agreeing to let her have a room for as long as she would need one; all the same, Suzannah's heart sank as Croft drove her away from what had seemed to her to be a haven of security. True, she had saved almost all her wages, but they weren't going to go far…

Mrs Coffin welcomed her with genuine pleasure, and over high tea, eaten after the shop was closed for the day, listened with sympathy to Suzannah's doubts about the future.

'Don't worry, love,' she said in her comfortable voice, 'something'll turn up, and you're welcome to stay here just as long as you want to.'

She patted Suzannah's hand over the table and went on, 'Now tell me all about your job? Was it interesting? Did you meet anyone nice?'

She meant young men, of course. 'No, but I'll tell you who I met, and I was surprised. That professor who came to see Aunt Mabel when she was so ill…' Her voice faltered for a moment. 'He's Lady Manbrook's nephew or something.'

'That was nice, dear…'

'Not really. He doesn't like me, you know, and he asked a lot of questions!'

'Did he, now? I do hear from the housekeeper at the manor that Miss Phoebe's in a rare bad temper these days. Everyone thought that the professor was going to marry her; she boasted about it too, but I met Mr Toms the other day and he said that he'd heard her telling some friend or other that she hadn't seen him in weeks. Don't know much about him myself, but he was always very civil to me and Dr Warren sets great store by him. I shouldn't think he'd put up with Miss Phoebe's nasty tempers.'

Suzannah wondered silently if he had a nasty temper too; she thought it quite likely. A man who liked his own way, she felt sure.

It was pleasant to be back in the village again, although

she didn't go near her old home. Indeed, she spent a good part of each day writing replies to the advertisements Mrs Coffin obligingly allowed her to look for in the papers and magazines which she sold. After three days she had two replies, both of them quite obdurate about pets. To leave him behind was impossible; Mrs Coffin liked him well enough, but she had a cat and a very elderly dog of her own, and although they tolerated Horace as a temporary lodger, there would be no question of him settling down with them.

Suzannah had taken over the cooking and some of the household chores from her kind landlady, anxious not to be too much of a burden to her, and each afternoon, after they had eaten their midday dinner, she took over the shop too while Mrs Coffin had what she called 'a bit of a lie down'. It was on the fourth day of her stay that Professor Bowers-Bentinck walked in.

She was adding up the items that Mrs Batch, from the other end of the village, had bought and, since Mrs Coffin didn't believe in new-fangled things like electric cash registers but wrote everything down on a bit of paper, any that came in handy, Suzannah was totting up her sums on the outside wrapper of the best back bacon she had just sliced.

The doorbell jangled as he went in and she looked up briefly, muttering, 'One pound fifty-three…' and then, at the sight of him, forgot how far she had got to.

She said vexedly, 'Oh, look what you've made me do—now I'll have to start again.' Which she did, adding her sums twice to make sure before giving Mrs Batch the total.

That lady knew the professor by sight, of course, she bade him good afternoon now, hoped he was well, remarked upon the weather and handed Suzannah a five-pound note.

Suzannah counted out the change, put her customer's purchases in her plastic carrier bag, and wished her good day, and when she had gone turned her attention to the professor.

'Good afternoon. Do you wish to buy something?'

He looked faintly surprised. 'Er—no. Have you taken over the shop from Mrs Coffin?'

'No but while I'm here I mind it for her while she has a short rest.'

'So you have no job?'

She didn't answer that at once, then she said briefly, 'No, not yet.'

'Then may I put a proposition to you and hope that you will overlook your dislike of me sufficiently to listen to it?'

'You don't like me either,' said Suzannah matter-of-factly.

He looked down his commanding nose at her. 'I am not aware that I have any feelings about you, good or bad, Suzannah.' He smiled thinly. 'Now, if you would listen to me and not interrupt.'

A high-handed remark which left her conveniently without words.

The professor pushed aside a basket of assorted biscuits, several tins of soup and a large card announcing that there would be a whist drive in the village hall next Wednesday, and sat down at the edge of the counter. He took up a great deal of room, and Suzannah had to look up to see his face, which rather annoyed her.

'I have a patient,' he informed her, 'who has recovered from a cerebral tumour which I removed some weeks ago. She is fit to return to her home—in Holland, I should add—but she needs a sensible companion with plenty of common sense to remain with her until she feels able to resume a normal life. She refuses to have a nurse, and quite rightly; she is no longer in need of nursing care, but she needs someone reliable to depend upon who, at the same time, will remain in the background unless she is needed. I believe that you would be absolutely right for the job.'

'You put it very clearly,' said Suzannah, digesting this opinion of herself. So she was just right to sit meekly in the background, was she, waiting until she was wanted? I'd like to show him, she thought, fiercely, I'd like just one chance to dine at the

Ritz with a duke wearing black tulle and diamonds and cut this wretch dead when he saw me there…

'Suzannah,' the doctor's voice was compelling, 'you are allowing your thoughts to wander. I trust you have understood me?'

'For how long?' she asked briskly, and, 'What would my salary be?'

He gave her an intent look. 'A few weeks at the most. The salary is adequate.' He mentioned a sum which seemed to her to be excessive.

She said, 'Isn't that rather a lot of money to pay someone to sit in the background, even if she is reliable and dependable and—what was the other virtue?—sensible?'

He said with scarcely veiled impatience, 'Oh, I'm sorry, I explained rather badly; I intended nothing personal.'

She said kindly, 'No, I don't expect you did, but you should be more careful you know, especially when you are talking to girls like me.'

'Why?'

'Well, just think for yourself, Professor: I'm no beauty, I've no money, no job and the future's a bit vague; I don't want to be reminded of any of those things. But it was kind of you to ask me, only of course I can't…'

'Why not?'

'Horace. He can't stay here with Mrs Coffin; she has a cat and a dog already and they put up with him, but only for the moment. No one else would want him.'

Professor Bowers-Bentinck was surprised to hear himself say, 'He can come to my home. I have a housekeeper who I know will welcome him and take good care of him.'

'Would she? He might escape…'

'There is a garden-room behind the house where he can roam without going outside. I assure you that I will be responsible for his safety.'

She was surprised to find that she believed him when he said that; he might be a disagreeable man, at least towards her, but she felt that he was a man of his word. She nodded her neat head. 'Very well, I'd be glad of the job; if I can save enough money I thought I might train as a nurse or a nanny…'

'And Horace?' he wanted to know.

'Oh, that's why I must save some money first, so that I can find a little flat or a room and live out.'

He stood up then and said with a return of his impatience, 'Have you any idea of the high rent you would have to pay?'

'Oh, yes, but I'd go to one of the provincial hospitals—Yeovil or Salisbury, somewhere like that.' She was aware that he was no longer interested; he had got what he had come for and her future was no concern of his.

'Will you let me know when I am to start work—I've no passport…'

He was at the door. 'You will get all the details in a letter. Send for a passport at once—better still, fill in the form and send it to me—I'll forward it with a note asking for the matter to be treated urgently.'

'Where shall I send it?'

'To Elliot's Hospital, London. Mark it personal and urgent.' He nodded a casual goodbye and closed the door quietly behind him, leaving her to wonder if she had dreamt the lot.

Mrs Coffin, when appraised of the afternoon's happenings, crowed with delight, assured her that her fortune was made and produced an application form for a passport from under the post office counter. 'You fill that in now, love,' she urged, 'and post it this very day. You can run across to the doctor's and the vicar's and get them to sign it for you. Get photos in Marlborough for it from the post office and send them off.'

She spent the rest of the day speculating as to the exact nature of the job Suzannah had accepted. 'Perhaps it's someone rich,' she observed, 'or a titled lady, living in Holland, too—let's hope you'll be able to understand her.' She glanced at Suzannah. 'You'll need some clothes, dearie.'

Suzannah supposed that even a faceless person sitting in the background would need to be decently clad. She had the new skirt, of course, and the sweater was half knitted. Her suit would have to do, but she would need a couple of blouses and another sweater and a decent dress besides.

'I'll have to buy one, there might not be time to make it,' she said out loud.

She was quite right, there was a letter for her the next day, giving the name of the patient, a Juffrouw Julie van Dijl, twenty-two years old, whose home was in the Hague. Unmarried, with parents and two brothers. There followed details of her condition and a veiled warning that she might be prone to short bouts of ill-temper and depression.

'Aren't we all?' muttered Suzannah, reading the business-like typing.

But the salary was written there clearly to be seen, and so were the conditions of her job; two hours to herself each day and a free day each week, though she must be prepared to be at her employer's beck and call at all hours, which seemed a bit ominous. But the money was generous and would make all the difference to her future.

She got the next bus to Marlborough and enriched her wardrobe with two blouses, a thin sweater, some underwear and a very plain silk jersey dress in pewter-grey. Well-satisfied, she returned to Mrs Coffin's and spent the next two days knitting like one of the furies, uncertain as to how long she would have before being summoned. The letter had ended with a curt request for her to be prepared to start work at short notice, so she packed the best of her clothes under the eye of a suspicious Horace and washed her hair and possessed her soul in patience.

She didn't have long to wait. Her passport arrived several days later; the professor must have a member of his family or a close friend at the passport office, she decided. And two days later there was another letter, requesting her in impersonal type to hold herself ready to leave in two days' time. She would be taken to London by car, Horace would be deposited as agreed and she would then join the lady she was to accompany. It was signed by the professor, his signature strongly resembling a spider in its death throes.

The driver of the car, when it arrived, proved to be a fatherly man, very spruce but certainly not a chauffeur. He introduced himself as Cobb, stowed her luggage in the boot, arranged Horace in his basket on the back seat and held the door open for her.

Suzannah gave Mrs Coffin a last hug and then asked to sit in front with him; he looked kind and perhaps he would give her some information about the professor.

In this she was mistaken; Cobb was kind, chatty as well, but not one word did he let drop about the professor other than to say that he was employed by him. So Suzannah passed the journey to town in trivial conversation, alternately feeling excited and apprehensive.

They had left early in the day and the morning rush was over by the time they reached London; all the same, it took a little time for Cobb to arrive at their destination: a quiet backwater of a street, tucked away behind Harley Street, lined with tall, splendidly maintained houses gleaming with paintwork, their brass door-knockers glistening with daily polishing. Cobb drew to a gentle halt before one of these houses, got out, opened the door and reached for Horace, and by the time he had done this the front door had been opened by a cosy-looking woman of middle age, dressed very neatly in black. She smiled at Suzannah as she mounted the few steps to the door.

'Good morning, miss. I'm Mrs Cobb, housekeeper to the professor. I'm to see that you have a cup of coffee before you leave, and I'll show you where your cat will live. Glad to have him, too; the professor's got a dog, but my old cat, Flossie, died a while ago and I do miss her.'

She had led the way into the house as she spoke, into a small hall, very elegant with its striped walls and polished floor. 'If you wouldn't mind coming to the kitchen, miss...'

There was a baize door beside the curving staircase at the back of the hall; they went through it, down some steps and through another door into the kitchen. The house, Suzannah realised, was a good deal larger than it appeared from the street, for the kitchen was large with a glimpse of smaller rooms leading from it and, through the window at the end, quite a long garden.

'He'll live here with me,' explained Mrs Cobb, 'but of course he'll have the run of the house, and through this door…' she opened another door and went down a short passage which in turn opened into a garden-room, 'there's all this for him to roam in. And be sure I'll take the greatest deal of care of him, miss. If you let him out so that he can look around…?'

The sun warmed the garden-room, and it was comfortably furnished with lounge chairs and little tables. 'You just have your coffee here,' advised Mrs Cobb, 'and let the little man roam.'

She bustled off and Horace, freed from his basket, sauntered around, sniffing at the greenery and finally settling in one of the chairs. Mrs Cobb, coming back with the coffee-tray, looked pleased. 'There! I knew he'd settle. Handsome, isn't he?'

Suzannah sat and drank her coffee and then, warned by Mrs Cobb that Cobb would be driving her to her employer in ten minutes' time, went away to tidy herself in the luxurious little cloakroom tucked away behind the staircase. From the glimpse she had of the house, the professor lived in the greatest comfort—more luxury. She would have liked to have seen more of the house. There were several doors leading from the hall, but they were all shut, and she resisted the temptation to open them and went back to the garden-room to say goodbye to Horace, who, curled up half asleep, did no more than open an eye.

'I'll be back,' she assured him, and followed Mr Cobb back into the hall once more and then out to the car. She felt terrible: like someone who had jumped into the deep end of a swimming pool and remembered at the last moment that she couldn't swim.

CHAPTER FOUR

THEY HADN'T FAR TO GO, but during the short drive Cobb, seeing her downcast face, talked cheerfully. 'The missus will love Horace,' he told her. 'Dotes on cats, she does. I dare say she'll drop you a line to let you know how he is.'

Suzannah said gratefully, 'Oh, do you suppose she would? I'd be very grateful; you see, I'm not quite sure how long I'll be away.' She added doubtfully, 'I hope I'll do.'

'Don't you fret, miss. The professor doesn't make mistakes; if he thought you were right for the job, then you'll be OK.'

He turned the car into a Belgravia square. 'Here we are.' He drew in his breath with a satisfied hiss. 'Just on time, too.'

The Bentley was gliding to a halt before one of the massive houses in the square, and Cobb drew up just behind it, got out, opened Suzannah's door and with a cheerful, 'Goodbye, miss,' left her with the professor, who had got out of his car too.

His, 'Good morning,' was curt but not unfriendly. 'I'll introduce you to Juffrouw van Dijl; you will leave with her in her car in about half an hour. Did Cobb give you an envelope?'

'Yes, I've not opened it.'

'Do so when you have the opportunity.' He didn't say what

was in it, but led the way through the imposing front door, held open by an impassive manservant. 'I have no time to waste, so don't dawdle,' he advised her unnecessarily.

They were led up a grand staircase to a room over looking the street, furnished in an opulent style which Suzannah found overpowering and in which were a number of people: an elderly man, a slightly younger woman, a youngish man whose eyes were too close together and a very pretty girl with dark hair and eyes, dressed dramatically in the very height of fashion and looking nervous and excited.

When she saw the professor she rushed to meet him and caught him by the arm. 'Guy—are you sure I'll be all right? You will come and see me? What will I do if I feel ill?'

He said gently, 'Why should you feel ill, Julie? You were always a remarkably healthy girl, and now that you are well again there is no reason why you should be anything else. Besides, I have brought Suzannah with me; she will keep an eye on you—and she is not a nurse, you know, just someone to keep you company and remind you from time to time that you're perfectly well again.'

The girl looked at Suzannah, taking in her neat, unfashionable appearance. 'Oh, hello.'

She nodded carelessly, not listening to Suzannah's polite, 'How do you do, Miss van Dijl?' and turned back to the professor.

'You will come, won't you, soon?'

'When I can arrange it, Julie. I'm tied up at the moment.' He left her and crossed the room to shake hands with the older man and woman and introduced Suzannah. 'Mr and Mrs South,' he told her, 'are aunt and uncle to Juffrouw van Dijl; she has been staying for a few days with them before returning home.'

Suzannah shook hands with them and wondered just where home was. Just as though he had read her thoughts, the professor said quietly, 'You will find all the information you need in the envelope, Suzannah.'

He went away presently, and shortly after that Suzannah accompanied her new employer out to the Rolls-Royce outside and got in beside her. Her luggage had been put in the boot, together with a great many cases belonging to Juffrouw van Dijl arranged there, and she sat quietly while tearful farewells were exchanged. No one had thought to bid her goodbye; she didn't mind that the aunt and uncle had overlooked her, but she chalked up another black mark against the professor for doing no more than nodding at her as he left. It had been a last-minute, absent-minded nod, too, as though he had remembered just in time that she was there.

The young man had stayed in the background; now he put his head through the open window of the car and spoke urgently to Juffrouw van Dijl; Suzannah tried not to listen but it wouldn't have mattered if she had for he spoke in some language she couldn't understand—Dutch, she thought—and her companion had answered just as urgently before they drove off.

They were going by hovercraft to Holland, and the drive to Dover took no more than an hour and a half. Juffrouw van Dijl made no attempt at conversation but sat, wrapped in thought, ignoring Suzannah, so that after a while she took out the envelope she had been given and read its contents: a detailed resumé of everything she needed to know while she was in Holland.

More information as to Juffrouw van Dijl's way of life, a reiteration of the hours she was to work and when she was to be free, the arrangement made to pay her salary each week, the currency, the name and telephone number of the family doctor, where she should go if she needed help…

Why should I need help? wondered Suzannah, and decided that was the professor covering all risks. There was even a short paragraph suggesting suitable dressing for the evening and the name of a bank where she might wish to deposit her money. All very helpful, she decided, folding away the letter carefully and tucking it into a pocket.

Their journey was uneventful, the chauffeur saw to everything and Suzannah had nothing more to do than follow her companion on to the hovercraft. Once on land again, they waited while the car was unloaded and then got into its comfort once again. Suzannah was surprised when Juffrouw van Dijl spoke. 'This is my father's car. He sent Jan the chauffeur to bring me home; I am not in the habit of travelling without a servant.' She paused. 'I suppose you know that I have been dangerously ill?'

'Yes, Professor Bowers-Bentinck has explained everything to me.'

'Good, it is tiresome having to tell people what has to be done. He told me that you aren't a nurse—I never wish to see another as long as I live.'

Which seemed a bit ungrateful to Suzannah, although she didn't say so.

Her companion went on, 'You are, of course, here to make yourself useful. You won't put yourself forward, I hope. It is only because Professor Bowers-Bentinck insisted that I should have someone sensible to be with me that I consented to employ you.'

Suzannah opened her mouth to answer this and then shut it again; she was quite sure that she wouldn't like the job. She certainly hadn't taken to Juffrouw van Dijl, but the salary was good, and according to the professor it would only be for a few weeks. Besides, she had every intention of letting him see that she was capable of coping with his patient; he must have known that she was self-willed and spoilt…

As she didn't answer, Juffrouw van Dijl turned to look at her. 'There is one thing I find agreeable about you,' she conceded. 'You don't answer back or chatter.'

A remark which Suzannah greeted with a faint smile and a well-modulated word of thanks.

Juffrouw van Dijl seemed disposed to talk. 'Of course, Professor Bowers-Bentinck is my surgeon, but he is also a very old friend of my family—we have been close for many years. I have not quite decided if I wish to marry him; for some time it was thought that he would marry some girl in Wiltshire, I believe, the niece of an English friend he had known for some time, but he sees her no longer and perhaps I shall decide to marry him, after all.'

Suzannah murmured and wondered what the professor would have to say to that. The girl in Wiltshire would be Phoebe, and she wondered why he was no longer interested in her. He could, she supposed, pick and choose among his women acquaintances; he was good-looking and successful and presumably, from what she had seen of his home, comfortably endowed with the world's goods. Perhaps he was content with his life as it was; he might even be hiding a broken heart behind that bland face of his. It seemed unlikely. On the whole, she reflected, it would be a pity if he were to marry the girl beside her; she didn't seem very suitable, but perhaps she was being unfair; she had been very ill and it must have cost her a great effort to get well again, even with the aid of the professor's surgery. She warmed towards her companion and said impulsively, 'I'm sure you will both be very happy,' not at all sure that it would turn out like that. Her warmth was wasted.

'I didn't ask for your comments,' said Juffrouw van Dijl sharply. 'Kindly keep your opinions to yourself in future.'

A future, thought Suzannah to herself, which wouldn't last too long if she could help it.

She looked out at the countryside; it looked flat, very green and rather uninteresting, but she reminded herself that this was only a very small part of Holland. Beyond the big cities there would be villages and trees and lakes. Perhaps she would get a chance to see them before she returned to England; it was such a small country, she would be able to see a good deal in a couple of days. She occupied herself with these pleasant thoughts until the Hague was reached and she turned her attention to her surroundings. It seemed a pleasant city and some of the old buildings looked interesting, but they passed them by and drove to the more modern sector of the city, turning away presently into a wide avenue, tree-lined, with large houses on either side. Into the gates of one of these the chauffeur turned the car, stopping on a sweep so pristine that it must have been combed hourly, and getting out to open the car doors. Suzannah nipped out on her own while he assisted Juffrouw van Dijl to alight, which gave her time to take a look around. She was disappointed: the house, built at the turn of the century, was ugly. It was of red brick, very large and hung around with a great number of balconies, and at each corner of its elaborate roof there were small turrets.

'Lookout posts?' Suzannah asked herself, craning her neck. 'But what is there to see in such a respectable neighbourhood?'

There was no one to answer her; following Juffrouw van Dijl's footsteps, she mounted the flight of stairs which swept grandly to the vast mahogany door and wondered what it would be like inside.

The door, opened by a man who murmured a welcome in a colourless voice, revealed a large hall, papered in crimson and hung with stuffed animals' heads, arranged in patterns between displays of nasty-looking spears and swords. She averted her eyes and trod across a vast expanse of Turkish carpet at the heels of Juffrouw van Dijl, to enter a room at one side of the hall. It was as overpowering as the hall, only this time the wallpaper was dark green, embossed and almost covered by paintings framed inches-deep in gilt. The furniture was large, solid and beautifully polished and there was too much of it—tables loaded with reading-lamps, silver-framed photos, china figurines and the like.

The lady who came to greet them was quite dwarfed by her surroundings; she was quite small, although stout, with a sweet expression on her face and an air of timidity. Surely not Juffrouw van Dijl's mother? wondered Suzannah. But it was; the little lady embraced her daughter with a good deal of emotion, begged her to sit down and not exert herself and looked at Suzannah. 'You must be the young lady who is to care for my daughter,' she declared in fluent, accented English. 'Such a relief to me, for I am not at all sure how much Julie may do. Professor Bowers-Bentinck did explain to me, but I am quite stupid about such things; that is why he suggested that a good, sensible girl might relieve me of worry.'

Suzannah shook hands and murmured appropriately; so many people had considered her sensible that she was beginning to believe it.

A maid had come in with a coffee-tray and Mevrouw van Dijl busied herself pouring it out while her daughter sat languidly, making monosyllabic replies to her anxious questions. Presently, with a word of apology, they reverted to Dutch and Suzannah sat drinking her coffee, listening to the meaningless words. She understood none of it, but it was plain then that Juffrouw van Dijl was laying down the law to her mother, who nodded her head meekly and presently turned to Suzannah.

'Julie is anxious to visit all her friends and continue with her old life,' she announced worriedly, 'but I think that is something the professor might not like. Did he say anything…?'

Suzannah, who had an excellent memory, quoted the parts of the letter which she felt could be mentioned harmlessly. 'He was most anxious that Juffrouw van Dijl should live quietly for at least two weeks; a few friends, but not any parties or dancing, and early nights with a rest after lunch each day. And she is never to go anywhere on her own, at least until he has seen her again.'

'You heard that, *lieveling*? It is hard, I know, but we will make it up to you as soon as we may do so. You have been so ill, and another week or two will restore you completely.'

Juffrouw van Dijl said something fierce in Dutch and turned to Suzannah. 'And suppose I refuse all this silly cosseting?'

'Professor Bowers-Bentinck has instructed me to tell him immediately if his instructions aren't carried out.'

Julie van Dijl tossed her lovely head. 'Oh, he did, did he?' She smiled. 'Dear Guy, he wishes me to get well quickly, so I will do as he says. But you will not stay a day longer than is necessary. I will put up with you because he wishes it, but only because of that. You had better go to your room and unpack…'

'Thank you, but first I must make sure that you go to your room too and rest. Do you wish me to unpack for you?'

'Certainly not. I have a maid. And I am not tired…'

Suzannah said in her calm voice, 'Perhaps not, but you have just said that you would do as the professor asked.'

Juffrouw van Dijl made a face and got up out of her chair, and her mother gave a relieved smile. 'We shall see you later, Julie. I'm sure Professor Bowers-Bentinck knows best, he is one of the most successful surgeons there is and he is, after all, a family friend.'

Her daughter gave her an impatient look, not speaking, and strolled out of the room with Suzannah trailing her.

The man who had opened the door was in the hall and with him a tall, bony woman, who exclaimed with pleasure at the sight of Juffrouw van Dijl and hurried her up the solid staircase. Half-way to the floor above, she turned and beckoned to Suzannah, who had been wondering what she should do. The man, some kind of butler she imagined, had ignored her and she didn't think she was supposed to go back to Mevrouw van Dijl. She went upstairs thankfully and crossed the wide landing to where the other two were waiting for her.

Julie van Dijl's room was a splendid one, overlooking the side of the house; it would have been a fitting background for a film star with its lush carpet, satin curtains and canopied bed. Suzannah stood uncertainly on its threshold.

'You have the room next to mine, through that door.' So she crossed the room and opened another door. The room beyond was very much smaller, nicely furnished but impersonal, rather like a hotel-room. But the view from the window was pleasant as it overlooked the garden too. Suzannah took off her jacket, peeped round another door leading to a small bathroom and went back to Julie's room.

She was surprised when she said, 'Your room's all right? The nurse was there when I was ill.' She was still more surprised when Julie added in an almost friendly voice, 'I like the door to be kept open at night.' She hesitated. 'In case I should want anything.'

'Of course. Can I do anything to help you now?'

The maid was unpacking at the other end of the room, her head bent over the piles of clothes she was folding carefully.

'I think that I am now tired. I shall lie down.' A signal for Suzannah to take the soft quilt from the daybed by the window and spread it out invitingly. She plumped up the pillows too, and then tucked her charge in without fuss. 'A book to read?' she asked.

'No, you had better unpack. I suppose you want tea.' She said something to the maid, who went away, annoyed at being hindered from her unpacking. 'We dine at seven o'clock—much earlier than in England—Anna will help me change. I suppose you have something fit to wear?'

Suzannah reminded herself that Julie van Dijl had been very ill. 'I have a dress,' she said calmly. 'I hadn't expected to take my meals with your family.'

Her companion said peevishly, 'Professor Bowers-Bentinck said that it was correct for you to do so.' She made an impatient sound. 'I am like a bear on a chain.'

'No', said Suzannah gently, 'you are someone who has made a miraculous recovery and needs to be cherished until you are quite well and strong again.'

Julie van Dijl said pettishly, 'How good you sound—a little prig…'

'I really don't know. I've never been quite sure what a prig was. But I have the professor's instructions and I shall do my best to carry them out.'

In her room she unpacked, drank the tea which had been brought, and took herself off to the bathroom where she lay for a long time in the blissfully hot water and thought about the weeks ahead of her. They weren't going to be easy…

Julie's father was at dinner, a stout, middle-aged man who had very little to say, although he was kind enough to Suzannah, but he left the talk to his wife and daughter and it was Julie who dominated the conversation. Naturally enough, it was mostly of herself and her stay in London and the hospital; she had little to say that was good about that. The fact that the professor had saved her life, aided by the skill of the nursing staff, seemed to have evaded her—probably she had been too ill to realise the care she had received. She enlarged at length about the awful food, and the fact that, even in a private room, she had not been allowed visitors for weeks. Her parents had been there, of course, but she didn't count them. 'All my friends,' she complained, 'coming to cheer me up, and that awful dragon of a sister sending them away.'

'But now you are back home, *lieveling*,' her mother pointed out, 'and almost your old self.'

She had smiled across the table at Suzannah as she spoke, wordlessly apologising for her daughter's criticism. 'I am sure that Guy will find a great improvement when he comes to see you.'

'Well, I intend to have some fun before then, Mama.' Julie shot a defiant look at Suzannah, who pretended not to see it. The salary was a most generous one; she began to see why.

The first few days passed tolerably well; various friends came to see Julie, and her wardrobe was combed through and pronounced unwearable, but she showed no desire to go anywhere or do anything other than lounge around in her room, reading magazines and chatting with her friends. Suzannah coaxed her to take a short walk each day and saw her firmly into her bed each evening. The worst part was getting her to rest after lunch, something which was only achieved after a stormy tussle ending for the most part in tears. But once tucked up on her day-bed with a novel or magazine she slept within minutes, leaving Suzannah free to take her few hours of freedom.

She didn't dare go too far. She had begged a street map from the butler, who, sour though he might look, was helpful, and set about exploring the neighbouring streets so that within a few days she had a good idea of where she was; ten minutes' brisk walk from the Scheveningseweg, the main road between den Haag and Scheveningen. There were parks to the left and right of the road, and trams trundling past every few minutes as well as buses. On her day off it would be an easy matter to get into the heart of the city. She looked forward to this; she realised after the first few evenings that a second dress was essential. Indeed, Juffrouw van Dijl had remarked tartly that when they had guests for dinner she would have to wear something more suitable. 'Even if you are in the background,' she pointed out, 'you can't look like a shop girl.'

Suzannah took her tongue between her teeth while rage bubbled. She said lightly, 'I should imagine that shop girls dress a good deal better than I. As soon as I have a free day I'll go shopping; something dark and very plain.'

Julie had looked at her suspiciously, wondering if she had meant it. 'But your hair,' she complained. 'It is so red...'

'Yes, isn't it? But don't ask me to dye it, because that's something I will not do.'

But before she had her day off Julie decided that she had to go shopping. 'You'll come with me, of course,' she said. 'I haven't anything fit to wear. There are several boutiques I go to, and we can stay in town for lunch.'

Suzannah made no demur; for one thing it wouldn't have been of much use, and for another, according to the letter of instructions she anxiously re-read each evening, Julie was to lead a normal life if she wished, provided she rested, went to bed at a reasonable hour and didn't tire herself.

Easier said than done, reflected Suzannah, but Julie showed no signs of tiredness, nor did she complain of headaches. Suzannah kept a brief record of each day and its happenings, for she felt sure that when the professor did come he would require her to give a detailed account of his patient's activities.

The day's shopping left Julie van Dijl more or less satisfied and Suzannah frankly envious. They had been driven to the heart of den Haag and deposited in Lange Voorhout, where a number of exclusive boutiques rubbed elegant shoulders. Julie van Dijl appeared to be a well-known client with them all: dresses and suits and ballgowns were displayed in a seemingly unending flow of colour and fabric while she chose what she liked without—as far as Suzannah could see—once asking the price. They sat on little gilt chairs and drank delicious coffee, and after a time Suzannah, sitting just behind Julie, ignored by everyone and not minding at all, began playing a kind of game with herself, deciding which of the outfits she would buy if she were in Julie's shoes.

They lunched in Le Baron restaurant at the Hotel des Indes, a stone's throw from the boutiques they had been visiting, and over the meal Julie van Dijl became quite friendly.

'I shall have that gold tissue dress with the roses,' she observed, 'and the pink satin with the tulle stole. I shall need at least two suits, and I liked the satin blouses with them… That grey knitted three-piece was quite nice, but the colour's wrong.' She paused to glance at Suzannah's bright head. 'Right for you though, but of course you would never wear anything like that. I dare say you shop at Marks and Spencer.'

Suzannah said without heat, 'Yes, when I can afford to.' A remark which left her companion without words for a few moments.

'What will you do when you leave here?'

'I have no idea at the moment, but there is always a job, you know—mother's help or domestic work…'

Julie said slowly, 'Guy—Professor Bowers-Bentinck told my mother that you were to have gone to a university. I suppose you are clever.'

'Oh, no. The best I could hope for was a degree in English so that I could get a teacher's post…' She paused because Julie had gone off into peals of laughter.

'But you don't look like a schoolteacher. Did you wish to be one?'

'Not particularly; it was a way of earning a living.'

Julie looked at her in astonishment. 'But if you do not wish to work, why do you not marry?'

'No one has asked me,' said Suzannah. The mildness of her voice belied the temper swelling inside her. 'Do you want to see if you can find anything instead of the three piece you don't like?'

There was one more boutique which Julie declared might have something to suit her, and happily she found what she was looking for there; just in time to walk the length of Lange Voorhout and find the car waiting for them.

Julie, content with her shopping, was easily persuaded to go to bed early and have her dinner there on a tray, which left Suzannah and Mevrouw van Dijl to dine together. At first the conversation was rather stilted, but presently Mevrouw van Dijl began to talk about her daughter. 'She is spoilt,' she said with an air of apology, 'but her father is so often away from home, and when he returns there is nothing he will not do for her, and of course she never listens to me. Her two brothers are both away, but they spoil her as well.' The good lady sighed. 'She needs a husband…there was someone, but he is in the diplomatic service and was posted to Shanghai—or was it Hong Kong? Anyway, too far…'

'He'll come back,' comforted Suzannah, 'I mean, they only stay in one place for a few years, don't they?' She frowned in thought. 'And surely they get leave?'

'Julie made me promise not to tell him about her—her disability.'

'But it's not a disability,' said Suzannah strongly. 'It was a tumour which Professor Bowers-Bentinck removed and she is completely cured.'

'Yes,' agreed her companion doubtfully, 'so we have been assured. Julie is very—how do you say?—enamoured of him.'

'Well, that's only natural, isn't it? He saved her life; besides he's very good looking and I dare say charming to her. But that won't last, at least, if she loves this other man, it won't.'

'You are a sensible girl,' observed Mevrouw van Dijl. 'Julie is a dear girl, but she is used to having her own way. You are not unhappy with us?'

'Certainly not, Mevrouw. Julie is making a splendid recovery. I'm sure Professor Bowers-Bentinck will be delighted with her progress.'

Which wasn't quite true; not that she was unhappy, but her days were filled with small pinpricks, some of them intentional. Alone with Julie she was treated almost—though not quite—as a friend, but when Julie's friends came to see her or she went to see them, Suzannah was ignored or treated with a careless indifference which she found hard to bear. She had been warned that she would expect to remain in the background and she hadn't expected anything else, but to be delegated there with an, 'And you can make yourself scarce, Suzannah,' or, what was worse, 'Go away until I ring for you,' was lowering.

But she was treated with courtesy by Julie's parents and the servants, and she began to wonder if Julie was being deliberately ill-mannered for some reason of her own. There was nothing to be done about it; she had accepted the job and the professor had told her that Julie was unpredictable at times.

She felt much better about it when at the end of the week she found an envelope in her room with her first week's wages. Moreover, she was to have a free day on the morrow. She accompanied Julie to a friend's house that morning and gave no sign of rancour when she was told casually to make herself scarce for an hour. She didn't go far, of course; she was there to keep an eye on her charge, which meant keeping out of sight but never so distant that she couldn't be summoned in a moment. She went and sat outside in the rather chilly autumn morning, listening to the murmur of voices and laughter from the drawing-room behind her.

Armed with her pay packet, she took a tram to the city centre on the next day; Julie was to spend the day with her parents at an aunt's house in the country and Suzannah, freed from her duties, spent a blissful few hours roaming round the shops. The grey jersey dress was no longer adequate; she had worn it each evening and was only too aware of the faintly mocking look which Julie cast at it. Boutiques were out of the question; she roamed C & A and then de Bijenkorf—rather more pricey, but she liked the clothes there.

The pretty dresses there were tempting, but she had to bear in mind that since she must keep in the background, something unassuming was called for. She found it presently—a soft grey-blue crêpe, long-sleeved with a discreet neckline, a mid-calf skirt and nothing about it to date it for a year or two. It was within her means, too; she found a coffee shop and made a frugal lunch in a glow of satisfaction.

She wore it that evening at dinner and Mevrouw van Dijl said kindly, 'That's a pretty dress, Suzannah, I like the colour,' so that she smiled with a pleasure which refused to be damped by Julie's rude,

'Spent all your money, Suzannah? Why don't you buy something pretty?'

Which made Suzannah wonder why she stayed to put up with such rudeness, even making allowances for Julie's recent illness. But the professor had said that the girl needed someone with her, although Julie had shown no signs of the depression he had mentioned. There had been plenty of ill temper, though!

Some of Julie's young friends had come in after dinner and stayed rather late, and by the time that Suzannah had made sure that Julie was in bed and half asleep it was well past midnight. She curled up in her own bed and closed her eyes and slept at once.

She wasn't sure what had wakened her. She sat up in bed to listen and then got out of bed; Julie was muttering and moaning softly. Suzannah went into her room and saw by the light of the bedside lamp that she was asleep but restless. As she reached the bed, Julie started up and burst into tears. 'Suzannah, don't go. I've had a dream—I'm not ill again, am I? I feel awful—I'm not going to die? Guy said I'd been cured, but perhaps he was only saying that…'

Suzannah sat on the side of the bed and put an arm round the girl.

'I'm quite sure that the professor wouldn't tell you something that wasn't true. He said you were cured, so you can take it that you are. You're not ill—you had a lively evening and you got overtired. I'm not in a position to say, but I think that perhaps you have been doing too much all at once. I know it's lovely to see all your friends again, but you have so many…'

'I don't care if I never see any of them again. There's only one person I want to see, and he's miles away.'

'But I expect he'll come back some day?' suggested Suzannah comfortably, 'If you didn't do quite so much…by the time he does see you, you will be perfectly well and prettier than ever.'

She fetched some water and Julie gulped it down. 'Don't tell Mother.'

'No, but if Professor Bowers-Bentinck comes to see you and asks, I must tell him exactly how you are—or you can…'

'He'll just look at me and say nothing very much, but he won't be pleased. I never know what he's thinking.' She added pettishly, 'He's so old…'

'Is he?'

'I don't want to marry him after all—I thought he'd do instead of…' She broke off and glanced at Suzannah, who kept an uninterested expression on her face so that Julie went on, 'Oh, well, it doesn't matter. Someone else can have him and I wish her luck. Heaven knows, plenty of girls have tried.'

'I dare say he's wedded to his work…'

Julie, her fright forgotten, laughed. 'You are green, aren't you?'

'I'm afraid so. Would you like a hot drink?'

'No, but will you stay here until I go to sleep? That chair's quite comfortable.'

She took a long time to doze off, but at last Suzannah was able to creep back to her own cold bed and fall into a brief, troubled sleep before it was time to get up.

Julie was still asleep when she went down to breakfast. Mevrouw van Dijl had coffee in her room and her husband had left the house some time before; Suzannah sat down to her solitary meal.

She had just poured her coffee and was contemplating the basket of bread and rolls when the door opened and Anna came in. 'Professor Bowers-Bentinck,' she announced, and he walked past her and crossed the room unhurriedly to stand by her chair.

He stared down at her for a few moments and she stared back. 'Good morning, Suzannah. Why are you so pale?'

It would take too long to explain just then, so she said, 'Does anyone know you're here? Should I tell Mevrouw…?'

'Anna will do that.' He turned to say something to the maid and then sat down at the table. 'You won't mind if I share your breakfast? I'm on my way to a seminar in Amsterdam—it seemed a good idea to call in on my way.'

And, when she had nothing to say, 'And now tell me why you look so whey-faced.'

CHAPTER FIVE

'WHAT A BEASTLY thing to say,' said Suzannah, finding her tongue at last. 'There's nothing wrong with me; we had rather a wakeful night.'

'Ah, yes, so I would imagine from the look of you…' He broke off as the butler came in with a tray: fresh coffee, eggs in a basket, toast, croissants and a variety of breads. He arranged these on the table before the professor, murmured '*smakelijk eten*' and went away.

The professor poured himself some coffee, examined the bread basket with interest, took an egg and helped himself to butter, perfectly at ease, and Suzannah, wishing to appear just as relaxed, asked, 'Do you often have breakfast here?'

He took a sip of coffee and added sugar, and although he spoke seriously she had the idea that he was amused.

'When Julie was ill, before I operated, I saw her frequently. This is a good time of day for a visit, before I start work…'

'Oh, yes—well. I thought you were in England.'

'So I was. I came over on the night ferry with the car; I've a couple of things to do while I'm here—I shall go back tonight.'

'Isn't that rather a rush?'

He shrugged. 'No, now let us apply ourselves to the matter in hand.' If he saw the quick colour come into her cheeks at his snub, he gave no sign. 'How is Julie? I want your opinion, Suzannah—nothing professional.'

She said tartly, 'Well, I can't be that, can I? I'm not professional. She's been good-tempered for most of the time, although she doesn't like me being here, you know, and really it must be tiresome for her to have me trailing round all the time. When we're alone we get on very well…' She paused, remembering the nasty little slights she had had to put up with. 'Until last night she has slept for at least eight hours at a time and gone to bed at a reasonable hour, although she hated that. But last night was different; some friends came to see her and they didn't leave until late; she was a bit excited by the time that she was in bed. She woke crying, afraid that she was going to die and that you hadn't told her the truth when you said that she was cured. It took some time to settle her and she asked me to sit with her until she fell asleep.'

'And when was that?'

'About five o'clock.'

'And what did you tell her?'

'I told her at once that she wasn't going to die and that you wouldn't lie to her.'

'She believed you?'

'Oh, yes, after a time.'

'Has she talked to you about a young man who is abroad?'

'Yes. I think she loves him, only she believes that he doesn't love her. Sometimes she says that she will marry…'

She stopped and went a painful pink, and the professor said, 'Go on, Suzannah,! It is important that I know everything.'

'She sometimes says that she will marry you, only then she changes her mind because you're too…'

'Old,' prompted the professor. 'As I am. I should point out to you that patients who have serious operations frequently believe themselves to be in love with the surgeon; it wears off the moment they realise that they are perfectly well again and resume a normal life.'

She stared at him thoughtfully. 'But isn't that awkward for you?'

'An occupational hazard, shall we say, and not all that frequent.' He took some toast and buttered it. 'Thank you for your help. And what about you?'

'Me? Oh, I'm fine.'

'You have your free time, your day off and your salary?'

'Yes, thank you.'

'I think that you have had to put up with Julie's occasional small rages; she can be shockingly rude.'

Suzannah said nothing and he went on, 'You feel that you can stay for another few weeks? Have you made any friends?'

She looked at him in astonishment. 'Good heavens, no—none of Julie's friends speaks to me.' And she added quickly, 'Well, why should they?'

'Why indeed?' He finished his coffee. 'Shall we go and see Julie now? Anna will have told her mother that I am here; I'll see her when I've examined Julie.'

'She's in bed.'

'Yes, I know that. I should like to see her before she has had time to realise I'm here.'

Julie was still asleep. She looked quite beautiful, her hair, grown again since her operation, framing her flushed face. The professor stood looking at her for a minute or two, and then picked up one arm flung across the counterpane. She woke then, staring at him, at first with bewilderment and then with delight. 'Guy—oh, I'm so glad to see you. Are you staying for a few days? Will you take me out one evening? Just us two?'

He leaned over the foot of the bed, smiling a little. 'I'm on my way to Amsterdam and it seemed a good idea to call in and see how you were. I'd like to take a look, if I may. It won't take long.'

She made a face. 'Don't you ever think of anything but your work? I feel fine.'

'Suzannah tells me that you have done exactly what I wished you to do; another week or two and you'll be out of my hands.'

He bent to examine her eye reflexes and then turn her head gently from side to side. 'Nothing hurts? You have a good appetite? Don't feel sick? Sleep well?'

Julie was sitting up in bed, her arms round her knees. 'I'm sure Suzannah told you everything. I can't move without her… I'm fine. Last night I had a bad dream, but it didn't last.'

The professor sat down on the side of the bed. 'You have nothing to worry about,' he told her, 'you have made a complete recovery but, just like anyone else, you need a little time to get over your operation. Do not do more than you have been doing; in a couple of weeks I'll let you off the hook for three months before I need see you again.'

'And Suzannah? Can she go?'

'In two or three weeks' time, yes.'

A remark which Suzannah heard with some trepidation.

He went away presently, and when Suzannah encountered Mevrouw van Dijl later in the morning it was to hear that he had gone again. He could have said goodbye, thought Suzannah forlornly, listening to Mevrouw van Dijl's gentle voice. 'Such a dear little boy,' she was saying. 'I knew him a very long time ago, before I married, and when Julie was born he was a schoolboy and so good and kind to her. She was a difficult baby.'

She's a difficult grown woman too, thought Suzannah.

A few days later Julie's two brothers came. The elder, a rather solemn man in his late twenties, was married and had left his wife at home as she was expecting a baby. He was called Cornelius and, while he was obviously fond of his sister, he viewed her with a hint of disapproval; his brother on the other hand was very like Julie: good-looking and not averse to drawing attention himself. They both worked in their father's business and were just back from America, and while Cornelius had little to say about their trip, Hebert was full of the places he had visited and the people he had met.

No one had thought of introducing Suzannah when they arrived. It was only when Julie said carelessly, 'I almost forgot, this is someone Guy wished on me until I'm perfectly well. Her name's Suzannah.'

Cornelius had said how do you do civilly enough, but Hebert had looked her over. 'Hello,' he said in fluent English. 'I wouldn't have your job for all the tea in China.' And he pulled a face and made her laugh. 'What do you think of Holland?'

'Well, I haven't seen enough of it to know,' she told him.

'Kept tied to Julie's heels? We must do something about that.'

He pulled up a chair and, oblivious to his sister's black looks, began to tell Suzannah something of den Haag.

They were staying a few days, he told her, and when he discovered that she was free the next day he offered to show her round the city. Suzannah felt flattered and touched by his kindness, and, although she had intended to spend the day filling the gaps in her scanty wardrobe, she agreed at once. It would be pleasant to have someone to show her the high points of den Haag and was a chance not to be missed; perhaps she wouldn't be there for very much longer, and she might never come to Holland again.

The day was a success, it seemed to her, happily unaware of Hebert's careless amusement at her enthusiastic sightseeing. He mentioned it casually to Julie that evening, not meaning to be unkind but impatient of what he considered to have been a rather boring day.

'Well, it was your fault for asking her,' said Julie tartly.

'The girl doesn't get much fun; you must be the very devil to look after.' He sounded sulky and Julie laughed.

'You've done your good deed anyway, Hebert. We must hope that she doesn't expect any more outings with you.'

She need not have worried; Suzannah had enjoyed her day with Hebert but she had no expectation of it being repeated; for one thing, he would be gone again within a week, and she had only one day off in each week. He had been a pleasant companion, but she had the good sense to know that she was as unlike his usual companions as chalk from cheese. She went to bed content, although her contentment might not have been so undoubting if she had known that the professor had telephoned while she was out with Hebert and, since she hadn't been there to answer him, he had been put through to Julie who, feeling bored and bad-tempered, had embellished Suzannah's day out with her brother. The professor was no fool; and the same, even allowing for Julie's airy exaggerations, he found himself surprisingly put out. Suzannah was one of the world's Marthas, reliable and undemanding, surprisingly sharp-tongued when the occasion arose, but sensible and kind too. She had no business spending her day with Hebert, who was bent on amusing himself with not much thought of others. The professor was vexed to find that the idea of Hebert turning on his considerable charm in order to attract Suzannah was distasteful to him. He had put down the receiver with deliberation, his handsome features cast in a disapproving mould.

'Silly girl,' he remarked to the empty room. A remark both unfair and untrue and, coming from him, surprising.

He went back to England that evening and two days later flew off to Cairo for an urgent consultation and subsequent operation on an influential member of Middle East politics. He operated successfully and stayed in Cairo until the patient was out of danger, and if he thought about Suzannah at all during that time it was fleetingly.

Back in London, he satisfied himself that Julie's family doctor was happy with her progress and plunged into a backlog of work, so that it was almost three weeks before he went to Holland again.

Suzannah had found the three weeks irksome; Julie was, as far as she could judge, quite well again, but since she had promised the professor to try and curb Julie's activities she went on cajoling and persuading her to lead a moderately quiet life. A thankless task which earned her Julie's increasing impatience and peevishness.

Moreover, it was becoming increasingly difficult to get even an hour to herself during the day. Julie, rebellious about an afternoon nap, would rest only if Suzannah read to her, pointing out that she might just as well sit quietly with her as moon around on her own. That Suzannah had no intention of mooning once she was free to go out made no difference to her; if Suzannah stood firm and insisted on a couple of hours to herself while Julie rested, she would return to find the girl either in a state of hysterical rage which took the rest of the day to calm, or she would have phoned one of her friends and gone off in her car, coming back home hours later by which time Suzannah's nerves, not to mention her mother's, were worn to threads.

When the professor came she was determined to ask him if she might go back to England. She had very little idea of what she would do when she got there, but she had some money saved and, armed with a reference from Mevrouw van Dijl and one from the professor, she would surely find work.

She had managed to get her free days, but only after a good deal of arguing, and now, with another one due the next day, Hebert had come home for a day or so and, very much to her surprise, asked her if she would like to go to Panorama Mesdag, a vast painting on a circular canvas of Scheveningen. The building in which it was housed was in the centre of den Haag, and he suggested that they might go in the afternoon.

'I dare say you will want to shop in the morning; I'll meet you outside the Ridderzaal at two o'clock.'

She had intended to walk along Scheveningen's lengthy boulevard, have a snack lunch somewhere and go window shopping in the afternoon, giving the shops in den Haag a wide berth so that she wouldn't be too tempted to spend any money. The future began to loom, vague and uncertain, and money was the one thing she would need. Perhaps on her very last day off she would splash out.

She spent the morning wandering round the department stores, and after a cup of coffee went to the Mauritshuis and studied the paintings it housed before finding a small café and making another cup of coffee and a *kas broodje* last as long as possible. And presently it was time for her to find her way to the Ridderzaal. It was a chilly day and there was no one loitering there, so she walked up and down for ten minutes or so and was on the point of giving Hebert up when she saw him coming towards her. But not alone; he had a young woman with him, a pretty, fair girl, wrapped warmly and fashionably; not quite as young as Suzannah had first thought but exquisitely made-up, with fair hair falling in a silky cloud to her shoulders.

Hebert took Suzannah's arm and began walking rapidly away from the Ridderzaal. 'This is Monique, Suzannah, an old friend of mine.' He turned his head to laugh at the girl. 'She will join us for the afternoon…' He started an easy conversation which allowed Suzannah very little chance to talk, and from time to time he and Monique exchanged a low-voiced talk in Dutch so that by the time they reached Panorama Mesdag Suzannah was beginning to get the impression that she was *de trop*. Indeed, once they were inside she wished heartily that she hadn't come. But for the moment at least she forgot her awkwardness. They had entered through a series of rooms hung with Mesdag's paintings, and then at the end of a narrow passage they climbed a few steps and emerged to find a vast circular painting of Scheveningen in the late nineteenth century, so lifelike that she felt she must get over the guard rail and join the fishermen mending their nets by the North Sea. She went slowly, and it wasn't until she was halfway round that she realised that her companions were no longer to be seen. There weren't many people there, and those that were were engrossed in the vast painting, and they hardly noticed her hasty search round the circle. They weren't there; perhaps they had gone back to look at the paintings and would return presently. She told herself with her usual common sense that since she wasn't likely to see Panorama Mesdag again before she went back to England, she might as well complete her visit.

Fifteen minutes later she made her way out again, to pause at the entrance and look up and down the street. Dusk was still an hour or two away, but the afternoon was already becoming dim and it was difficult to see any distance. She waited for a few minutes and then turned her steps towards Noordeinde. She would have an early tea and then take a tram back to Scheveningen. She had gone only a few steps when she saw Hebert and Monique coming towards her.

'Suzannah, Monique remembered that she had to collect something from the chemist and it seemed a good chance to go while you were looking at Panorama Mesdag; we did try to attract your attention inside, but you were so engrossed...' He laughed too loudly and went on quickly, 'Shall we have tea? There's a splendid place close by...'

Suzannah didn't believe a word; not only did he look guilty, Monique was looking decidedly uneasy. She agreed cheerfully to having tea, reminding herself that it was none of her business anyway, although she wondered why Hebert had asked her to be such an obvious third when he and Monique were, for the most part, unaware of her company.

The café to which he led them was hardly splendid. It was in a side street, clean as Dutch cafés were, however humble, and almost empty of customers. Hebert ordered tea, which came as glasses of hot water with a tea bag in each saucer, and a plate of little biscuits, and then, with a muttered excuse, carried on a low-voiced conversation with Monique.

Suzannah sipped her rather tepid tea and ate a biscuit, feeling lonely. When the other two paused for a moment she said, 'Well, thank you for showing me Panorama Mesdag and for my tea...' She intended to get up, but Hebert put out an urgent hand.

'Suzannah, you are a kind girl; will you do something for me—for us? I—we, that is—can only see each other secretly. Monique is married and I am engaged, but neither of us is happy. This is the only way we can meet. I ask you not to say anything to my parents—if you would let them think that we have spent the afternoon and evening together.' He added, 'They do not approve.'

'Well, I don't suppose they do,' said Suzannah. 'It seems rather hard on your fiancée and on Monique's husband. I won't tell. But don't think that I'll do this again for you, for I won't.'

She got to her feet, nodded briefly at them both and went into the street. It was almost dark by now and she wondered what she would do for the next hour or so. The shops were shutting and she was shy of going to a café on her own. It would have to be the cinema. She sat through an American film with Dutch subtitles, a combination which confused her, for a couple of hours, and then walked to the nearest tram stop.

The professor, driving through the city on his way to see Julie, stared at her small, hurrying figure, unable to stop because of the traffic lights. Her free day, he decided idly.

He was there sitting with Mevrouw van Dijl and Julie when Suzannah went into the drawing-room. He got to his feet, but before she could do more than greet them Hebert came in. The professor nodded coolly, having a poor opinion of him, but Hebert was effusive.

'Come to check on Julie, have you?' He wanted to know. 'She looks pretty fit to me.' He sat down close to Suzannah. 'I've been putting the car away. Suzannah and I had a delightful time in town—saw a few sights and had lunch and tea—introduced her to some of our famous cream cakes at Saur's and had a stroll round the shops afterwards.'

He laughed for no reason at all and glanced at Suzannah. 'We had a delightful time, didn't we, Suzannah?'

She didn't look at him and, since she was aware that the professor was watching her, she addressed her feet. 'Oh, very,' she agreed.

She was saved from saying more by Julie's rather petulant, 'Well, if you want to take a look at me, Guy, I suppose you'd better do it now. Suzannah, come with us—you can tidy up afterwards.'

Suzannah was only too glad to escape; perhaps by the time the professor had finished his examination Hebert would be gone. At least the professor wouldn't be there to hear her fibbing about her outing with Hebert.

He was in no hurry; he went over Julie with calm thoroughness, then sat down to talk to her while Suzannah fidgeted uneasily in the background. The moment she could, she would escape, she told herself, and was frustrated by the ringing of the telephone by the bed. When Julie went to answer it the professor said quietly, 'We'll wait outside,' and scooped Suzannah out of the room before she could think up a reason for staying.

He went to lean against the gallery rail overlooking the hall and turned to look at her. 'You had a delightful time with Hebert?' he wanted to know.

Suzannah turned a little way from him and became engrossed in the hall below. 'Yes.'

'It doesn't sound like him at all, looking into shop windows.' There was something in his voice which made her uneasy. 'I'm glad he gave you a good tea, though. Saur's is a delightful café—did you go upstairs?'

'Yes, yes, we did,' declared Suzannah, 'and the tea was splendid.'

'Although I don't care for that pink and gold china,' observed the professor.

The blandness of his voice made her glance quickly at him. He returned the look with a smile as bland, and she was emboldened to say with foolish *sang froid*, 'I thought it rather pretty…'

He spoke very quietly in a voice to chill her to her bones. 'Suzannah, Saur's has no upstairs tea-room and certainly no pink and gold china; moreover, Hebert was not with you when I saw you walking down Lange Voorhout. Who did you spend the time with?' He watched her face. 'And don't waste time thinking up more lies—Oh, I dare say you were at Panorama Mesdag, it's an ideal place to meet and slip out again unobserved. But why, I wonder, did you and Hebert connive together?'

She very nearly choked. He had taken it for granted that she was meeting someone—a man—on the sly, and if that was what he thought of her he was even worse than she had always thought him to be, arrogant, narrow-minded, cold-blooded. 'It's none of your business,' she told him, but her voice, despite her best efforts, shook a little.

'Oh, but it is. I asked you to come here…' He stopped as two tears rolled down Suzannah's cheeks. She turned her back and wiped them away with a finger like a child. He said suddenly, 'I have it all wrong, haven't I? Hebert's up to his nasty tricks again and is using you. Oh, you don't need to fib any more, my dear, I shan't give him away, but neither will I permit him to do that to you.'

He turned her round to face him and lifted her chin to stare into her unhappy face. 'You don't like me, do you? But believe me, I wouldn't wish you any harm or any unhappiness.'

She made a small sound, a watery hiccup followed by a sniff, and he offered her a very white handkerchief. 'When do you have your next free day?'

'Julie is going to visit an aunt next Thursday, Mevrouw van Dijl is going with her, and so it's convenient for them if I have my day off then.'

'Nine days' time…' He thought for a moment. 'I'll be over again on the Wednesday for a final visit until Julie's routine check-ups; I'll have the car and we will make a tour of some of the country.'

She regarded him with astonishment. 'But there's no need,' she told him urgently. 'Such a waste of your day, taking me out.'

'Oh, no, I shall enjoy seeing something of the Veluwe, it is a favourite time of year for me. And I dare say if we are very careful we shall manage not to disagree for an hour or so.'

He smiled then and she was quite taken aback to see his whole austere face alter; he looked kind and friendly, and at the same time comfortably detached. Perhaps, she thought confusedly, I shall like him after all. She nodded her bright head. 'I'd like to do that,' she told him, 'if you're sure it's not spoiling your leisure.'

He thought of the lunch with medical colleagues he would have to put off and the dinner he had intended to give to the charming daughter of an old family friend, and wondered why on earth he had so rashly committed himself to a day with this small, plain girl with the sharp tongue and the bright hair. He remembered the tears and smiled ruefully and, seeing her sharp look, said cheerfully. 'It is always a pleasure to show off one's adopted country.'

'I thought you were English.'

'I am, but my aunt married a Dutchman, as you know, and I spent all my school holidays here, as well as taking a medical degree at Leiden.'

He spoke casually, and she thought that he might be getting bored; it was providential that Julie should join them then and presently all three of them went back to the drawing-room. After a little while the professor went away.

Suzannah contrived not to speak to Hebert during the evening; indeed, she rather felt that he was avoiding her while he talked loudly and at length about his work and the holiday he was planning to take. He gave so many details about it that it amounted to a timetable of his movements while he was away, so that Suzannah began to wonder if he and Monique had planned something together and he was trailing red herrings for his mother. That lady remarked during the evening that he was giving them such a detailed account of where he would be and what he would be doing that there would be no need for him to send postcards.

He had laughed heartily, and Julie had given him a quick look and giggled.

He stayed one more day and, since his father was at home, he spent a good part of it closeted in the study, discussing business. Beyond an occasional word, Suzannah had been able to keep away from him.

Julie had said nothing to her about her supposed outing with Hebert, and she decided that the girl knew more about it than she intended to say. She was growing impatient of Suzannah's company; although she rested reluctantly during the day and agreed to go to bed by midnight, there was always a tussle between the pair of them, with Julie lazing around her bedroom, lying for ages in the bath and then calling Suzannah back once she was in bed to fetch a book or a drink or whatever.

Suzannah didn't allow it to annoy her; the professor had said that his next visit would be the last until the three-monthly check-ups which meant that she would be leaving very soon now, and although she had been more than thankful for the job and she had been able to save most of her wages, she looked forward to being back in England. It would be lovely to see Horace again; the professor had told her that he was happy and had settled down very well, but the sooner she found a room so that he could be with her again, the better. The question of where she was to go on her return worried her; as soon as she knew when she was to return she would have to write to Mrs Coffin and ask if she and Horace might stay with her until she could find another job. She would have to collect Horace on the way, of course; she spent some time poring over timetables trying to fit in her journey to suit collecting him and going on to Mrs Coffin's on the same day.

True to his promise the professor arrived on the Wednesday, walking in as she sat at breakfast just as he had done previously. He wished her good morning civilly enough, ate his breakfast with only the modicum of conversation and asked her how Julie was.

He looked impatient, so she made her replies brief before they went upstairs to Julie's room. She was awake, drinking her morning tea and reading her letters, but she bounced up in bed as he went in flung her arms round his neck.

'Very much better,' commented the professor. 'I wonder why.'

She waved a letter at him. 'He's coming home,' she told him in an excited voice. 'Evert—you remember him?'

'Of course I do.' He added deliberately, 'You refused to let anyone tell him that you had a brain tumour…'

'Yes, but he says in his letter that he would never have gone away if he had known—how did he know?' She paused to puzzle over it.

'I wrote and told him,' said the professor placidly. 'You may have forgotten, but you never made me promise not to tell. He has been having weekly reports from me since I operated. I told him not to come back until you were quite cured. And you are. When does he get here?'

'Guy, oh, Guy—in two days' time. I thought I'd never see him again, and I didn't care what happened. I even thought for a little while that I'd marry you.'

The professor received this remark calmly. 'Well, now you won't have to, and as it happens I don't think I want to marry you; much as I find you very beautiful and charming! Now let us be serious for ten minutes and take a final and thorough look at you.'

Suzannah had been standing quietly a little apart, listening with the greatest interest, pleased that Julie's future was so rosy, and vaguely wistful and sad that something like that didn't happen to her. How easily her problems would be solved if a man were to appear, sweep her off her feet, marry her out of hand and never allow her to worry again for the rest of her life. She stood there daydreaming while the professor and Julie watched her. It wasn't until he had said, 'Suzannah,' for the third time that she came back to her senses.

'If you don't mind,' observed the professor, 'I would be glad if you would fetch Julie's pills—they need to be changed.'

She blushed and went to the bathroom to fetch them from the cupboard there. She thought he looked impatient again; she must vex him very much. He certainly wouldn't want to take her out as he had suggested. He must have been comforting her; people said all kinds of thing upon occasion and didn't mean them.

She offered the little bottles and Julie asked, 'When can Suzannah go? I don't need her now, you know. And when Evert comes…'

The professor didn't even look at Suzannah. 'He comes in two days' time—so, let me see, Suzannah can leave on the day after tomorrow. I will talk to your mother before I go.'

Julie flung her arms round his neck again. 'You really are a darling; you would make a lovely husband, only I can't think of a girl nice enough for you.' She looked at Suzannah. 'I don't suppose you've had much fun,' she commented. 'You'll be glad to get home and go out and about.'

Suzannah agreed smilingly. It was quite true, she reflected, half the world had no idea how the other half lived, and there was no point in enlightening Julie.

The professor patted Julie on the shoulder. 'Be a good girl,' he begged her. 'I'm going to see your mother now. You know where I am if you need help. Suzannah, come downstairs with me.'

In the hall he said, 'I'll be here at nine o'clock tomorrow; that will give us a long day out.'

'Oh, well, I thought…that is, I have to pack and look up trains and things.'

He swept an eye over her person. 'Packing will take you half an hour, perhaps less; you haven't a very large wardrobe, have you? And you'll travel back with me—on the day ferry to Harwich—I booked you on in it.'

She goggled at him. 'But how did you know I would be leaving?'

'Well, of course I knew. Evert had told me that he would be coming and I was almost certain that I could discharge Julie, at least for the three months. You're no longer needed and I imagine you would wish to return to England. Unless you have some other plan?'

She shook her head. 'No. I mean to go to Mrs Coffin, if you wouldn't mind me picking up Horace on the way?'

'We'll talk about that tomorrow.' He studied her tweed skirt and jumper. 'Have you a winter coat? We might want to walk tomorrow and it has turned cold.'

She went a bright pink. 'Yes, thank you…'

'Good. I'll see you in the morning.' He nodded goodbye and crossed the hall to the drawing-room, leaving her to stand there, relief flooding through her because she wouldn't have to worry about the journey back. Even stronger than her relief was annoyance at his careless remarks about her clothes. 'It's all very well for him,' she muttered, going back upstairs, 'with his Bentley and his Savile Row suits and silk ties. Arranging things to suit himself.' An unfair remark, she admitted reluctantly; he had, after all, arranged for her return.

CHAPTER SIX

SUZANNAH STOOD IN front of the dressing-table looking-glass and studied her reflection. It didn't please her. Her coat was a useful brown; it had been a good one some years ago, but it was faintly threadbare around the cuffs and down the front, and the brown dress beneath it did nothing to improve her appearance. She tucked a leaf-green scarf into the collar of the coat and, cold weather or not, decided not to wear the only hat she had: brown again and presumably prudently purchased with an eye to its usefulness rather than any pretentions to fashion. At least her gloves and handbag were passable. She wished suddenly that she hadn't accepted the professor's invitation, but it was too late to change things now and, thinking about it, he hadn't given her much chance to refuse. At this very moment he might be wishing that he wasn't to be saddled with her for a whole day.

His thoughts weren't quite as drastic as that; but as he drove through den Haag to pick her up he wondered why on earth he had asked her out. They had never had a real conversation, and for all he knew she would be tongue-tied, or, worse, chatty, and yet he found himself wishing to know more about her. And her eyes were beautiful. He thumped the door-knocker of the van Dijls' house and went in.

Suzannah came down the stairs, outwardly calm. She had been to see Julie, sitting up in bed enjoying her breakfast, and that young lady had thoughtlessly remarked that brown was all the wrong colour for Suzannah. 'You should wear green or that lovely greeny-blue tweed', she observed blithely, 'and of course you could wear black with that hair. Still, I don't suppose Guy will take you anywhere where he'll see anyone he knows.'

Suzannah had been quite unable to answer this; she had ducked out of the room and waited a moment before going down to the hall, rather pale with suppressed rage and humiliation. She crossed the hall to where the professor was standing and said good morning in a tight little voice, wanting very much to turn and run, only he said just the right thing. 'It's a cold, dark day and that hair of yours is like a ray of sunshine.' His smile was so warm that she found herself smiling in return, and suddenly the brown coat didn't matter at all.

In the car, sitting beside him in the greatest comfort, she was told to take the map from the pocket beside her. 'We shall go to Utrecht and then Appeldoorn and Zwolle, Kampen Sneek, across the Isselmeer, then across to Bergen and down the coast to Haarlem, across to Hilversum, then down the river Vecht—that's a beauty spot—and back here.'

'All in a day?'

'Holland is a small country, and we have eight or nine hours.' He smiled at her again, and she knew that the day was going to be fun, after all.

A few miles out of den Haag, the professor turned off the motorway, drove slowly through Gouda and took a secondary road through Oudewater, where he stopped the car to tell her about the witches' weighing scales there. She was surprised to find that he was both interesting and amusing, and when they reached Utrecht, although he didn't stop, he told her a good deal about the city as they drove through it.

Once out of the city he took another secondary road through the Veluwe, driving slowly so that she might enjoy the woods all around them, circumventing Appeldoorn and turning north to Vaasen where they stopped for coffee at a restaurant—'T Neotshuis. Its interior was spectacular and besides, close by was Kasteel Cannenburch, with its beginnings in the fourteenth century. The professor knew its history well, and over coffee he related it. 'Such a pity that it is closed, but the grounds are open if you would like to see them?'

'Yes, oh, yes, please,' said Suzannah, and skipped happily beside him out of the restaurant; she was feeling quite at ease despite her initial fears, and if her companion wasn't enjoying himself he was dissembling very successfully.

They drove on presently, to Zwolle and across the bridge to Kampen and then on to Sneek, where they stopped so that he might show her the harbour, crammed with yachts, and the Hoogeindster Waterpoort, an ancient water gate with two towers. She would have lingered there, for there was a great deal to see, but he whisked her back into the car and drove along narrow country roads winding beside the lakes stretching in all directions until they came to Beesterzwaag where they stopped for lunch. The hotel had a fine restaurant set in grounds which were still attractive, even at the tail end of the year. The food was delicious: smoked eel on toast, roast pheasant and red cabbage, and paper-thin pancakes with syrup. Over coffee, the professor said, 'We are about half-way; we shall drive over on the Afsluitdijk and cross over to the coast, the country there is pretty and the road is quiet until we reach Haarlem. We don't need to go into the town, we'll go south to Aalsmeer and turn off before we reach Hilversum and go down the river Vecht; the light will be going by then, but you will be able to see some of it. We can use the motorway from there, as it will be too dark to see any more.'

'We've been over almost all of Holland,' said Suzannah.

'It may seem like it to you; there are so many villages and small hidden roads still to discover.'

The weather stayed kind, although the afternoon was already darkening; the Afsluitdijk stretched unendingly, it seemed, but the Bentley made nonsense of its length. Then they were on the mainland again, taking a narrow road to the east coast. The professor had been right, it was pretty, with the sea never far off and small, isolated villages, but presently they reached the outskirts of Haarlem and turned inland on a main road now. But before they reached Hilversum he turned into a narrow, winding road running by a charming river, lined with trees and with splendid houses on either side of it; it was dusk now and they were lit, their high, wide windows uncurtained so that Suzannah longed to stop and walk up their wide driveways and peer inside. The professor knew several families living there and, seeing her interest, told her something of their history.

'It would be very nice to live here,' said Suzannah wistfully, 'but of course you live in England.'

He smiled a little and agreed. 'Shall we have a cup of tea? There's a café in Loenen.'

It was beginning to rain as they left the café, and there was a mean, cold wind blowing. The day was almost over and Suzannah was aware of regret; she had loved every minute of it and, surprisingly, she had liked being with the professor, although she still harboured the suspicion that he had given her a treat to make up for the small snubs and slights she had had. He was kind, she reflected, staring ahead of her into the dark, made darker by the car's headlights. They would be back in den Haag very soon now. She would spend the evening packing—well, she amended, part of the evening, for there was very little to pack. The professor had fallen silent and she began to brood over what she should do when she got back to England. But her thoughts were brought to an end by the professor's voice.

'I thought we might have dinner in Leidschendam, it's far too soon to go back.'

'Oh, yes—but I'm not dressed… I thought—that is, you might meet someone you know.'

'My dear girl, what are you talking about? I probably shall, but what has that got to do with us having dinner?'

'I think you might be ashamed of me,' she said in a cool little voice. 'I'm rather shabby, you know.'

His voice, very quiet, came to her through the dimness of the car.

'You must have a very low opinion of me, Suzannah.'

'Oh, no, I haven't, only…' She stopped just in time from telling him what Julie had said.

He finished for her, 'Ah, Julie in one of her bad moments planted the idea in your head.' He added coldly, 'And you believed her?'

'Not like that, I didn't.' She was anxious to explain, because she could hear the anger in his voice. 'I just didn't want to embarrass you. I don't think you'd mind a bit what I was wearing, but if you saw someone you knew they might—well, be surprised. I haven't explained very well, but I'm sorry you're angry, only it's true, I wouldn't want to embarrass you, truly I wouldn't.' She sniffed, a small, forlorn sound. 'It's been such a lovely day…'

'Indeed it has, and we are not going to spoil it now. We will dine at our ease and discuss what you are going to do next, and I promise you that you are quite adequately dressed: Julie's idea of shabby is wearing a dress for the second time, and hardly to be taken as a general rule.'

The restaurant, when they reached it, was a splendid one, and Suzannah cast the professor a reproachful look as her coat was taken from her, revealing the brown dress. A look which he ignored, and from the way the head waiter led them to a table with deferential respect she might just as well have been wearing a couture gown and diamonds.

The restaurant was already half full, and indeed the professor nodded to several people on the way to their table, but no one stared at her. Perhaps the dress wasn't so bad, after all.

The professor asked her what she would like to drink, ordered the sherry she asked for and a *jenever* for himself, and watched her while she studied the menu. The dress *was* terrible, he thought—someone should tell her to wear green or blue or grey—but he had to admit that her ordinary face, its colour heightened with excitement and, he suspected, misgiving, had a certain appeal; certainly her eyes were beautiful and the burnished copper of her hair was quite unusual. And she was a good companion… He smiled as she glanced up and asked her what she would like to eat.

'We had rather a large lunch,' she observed doubtfully, unaware that he had decided before they set out that he would at least give her a good lunch and dinner. Never one to do things by halves, and despite the fact that he had been regretting his invitation, he had kept faithfully to his plan.

He now found, rather to his surprise, that he was enjoying her company.

He said, 'That was hours ago. They do a very good salmon in lobster sauce—shall we have that? And perhaps a *mousseline* of chicken with caviare for starters? And, since we are celebrating Julie's complete recovery, I think we might have some champagne, don't you?'

Suzannah, relieved not to have to decide for herself, agreed and added artlessly, 'I had champagne once, on my mother's birthday…'

'And how long ago was that?' he asked gently, and led her on to talk about her childhood before asking casually, 'so what do you intend to do when you get back to England?'

It wasn't the first time he had asked her that. She reminded him that she would go to Mrs Coffin with Horace, and he said easily, 'Have you anywhere to stay in London? It occurs to me that it might be easier and far quicker for you if you were to leave Horace with Mrs Cobb for a few more days while you find a job.'

The champagne was having its effect; for the moment at least, life was benefiting from rose-coloured spectacles. 'Well,' said Suzannah cautiously, 'that would be much easier, wouldn't it? I could go straight to some employment agencies…'

'What do you have in mind?'

'I can't do shorthand and I don't know how to be a secretary, so I thought I'd try to get work as a receptionist at a doctor's or dentist's, but I'll take anything where I can have a room and keep Horace.'

'You have friends in London where you can stay when we get there?'

He reflected that he had helped her twice, and it looked as though he would be doing that for a third time. He didn't know whether to be relieved or not when he replied promptly, albeit untruthfully, 'Oh, yes. If Horace might stay until the next day with Mrs Cobb, just while I can get settled in.'

He frowned. 'Did you not say that you would stay with Mrs Coffin until you found work?'

'Yes, I did. But it seems a waste of time not to stay just a day or so in London first; I might get a job immediately.'

She spoke with conviction, made seemingly positive by her desire not to impose upon him a moment longer than she need. There must be lodgings somewhere in London where she could stay with Horace. Once there, even though it would be evening by then, she could say goodbye to the professor and find a place, if only for one night. Further than that she refused to think, shying away from a mental picture of her touring London with Horace in his basket, looking for work and a place in which to lay their heads. But, of course, if her search was fruitless she could get an evening train to Mrs Coffin's… She uttered a small sigh of relief and the professor wondered why, convinced that she was only telling him what she thought he would want to hear.

A patient man as well as a clever one, he began to talk about something quite different. Suzannah followed his lead so eagerly that he was more than ever sure that she was prevaricating. Time enough to find out when they got back to London. Hard on the thought came another; there was no earthly reason why he should concern himself with her future; he was seeing her safely back, she wasn't penniless and she had assured him that she would find work without any apparent difficulty. She was a sensible girl, well-educated and able to stand on her own two feet, and he could think of no reason for feeling concern for her future.

It wasn't mentioned again; the rest of dinner passed pleasantly, the talk of any number of subjects but never of her.

It was only a short drive back to the van Dijls' house, and once there he went in with her to spend half an hour in small talk with the van Dijls and Julie. When after ten minutes or so Suzannah excused herself on the grounds of packing her things, no one attempted to stop her from doing so. Beyond a brief nod of goodnight and the warning to be ready for him when he came to fetch her in the morning, the professor had nothing to say to her save to murmur a conventional rejoinder when she thanked him for her day. Perhaps he hadn't enjoyed himself as much as she had thought he had, she mused, getting ready for bed; it was difficult to know exactly what he thought about things at times. She went to sleep feeling vaguely worried, although she wasn't at all sure why.

He was exactly on time the next morning, and they wasted very little time on goodbyes. Mijnheer van Dijl was already at his office, but his wife thanked Suzannah, kissed her and pressed a small packet into her hands. 'You have been so good,' she murmured. Julie trailed down in her dressing-gown to kiss the professor and shake Suzannah's hand with a casual, 'Well, have fun wherever you are going. I won't stay; I must get ready for Evert.'

'I hope you'll be very happy,' said Suzannah, and got into the car, with the professor taking her case to stow in the boot.

The journey was smooth and untroubled; the professor travelled without fuss, but with every detail dealt with in advance. It was as they were nearing London in a dark early evening that she said, 'If you would drop me at Charing Cross station…'

He interrupted her. 'Certainly not, at this time of the day. There is no question of you traipsing around London on your own. It will be best if you come back with me for the night; you can go to your friend's house in the morning, and then come back and collect Horace.'

'There is no need…' began Suzannah in what she hoped was a firm voice.

'Don't argue.'

It was obvious to her that nothing she said would alter his plan, so she said, 'Very well, Professor,' in such a meek voice that he laughed.

They arrived at his house soon after that, and she was ushered into its warmth and in no time at all found herself sitting opposite to him at an oval dining-table in an elegant dining-room, eating delicious food Mrs Cobb had conjured up without any sign of fuss. And when they had finished she was taken to the kitchen to see Horace. He looked sleek and content, but he was pleased to see her. He lived in great comfort, that was obvious, and she wondered how he would like the humbler home she hoped to find for them. The professor had gone to his study and she explained that in the morning she would go and see her friend, now so vivid in her imagination that she seemed real. 'And then I'll come back for Horace; I expect it will be after lunch…'

'That's all right, miss. The professor won't be here, but he said to expect you.'

Presently they said goodnight and Suzannah went out into the hall. She had been shown her room when they had arrived and she started up the stairs, uncertain whether to knock on the study door. It opened while she stood trying to make up her mind, and the professor stuck his head out.

'Going to bed? Sleep well. I shall be gone early and shan't be back until late in the evening. Collect Horace when you like; I've told Cobb to drive the pair of you and your case to your friend's house. Just let him know when you want to go.'

She said faintly, 'Oh, but there's no need,' and at his, 'Don't argue,' didn't finish but uttered her thanks for the journey. 'It was very kind of you,' she finished. 'Goodbye, Professor Bowers-Bentinck.'

He came out into the hall and stood looking up at her. 'We say goodbye rather frequently, don't we?' He added with a touch of impatience, 'Let me know if you need help. Have you sufficient money to keep you until you find a job?'

'Yes, thank you.' London was very much dearer than her own small village; she pushed the worrying thought away and said cheerfully, 'And I can stay with my friend…'

He eyed her narrowly and was about to speak when the study door was pushed wide and a dachshund trotted out and sat down beside the professor. 'You haven't met Henry—come and say hello to him.'

She crossed the space between them and stooped to pat the little dog.

'Hello and goodbye, Henry,' she said, and rubbed a silky ear.

She stood up and offered a hand to the professor. 'Goodbye, Professor.'

He took her hand and bent and kissed her; she had been kissed before, though not often, casual kisses which had meant nothing, but this was different. The thought flashed through her mind that he was an older man, a man of the world, and must have had years of practice. It would be delightful to be kissed like that every day; she would have to be content with once in a lifetime. She said goodnight and goodbye in a brisk voice and went upstairs without a backward glance, reminding herself that there were a great many things about him that she didn't like;

she couldn't call any of them to mind just at that moment, but she would certainly remember them later.

A pleasant girl brought her tea in the morning, told her that breakfast would be in half an hour and suggested she go to the breakfast-room on the left of the hall and warned her that it looked like snow. 'Just right,' she said cheerfully, 'with Christmas so near.'

Suzannah was met at the bottom of the stairs by Cobb with a cheerful good morning and the hope that she had slept well. 'I understand that you'll be going to your friend, miss. When you come back for Horace, I'm to drive you wherever you wish to go.'

She thanked him nicely and worried about it while she ate a splendid breakfast, went to say hello to Horace and presently got into her outdoor things and left the house.

It was now that she needed a kindly fate to step in and give her a hand, but in the meanwhile she would study the situations vacant columns of the daily press. She went into the first newsagents she came across once she had left the calm backwater where the professor lived, and, armed with several newspapers, walked on in the direction of Regent Street and in a small side street found a small, rather seedy café. With a cup of coffee before her, she opened the first of the papers and began searching.

Fate had decided to be kind; her eyes lighted upon an urgent demand for a young educated woman to help at a nursery school close to the Tottenham Court Road. The position was vacant due to illness and an address was added.

She left her coffee and crossed to the counter. 'Is Felix Road, just off the Tottenham Court Road, far from here?' she asked the man behind the coffee machine.

He scratched his head. 'Felix Road—that'll be near the 'ospital. Get on the underground to Goodge Street, it'll be close by. Yer can take a bus if yer want.' He thought a minute and told her the number. 'Might be 'andier.'

She thanked him and set off smartly, found a bus stop, caught a bus and presently got off again when the conductor warned her. She found Felix Road without much trouble; a narrow street in the warren of similar streets between the underground station and the hospital. The nursery school was half-way down it, a tall brick house needing a coat of paint, its neighbours on either side, apparently empty, even shabbier. But the windows were clean and curtained, and the neighbourhood was more or less traffic-free. She mounted the steps to the front door and rang the bell.

She could hear children's voices from behind the door, and someone singing nursery rhymes, and when the door opened the woman standing there was reassuringly middle-aged and motherly.

She eyed Suzannah. 'Yes?' she asked.

'There is an advertisement,' began Suzannah, and before she could say more she was invited in.

'Perhaps it is already filled?'

The older woman held out a hand. 'Mrs Willis, I own this place.'

'Suzannah Lightfoot.'

They shook hands and the woman said, 'No, there have been several girls after it, but it's too much like hard work for most, and they don't like the idea of living here.'

She opened a door in the hall. 'Come in and I'll explain.'

They sat facing each other across a small table in the rather bare room. 'I've lost two of my helpers in the last week: one is ill, the other got married. There are thirty children here, toddlers; most of the mothers work at the hospital and the toy museum down the road. They come at eight o'clock in the morning and most of the kids are called for by six o'clock each evening. It's hard work and the pay's not much—it's not state-run—'

She mentioned a sum which Suzannah thought she could manage on if she were careful. 'There's a bedsit in the basement, and you'd have to live in. Sundays off and most Saturday afternoons. It's quiet here, not a bad area, although it's a bit run-down. I live at the top of the house, but I must warn you that once I'm there of an evening, I don't want to be disturbed.' She stared across the table at Suzannah. 'Have you references?'

Suzannah handed them over. A letter from Lady Manbrook, another one from Mijnheer van Dijl and one from the vicar at home. Mrs Willis read them carefully. 'Done any teaching?'

'No. I have four A-levels and have been offered a place at a university. I couldn't take it up because the aunt I lived with became ill.'

'I usually check references, but I'm pretty desperate for help. How do you feel about coming here? A month's trial?'

'I should like to work here. I have a cat; may he live here in the bed-sitting-room?'

'Why not, as long as he's not a nuisance? You'd better come and see the place.'

She led the way out of the front door and down the area steps to another door beneath them, took a key from her pocket and unlocked it. The room was rather dark and cold, but it was clean, with a small gas stove in one corner and a door leading to a toilet and shower-room. The furniture was sparse and cheap, but the curtains were cheerful and there was a small gas fire in front of the old-fashioned grate.

'It's rent-free,' said Mrs Willis. 'Goes with the job. You can bring any bits and pieces of your own.'

'I haven't any. I'd like the job, Mrs Willis, and I could move in today if you would like me to. If I could have an hour or two to settle in and get some milk and bread and food, I could start first thing in the morning.'

'Want the job that bad?'

'Yes, I do. And I'll work hard.'

Mrs Willis smiled. 'Let's hope you can kept it up. We don't have holidays here like the schools. I close on Christmas Day and Boxing Day and at Easter for a couple of days, but the women around here work most of their days and there's nowhere to take the kids. Any plans for Christmas?'

'None, Mrs Willis.'

'Good. I'm going over to my sister's at Northolt as soon as the last child's gone on Christmas Eve, and I'll be back late on Boxing Day. Mind being here alone?'

'No, I don't think so.'

'The houses on either side, they're used as warehouses for small firms, but there are folk living across the street and further down the road.'

She handed Suzannah a key. 'Let yourself out and come back when you're ready. You'd better see round the place then. I can't spare the time now.'

Well, she had a job and somewhere to live, thought Suzannah on her way back to the professor's house. Not ideal, but better than nothing, and since she was to be paid weekly she could afford to lay out some of the money she had on a store of groceries and one or two small comforts.

She had some difficulty in persuading Cobb to allow her to leave in the taxi she had prudently hired. 'I don't know what the professor will say,' he said worriedly. 'I was to see you safe and sound at your friend's house…'

'Well, he didn't know—and nor did I—that my friend would get a taxi to bring me back here to collect Horace and my things. It's outside now, waiting. Could you explain that to the professor? And tell him that I've got a good job with a nice little flatlet.' She shook his hand. 'Thank you and Mrs Cobb, and please thank the professor for me; I'll write to him.'

So Cobb had let her go, looking doubtful still and presently she was back in the basement room, making a list of the things she would need, with Horace, glad to see her but not best pleased with his surroundings, sitting suggestively before the unlit fire.

She put fifty pence in the slot and lit it before she hurried out to the few shops she had seen at the end of the street. At that hour of the afternoon there weren't many shoppers; she bought what she needed, prudently stocking up on tins of soup, then she ordered milk and collected bread and food for Horace and hurried back again. With the curtains drawn and the light on, the room didn't look too bad. She fed Horace and made a cup of tea for herself, filled the hot-water bottle she had bought and put it in the divan bed in one corner and went back up the steps to the front door.

It was open now and there were women coming and going, collecting children after their day's work. Mrs Willis saw the last of them away, said goodnight to a dispirited-looking girl who followed them out and who, it transpired, was another teacher, and led Suzannah round the house. The rooms were given over to the children: four quite large rooms on the ground floor, although with two helpers short she and the girl had been managing between them in two of the rooms. 'We'll split the children up tomorrow, that will mean ten or twelve each. They play and learn a bit until noon, then they have their dinners and you and Melanie take it in turns to keep an eye on them all while they rest for an hour. So every other day you'll get a bit of free time for shopping. We close at five o'clock, though sometimes I'll keep a child until six if the mother can't get here before then.'

All the while she had been talking she had been marching round the house, pointing out where everything was kept. It was all very clean and there were small hand-basins in the cloakroom and a long, low table with small chairs for the children's meals.

'You and Melanie eat with the children, but you get your own tea and take it in turns to have it. We open at eight o'clock, so have your breakfast first.'

They were back at the front door again. 'I said before that it's hard work but I treat you fairly, and if you can't stick it, just say so.'

It was nice to have Horace to talk to; Suzannah aired her plans and doubts to him while she got her supper ready. The contrast between their new home and her comfortable bedroom at the van Dijls' was cruel, but that was something she could remedy, given time and money; in the meantime, she assured him, they would be cosy enough. He was a docile cat and had quickly discovered that, although he might go into the concreted area, that was his limit. She arranged an old woolly scarf before the fire and he curled up without fuss.

At least the water was hot in the shower and the room had warmed up nicely; she ate her supper, made a list of shopping and went to bed. To her surprise her last thoughts were of the professor. Rather sad, although she didn't know why.

He was thinking of her too, but without sadness. Cobb, when questioned, had been unable to give any accurate information as to where Suzannah had gone, and the professor was fair-minded enough not to blame him for letting her leave without giving an address, but he was annoyed that she should go in such a fashion. Almost as though she didn't want him to know just where she had gone; she should have remained at his house until he had made sure that this good job really was good. He frowned; the wretched girl was intruding too deeply into his busy life and it was nonsensical of him to concern himself with her; she had shown clearly enough that she was quite capable of looking after herself. But a nagging doubt remained; he felt compelled to telephone first his aunts and then Mrs Coffin, asking them to let him know if Suzannah should get in touch with them.

Suzannah was up early, breakfasted and tidied her room and had seen to Horace and was ready in the hall when the first of the toddlers arrived. And after that the day became too busy to think. The children for the most part were good, but they needed amusing, and the older ones had to be given simple lessons. Midday dinner was chaotic but thankfully, when it was over, the children were ready to rest for an hour or so. Suzannah had agreed to mind them while Melanie had her free hour, and Melanie, glad to have someone to help her, agreed to Suzannah slipping down to her room to see Horace before she went. She was a melancholy girl but, like Suzannah, needed to earn her own living, and she was good with the children. She lived with a widowed mother at the other end of the street and had a boyfriend who wanted to marry her. 'Only of course there's Mother,' said Melanie. 'She doesn't like him overmuch and won't have him to live at home, so we have to wait until we can find rooms or a small flat.'

Suzannah listened with sympathy, begged her not to hurry back and settled down to watch over the toddlers, arranged in neat rows to sleep. The day seemed endless, but the next day was easier; it was her turn to be free while the children rested and she went shopping with an eye to Christmas, now so close. She found the public library too and chose two books. When she returned she spent a short time with Horace and went back to sing nursery rhymes with the ten children she was looking after.

She saw very little of Mrs Willis, but on the second day, as they passed each other in the hall, she paused long enough to ask if Suzannah was managing and was she warm enough in her room?

Suzannah said cheerfully that she was perfectly happy and everything was fine. All the same, she cried herself to sleep that night. Even with Horace for company, she was lonely.

On Christmas Eve the children had a party so that they were fetched a little later than usual, and when they had all gone the three teachers cleared away the cardboard plates and mugs, tidied the place, wished each other a happy Christmas and went their separate ways. By early evening the house was quiet, for Mrs Willis had gone and so had Melanie, and Suzannah was very conscious of the silence, even with the radio on. She had bought a chicken already cooked, sausage rolls and a few mince pies and a few sprigs of holly. She would go to church in the morning, she decided, and on Boxing Day go for a walk in one of the parks.

She ate a mince pie, gave Horace an extra snack of sardines, drew the rather down-at-heel armchair close to the gas fire and settled down to read.

She wasn't a girl to mope; all the same she was quite glad to think that the place would be open the next morning as she got ready for bed on Boxing Night. She had gone to church on Christmas morning and come back to share the chicken with Horace and listen to the radio, and on Boxing Day she had gone for a really long walk, finding her way to Green Park and then into St James's Park and walking all the way back again. She had had a good think as she walked, and she knew what she was going to do: stay with Mrs Willis for six months and then apply to one of the London hospitals to train as a nurse. She would have liked to have done that sooner, but there was the problem of Horace; she would need to save enough money to rent a room so that she could live out while she trained, and if she was careful and saved every penny she could spare and added it to the money she already had, she would be able to manage on a student nurse's pay. She had walked the long way back, doing mental arithmetic and pondering ways and means; the results weren't always very clear, for the sums kept coming out differently because she found that her thoughts were side-tracked far too often by thoughts of Professor Bowers-Bentinck.

'And I can't think why,' she observed crossly to Horace, 'for he was a ship passing in the night, as they say.'

She was more than busy when the children arrived in the morning; most of them were tired, queasy from too many sweets and pettish and whiney in consequence. She spent a good deal of her day mopping up after puking toddlers, and the rest-hour was a nightmare of grizzling moppets. They were feeling more themselves on the next day, and since it was her turn to have an hour off in the afternoon she was able to go to the shops and stock up once more, and after that everyone fell easily enough into the usual routine. It was broken again at the New Year, but only for a day, and Suzannah, now quite at home in her job, hardly noticed the small upsets caused by upset tummies and a rash of head colds.

She had been there rather more than a month when Mrs Willis decided that the children, well wrapped up against the cold, should be taken for a short walk twice a week. Suzannah and

Melanie welcomed the idea; it would fill in the later part of the morning before dinner, and it would be nice to have a breath of air. A schoolleaver glad of the pocket money agreed to give a hand, and the first expedition went well. The children were, on the whole, good, and the weather, though cold, was bright and it made a nice change for everyone.

The dry, cold weather held and the morning walks became part of the week's regime, down side streets, across the Tottenham Court Road and ten minutes running around in the grassy square on the other side and then back again.

It was when the procession of small children was wending its toddling way back, with Melanie in front, the teenager in the middle and Suzannah bringing up the rear, carrying a reluctant walker, that Professor Bowers-Bentinck, waiting at the traffic lights for the slow-moving procession to trot across the road, saw Suzannah, one toddler clinging round her neck, another held by the hand, making her careful way behind the string of small people.

Shaken from his usual calm, he uttered a startling sound between a groan and a great sigh, and only when the driver behind him hooted urgently did he see that the lights were green again and the wavering crocodile was disappearing down a street on the opposite side. He had perforce to drive on, but presently he found a side turning, reversed the car and drove back the way he had come, to stop by a parking meter, get out and make his way to the row of shops across the pavement.

He tried several shops before he found somebody who could answer his questions. Oh, yes, said the beady-eyed old lady behind the counter in the general stores, there was a nursery school not too far away. 'Want to send the little 'uns there?' she wanted to know. 'Well, you could do worse than Mrs Willis. Takes the kids when the mums go to work, and one or two besides.' She paused infuriatingly to think and scratch her permed head with a pencil. 'Felix Road, that's where she is. Near the hospital.'

The professor thanked her with a suave charm which left her

smiling, and went back to the Bentley. He had no difficulty in finding Felix Road, and he drew up outside the house, spent a few minutes telephoning to his registrar and sat, a prey to a number of thoughts. But when he saw the door open and Suzannah go down the steps to her basement, he got out and followed her without hurry.

It was her turn to have an hour off. She was feeding Horace when the door-knocker was thumped. She opened it and the professor walked in.

CHAPTER SEVEN

THE PROFESSOR WALKED in without hesitation, so that Suzannah retreated before him until she came up against the table and couldn't go back any further. It took her a moment or so to find her voice, surprise and a sensation she had no time to guess at had taken her breath, so that her, 'Hello,' was uttered in a strangled squeak.

Rather disconcertingly, he said nothing, merely stood there, looming over her, his ice-blue eyes cold. Presently he took his gaze from her face and studied his surroundings. When he spoke, his voice was quiet and gentle.

'You were going to write,' he said mildly.

She could see that he was coldly angry, despite his tolerant tones.

'Yes, well, I did mean to, and then I thought it was a bit silly…' He raised his eyebrows and she hurried on, 'I mean, you're busy, going here and there and everywhere, and important too, I dare say, and you must have a great many friends. We weren't likely to see each other again—there seemed no point…' Her voice petered out under his stare.

He said harshly, 'I see. But was it necessary to lie to me, Suzannah?'

She went red. 'I'm sorry about that, but I didn't want to be a nuisance; you have done such a lot for me—I can't think why.'

'Nor can I.' A reply which she found disconcerting.

She said politely, 'Will you sit down. I have to go back to the children in half an hour or so; it's my free hour—we take it in turns.'

He sat down on the wooden chair at the table and it creaked alarmingly. He asked casually, 'You live here? The other teachers too?'

'Mrs Willis, the one who owns the school, lives on the top floor in a proper flat. Melanie, the other helper, lives with her mother at the end of the street.'

'And do you intend to make this your life's work?'

'Oh, no. I thought I'd stay here for six months, then I can train as a nurse.'

'Why not sooner than that?'

'Well, I'll need to have a room and live out because of Horace.'

She was sitting on the edge of the divan, her hands in her lap. 'I've had time to think about it. I don't want to teach; I like children, but I don't think I'd make a good teacher.'

'So you have your future settled.'

'Yes. How did you know I was here?'

'You crossed the road with a string of infants a short while ago; I was waiting at the traffic lights and my curiosity got the better of me.' He gave her a hooded glance. 'Are you lonely, Suzannah? Where did you spend Christmas?'

'No. I'm too busy to be lonely.' She said it too quickly, without looking at him. 'I spent Christmas here.'

'Alone?'

'I had Horace.' She spoke defiantly, uneasy at his questions. 'I really am very happy.'

He got to his feet, dwarfing everything around him. 'I am delighted to hear it.' He smiled thinly. 'Do you want me to go?'

'Yes. I have a great deal to do…'

'You said that once before,' he reminded her. 'And once before I came to see if I could help you, but it seems that I am once more mistaken.'

He went to the door and with his hand on the door knob turned to ask, 'There was no friend, was there, Suzannah?'

'No.'

He nodded his head and opened the door, and went up the steps, got into his car and drove away.

She stood listening to the Bentley's quiet departure and made no move to sit down. 'I don't suppose I shall ever see him again,' she told Horace. 'I said all the wrong things, didn't I? I didn't even thank him for coming to see me, and there was no need for him to have done that. I thought I didn't like him, but I think I do, even when he's angry and goes all icy and quiet!' There seemed no reason why she should burst into tears, but she did, so that when she went back presently and Melanie commented upon her puffy eyes and red nose, she had to pretend that she had a cold.

She found the days passing very slowly. They were not monotonous, for thirty small children each doing his or her own thing hardly made for monotony, but they needed to be played with, taught their letters, how to count, how to feed themselves, and they needed to be cuddled and amused and kept clean. Suzannah was tired by the end of the day, and yet she went to her room reluctantly when the last of the children had been fetched home. She had told the professor stoutly that she wasn't lonely, but that hadn't been true; despite Horace's cosy presence, she longed for someone to talk to. Preferably the professor; she admitted that, to her own astonishment. They might dislike each other, but even while he was poking his nose into her affairs he was reassuringly large and dependable; moreover, when he chose, he was a delightful companion. 'Although I don't like him,' she told Horace, too often and too loudly.

It was a couple of weeks later, well into the middle of a snowy February, that fate took a hand once again. The children hadn't gone out that morning—the weather was too bad. They sat at their little tables, painting and modelling with clay, evenly divided between Suzannah and Melanie while Mrs Willis had gone to supervise their dinners being prepared in the kitchen at the back of the house.

Suzannah, scraping modelling clay off an overenthusiastic moppet, twitched her small nose and then frowned. There was a faint smell of burning and not from the kitchen, for it was acrid, like scorching cloth.

Melanie was in the adjoining room with the door half-open. Suzannah opened it wide and called her, and then, as the smell was suddenly stronger and she could hear a faint crackling, she shouted urgently.

Melanie came across the room, frowning. 'That's no way to talk in front of the kids,' she began. 'Someone's burning the dinner…'

'I'm going to see what it is; look after my lot,' said Suzannah, and didn't wait for an answer. She shut the door after her and went into the hall. The kitchen was beyond the staircase and she could hear voices from it; the crackling was coming from somewhere upstairs, and as she began to run up them a puff of smoke eddied from under a door on the landing.

It was the door leading to Mrs Willis's flat, and it was locked. She tore down the stairs again, breathless with fright, flung open the kitchen door and found the room empty. Mrs Willis and the cook were in the small room beyond where the bowls and the spoons were kept.

'There's a fire in your flat, Mrs Willis,' said Suzannah, and without waiting for an answer she raced back again to where Melanie was rounding up the children for their dinners.

'Don't ask questions—there's a fire upstairs, get the children's coats and get them out—quick!'

Melanie was a nice girl, but not quick on the uptake. 'Fire?' she asked. 'I thought it was the kitchen burning something…'

'Oh, be quick, do!' cried Suzannah, quite out of patience as well as being scared to death. She went to the small cloakroom off the hall and hauled out coats and hats and scarves and began putting them on the children whether they belonged or not. She was aware that Melanie had rushed up to her, clutching her arm, shouting that there was a fire and they must get out of the house, but she shook her off, still bundling the children into coats. 'Of course there's a fire!' she shouted. 'The children will catch their deaths without coats; for heaven's sake wrap them up and get them out.'

Mrs Willis and the cook were there now, marshalling the children into the hall and out through the door and down the steps.

'I've phoned the fire brigade,' shouted Mrs Willis. 'Get the children counted.' A blast of unpleasantly hot air billowed down the stairs and she coughed. The last of the children were being hustled out when one small boy turned and ran back into the second of the playrooms. The smoke was thick now and a small tongue of flame whipped round the top of the stairs. Suzannah snatched up a woolly scarf, wound it round her face and plunged into the smoke. The child was at the back of the room, still comparatively free from smoke, searching frantically through the box of toys in one corner. Suzannah saw who it was then: Billy Reeves, small and undernourished and inseparable from the grubby teddy bear he dragged with him each day. Common sense told her that it was madness to delay there, but it might be quicker to find the bear and hurry Billy away from danger than try and prise him loose from something he was determined to do. She had learned a lot since she had joined the staff at the nursery school.

Spurred on by the child's frustrated screams and sheer terror lest they wouldn't be able to get out of the house, she hurled toys in all directions, found the bear, snatched up a suddenly happy Billy and rushed out into the hall. The stairs were well alight now, although the flames were not yet half-way down, but the smoke was worse. She clapped a hand over Billy's mouth and nose and ran to the door just as the wooden ceiling above their heads began to fall in. A smouldering plank fell across them, and she pushed it away with a free hand, not noticing the pain as it scorched her. She almost fell through the open door and pushed Billy into Mrs Willis's waiting arms.

'Horace,' she shouted to no one in particular, and galloped down the area steps to scoop him into his basket and rush back again. There was quite a crowd by now, and the fire engine's reassuring siren very close, and hard on its heels a police car and an ambulance.

None of the children was hurt, but they were terrified and cold; they were stowed into the ambulance and taken the short distance to the hospital and a second ambulance took the rest and Melanie. Mrs Willis refused to go, and Suzannah, shivering with cold and well aware of her throbbing hand, stayed with her. Mrs Willis, usually so efficient, looked as though she would faint at any moment. She clutched Suzannah as the fire took hold. 'My flat,' she muttered, 'and all the work I've put into the place...'

Suzannah put an arm round her. 'The children are safe; you'll get insurance and be able to buy another house. And there must be an empty hall or rooms where you can carry on—the children will need you.'

Mrs Willis blew her nose and wiped her eyes. 'You're right, it isn't the end of the world. I've plenty of friends, too.'

She saw that Suzannah was shivering and noticed her hand. 'You're hurt, you must go to hospital and have that burn dressed. You were very brave to go after Billy I should have gone...'

'I was the nearest,' said Suzannah, and broke off as a police officer tapped her on the shoulder. 'We'll run you to the hospital, miss. That hand needs seeing to. There's nothing more to do here. And you too, ma'am. You're the owner? No need for you to catch your death of cold; we'll drop you off if you've friends who'll put you up until things are sorted out.'

'At the end of this street.' Mrs Willis got into the car beside Suzannah. 'And what about you, Suzannah? Have you somewhere to go when you've had your hand seen to?'

Suzannah had Horace's basket on her lap; his head was pressed up to the wires at its end and she was stroking him with a finger. She said cheerfully, 'Oh, yes, I'll be all right, Mrs Willis.' The poor woman had enough to worry her.

The accident room was busy. Suzannah was sat down in a chair and told that someone would see her in a few minutes. The minutes ticked away while two road accidents were dealt with one after the other, which gave her more than enough time to wonder what she would do. She had no money and no clothes, only Horace, quiet in his basket beside her. She supposed that someone would tell her where she could get a bed for the night; the Salvation Army or perhaps the police would help. A cell, perhaps… She giggled tiredly and closed her eyes.

And that was how the professor found her; he had been called down to give his opinion of a severe head injury, and on his way back to the consultant's room he saw her. She was a deplorable sight and smelled horribly of smoke. Her hair was full of bits and pieces and specks of soot, and there was a smear down the front of her skirt and the sleeve of her sweater was badly scorched. She had laid her burned hand across her chest to ease the pain, while the other hand clutched Horace's basket.

The professor said something forcibly under his breath, and the house doctor with him said quickly, 'I expect she's from the nursery school. There's been a fire there—the children came here to be checked, none of them hurt, luckily.'

'When was this?'

'Oh, an hour or so ago, sir.'

The professor swore quietly and the young surgeon looked at him in surprise. Professor Bowers-Bentinck never swore and seldom raised his voice, certainly never before a patient; he had the reputation of being a rather cold man, brilliant at his work and certainly very sure of himself.

'I know this young lady,' said the professor. 'I want her taken up to theatre—they'll be busy in the two main theatres, so put her in the surgery at the end, will you? Get a porter and do it now, if you please.'

She woke up when the porter brought a chair and still clutching Horace's basket, only half awake, she was transported to the fourth floor where the theatre block was.

The surgery was a small room used for taking out stitches and minor cuts and dressings, and the young surgeon hovered round her, not quite sure what to do. He had suggested leaving the cat basket outside, but Suzannah had clung to it and even tried to get up and go. And, since the professor had left her in his care, the young man was in two minds as to what to do.

Suzannah sat watching him; any minute now he might snatch Horace from her and he was all she had left in the world. Two large tears trickled down her dirty cheeks.

The professor, coming quietly into the room with everything needed to deal with her hand, dumped the lot on his houseman, whipped out a very white handkerchief and wiped her face.

'Oh, it's you,' wailed Suzannah, and gave a really tremendous sniff.

He took Horace's basket from her and put it on the floor.

'Indeed it is I. No, don't worry about Horace, he'll not be taken away. I will see to that hand before I take you to Mrs Cobb for the night.'

Suzannah sniffed, blew her nose, wiped her eyes once more and said, 'No,' and because that sounded rather rude, 'Thank you very much, but I'll be all right.'

The professor didn't bother to answer. He beckoned his houseman nearer and began to clean her hand and dress it. He was gentle, but it hurt all the same. When she spoke it was because she felt that someone should say something. 'I thought you were a brain surgeon.'

'Oh, I am, but one does acquire the rudiments of first aid as well.'

A remark which drew forth an outraged snort from the house doctor.

The professor finished the job to his satisfaction and said, in the kind of voice which brooked no arguing, 'You will wait here, Suzannah, with Horace. I shall return in about ten minutes.'

Whatever he had done to her hand had soothed it; the throbbing pain had eased and her one wish was to be allowed to sleep. She was scarcely aware of his going, and dozed off while the house doctor, left to mount guard, tidied away the considerable mess the professor had made.

She awoke when the professor came back, this time with a porter and a chair, and although she attempted to remonstrate with him he took no notice, but disappeared again. She was wheeled through endless corridors and into lifts and at last was trundled through a side door of the hospital.

The Bentley was there; the professor shovelled her carefully into the seat beside his, put Horace in the back of the car, thanked his assistants gravely and drove away.

Suzannah, more or less free from pain and her lungs clear of smoke, had revived. She said worriedly, 'I smell awful,' and then, 'Where are you taking me?'

'Back to my house. Mrs Cobb will take care of you. Tomorrow you can decide what you want to do. A little while ago you told me that you would be quite all right, but at the moment you are in no fit state to go anywhere but to bed.'

The word bed conjured up the blissful thought of sleep. 'And you don't mind having Horace, too?'

'I have no doubt that Mrs Cobb will be delighted.'

He sounded impatient and she said nothing more; once she had had a good sleep, she told herself, she would think of what to do.

At his house he handed her over to Mrs Cobb, who tutted softly, gave Horace into Cobb's care and led Suzannah upstairs. 'A nice warm bath,' she said comfortably, 'and something tasty for your tea and then bed.'

'Tea?' asked Suzannah, 'I don't know what the time is…'

'You poor child, you're worn to a thread. The professor said you had been in a fire and got burnt, and very nasty that must have been.'

She began to remove Suzannah's clothes. 'And I'll do what I can with this skirt and jumper of yours, but they are really beyond my skill. Of course, you've no clothes… Did they save anything from the fire?'

Suzannah was in the bath, her injured hand resting on its side. 'I don't know.'

She sounded near to tears, and Mrs Cobb said quickly, 'Well, no matter, but I'll wash that hair of yours.'

And presently, tucked up in bed, a light meal and a pot of tea disposed of under Mrs Cobb's motherly eye, she curled up and slept. The bed was soft and warm, and she had no doubt that the room she was in was delightful, only she was too tired to bother to look.

The professor, coming home an hour or so later, was led upstairs by his housekeeper. 'Just so's you can see the young lady's all right,' said Mrs Cobb. 'Very tired, she was and, begging your pardon, sir, filthy dirty.'

They stood together looking at Suzannah, deeply asleep—indeed, snoring very delicately.

'I hear at the hospital that she went back into the fire to fetch a small boy who had escaped to find his teddy bear.'

'Well, fancy that!' declared Mrs Cobb. 'Poor lamb, it's a wonder that her wits aren't turned.'

The professor said gravely, 'Fortunately I believe Miss Lightfoot to be a young lady who will always keep her wits about her.'

They went back downstairs and he passed her and paused

on his way to the study. 'I'm dining out, Mrs Cobb. Don't wait up—tell Cobb to lock up if I'm not back by eleven o'clock.'

It was a long-standing engagement he couldn't put off, but he excused himself as soon as he reasonably could, getting home just before Cobb began his evening round.

'I'll be in the study, Cobb. Ask Mrs Cobb to look in on Miss Lightfoot before she goes to bed, will you?' He opened his study door. 'I'll take a look as I go to bed.'

He said goodnight and sat down behind his desk. There were letters to answer and reading to be done. It was almost one o'clock when he got to his feet at last and went upstairs.

Suzannah, refreshed by her sleep, sat up in bed and looked around her. There was a rose-shaded lamp by the bed and the room looked charming in its soft glow. The furniture was maple, and the curtains and bedspread were rose-patterned in some heavy silk fabric. She examined it all slowly, aware at the same time that her hand was increasingly painful, and not only that, she was hungry. The dainty little carriage clock on the tallboy said half-past twelve. Everyone would be in bed by now. She lay back again and closed her eyes, but now sleep eluded her, and if she shut her eyes she could see the flames creeping further down the stairs and remember how terrified she had been while she and Billy searched for his teddy bear; the picture was so clear that she could smell the smoke…

The hands of the clock crawled round to one o'clock, which meant that there would be no one about for six hours. Looked at from one o'clock in the morning, the night stretched endlessly ahead.

She shut her eyes again and tried not to think about buttered toast and mugs of milky cocoa. She opened them quickly when the door opened and the professor walked in.

Anyone else would have said unnecessarily, 'Awake?' She was immensely cheered when he asked, 'Hungry?' and came to stand by the bed, looking down at her.

She nodded. 'Oughtn't you to be in bed?' she asked.

He sat down on the bed. 'I had to go to a very dull dinner party, and then I had some letters to write. I'm hungry, too. How about some sandwiches and a drink? Cocoa, tea, milk?'

'Cocoa, please.'

He said, to her surprise, 'I'm a dab hand at sandwiches. Give me ten minutes.'

He was very soon back, carrying a tray with mugs of cocoa and a plate piled high with sandwiches. He put it down on the bedside table and handed her a mug, and when she had drunk some of it he took it from her and put a sandwich into her hand. 'Chicken,' he told her, and took one himself, pulled up a chair and sat down. 'Are you very wide awake?'

'Yes.' She spoke thickly through the sandwich.

'Good. Listen to me. You will stay here tomorrow; you can't get a job until your hand is better, and it will give you time to decide what you want to do. If you're dead set on training as a nurse, I'll see what I can do, though I don't think it's the life for you.'

'Would I be a better teacher? Some small school…'

'It needs careful thought,' he said smoothly. 'I think the best plan is for you to go and stay with my aunts and think about it—after all, it is your whole future—you don't want a dead-end job.'

'But I can't go there.' She accepted another sandwich and took a bite.

'They will be glad to have you, and you can make yourself useful, picking up balls of wool, and finding their spectacles. They liked you.'

'You are very kind, but I can't impose on them, or you. I'm so sorry it's always you who finds me.' She finished the sandwich and he offered her the mug again, and she finished its contents down to the last drop.

'Your hand is hurting?'

'Well, yes, but it's better now that I'm not hungry.' She had a third sandwich in her hand, but with it halfway to her mouth put it down again. 'I feel sleepy…'

The professor put down the plate and picked up the mug and studied its emptiness with satisfaction, and she muttered, 'You put something in my cocoa.'

'Naturally I did. You need a night's dreamless sleep. Goodnight, Suzannah.'

She closed her eyes, mumbled something and fell deeply asleep.

He picked up the tray and stood looking at her. Her face was still pale, but her newly washed hair gave it a glow. She looked a great deal better than she had when he had found her at the hospital; all the same, there was nothing about her ordinary face to attract a man's attention. He shrugged his massive shoulders and took the tray downstairs and went to his bed.

He was up early, for he was operating that morning, and he and his senior registrar would hold outpatients in the late afternoon, but before he left the house he went to the kitchen where he spent ten minutes talking to Mrs Cobb.

'You just leave it to me, sir,' she told him. 'I'll pop along to Harrods and get all the young lady needs. A size ten, I should think; just a slip of a thing, she is.'

'I'll leave the matter in your capable hands, Mrs Cobb, but I beg of you, choose nothing brown or grey…'

'A pretty blue or green, sir.'

When he had left the house and Cobb had come back into the kitchen, she was at the table making a list. 'Mark my words,' she observed to her husband, 'he doesn't know it yet, but he's sweet on her. She's just right for him, too—she'll make him a good wife. It'll be nice to have children in the house.'

Cobb sat down at the table. 'Running ahead a bit, aren't you, my dear?'

'Maybe I am, but you mark my words…'

Presently she took up a splendid breakfast to Suzannah, sat her up against her pillows, and advised her to stay in bed for a while. 'I'll be back presently with some clothes for you, Miss Lightfoot, and give you a hand with a bath. You mustn't get that hand wet. The professor left some tablets for you; you're to take them if you have any pain.' She beamed at Suzannah. 'Now I'll be off and see what I can find for you to wear.'

'I haven't any money,' said Suzannah.

'Don't worry about that. You'll get compensation.'

Mrs Cobb had gone before Suzannah could ask any more questions, so she went to sleep again.

She woke up to see Mrs Cobb standing by her bed, bearing a small tray daintily laid with cup and saucer, small coffee-pot, cream and sugar.

'There, you've had a nice sleep. Just you drink your coffee while I show you the things I've bought.' She beamed with pleasure as she laid her shopping on the bed. 'Size ten—I checked; I told the professor that's what you'd be, so small you are.' She gave a glance of good-humoured envy at Suzannah's person, enveloped in one of Mrs Cobb's voluminous nighties.

There were undies: scraps of silk and lace in pale colours, the sort of garments Suzannah had drooled over when she had had occasion to go to the shops. There was a skirt, tweed, in a glowing blue-green, and a matching sweater, a couple of ivory silk shirts and a thick tweed top coat in a shade just a little darker than the skirt. There were shoes too, and a pair of slippers as well as a quilted dressing-gown.

Suzannah looked at them all in amazement, and then with regret. 'But I can't wear these,' she pointed out. 'I haven't a penny to my name; besides, I've never had anything like them. Even if I had some money, I doubt if it would be enough…'

'Now you're not to worry your head, Miss Lightfoot. The professor said you were to be fitted out so's you can go to his aunts for a few days, just while you get over that nasty fire. He said Harrods, and it's more than my job's worth not to do as he says.'

She saw Suzannah's questioning look. 'Not but he isn't the

kindest man on this earth, but when he wants something done, then it's done, if you see what I mean.'

'Yes,' Suzannah almost wailed, 'but I can't take clothes from someone I hardly know.'

'Well, you can't stay in bed for ever, love, can you? Nor can you leave this place mother-naked. Your own clothes were in a fine state, past cleaning and mending, and I don't suppose that you noticed that you'd lost a shoe.'

'Did I? To whom do I go, I wonder, to find out about my clothes and things?'

'I'd leave that for the professor,' advised Mrs Cobb comfortably.

So presently Suzannah got up, had a bath and with Mrs Cobb's help got into her new clothes. Everything fitted, even the shoes, and when Mrs Cobb sat her down in front of the triple mirror on the dressing-table and brushed her hair smooth and tied it back with a blue ribbon Suzannah heaved a great sigh. 'Clothes make a difference, don't they?'

'Indeed they do, miss, and the colour's just right for you, with that hair. Cobb will have lunch ready for you downstairs if you would like to come down.'

So Suzannah went downstairs to eat her lunch under Cobb's fatherly eye, and then sit in the drawing-room with Henry and Horace for company. They shared her tea too, and presently Cobb came in to collect the tea-tray and turn on the six o'clock news.

The professor came in half an hour later, so quietly that at first she wasn't aware that he was there, standing just inside the room. It was Henry trotting over to greet him that caused her to turn round and see him there.

He wished her good evening in a cool voice that instantly deflated her, so that she responded shyly and then rushed in with her thanks, getting more and more muddled until he stopped her with a curt, 'Never mind that, Suzannah. I'm glad to see that you are feeling more yourself. My aunts will be delighted to have you to stay for a few days. Cobb shall drive you down tomorrow.'

Which chilling speech, coupled with the fact that he hadn't appeared to notice her new outfit, caused her to retire behind a polite manner which even to her own ears sounded wooden. She sat there, trying to think of some well-turned phrase which would get her out of the room; it seemed obvious to her that, although he had given her shelter and clothes most generously, he had no wish for her company. But when she suggested that she was tired and would go to bed, he sat down opposite her with the quelling observation that it should be possible for them to dine together without the danger of them falling out, at least for an hour or so.

This annoyed her. 'I have no intention of falling out with you, Professor, you have been very kind to me and I'm grateful, although I must say you have made it very difficult for me to thank you.'

'Have I?' he smiled a little. 'Do the clothes fit?'

She refrained from breaking into a paean of delight about them. 'Perfectly, thank you. If you will let me have the bill, I will pay you back when I get a job.'

He agreed carelessly and got up to get her a drink, but he had barely sat down again when Cobb came in to say that he was wanted on the phone. And when he came back after a few minutes it was to say that he would have to go out again and would probably not be back for dinner. 'So I'll say goodbye, Suzannah. I have asked my aunts' doctor to take a look at that hand, and in the meantime you can decide what you want to do.'

She stared at him. How on earth was she to get a job, or even start looking for one, without a penny in the world? She hadn't the price of a stamp, let alone the money to take her to any interview she might be lucky enough to get. She had an urge to fling herself on to his great chest and tell him that, but all she did was sit very upright in her chair and wish him goodbye in a quiet voice.

It took her completely by surprise when he came over to her chair and bent and kissed her quite savagely before he went.

'Well,' said Suzannah, and, since she was bereft of words, 'Well, whatever next?' The answer to the question came out of the blue to shock her. There would be nothing next; he didn't like her, he found her a nuisance, and it was his misfortune that she invariably ended up on his doorstep. And, far worse, she had fallen in love with him. 'And I can't think why,' she told Horace and Henry, for she had to tell someone and there was no one else there. 'He's tiresome and ill-tempered and impatient, and he must hate the sight of me.'

A good cry would have been a comfort, but Cobb came in then to tell her that dinner was waiting, so she went to the dining-room and ate her lonely meal, choking down tears with the delicious food, and presently, with the plea that she was tired, she went to bed.

'What time do we go in the morning?' she asked Cobb as she wished him goodnight.

'We're to be there for lunch, miss. If we leave around ten o'clock, that should give us plenty of time. Mrs Cobb's found a case for the rest of your things, and we wondered about Horace…?'

'Oh, do you suppose that Lady Manbrook would mind if I took him with me? I expect I'll have that little flat again…'

'I couldn't say, miss, but I'm sure no one would object to Horace—a well-behaved cat.'

'Yes, he's a great comfort to me. Thank you and Mrs Cobb for looking after him so very well.'

'A pleasure, miss. Henry will miss him.'

She went upstairs to bed and lay thinking about the future. Something domestic, she decided, for there was always work for such; for the moment she would have to give up her idea about training as a nurse. First she must save some money and find herself and Horace somewhere to live as quickly as possible. It was kind of Lady Manbrook to have her, but she had no intention of staying a day longer than she had to. She was already beholden to the professor, and she wanted to get away from him as soon as possible. Out of sight, out of mind, she told herself, and burst into tears at the thought of never seeing him again. Somehow that mattered far more than her precarious future.

CHAPTER EIGHT

LONG BEFORE SUZANNAH went downstairs the next morning, the professor had left his house. She ate the breakfast set before her, gathered Horace into his basket, and, when Cobb had put her few possessions into the boot, got into the car beside him.

The journey was uneventful and rather silent. Suzannah discussed the weather at length, the state of the road and the perfection of Mrs Cobb's cooking, but presently she fell silent and Cobb, beyond the odd word now and then, didn't disturb her.

She thought it unlikely that she would see the professor again; he had wished her goodbye without expressing any hope that he might meet her in the future, and although the thought of never seeing him again was almost too much to bear, she intended to do her utmost to avoid that happening. Unkind fate had thrown her into his path and he had been too kind to ignore her; all the same, she guessed that he must be heartily sick of seeing her. Once she was at Lady Manbrook's house she would contrive to phone Mrs Coffin and persuade her to write and beg her to go to her—a broken arm, flu, varicose veins? thought Suzannah wildly; anything which would make it necessary for Mrs Coffin to call upon her for help. Once there, she could set about finding a job, preferably miles away where she was unlikely to encounter the professor ever again. She had it all most nicely sorted out in her head by the time they reached Ramsbourne House, so that she was able to wish Cobb a cheerful goodbye and greet her hostess with calm.

Lady Manbrook and Mrs van Beuck welcomed her warmly, expressed their admiration of her conduct at the fire, commiserated with her over her burnt hand and hoped that she would stay for as long as she wished.

'And you have brought your cat with you? He won't mind being in the house? We have given you a room with a balcony, so that he may feel free to take the air.'

Parsons took her upstairs presently, to a charming room overlooking the grounds at the back of the house. 'It's nice to see you again, miss,' said Parsons. 'We're all so sorry that you burnt your hand. The ladies were ever so upset.'

She tweaked the bedspread into exactitude, put Suzannah's small bag on the low chest by the closet and went away.

Suzannah took off her coat, tidied her hair and examined her room, while Horace explored his territory, decided on the most comfortable chair, and curled up and went to sleep, leaving her to go downstairs to the drawing-room to drink a glass of sherry with the old ladies before lunch.

She had no opportunity to telephone Mrs Coffin that day, nor the following day either; it would have been simple enough to walk to the village, she supposed, and phone from there, but she had no money and for the moment she had no idea how to get any. She spent the next day or two devising ways and means of getting hold of even a few coins, enough even for a stamp, but none of them were sensible enough to carry out. And she had nothing to sell…

Life was pleasant at Ramsbourne House, slow-moving, gracious living which was very soothing. Suzannah's pale cheeks were pale no longer, her hand healed, even her hair seemed to glow more brightly, but it couldn't last, she told herself. In two days' time, she, promised herself, she would talk to Lady Manbrook and explain, and ask her if she could borrow some money from her. But first she would try and telephone; she was sure that Mrs Coffin, once she had understood how Suzannah was placed, would help.

The professor had had a busy week which perhaps accounted for his slightly testy manner and his thoughtful silences. Mrs Cobb, noticing this, nodded her head in satisfaction, pointing out to Cobb that she had told him so, hadn't she?

To which he replied that she was fancying things, for the professor had given no hint that he intended seeing Miss Lightfoot again. Which was true, although he had thought about her a great deal; not very willingly, it had to be said, but her small image frequently danced before his eyes, reminding him that even though she wasn't in his house, she had left something of herself behind. It had been with difficulty that he had refrained from telephoning his aunts to find out how she was, but he had eventually decided to wait for at least two weeks, and in the meantime he would see about finding her a job. There was no reason why he should do that, but the thought of her struggling to start all over again was a continuous nagging worry to him. He sat at his desk, considering what he should do; probably, he told himself with a shrug, he would end up with Horace back with Mrs Cobb and Suzannah at the other end of the country. He frowned, for the idea didn't appeal to him.

He looked at the papers on his desk waiting for his attention and then ignored them, deep in thought and only disturbed when Cobb tapped on the door, but before he could speak he was pushed aside and Phoebe went past him to fling herself at the professor.

'Guy—darling—it's ages since I saw you last. I'm in town to do some shopping and I thought we might go out—take me out to dinner, will you?' She jerked her head at a disapproving

Cobb, still standing in the doorway. 'He said you were busy, but you're never too busy to see little me, are you?'

The professor had got to his feet. 'It's all right, Cobb,' he said, and pulled up a chair for his visitor. 'This is a surprise, Phoebe. I'm afraid it's out of the question to take you out, though. I've a backlog of work which simply has to be done.'

She pouted prettily. 'Oh, Guy—and I was certain you'd give me dinner.' She saw his bland face and changed her tactics. 'Well, anyway, I'll give you all the news. Uncle keeps fit enough, I suppose, though I'm sure he'd be glad to see you—you must come down for a weekend soon. I've made quite a few changes, too. Old Toms doesn't approve, but who cares what he thinks? We need someone younger in his place; I'll be glad when I can find an excuse to get rid of him. Which reminds me—I saw something on the television about a fire in a kids' nursery school and that red-haired girl I sacked was on the screen with some woman or other. So she fell on her feet, didn't she? Her sort always do.'

The professor had no comment to make upon this, and Phoebe rattled on, 'I must say she looked positively dowdy.'

The professor leaned back in his chair and put his hands in his pockets. 'I dare say she did. She had just been back into the fire to rescue a small boy. Her hand was burned and I found her at the hospital waiting to have it dressed.'

'You saw her?' Phoebe said quickly. 'How interesting.'

'Not interesting; pathetic if you like, and extraordinary.' He ignored her sharp look. 'She is at present staying with Lady Manbrook until she is quite well again.'

He had spoken very quietly, but something in his voice made her frown. She said lightly, 'You sound quite concerned about her; after all, she's only a girl from the village.'

He said evenly, 'A rather special girl, Phoebe. And now, if you will excuse me, I really have to work.'

She flounced off her chair, stood up, opened the door and saw him rise to see her to his front door. She stood a minute, looking at him, conjuring up a smile. 'Well, I hope she gets well soon and finds a decent job. I expect meeting her unexpectedly like that was a bit of a surprise. It sounds very romantic, plunging back into the fire, and actually saving the child; no wonder you think she's a bit special...'

But, although she smiled, her eyes were cold. She didn't make the mistake of kissing him, but offered a hand and said cheerfully, 'Don't forget to visit Uncle William some time—bye for now.'

There was a cruising taxi passing; the professor lifted an arm, crossed the pavement with her and saw her into it, and then went back to his desk. He sat there—making no attempt to work—and presently, when Cobb came to tell him that dinner was served, he wandered into the dining-room and sat down while Cobb handed him his soup.

'I'll be away this weekend, Cobb,' he said presently. 'I'm spending it with Lady Manbrook.'

A titbit of news Cobb lost no time in conveying to his wife.

The professor drove himself down on Saturday morning under a lowering February sky and in the teeth of a howling wind. He had decided to break his journey and lunch on the way, for he remembered that his aunts were in the habit of taking a nap after that meal, which meant that Suzannah would probably be alone. He wasn't at all sure why he was so anxious to see her; she was, he supposed, on his conscience, and for some reason he felt bound to do something about her future.

Snow opened the door to him, took his coat, mentioned that his aunts were resting and in their rooms, but that Miss Lightfoot was in the drawing-room and ushered him across the hall.

'I'll see myself in,' said the professor, and opened the door and walked without haste into the room.

Suzannah was sitting by the fire with Horace on her lap, her head full of ideas and plans, none of which were of any use unless she had some money. She turned round as the door opened to see who it was, and when she saw the professor said what was uppermost in her mind.

'Would you lend me a pound?'

If he was surprised, he didn't show it; his lip twitched briefly but his voice was quite steady. 'Of course.' He fished around among his loose change and offered two coins. 'Though I think two pounds would be more sensible, you might lose one.'

'I'll pay you back as soon as I've found a job.' She saw his faint smile and blushed. 'I'm sorry, you must think I'm mad, but I was thinking that if I had some money I could telephone, or take a bus or something; you have no idea how awkward it is when one hasn't a penny piece in the world.'

'My fault—I overlooked that fact when you came here. I do apologise.'

'Oh, I'm not blaming you, indeed I'm not, you've done so much for me and really it must be so vexing for you, my always turning up to annoy you.'

He came and sat down opposite her. 'But you don't annoy me, Suzannah; indeed I find that I miss you…'

A great surge of love threatened to explode in her chest, but she kept a calm face. 'Well, perhaps you do, like missing an aching tooth!'

He laughed. 'You're happy here? I see that your hand is better. If you will be patient for a little longer, I will see what I can do about getting you into a teaching hospital where you can live out.'

As he spoke, he was aware that he had no intention of doing any such thing; he badly wanted to have a finger in the pie when it came to her future.

He hadn't expected her refusal. 'That's awfully kind of you, but I thought I'd get some kind of domestic work in the country; I'd quite like to go to Scotland, or if there's nothing for me there, Yorkshire. Somewhere miles away.'

He was astonished at the wave of dismay that swept through him at the news. 'A long way for Horace,' was all he said.

'Yes, but once we're there we'd stay.'

He said evenly, 'So you want to start again, Suzannah? A new life with new surroundings and new friends?'

She nodded. 'Yes, oh, yes, you have no idea how much I want to do that.'

The professor looked at her, sitting neatly opposite him, hands folded over Horace's furry body; certainly no beauty, but possessed of something most of the women of his acquaintance didn't have—charm and a certain kind of gentleness which masked a sturdy independence. And the most beautiful eyes he had ever seen. He had been tolerably satisfied with his life until now, but he knew that that wasn't true any longer. Life wouldn't be the same if Suzannah were to go away; what he had supposed had been concern for a girl who had been left to fend for herself had evidently developed into something else, something he wasn't going to put a name to until he was sure, and it looked as though he would have no need to do that, for she had spoken with a quiet conviction; she wanted to go away, a long way away, too, and seeing him again hadn't entered into her head.

He was a patient man and he had made up his mind; moreover, he liked to get his own way. He said smoothly, 'Now, let me see, I should think somewhere like York would suit you admirably—do you know the city?'

He began to talk effortlessly about that part of England, never mentioning her future; he was still chatting idly when the old ladies joined them and they had tea, talking of other things.

Suzannah, in her room, doing her face and hair before dinner, told herself that he really had no interest in her, only a polite concern, and as for his coming for the weekend, probably he did that regularly. It was heavenly to see him again, but she must get away before he came again or offered to find her work. If she were several hundred miles away, life would be so much easier. She didn't believe that, but it sounded sensible.

The evening passed pleasantly enough. The old ladies discussed art, the repairs to the church and if it would be possible to have the tapestry curtains in the small sitting-room repaired by an expert. The professor took a polite interest, while sitting watching Suzannah, his mind on other things, and presently, while they were having their coffee, he invited her with just the right amount of casualness to accompany him the next morning to his house. 'I need to check on the barn roof,' he explained, 'and it will be a pleasant drive even in February.'

It would have seemed strange for her to refuse. She agreed calmly and asked where he lived. 'I thought your home was in London?'

'Well, it is, but my home—where I was born, is at Great Chisbourne, on the edge of the Savernake Forest. I think you may like it.'

She would have liked a two-up and two-down with no mod cons if he had lived in it; but she said politely, 'I'm sure I shall.'

They left after breakfast, a meal at which the professor had chatted about this and that without saying anything to the point, while eating with a splendid appetite. Suzannah, a prey to a fine muddle of thoughts, did her best with her scrambled eggs, crumbled toast and drank several cups of coffee while making polite replies when necessary. She was in a state of euphoria at the very idea of spending several hours with the professor, so that she was a trifle absent-minded.

The weather had shown little improvement since the previous day and there was little traffic; the professor drove fast, slowing down to go through Marlborough and then turning on to a side road which led them through the centre of the forest, until the trees thinned and they reached Great Chisbourne, a small village with the forest at its back and rolling country beyond. The main street was wide and lined with nice old houses, and at its end the professor turned the car through an open gateway and stopped before the house at the end of the short drive.

It was of a comfortable size, of mellow red brick, and with an ancient slate roof which rose in a series of irregular gables, interspersed with tall, elaborate chimneys. It stood in large grounds with trees grouped behind it and a grass lawn before it, ringed around with flower-beds; even on such a dull day, it looked charming.

Suzannah went with the professor to his front door, which was opened as they reached it by a small dumpling of a woman with white hair and black beady eyes. He greeted her with a hug and a kiss and turned to Suzannah.

'This is Trudy, my old nanny; she lives here and looks after me when I come here.'

Suzannah shook hands, conscious that she was being studied closely, but not, she thought, unkindly.

'There's coffee waiting,' said Trudy. 'I'll show you where you can put your coat, Miss Lightfoot, and you, Mr Guy, be sure and hang yours up in the closet.'

Suzannah was borne away and shown a well-appointed cloakroom at the back of the hall, and presently returned to find the professor lounging on the gilt and marble table standing against one wall of the hall, his hands in his pockets, whistling. The hall was warm and welcoming and had wood-panelled walls and a polished floor with thick Turkish carpet down its centre. There were high-backed, rush-seated chairs on either side of the table, which held a great bowl of hyacinths, and wall-sconces with mulberry silk shades. A pleasing sight, although it was the sight of the professor which pleased her most.

The room which they went into was long, reaching from the front of the house to the back, with a low-beamed ceiling, a huge fireplace and bay windows at each end. The floor was as highly polished as the hall and strewn with silky rugs in faded jewel colours, which were reflected in the swathed curtains at the windows. The furniture was a pleasing blend of comfortable armchairs and sofas and much polished dark oak. There were wall sconces here too, capped in ivory silk, and some splendid paintings in elaborate gilt frames, mostly portraits Suzannah hoped that she might have the chance later of inspecting them.

They sat by the log fire and drank their coffee, the dog between them, and once again the professor didn't allow the conversation to stray from general topics. Perhaps that was just as well, reflected Suzannah, for otherwise she might find herself saying more than she meant. But even so she was enjoying herself; she was discovering that when the professor was there nothing else seemed to matter; the fact that she had no money, no clothes and a hazardous future seemed unimportant. She decided, as she sat there, that she would enjoy every minute of the day and never mind anything else.

Presently he fetched their drinks from the Jacobean oak court cupboard before, at Trudy's invitation they crossed the hall to have their lunch. The dining-room was furnished in the Stuart style, with a long side-table, its burr-walnut inlaid with floral marquetry, the chairs around the table elegant William and Mary. There were long crimson curtains at the windows and above the fireplace was a wooden carving of fruit and flowers. Suzannah paused to look at it. 'That looks like Grinling Gibbons,' she ventured.

'Well, I hope so, since he carved it.' He smiled at her. 'Come and sit down and let us see what Trudy has got for us.'

Trudy, besides being a nanny, was an exceptional cook; no frills, no *nouvelle cuisine*, but little cheese soufflés for starters, followed by steak and kidney pudding, properly made with oysters and mushrooms and accompanied by boiled potatoes and sprouts, and for a pudding a bread and butter pudding which qualified as ambrosia.

'I dare say you come here as often as you can,' observed Suzannah, as she poured their coffee.

The professor had watched her tucking in to the good food with hidden delight. 'Indeed, yes. When I marry I shall make a point of coming here each weekend; this is, after all, my home, and I should like my children to grow up here.'

She was just a little bit muzzy from the sherry and the wine. 'You are going to marry, Professor?'

'Certainly. Would you like to see the gardens before it becomes too dark?'

And if that wasn't a snub, she reflected, what was?

She got her coat and they went through a door at the back of the hall, into a glassed-in patio which in turn led to the gardens beyond. Even in mid-winter they were a delight: narrow paths bordered by shrubs and trees, a gazebo at the end of a long walk edged with flower-beds which in the summer would be a blaze of colour.

'You like it?' asked the professor.

'It's heaven,' declared Suzannah. 'I don't know how you can bear to be away from it.'

'I am able to come for most weekends,' he pointed out. 'We aren't far from the motorway, you know, it's a quick run up to town.'

She was dying to ask him if he would drive up to town each day—surely not?—or live in London during the week and rejoin his family at weekends. He must have read her mind, for he said idly, 'Of course, my wife and children would have to divide their time between London and here...'

'Yes, but when they start going to school,' she pointed out seriously.

'Ah, then I should have to commute.' He smiled at her. 'There's a charming little pond at the end of the garden; shall we have a look at it?'

He wasn't going to allow her to see into his private life. She went rather red at the idea of prying into it. She said briefly, 'I'd like to see it. How big is your garden?'

'About four acres—there's a kitchen garden and a small orchard beyond.' He took her arm. 'There's a paddock, too. There are a couple of worn-out donkeys there; no one wanted them, so they live out their elderly lives here...'

'Oh, how nice. Will they do for the children when you have them?'

'Admirably. You are not bored with my aunts, Suzannah?'

'Bored? Goodness, no. It's heaven, not having anything to bother one, you know. But now I have some money I shall go into Marlborough and get the papers and find work.'

He came to a halt, and still he was holding her arm, so she stopped too. 'Ah, yes, I was wondering if you could see your way to staying at Ramsbourne House for a little longer; I believe that I know of something which might suit you.'

The last thing she wanted. Especially if it were to be near his home. She must get away at all costs. She said, 'I really had made up my mind to go right away from here.'

'Why?'

She went rather pale. 'Well…it would make a nice change.'

'You have a reason,' his voice was very even, 'but you don't want to tell me, do you, Suzannah?'

'No. No, I don't, if you don't mind.'

He nodded and started to walk on again. 'Shall we go and take a look at the donkeys?'

'Yes, please. Who looks after them when you're not here?'

'Trudy's nephew. She was born and brought up in the village, and most of her family have looked after us. She never married, but she has three sisters and any number of nephews and nieces; they run my home between them.'

He opened a wicket gate at the end of the path and entered the paddock. There was a large shed at its farther end, and along one outside edge was a high brick wall, crowned with tiles. He nodded towards this. 'The kitchen garden is on the other side; that leads to the back yard and the garages. That roof you can see is the barn; we'll take a look at it presently.'

The donkeys were in the shed, standing contentedly side by side. They were elderly but well cared for, and ambled over to meet them as they went in. The professor reached up to a wooden box on a ledge above his head and pulled out a handful of carrots. 'This one's Joe—the one who is eating your carrots is Josephine.'

They stayed a little while with the gentle beasts, and then

crossed the paddock and went through a narrow wooden door into the kitchen garden, walled and sheltered, with peach and pear and nectarine trees against the red brick. There was a greenhouse, too, with a vine wreathed around its walls. 'Been there for ages, long before my time,' observed the professor. 'We get good grapes from it.'

The garden was a model of orderliness, with rows of cauliflowers and winter cabbage, leeks and Brussels sprouts and, under cloches along one wall, neat rows of seedlings. The professor took his time looking at everything which rather surprised Suzannah; it seemed to her that he had enough on his hands, operating and presiding over out-patients and checking on his patients in the wards. She asked, 'Don't you get tired? I mean, you have a busy week at the hospital, I expect, and then you come down here…'

'Ah, but you see, this is my real life. I love my work, but I believe that I am a country man at heart. I count myself very fortunate that I have the best of both worlds.'

They wandered out of the kitchen garden and into the yard behind the house, and he inspected the barn roof and then took her back into the house through the back door.

It was getting dark already; there were lights into the stone passage which led to the hall. He took her coat and Trudy came from the kitchen with the tea tray.

'Muffins, Mr Guy,' she told him as she went past, 'and a nice chocolate cake I made this morning, seeing that you were coming. There's sandwiches with Gentleman's Relish, and some nice thin bread and butter.'

Suzannah, sitting by the fire again, could think of no way better to spend a winter's afternoon than by a blazing fire, eating muffins and listening to the professor talking about nothing in particular.

She sat, looking into the flames and wishing she could stay forever, envying from the bottom of her heart the girl she thought he was going to marry. She took a quick peep at him, sitting there, his long legs stretched out before him, the dog with his head at his master's feet. In the firelight he was better-looking than ever. She remembered the first time she had met him and his cold stare… He looked up and the stare wasn't cold now; indeed, it caused her to frown a little, so that he said casually, 'I suppose we must think about going back to the aunts. They expect us for dinner.'

She got up with the vague feeling that he had been going to say something else and then changed his mind. 'I've had a lovely day; thank you very much for inviting me.'

He went unhurriedly to the door and held it open. 'I shall be coming down again very shortly: I promised Phoebe that I would take a look at Sir William; she seemed rather worried about him. She asked after you, by the way.'

Suzannah was surprised. 'Did she?' She sought for something suitable to say. 'That was very kind of her.'

'Possibly,' said the professor, and followed her into the hall.

He left Ramsbourne House very shortly after dinner that evening. He had wished his aunts goodbye and then invited Suzannah to see him out of the house. She went with him, thinking that perhaps she wouldn't see him again, for she fully intended to be away before he came again. At the door he turned her round to face him, his hands on her shoulders.

'Next time I come we will settle your future, once and for all. No more jobs which lead nowhere—something permanent.'

He bent and kissed her hard, and was gone before she could utter a sound.

His kiss shook her badly, so that she didn't remember his words until some time in the middle of the night. Something permanent, he had said, but perhaps it would be somewhere she would see him, and that was something she was determined not to do, not even if it was only on rare occasions. He had mentioned training as a nurse and probably he had spoken to someone at his own hospital where his word was taken heed of, and that wouldn't do at all. 'I must make a clean break,' she told a drowsy Horace, and then lay awake until it was getting light, wondering how best to do it.

She had had an almost sleepless night for nothing, for fate had taken a hand again. It was the following afternoon while the old ladies were taking their post-prandial nap that Suzannah was sitting in the drawing-room writing out an advert to put in *The Lady* magazine and another one for the local weekly paper, made possible by fifty pounds in the envelope Snow had handed her that morning with the murmured observation that the professor had asked him to let Suzannah have it when she came downstairs. There was a scrawled note with the money, begging her to accept it, 'just to tide you over; you can repay me later.'

She had been reluctant to accept it, but with money she could do so much more, not only advertise but travel to interviews should they be forthcoming.

She was making a fair copy when Snow came softfooted into the room. 'Miss Davinish has called, miss. She would like to see you; I told her that the ladies were resting, but she said she had come to see you.'

'Me?' Suzannah jumped up in surprise. Perhaps Miss Davinish wanted her back—perhaps the cottage was vacant again and she could go there to live, only she couldn't: it was too near the professor's home…'Thank you, Snow; would you ask her to come in? Lady Manbrook wouldn't mind?'

'Certainly not, miss. She is acquainted with Miss Davinish.'

Phoebe Davinish came into the room with an air of being entirely at home there. She stood for a moment just inside the door, studying Suzannah, who was standing uncertainly by the table. She said, 'Hello. I'm on my way home and it seemed a good opportunity to see you.' She sat down and undid her fur coat. 'I dare say you're wondering why I've called to see you?'

'Yes, I am rather.'

Phoebe smiled as she watched her. 'Did Guy—Professor Bowers-Bentinck come to see you this weekend?'

'Not me specially. He came to visit his aunts.'

Phoebe went on smoothly, 'Oh, I understood him to say that he would be seeing you. He's concerned about you; thinks you should have a chance to get a permanent job…'

She paused to watch Suzannah's reaction and smiled when she replied, 'Well, yes, he did say that he would like me to stay here, as he thought he knew of something…'

Pheobe went on chattily. 'Did he tell you that we are to be married?' She paused again and watched the colour leave Suzannah's cheeks. 'I see that he didn't. Well, I can understand that—you do show your feelings rather openly, and he does dislike hurting people's feelings.'

Suzannah thought wildly that that didn't sound like the professor at all; he was kind, certainly, but quite ruthless about getting his own way. But she said nothing, sitting there listening to Phoebe whom she knew didn't like her, but who sounded so plausible now.

'Well, we have had a splendid idea. We shall need more staff, of course; I suggested that you might like to come as Girl Friday—you know, answer the phone, write letters, take calls for Guy, help around the house. You would have a room to yourself, of course, and wages…'

So that was the permanent job he had had in mind, thought Suzannah, and anything less possible she had yet to think of. She wished very much that she could scream with rage and misery and throw something at the girl sitting opposite her, but instead she said in a calm voice, 'That's very kind of you, Miss Davinish. It's rather a surprise, and not quite what I had planned to do…'

'Oh and what was that?'

Phoebe sounded quite friendly; everything was going very nicely. She had banked on Suzannah's refusing; she wasn't the kind of girl to let a man know that she was in love with him—she would want to put the whole of England between them.

'I mean to go right away, and as soon as possible.'

'Well, I dare say that might be a good idea, after all, although I'm sure Guy will want to help in any way he can. You'll need money.'

Suzannah thought of the fifty pounds. 'I think I can manage.'

Phoebe started to do up her coat.

'Well, do let us know if you need help. Guy is a great one for helping lame dogs over stiles, you know.'

She got to her feet and Suzannah got up too and put Horace on the floor. He had been staring unwinkingly at Phoebe; now he crossed the space between them and sank his claws into her coat, and then drew a vicious claw down her tights, ripping them neatly.

Phoebe whirled round and aimed a blow at him, although he had prudently retired under the table by then. 'You damned brute,' she screamed, 'you've ruined my tights and probably my coat as well! You're dangerous—' She glared at Suzannah. 'You should have him put down… You'll pay for this.'

She stormed out, brushing past an astonished Snow and banging the front door behind her, and he returned to the drawing-room to ask, 'What was all that about, miss?'

'Horace scratched her, Snow.' Suzannah had stopped to pick up Horace who looked as though butter wouldn't melt in his mouth. 'She said he should be put down.'

Snow's stern face relaxed very slightly. 'A more docile beast I have yet to meet, miss. A very nice cat, if I may say so.'

When he had gone, Suzannah sat down again with Horace on her knee. She said softly, 'I don't blame you, Horace; if I had claws I would have done exactly the same.'

He settled down, purring loudly, and when he felt the top of his head getting damp from her tears he took no notice.

CHAPTER NINE

THERE WAS TIME for Suzannah to go to the village and post her letters off to the magazine and newspaper she had chosen. She left Horace snoozing before the fire, got her outdoor things, and walked briskly to the general stores with its additional small sub-post-office. The shop was full, and only Mrs Maddox who owned it was there to serve, discussing the merits of streaky bacon with a customer. Suzannah wandered over to the corner where the newspapers and a variety of magazines were on display, and picked up the morning's paper. She put it down again as her eye lighted on the board hanging on the wall behind the paper stand. It was full of cards: local teenagers wanted to pick watercress, a carrycot for sale, kittens wanting good homes, charming widow in her forties would like to meet a friendly gentleman of a similar age for outings, and then, wedged in among the prams, kitchen tables and winter coats on offer was something Suzannah felt was meant for her. It was written in black ink and heavily underlined. Strong young woman required at once to assist in moving family to York. Emergency post, temporary until nanny has recovered from illness. To be responsible for two small children and a baby. There was a phone number and an address in Avebury.

Suzannah wasted no time. She was across the street and in the telephone box as fast as her legs would carry her, only once there she remembered that she hadn't any small change. A precious ten minutes was wasted while she went back to the shop and wheedled the queue to let her get change from Mrs Maddox, but finally she got through to Mrs Coffin. That lady listened to what she had to say, and then stayed silent for so long that Suzannah was dancing with impatience. Finally, she said in her comfortable country voice, 'All right, love. If you get this job I'll have Horace; just so long as it's not for more than a week or two.'

Suzannah let out a sigh of relief, thanked her old friend and then dialled the number on the card. A distraught voice answered, and when she asked if the post had been filled, the owner of the voice broke into a long speech in which the baby being sick, the two children making off with a cake cook had just made and the removal men due to arrive the next morning, were jumbled together in a mournful diatribe. Suzannah waited for a pause. 'Then may I come and see you? Perhaps I might do if there is no one else?'

'When can you come?'

Suzannah peered across the street at the church clock. 'Well, I'm not sure about buses, I'm at Ramsbourne St Michael…'

'I'll send the gardener to fetch you. Where are you?'

Suzannah told her. 'But I'm afraid I must ask to be brought back here again.'

'That's fine. He'll be along in a few minutes. It's only a mile or two.'

The gnarled old man who drove up presently in a Land Rover had little to say, although he wasn't unfriendly. He turned off the road about a mile out of the village, down a lane full of potholes and then in through an open gate to stop before a rambling house; there were no curtains at the windows and the front door was open even on such a cold day. A skip half-full with odds and ends of broken furniture and rubbish was in the drive, and someone was hammering in a demented fashion.

Suzannah got out, thanked her driver and knocked on the open door.

A voice from somewhere in the house begged her to come in and she threaded her way between packing cases, up-ended chairs and tidy stacks of pictures towards it.

The kitchen: a pleasant, cluttered room, but warm and cosy too and at the moment rather crowded. Two small children were sitting at the table eating their tea, an older woman was at the sink, cleaning vegetables, and the owner of the voice was sitting by the Aga with a baby on her lap.

'Sorry for the mess. We're moving house,' she added quite unnecessarily. 'Of course, Nanny would get measles just when she's most needed. Are you strong? The children are awful. Have you any references? Do you live locally—I don't remember seeing you around? My name's Meredith, by the way. My husband's already at York—we've bought a house there but he can't get back to give me a hand. He doesn't know about Nanny.'

There didn't seem to be any necessity to answer any of this; Suzannah picked up the slice of bread and butter one of the children had hurled on to the floor and waited patiently. When Mrs Meredith stopped talking, she said, 'My name is Lightfoot, Suzannah. I lived for a long time with my aunt near Marlborough. She died recently and I want a temporary post while I decide what to do.'

'When can you come? We move the day after tomorrow. I suppose I must ask you for references.'

Suzannah gave the names of Mrs Collin and Dr Warren.

'And when could you start?' asked Mrs Meredith again. 'I warn you it will be pretty ghastly—Nanny will be away for two weeks and I'm no good with the children.' She smiled suddenly. 'The pay's quite good, and of course we'll pay your fare back.'

She was a pretty woman, not used, Suzannah guessed, to

doing things for herself; she rather liked her. 'If my references are all right, I could come early on the day you move, if that would do?'

'My dear girl, you have no idea what a relief it will be to have someone to look after the children and the baby. Can I phone you?'

Suzannah gave her Mrs Coffin's number; the less Lady Manbrook knew the better, just in case the professor should ask. She didn't like fibbing to the nice old lady, but she couldn't think what else to do if she wanted to disappear completely.

Presently she was driven back by the old gardener and set down outside the telephone box, and during the short journey she had time to reflect upon her good fortune. She had time, too, to worry about the fibs she was going to tell old Lady Manbrook; a truthful girl by nature; she was irked at having to deceive the kind old lady, but she could think of nothing else to do. To get away quickly so that she need not see the professor again was paramount in her mind; a few fibs on the way were inevitable.

She thanked the old man and walked back to Ramsbourne House, and at dinner that evening explained that she would have to leave in the morning to look after an old friend from her village. She spoke uncertainly, but the old ladies put that down to her worry about her friend, and since they were both short-sighted they failed to see the guilt written all over her face.

With her few possessions and Horace in his basket she boarded the bus in the morning after bidding the old ladies goodbye. She had told no one where she was going and no one had asked her; that she came from a village not too far away was common knowledge, but its name had never been mentioned. The bus was half-full and no one on it knew her. She felt more and more secure the nearer she got to Mrs Coffin and the village.

She would only be staying for two days, she told Mrs Coffin, paying that lady the modest sum she asked for her lodging. 'And

I'll pay you for Horace's food before I go,' promised Suzannah. 'Mrs Meredith said two weeks at the most, if you don't mind.'

'Lor' bless you, love, of course I don't mind and nor does the dog, though I dare say my Tiger will.' She chuckled easily and went to serve a customer, leaving Suzannah to settle Horace by the fire in the sitting-room and unpack her bag.

She hated saying goodbye to Horace; he had been leading a very unsettled life for the last month or so, and he gave her a reproachful look as she stroked his elderly head. 'Don't you fret,' said Mrs Coffin. 'I'll keep an eye on him, and you'll see, something will turn up for you when you get back.'

Suzannah gave her a hug. 'Don't let anyone know where I am,' she begged.

'Well, there is no one to ask, is there, love?'

Suzannah bent down to examine a shoe. 'No, of course not.'

This time she was to be picked up in Marlborough, again by the old gardener, who, beyond observing that the house was in a rare pickle and he doubted they'd get away before the following day, only said, 'The missus can't seem to manage without nanny or the master, and them children run wild.'

Hardly an encouraging start, reflected Suzannah, but beggars couldn't be choosers and if she were kept busy for the next couple of weeks she might be able to forget the professor. She had been singularly unsuccessful at that so far.

The house, when he reached it, was in a state of chaos; Mrs Meredith had recruited two women from the village to help get the house emptied, and the elderly woman, the cook, was in the kitchen banging pots and saucepans into wooden chests, declaring that she would give in her notice the moment they got to York. The furniture movers were already busy, tramping to and fro, taking no notice of anyone else, calling cheerfully to each other with a good deal of, 'To you, George, and back to you, Tom,' as they manoeuvred weighty pieces of furniture out of the house and into the van.

Mrs Meredith was in her bedroom, trying to decide what to

wear. Her face broke into a wide smile when she saw Suzannah. 'Oh, good, you're here. If you could catch the children and get their outdoor clothes on, and then could you possibly change the baby? Cook's going to make tea for everyone before we go. The men say we'll be there by six o'clock...'

'But isn't York about a hundred and eighty miles from here?' Suzannah had a mental picture of the two vans and Mrs Meredith racing up the motorway at seventy miles an hour, and even then they'd never get unloaded before midnight. It was a relief when Mrs Meredith laughed. 'Oh, we shall spend a night on the way. We're going across country to the M1 and spending the night at a small place called Crick just off the motorway. My husband has got rooms for us all at the Post House there. It's about half-way, so we should be in York during the afternoon. My husband will be there to meet us and the men will stay overnight at the local pub.'

She turned away to hold up a pale grey trouser suit. 'This would be sensible to travel in, don't you think? I'll be driving the station wagon, Cook can sit beside me and you and the children can sit in the back.'

Sinking her weary head on to the pillow that night, Suzannah went over the day. They had managed to get away somehow; the vans had lumbered off first and then Mrs Meredith, after a last-minute frantic rush around the house to make sure that everything was gone. She was a good driver and they soon overtook the vans, all of them stopping for lunch at a wayside hotel, where she had been kept busy seeing that the children ate their meal, leading them to and from the loo, feeding the baby and changing it and snatching a quick meal for herself. The baby was a good child and slept peacefully for hours at a stretch, which had left her free to amuse the children, both bored stiff by the afternoon. A brief break for tea and they went on again and came at last to the hotel. Mr Meredith had organised everything very well: instructions had been written down, hotels had been advised of their coming and their rooms were comfortable. Suzannah, with the baby in its carry-cot beside her bed and the door open to the children's room, slept the sleep of someone who had done a hard day's work.

The rest of the journey went well. The worst was over, Mrs Meredith assured her; they would stop for lunch on the way and be at their new home before tea-time. And so they were.

The house was a few miles from York—a converted farmhouse, roomy and pleasant to the eye and set in several acres of ground. There were lights streaming from its windows as they drove up, and Mr Meredith came to meet them. An efficient man, Suzannah guessed, for he had tea organised and a sturdy girl to serve it, and in no time at all the room where the children were to sleep had its essential furniture so that she was able to bath and undress them and bring them their suppers in bed before turning her attention to the baby.

She had had her supper with Cook, and Mr Meredith had thanked her for being of such help to his wife. He was a kind man, a little pompous, but highly successful in life and he was fond of his wife; anyone could see that. It would be nice to be married to someone who doted on you, she mused drowsily, and inevitably thought of the professor.

She had intended to ponder her future during the weeks she would be with the Merediths, but she had little time to think, let alone ponder. The children were endearing, full of spirits and extremely naughty. They disappeared a dozen times a day, hiding in the attics or the enormous cupboards; they fought like two puppies and cried loudly if they were thwarted. It was fortunate that the baby was one of the most placid creatures she had ever encountered. All the same, her days were crammed; there was certainly no time to decide her future.

With the help of curtain hangers, window cleaners, carpet layers and the like, the house was quickly a home. The children had their nursery in one wing of the roomy old house, and since there was a side entrance leading to the back stairs Suzannah saw little of Mrs Meredith, although each evening after the children were in bed and the baby settled until the ten o'clock feed, Suzannah was invited to go downstairs for drinks and dinner. And, by the time she had bidden the Merediths goodnight and gone to her own room, she was too tired to think about anything much. Only the professor, and that was a waste of time, she told herself crossly, when she should be planning what was the best thing to do next. Invariably at this point she fell asleep.

The professor, back home after an urgent summons to go to the Middle East and perform an intricate operation upon the small son of an oil sheikh, picked up the letters waiting for him, exchanged a few words with Cobb and went to his study. Cobb followed him in with the whisky he had asked for and the assurance that Mrs Cobb would have dinner ready within fifteen minutes and retired silently, leaving the professor to glance through his post. There was a letter from Lady Manbrook—he recognised her copperplate handwriting—but before he read it he reached for his appointments book. There were private patients to see at his rooms in the forenoon, and before that a ward round at the hospital as well as an outpatients clinic in the afternoon. He sighed faintly, his mind full of Suzannah whom he wanted to see above all people; she had captured his heart and his mind, and he had to steel himself against getting into his car and going down to his aunt's to see her. He opened the letter; at least he knew where she was until he could be with her again.

No one, watching him reading, would have guessed at the great surge of strong feeling which shook him as he deciphered Lady Manbrook's rambling missive. His face was as calm as it always was, only his mouth had tightened and a muscle twitched in his cheek. He had been mistaken; he no longer knew where Suzannah was, if he was to believe his aunt's gentle regret at her guest's sudden departure, and he had no reason to doubt it. He read the letter once more, sat for a little while deep in thought and once more picked up the telephone. His secretary,

Mrs Long, would have left his rooms by now; he phoned her home and she listened to what he had to say.

'Two patients in the forenoon, sir,' she assured him, 'and no one in the afternoon; it's your outpatients in the afternoon and you're operating.'

'I'll see to all those, but rearrange the other appointments for the next two days, will you? I have to go away for a couple of days. There wasn't anything desperately urgent, was there?'

'No, sir, I'll do that—will two days be enough?'

'I'm not sure. I'll keep in touch.'

He rang off and then rang the hospital to talk to his registrar. 'I'll be in tomorrow,' he told him, 'but I shall want you to take over for the next two days after that. Sort it out, will you? I'll give you a ring on the second day.'

Cobb tapped on the door to tell him that dinner was ready and the professor said, 'Cobb, Miss Lightfoot has disappeared. I intend to go down to Great Chisbourne tomorrow evening and stay a couple of days. Will you have a bag packed for me when I get back? And a quick meal?'

Cobb looked shocked. 'Of course, sir. Missing, you say? Such a pleasant, level-headed young lady. Mrs Cobb will be quite upset…'

The professor smiled grimly. 'Well, tell her not to get too worried; I intend to find her.'

His day was long and hard; he had bent his powerful brain to the delicate task of removing a blood clot from his patient's brain, examined his two private patients and his ward cases and dealt with a number of outpatients before he finally let himself into his house that evening. The faithful Cobb met him in the hall. 'Mrs Cobb has a light meal ready, sir, and your bag is packed. Is there anything further?'

The professor took off his coat and stretched his great arms. 'No, Cobb, thank you, only phone me if you should get any news—I'll be at Great Chisbourne—if I'm not there, give a message to Trudy, will you?'

He went to his room and showered and changed, ate his meal and was back in his car within the hour.

It was late by the time he reached his house, but on the way he had phoned Trudy and she was there, waiting for him, wrapped in a red woolly dressing-gown, reassuringly matter-of-fact and comforting.

'There's coffee and sandwiches, Mr Guy,' she told him, and, after one look at his tired face, 'You're tired to the bone. Something's wrong, isn't it? And you so happy with that nice young lady…'

'The nice young lady has run away, Trudy. I have to find her.' He flung his greatcoat down and sat down at the kitchen table while she poured the coffee.

'Well, of course you do. And I'll be bound she's run away for a good reason. If ever I saw a girl in love…of course you'll find her.'

The professor said quite meekly, 'Yes, Trudy. I'll go over to Lady Manbrook's in the morning and find out just what happened.'

'You do that, Mr Guy, but first you're going to have a good night's sleep or you won't have your wits about you in the morning.'

His aunts were delighted to see him; they were also vague, but then they always were. It took time to discover that Suzannah had gone to look after an old friend and had taken Horace with her. 'We're not quite sure why she had to go,' they told him, 'but it seemed to be a matter of extreme urgency, for the dear child left very shortly after she had gone down to the village—you remember, dear?' Lady Manbrook asked her sister. 'It was only ten minutes or so after Phoebe Davinish came to see her—we didn't see her, of course, but Parsons told us and Snow did say that Phoebe left looking put out.'

It wasn't much, but it was a start; the professor stayed a little while with the old ladies and drove himself back to his home. Over his lunch he assessed the information he had gleaned; it was obvious to him that Phoebe had been the cause for Suzannah's sudden flight to heaven knew where.

He drove back to Ramsbourne St Michael after lunch, parked the car and entered the village stores. Mrs Maddox was behind the counter, waiting for customers, and it was here that he had success, for she remembered Suzannah. 'Lovely red hair,' she observed chattily, 'though she did look a bit worried. The shop was full and she was looking at those adverts I keep by the door. Next time I looked up there she was across the street, phoning from the box, and presently along comes the old gardener from Mrs Meredith's and she gets in and off they go.'

'Did she have a cat basket with her?'

Mrs Maddox looked surprised. 'Oh, no, nothing at all with her. I didn't see her come back…'

'And this Mrs Meredith—where does she live?'

He was given a suspicious look. 'Well, sir, I don't rightly think I should say, for its none of my business.'

The professor, when called upon, could exert great charm. 'I'm Lady Manbrook's nephew. I am a friend of Miss Lightfoot's and I do need to see her as soon as possible.'

'Oh, well, that's different, sir. Mrs Meredith's gone—somewhere up north. Wait a minute, I've got the forwarding address somewhere. They went a week or more ago, and a fine muddle it was getting them moved, so I hear from all accounts, Mr Meredith not being able to come here and direct things and Mrs Meredith, nice though she is, always up in the clouds, no method if you see what I mean, as well as two of the naughtiest children I've ever met and a baby, too. Her Nanny got the measles and she was at her wit's end for help…' She rummaged around on the shelf behind her and produced a paper. 'Here we are—everything is to go to Mr Meredith's place of business for the time being—I suppose they've not settled in yet—I heard tell that it was a place in the country.'

The professor had listened with patience; he was getting somewhere, but far too slowly for his peace of mind. He thanked

Mrs Maddox and got into his car. Mrs Coffin seemed a likely link in the chain. He walked into her little shop and was relieved to see the look of guilty consternation on her face.

'Well,' said Mrs Coffin in an agitated voice, 'fancy seeing you here, sir, however did you…?' She stopped and started again. 'Come to look up Dr Warren, I dare say—he'll be back from his rounds by now.'

'I've come to see you, Mrs Coffin, if you could spare me five minutes?'

She made a great thing of looking up and down the village street. 'Well, sir, it's my busy time…' She caught his eye; he was smiling, but there was going to be no putting him off, she could see that.

'Come through into the back room, sir,' she invited him unwillingly, and lifted the counter flap for him to join her.

The little room was crammed with furniture and a bright fire burned in the small grate. An elderly dog sat in front of it, a large black cat sat on one side, and on the other Horace was perched, looking uneasy.

The professor stooped to twiddle his ear. 'Hello, old fellow,' and Horace brightened visibly. 'Yes, all right, I'll take you back with me, we shall be glad to have you with us again.'

Mrs Coffin looked relieved. 'Oh, you've come for Suzannah's cat. She was so worried when she left; you see, she wasn't sure how long she would be gone, and him and my Tiger don't get on, only there wasn't anywhere else to take him.'

'That was very kind of you, Mrs Coffin,' said the professor smoothly. 'If you will let me have her address, I'll let Suzannah know that he's back with me.'

'I've got the address somewhere—sent me a card last week, just to let me know she was all right. Here we are—Tidewell House, Tidemore, York. In the country, she said. I was to let her know how Horace was, but perhaps you'd be kind enough to do that if he's going with you?'

She glanced at the professor; he seemed, in the last few minutes, to have got younger, or perhaps it was because she hadn't got her glasses on.

'Certainly I'll tell her, Mrs Coffin; I shall be going back to London with him this evening.'

'All that way!' marvelled Mrs Coffin, who didn't believe in travel. 'You'll give her my love, won't you, sir?' She produced Horace's basket and he stowed him inside. 'Such a dear girl, and never a grumble, though she looked that sad.'

'Then I must find her and do my best to cheer her up,' declared the professor blandly, and bade Mrs Coffin goodbye.

He drove himself back to his house, ate the meal Trudy had got for him, fed Horace and telephoned his registrar, to be told that a severe head injury sustained by a little girl in a street accident had just been admitted and would need surgery. 'Otherwise everything's fine,' observed his right hand.

The professor suppressed impatience. 'I'm on my way in ten minutes or so. I'll come in as soon as I get back.' They discussed the case for a few minutes and he hung up. 'I'll have to get back,' he told Trudy, 'but first I must tell you that I know where Suzannah is; as soon as I'm able, I'll go to York and fetch her.'

'You don't know why she went?'

He shook his head. 'No. Though I think I can guess.' He gave her a hug. 'I'll be in touch, Trudy.'

It was almost eleven o'clock by the time he got home. He handed Horace over to Cobb, told him that he would be at the hospital if he was wanted, assured him that Suzannah was safe, and took himself off to the intensive care unit. He spent the greater part of the night operating on the child and, satisfied with his work, went home at last to sleep like a log.

He was back at the hospital in the morning, to find the child greatly improved and nothing urgent waiting for him. 'I'm going up to York,' he told his registrar. 'I've a couple of patients to see at my rooms, and I'll leave my address with Mrs Long—you can always get me in the car. I want to leave very early in the morning, and if all goes well I shall be back here in the evening of the next day.'

Thrusting all thought of his Suzannah from his mind, he worked without pause all day, catching up on letters, seeing his patients and doing a quick round at the hospital, but once home again he allowed himself to think of her. 'We really can't go on like this, can we?' he asked the faithful Henry, and Henry, who hadn't been allowed to travel down to Great Chisbourne, thumped his tail in agreement. The professor bent to stroke him. 'You shall come with me to York,' he promised. 'I dare say I shall need all the moral support I can muster.'

The pair of them left very early the next morning. It was a cold, bleak day, but the roads were dry and the Bentley made light of the miles. The professor stopped at a service station after a couple of hours, and then drove on into a day which was now almost as dark as the night, with thick clouds racing across the steel-grey sky and a fine rain beginning to fall. But presently the rain ceased, and by this time he had almost reached York and the sky was clearing.

'A good omen, Henry,' observed the professor to the little dog curled up on the seat beside him.

He had no need to go into the centre of York but skirted its edges, and after a few miles turned off the main road and took a narrow lane which led him to Tidemore. Tidewell House, he was informed when he stopped to ask, was less than a mile along the road, and he found it easily enough; a farmhouse at one time, it was now a comfortable dwelling set in a good-sized garden with paddocks on either side. He drove up the short drive and got out, rang the old-fashioned bell beside the solid front door and waited, the picture of calm patience, for it to be opened.

He said to the rather severe elderly woman who opened it, 'Is Mrs Meredith at home? I should like to speak to her.'

'She's in. What name shall I give, sir?'

'Bowers-Bentinck.'

She ushered him inside and opened a door in the hall. The

room he entered was small and only partly furnished, with packing cases lining a wall. He contemplated them without much interest, seething with an inward impatience now, and it was with relief that he heard the door open and turned to see Mrs Meredith.

They shook hands while he made the usual civil excuses for disturbing her. 'I believe you have Miss Lightfoot working for you; I am anxious to see her.'

Mrs Meredith, airy-fairy though she was, had sharp eyes; not a man to show his feelings, she decided, but boiling over inside. 'Yes, she's here—how fortunate you came today, for my permanent nanny is returning tomorrow and Suzannah is going back. She's out with the children, but they'll be back any minute. Have you come a long way?'

'London.' He hesitated. 'I hope to take her back with me, if that would be possible?'

'I don't see why not.' She smiled at him, scenting romance in the air. 'I'll get a coat and go and meet them, and take over the children and leave you free to talk.' She was half-way to the door. 'She's been marvellous—I don't know what I'd have done without her, and the children love her. I won't be a moment.'

They went through the house, out of the back door and through the door in the garden wall. There was a paddock beyond and fields. The professor came to a halt and heaved a great sigh; his Suzannah was in the field, tossing a ball to the two children with her; they were shouting and screaming and racing around her, and Mrs Meredith and the professor were quite close before she looked up and saw them.

She stood, the ball fallen from her hand, staring at him, her mouth open, the colour creeping into her face and then ebbing away, leaving it pale. She said in a squeaky voice, 'How did you get here?'

'In the car. Hello, Suzannah.' He had come to a halt before her and took her hands in his, and neither he or Suzannah noticed Mrs Meredith dragging the children back to the house.

'How did you find me?' she whispered.

'It wasn't too difficult, my darling—your hair—people notice it. What did Phoebe say to make you run away?'

She gave her hands a little tug, but he tightened his gentle hold, and when she looked up into his face she could see that she would have to answer him. 'Well,' she began, 'she said that you and she were going to be married and that you were sorry for me and felt that you had to help me and that I was an embarrassment to you…'

She sniffed and her eyes filled with tears.

'Oh, dear, oh, dear,' said the professor at his most soothing. 'And, of course, you believed her.'

'Well, I didn't want to, only you didn't seem to like me…'

'My dearest love, I not only like you, I love you. I fell in love with you the very first time we met, but I must confess that I didn't realise it for some time, although I was plagued by an urge to look after you from the moment Phoebe told me that she had sacked you. But you refused my help in no uncertain manner, didn't you? It was then that you took possession of my heart and mind.'

'You never said anything,' she said sharply. She gave another tug and he laughed softly.

'Don't get cross, my darling; several times I thought I would take a chance, and always you backed away and started talking about the weather. But now no more of that. Will you marry me, Suzannah? And I want the answer now, so don't start arguing!'

'I never…' She began and saw the look in his eyes. 'Oh, Guy, of course I'll marry you, and I'm sorry I ran away, only I love you and I thought that you didn't love me…'

The professor let her hands go at last and wrapped his great arms around her. 'And that, my darling, is something I must disprove to you.'

He kissed her slowly and then quite fiercely, so that she had no breath to speak, only just enough to kiss him back.

The sun had gone in and a fine drizzle was drifting down.

Suzannah couldn't have cared less; she was in heaven, and as for the professor, that most observant of men, he hadn't even noticed; he had his heart's desire.

* * * * *

Keep reading for an excerpt of
The Prince's Outback Bride
by Marion Lennox.
Find it in the
Outback Journey anthology,
out now!

PROLOGUE

'WE HAVE NO CHOICE.' Princess Charlotte de Gautier watched her son in concern from where she rested on her day-bed. Max was pacing the sitting room overlooking the Champs-Elysées. He'd been pacing for hours.

'We must,' Charlotte added bleakly. 'It's our responsibility.'

'It's not our responsibility. The royal family of Alp d'Estella has been rotten to the core for generations. We're well rid of them.'

'They've been corrupt,' Charlotte agreed. 'But now we have the chance to make amends.'

'Amends? Until Crown Prince Bernard's death I thought I had nothing to do with them. Our connection was finished. After all they've done to you…'

'We're not making amends to the royal family. We're making amends to the people of Alp d'Estella.'

'Alp d'Estella's none of our business.'

'That's not true, Max. I'm telling you. It's your birthright.'

'It's not my birthright,' he snapped. 'Regardless of what you say now. It should have been Thiérry's birthright, but their corruption killed Thiérry as it came close to killing you. As far as anyone knows I'm the illegitimate son of the ex-wife of a dead prince. I can walk away. We both can.'

Charlotte flinched. She should have braced herself earlier for this. She'd hoped so much that Crown Prince Bernard would have a son, but now he'd died, leaving… Max.

Since he was fifteen Max had shouldered almost the entire burden of caring for her, and he'd done it brilliantly. But now… She'd tried her hardest to keep her second son out of the royal spotlight—out of the succession—but now it seemed there was no choice but to land at least the regency squarely on Max's shoulders.

Max did a few more turns. Finally he paused and stared down into the bustling Paris street. How could his mother ask this of him—or of herself for that matter? He had no doubt as to what this would mean to their lives. To put Charlotte in the limelight again, as the mother of the Prince Regent…

'I do have a responsibility,' Max said heavily. 'It's to you. To no one else.'

'You know that's not true. You have the fate of a country in your hands.'

'That's not fair.'

'No,' Charlotte whispered. 'Life's not.'

He turned then. 'I'm sorry. Hell, Mama, I didn't mean…'

'I know you didn't. But this has to be faced.'

'But you've given up so much to keep me out of the succession, and to calmly give in now…'

'I'm not giving in. I admit nothing. I'll take the secret of your birth to the grave. I shouldn't have told you, but it seems…so needful that you take on the regency. And it may yet not happen at all. If this child can't become the new Crown Prince…'

'Then what? Will you want to tell the truth then?'

'No,' she said bluntly. 'I will not let you take the Crown.'

'But you'd let an unknown child take it.'

'That's what I mean,' she said, almost eagerly. 'He's an unknown. With no history of hatred weighing him down…maybe it's the only chance for our country.'

'Our country?'

'I still think of it as ours,' she said heavily. 'I might have been a child bride, but I learned early to love it as my own. I love the people. I love the language. I love everything about it. Except its rulers. That's why... That's why I need you to accept the regency. You can help this little prince. I know the politicians. I know the dangers and through you we can protect him. Max, all I know is that we must help him. If you don't take on the regency then the politicians will take over. Things will get worse rather than better, and that's surely saying something.' She hesitated, but it had to be said. 'The way I see it we have two choices. You accept the regency and we do our best to protect this child and protect the people of Alp d'Estella. Or we walk away and let the country self-destruct.'

'And the third alternative?' he asked harshly. 'The truth?'

'No. After all I've been through... You don't want it and I couldn't bear it.'

'No,' he agreed. 'I'm sorry. Of course not.'

'Thank you,' she whispered. 'But what to do now? You tell me this boy's an orphan? That doesn't mean that he's friendless. Who's to say whoever's caring for him will let him take it on?'

'I've made initial enquiries. His registered guardian is a family friend—no relation at all. She's twenty-eight and seems to have been landed with the boy when his parents were killed. This solution provides well for him. She may be delighted to get back to her own life.'

'I guess it's to provide well for him—to let him take on the Crown at such an age. With you beside him...'

'In the background, Mama. From a distance. I can't take anything else on, regardless of what you ask.' Max shoved his hands deep in the pockets of his chinos and, turning, stared once more into the street. Accepting what he'd been thinking for the last hour. 'Maybe he'll be the first decent ruler the country's had for centuries. He can hardly be worse than what's come before. But you're right. We can't let him do it alone. I'll remain caretaker ruler until this child turns twenty-one.'

'You won't live there?'

'No. If there wasn't this family connection stipulation to the regency then I'd never have been approached. But Charles Mevaille's been here this morning—Charles must have been the last non-corrupt politician in the country before the Levouts made it impossible for him to stay. He's shown me what desperately needs to be done to get the country working. The law's convoluted but it seems, no matter who my father was, as half-brother to the last heir I can take on the regency. As Prince Regent I can put those steps into place from here.'

'And the child…'

'We'll employ a great nanny. I'll work hard on that, Mama. He'll be brought up in the castle with everything he could wish for.'

'But…' Charlotte hugged Hannibal—her part poodle, part mongrel, all friend—as if she needed the comfort of Hannibal's soft coat. As indeed she did. 'This is dreadful,' she whispered. 'To put a child in this position…'

'He's an orphan, Mama,' Max said heavily. 'I have no idea what his circumstances are in Australia, but you're right. Once Alp d'Estella's run well then this may well be a glorious opportunity for him.'

'To be wealthy?' Charlotte whispered. 'To be famous? Max, I thought I'd raised you better than that.'

He turned back to face her then, contrite. 'Of course you did. But as far as I can see, this child has no family—only a woman who probably doesn't want to be doing the caring anyway. If she wants to stay with him then we can make it worth her while to come. If she doesn't, then we'll scour the land for the world's best nanny.'

'But you will stay here?'

'I can't stay in Alp d'Estella. Neither of us can.'

'Neither of us have the courage?'

'Mama…'

'You're right,' she said bleakly. 'We don't have the courage, or I surely don't. Let's hope this little one can be what we can't be.'

'We'll care for him,' Max assured her.

'From a distance.'

'It'll be okay.'

'But you will take on the role as Prince Regent?' She sighed. 'I'm so sorry, Max. That's thirteen years of responsibility.'

'As you say, we don't have a choice. And it could have been much, much worse.'

'If I hadn't lied… But I won't go back on it, Max. I won't.'

'No one's asking you to,' he told her, crossing to her day-bed and stooping to kiss her. 'It'll be fine.'

'As long as this woman lets the child come.'

'Why wouldn't she?'

'Maybe she has more sense than I did forty years ago.'

'You were young,' he told her. 'Far too young to marry.'

'So how old is old enough to marry?' she demanded, momentarily distracted.

'Eighty maybe?' He smiled, but the smile didn't reach his eyes. 'Or never. Marriage has never seemed anything but a frightful risk. How the hell would you ever know you weren't being married for your money or your title?' He shrugged. 'Enough. Let's get things moving. We have three short weeks to get things finalised.'

'You'll go to Australia?'

'I can do it from here.'

'You'll go to Australia.' She was suddenly decisive. 'This is a huge thing we're asking.'

'We're relieving this woman of her responsibility.'

'Maybe,' Charlotte whispered. 'But we might just find a woman of integrity. A woman who doesn't think money or a title is an enticement, either for herself or for a child she loves. Now wouldn't that be a problem?'